MW01131426

Riga Mortis

by

ILZE BERZINS

authorHOUSE™

1663 LIBERTY DRIVE, SUITE 200
BLOOMINGTON, INDIANA 47403
(800) 839-8640
WWW.AUTHORHOUSE.COM

© 2005 ILZE BERZINS. All Rights Reserved.

No part of this book may be reproduced, stored in a retrieval system, or transmitted by any means without the written permission of the author.

First published by AuthorHouse 05/13/05

ISBN: 1-4208-3544-0 (sc)

Library of Congress Control Number: 2005903297

Printed in the United States of America
Bloomington, Indiana

This book is printed on acid-free paper.

Riga Mortis

ALSO BY ILZE BERZINS

Happy Girl
Death in the Glebe
Revenge on the Rideau
A Tear in God's Eye
Riga Blanca
Kolka

http://www.ilzeberzins.com

Chapter One

Outside, on Valdemara Street, snow was falling. Bunches of big weightless flakes slowly slipped from the sky, smoothing a fresh white eiderdown over the ancient cobblestones, the sidewalks, the magnificent old buildings and the trees which lined the Esplanade.

By the time evening came, a hush had descended. Familiar sounds—the laughter of children, pedestrian footfalls, the clatter of tramways—all faded away to a distant whisper. When the snow stopped, there would be stars, perhaps a moon and the city would glitter like an immense milky jewel.

From far off, a dog barked, the noise soft and muffled. Arnie poured himself a refill, stretched out on the hobnailed leather couch by the window and gazed at his glass hoping the contents would help to dispel the winter's chill. For a long moment, he lay motionless, luxuriating in the comforting daze that came over him as the alcohol reached his brain and relaxed his nerves. It was Tuesday evening, almost seven o'clock, January the twenty-fourth.

After the kind of day he'd had, Arnie deserved at least a few minutes to himself even though, somewhere in the back of his mind, he knew he had a date with a deadline. He had always been a procrastinator, a member of the last-minute club and he had been able to pull it off, although lately, he noticed that it was becoming more of a struggle.

Today he had eaten lunch with a boring blue blazer type from the American Embassy, a guy nicknamed Teflon Don. Arnie had noticed that the guy's hands were manicured and that his Timberland all season brogues looked as tefloned as their owner—not a fleck of winter crud on either of them.

Some of the expats from Chicago had muttered darkly about the circumstances surrounding Commercial Attaché Donald C. Fischer's appointment in view of the circumstances surrounding his wife's death. At the time he had heard these rumours, Arnie had paid little attention but all through their lunch, he couldn't put them out of his mind. Fischer had invited Arnie and, over the first drink, he let it all hang out. He was diplomatically asking for a retraction of a story Arnie had published about some expat a couple of weeks before. How tacky, Arnie thought. All the same, he said he would try to find space in an upcoming edition of his magazine, having no intention of doing so. Let the bastard squirm.

After lunch, coming out of the Hotel Latvija, Arnie had chuckled as he walked past the strip where Lenin's statue had once loomed over the landscape. He always got a charge remembering his perfect expat moment. And tonight was no exception.

After a pub crawl late one warm spring night, he had been caught short while walking along Elizabetes Street and had stopped at this same patch of lawn in front of the Courthouse.

He could still feel the indescribable pleasure of urinating on the spot where Lenin's statue had stood. He promised himself that he would do it again but he would wait till the weather was warmer.

And he would never forget the photograph he had clipped from a magazine which showed one of the many Lenins being dismantled in 1991. He wished he had been there. Lenin, all two thousand pounds of him in blackened cast bronze, was being strung up by a rope under his armpits, pigeon shit decorating his shoulders. There he was in mid air, fat and corpulent in his three-piece suit and tie, pompous yet helpless. It comforted Arnie to think that the heaven this Lenin was going to was the blast furnace reserved for all statues of out-of-favour politicians. And it would be hotter than Hades.

Shivering as a draft of cold air rushed through the cracked windowpane, he cursed the lace curtains. Useless against the arctic blasts, they had come with the apartment, remnants of the previous tenant's occupation and now were grey with age and fatigue. He had meant to change them first thing but it was one of those jobs that had fallen to the bottom of his list as he struggled to get *WOW!* magazine off the ground. He would have to get up to turn on the space heater but he just didn't want to quite yet.

Even though his apartment had not been renovated, Arnie felt lucky to have found it. High up on the sixth floor of one of Riga's ornate Art Nouveau buildings, its windows looked out on the faded elegance of Valdemara Street. It was not, thank God, in the working class stretch of Valdemara further down towards the boonies but right in the heart of the prestigious *Centrs*. Arnie smiled to himself thinking, 'tell me where you live and I'll tell you who you are'. He had heard about this Valdemara gem through an expat friend of an expat friend who was relocating. As his arrival in Riga coincided with the expat's departure, Arnie had nabbed the apartment immediately, sight unseen.

Letting out a huge sigh, Arnie clenched his eyelids closed and massaged the arch of his nose. He knew that he would be spending the next couple of hours staring at his computer screen. From the hallway, a sound made him lift his head. It was the faint pitapat of four little feet. He smiled. A dark form slipped out of the shadows and oozed toward him. With a sharp little chirp, his cat leapt up on the couch, kneaded his stomach with her insistent white paws and settled herself into the cushy warmth of his armpit.

The light, such as it was during the winter months, had vanished. Night descended, its deep mauve shadows creeping into corners, dissolving all edges and boundaries.

Gazing into the pools of darkness, Arnie drifted back to the past and wondered how the room must have looked in the era of his grandparents. Usually, two drinks was all it took to set his imagination soaring. The room felt watchful, as if the ghost of a previous tenant was standing silently in a corner waiting to speak.

Damn! He nearly jumped out of his skin as the nerve-shattering burr of the phone ripped through the silence. Why hadn't he switched off the blasted ringer! Muttering to himself, Arnie turned to look over at the offending machine and wondered whether or not to answer it. Finally, deciding he had better find out who it was, he swung his legs over the edge of the sofa. Gerda, disturbed in the process, made her feelings known as she dug in her fishhooks. *Damn cat!* Arnie yelped giving her a swat that sent her flying across the room. He examined the claw rips in his sweater, rubbed at his arm and decided he'd catch her later and choke her to death.

By now the phone was on its fifth burr. Watching his glass to make sure he didn't spill a drop, Arnie lumbered to his computer desk, sat down and placed the glass beside him. Snatching the receiver from its cradle, he snarled, "Who is it?"

"Be cool, man," came the familiar male voice.

Oh, no! Arnie muttered. Why me? It could only be Mike, the Puff Daddy impersonator, who also happened to be his one and only employee. No matter how weird, Mike was a dynamite photographer and Arnie needed him. He decided not to hang up.

"I got you the Pulp Fiction video with John Revoltin, man."

"No, Mike. It's *Tra*volta. How many times do I have to tell you? You know I don't have a VCR and where the hell did you come up with a copy of Pulp Fiction? It hasn't even been released yet."

"No VCR? You're shittin' me, right?"

"No, I'm not. What's up, Mike?"

"*What's up*" Mike repeated. This was new vocabulary. There was silence at the other end and Arnie knew that Mike was scribbling down the words in his phrase book. He groaned inwardly. He would have to listen to Mike practising this phrase over and over and he knew it was going to drive him crazy.

Arnie's patience cracked. His tone became sharp and un-friendly.

"Look, I've got a deadline to meet."

"Chill, man."

"I'm listening, Mike! What is it, for godssake?"

"Hey, wait'll you hear this." Mike started to sound short of breath, a sign that he thought he was onto something big. "I got some *real* interesting photos for you. You're going to be like *so* wowed by this stuff."

Mike was almost panting with excitement.

"Okay, Mike. No details on the phone," Arnie said tightly.

When they first met, Mike had told Arnie that his life-long ambition was to become an American-style hipster. North American crime movies and videos were his inspiration. Arnie decided that Mike was succeeding quite well.

"Bring them over. I'll be working late tonight."

"Sure thing, bud."

"Bye, Mike."

"Catch you later, dude."

After the disconnect clicked in his ear, Arnie let out a groan. The mood of the evening was broken and now there was no way he could ignore his deadline. He looked at his watch and grimaced. Another brewski? Okay, just a little one and just one more cigarette. He lit up, sucked in, exhaled and, as he watched the smoke curl up towards the ceiling, wondered what Mike would have for him. He knew that whatever it was, it would be good. Crazy ol' Mike had sounded really excited.

A few minutes later, Arnie butted out, shook off his lethargy and forced himself to turn on the computer. He examined the contents of his pockets, thumbed through some papers on his desk, re-arranged a clutch of ballpoints in their ceramic holder, cleaned out an ashtray and set it on his computer table. Then coffee. He must have coffee and lots of it. He poured himself a mug-full, added a liberal splash of Balzams, heaved a big sigh and sat down in his swivel chair. He cut his eyes to his watch. God! Where had the time gone! His deadline was minutes, not hours, away.

Just about now, Arnie should have felt something—a tremour of dread or a sense of foreboding. In fact, had he been psychic, he would have been terrified. But Arnie didn't go in for premonitions, never picked up on vibes or omens of any kind. He remained blissfully unaware that Fate was getting ready to snooker him.

It was rough going. Arnie shut his eyes, held his breath. A to-die-for sentence floated in his subconscious, just beyond his reach. Where were those words? *Where were they?* Oh, they were coming, coming… *Now!* Adrenaline surged through his body, his fingers poised over the keyboard. The words were perfect. His fingers coiled like talons about to strike.

Then it happened. Right on cue, a ferocious commotion exploded at the door. *Christ!* Arnie screamed, beside himself with rage. The words that had been right on the proverbial tip of his tongue slipped back into the dark recesses of his subconscious. *Christ! How am I ever going to make that deadline!*

The goddamned things always knew when a deadline was imminent. They just knew. Some feline intuition had alerted the cats in the hallway that he was sweating blood. Like a Greek chorus, they had assembled, had waited for just the right moment. As if on cue, they had hunched down low to align themselves with the crack under his door and had started the most bloodcurdling yowling Arnie had ever heard.

Turning away from the monitor, Arnie flushed with rage. He clenched his fists. *That fucking fucking Cat Lady! He'd get her!* He'd kick out that Cat Lady and her cats if it was the last thing he ever did. He'd boot them off this planet. His mind on the cats, he forgot his headline, forgot the whole story. What the hell was she doing letting her hormone-hyped scrags roam free in the corridors? And if that wasn't bad enough, they left their disgusting shit logs at his front door so that he would step in them as he rushed out to be on time for an appointment.

Arnie could smell the cat piss, could feel his skin start to itch, his blood pressure soar. For one horrible moment, he saw himself being jumped on when he opened the door. He imagined claws digging and kneading, sandpaper tongues licking and the smell of sardines reaching his nose as the deep purrs of feline excitement resounded in his ears. What a nightmare!

Arnie breathed deeply. *Calm down. Calm down.* He inhaled slowly, paused, then exhaled, just as he had learned to do in his yoga class. Closing his eyes, he said the Serenity Prayer, took another yogic breath, smiled and went into the kitchen. He decided that the cat problem was one of the things he *could* change and made a mental note to borrow a dog for a day or two. He would keep his eye out for any local he'd meet with a Rottweiler or a pit bull.

Arnie never faced crisis without food or drink. Humming softly to himself, he took one of his hamburger specialities from the freezer, set it on the counter to thaw and thought to himself that he would willingly share this gourmet blend delicacy with any neighbouring pit bull he could enlist to take care of the cats.

As he turned away from the fridge, Arnie allowed himself a half-minute reflection on food and his early days in Riga. How he had missed his neat little stacks of Lean Cuisines that he'd always find in his freezer back in Ottawa! The first few months had been hard. He'd get mad uncontrollable urges for gigantic juicy Dunn's smoked meat sandwiches, drive-through Harvey's double burgers bursting with bacon, tomatoes, pickles and onions, greasy cheesy steak subs and Tim Horton's doughnuts. But, like everyone else, he had adjusted.

A few murderous thoughts, a good belt of vodka, a cigarette and he was back in his squeaky swivel chair. *Focus, discipline. Keep your mind off food. Keep your mind off the cats.* All he had had to do was pound on the inside of his door and the cats outside had scattered. The hallway was quiet again. He promised himself that he'd deal with the Cat Lady first thing in the morning.

Breathing some of the positive affirmations he had learned in his stress management class back in Ottawa, Arnie psyched himself up for the final stretch. There was still time. He knew that each issue had to have zing, a twist, some salty little tidbit to make all the gossip and innuendo fun to read. Looking over his story, Arnie exhaled a puff of smoke and grinned. Things were falling into place nicely. He'd lead with the sex stuff, then do community, then the ads. He took a manila folder from his briefcase. The pictures for the February issue were great. When Mike arrived with the latest photos, he would put in another order.

And now for the clincher. At some moment, while Arnie had been doing research on another story, one of his sources had let drop a gem. Waitress-from-Milwaukee-turned-socialite, Maija Fischer, was having her Valentine's Day birthday bash at the Pussy Kat in Pardaugava. And did he ever have a great shot to go with *that* bit of news! Mike had managed to get his hands on a Maija close-up from the Milwaukee cocktail waitress days. There she was wearing her cute little outfit with its nipple-skimming bodice. Then another shot. The winner. Maija totally topless!

How in the world had the kid bagged that one? Brains, talent, ambition, connections. And money. Arnie paid well, factoring in the bribes without which you'd get nowhere in Latvia. No matter how annoying Mike could be, Arnie knew he couldn't do without his star photographer. Then and there, he decided to give the guy a raise. If he ever gets here, Arnie muttered to himself biting back his impatience.

He re-examined the topless. It was a beaut but where would it have come from? Perhaps Maija had been a nude model in some Milwaukee Art School. Well, wherever the photo had been taken, Arnie was sure it had circulated among the senior male Latvian population in Milwaukee, complete with the caption: *I need money for college...for my grandmother's hip replacement...for my father's open-heart surgery.* But this kind of thing wouldn't work in Latvia. Now, as Mrs. Donald C. Fischer, wife of the Commercial Attaché at the American Embassy, Maija didn't need to bend over quite this far. Arnie looked closer. Could the topless be a fake? A clever cut and paste job?

Other possibilities surfaced. Perhaps Maija had modelled at the Art Academy when she had first arrived in Riga. Perhaps the shot had been taken at a nude beach or at one of the spas in Jurmala. Arnie pondered for a minute, then smiled to himself relishing the thought of others doing the same. With a final shrug, he put the topless aside and decided on the nipple-skimmer. ALMOST TOPLESS would have to be the headline, a teaser, whetting appetites for another issue.

As Arnie kept working, he listened with one ear for the buzzer at the door. Where the hell was Mike? What were these sensational photos he had been so excited about? But he couldn't afford to get too distracted. There was still more stuff to fit in.

9

He glanced at the tidbit about Father Gregory at some church in Pardaugava who had been caught fondling an altar boy. *Boh-ring*, he mouthed, stifling a theatrical yawn as he typed up the item. He would have to slot that somewhere in the Community section.

Was there an item he could get sued for? It didn't matter. Each issue was incorporated as a separate company. That way, if there were legal problems, he was financially liable for only the one issue. He would simply close it down and open a new one the very next day.

A half-hour later, Fate finally struck. It was the end of the world. The blackout. The crash.

"FUUUCCCKKK!"

Arnie's scream sliced through the black silence, resonating like a siren's wail. He was going crazy, having a heart attack, hallucinating. Or had his body been snatched by aliens, sucked dry and only his mind remained? In horror, he kept staring into the black pit that had swallowed up his world. His article had vanished from the face of the earth. Stunned, he sat there hoping that any second now the words would reappear. But nothing happened. The black hole gaped at him, mocked him. The words were gone forever.

A second scream built up in his throat. He controlled himself. Just barely. As if in prayer, he lowered his head, clenched his hands together and bit down hard on his lower lip. He fought the urge to hurl his fist at the monitor. *My God! A power outage and I didn't save!* Clutching his head, he shuddered in horror as his deadline went out the window.

Chapter Two

A thread of moonlight shone through the window giving the room an eerie glow. Arnie's eyes took a minute to adjusted to the dark. He shivered feeling cold sweat popping on his scalp. Now what? Holding his right hand out in front, he made his way into the kitchen and groped for a candle and matches which he kept in a drawer. He lit the candle and moved slowly towards the apartment door expecting the hallways to be dark.

He winced as a blast of cold air slapped him in the face, almost blowing out the candle. Amazing! The light was on, the same dim light from the dusty bulb that hung above the stairwell. He heard the faint din of TV noise coming from the apartment across from his. There was light under the door. Shaking his head in bafflement, he made his way back into his dark kitchen and checked his fuse box. Everything appeared in order. Could it be the breakers in the basement? He scrunched up his face in annoyance knowing he'd have to go down there and see what was going on.

For a few seconds Arnie stood with one foot still inside across the lintel, the other out in the hall and shuddered, not believing how cold it was outside his apartment. Then, leaving the candle burning on his kitchen counter, he grabbed a jacket, locked his door and started down the stairwell. On the landing of the fourth floor, he encountered an old couple lugging up their heavy shopping bags. Russians. There was no point telling them about his power outage. He moved past giving the couple a quick nod.

He reached the main floor. There was dead silence. He could hear a pin drop. A low wattage bulb lit the front entrance. Pulling up his jacket collar, he moved down one more flight to the basement. The light was even dimmer here. As he pulled open the door to the garage, his nose was assailed by the dank smell of mildew, garbage, and exhaust fumes. Holding his breath, stepping around puddles of black oily gunk, Arnie made for the hydro panels. Bloody hell! Just as he thought. Someone had thrown his breaker. But who was the big question.

His first choice was the Russians, owners of a Great Dane who ritually deposited elephantine turds all over the place. Between the Russians and the Cat Lady, he felt overwhelmed. As well, for some reason, they had picked a fight with him over a parking space back in the days when his car still worked. Yeah, it was probably them, revenge-driven because he had left an unsolicited collection of dog turds at their door.

Shaking his head, he reset the breaker switch. The dust and dirt disgusted him. He shivered not from the cold but from a sense of mounting dread. He took a quick look around. And that's when he saw it. A dark shape wedged behind a badly parked orange Lada. He moved closer. Three seconds later, he froze. His mouth opened wide in silent terror. Sweat popped out on his upper lip and he swayed forward, gaze locked on a heap of rags. In the dim light he could make out a dark puddle oozing its way out of the heap. He held his breath and stared in horror at the stain spreading around his feet. His heart gave a sickening thud. *It's blood!* He was standing in it. *God!* His voice, high-pitched and terrified, echoed in the deserted basement.

Taking in gulps of the fetid air, he waited to come back to his senses. Sweat rolled off him. He shuddered uncontrollably. Had someone killed Mike? Was he next? The darkness stirred and the feeling came over him that there was someone else in the garage. Hiding in the shadows. Watching him. Waiting. Suddenly a whirring sound broke the silence. Arnie's body gave a jerk, as if he'd been given an electric shock. His heart jack-hammered. The automatic garage door came to life creaking and banging as it began to roll up. A car was about to pull in. Instinct said don't get involved. Get the hell outta here!

He took two seconds to give his feet a quick wipe on the mat at the garage entrance and bolted out the door. Hugging the wall, he snaked his way toward the staircase. Thank God it was deserted. Clenching his teeth, he dug his nails into the palms of his hands. It felt as if he had just run a mile. His breath came in painful puffs, the only noise he could hear besides the thudding of his own heart as he staggered up the six flights to his apartment.

He made it to his door, unlocked it, snapped the deadbolt behind him and flung himself on the couch. He grabbed for his cigarettes, his hands shaking so badly that he had trouble with the lighter. He sat there, bent over, hugging himself, inhaling smoke. With an effort, he forced his mind to work. What was going on? He had seen a dead body, at least he presumed it was dead. And who had been tampering with his breaker? Was it really the Russians? Or had he been lured down to the basement by a killer? He let possibilities run through his mind, unchecked, uncensored. For an instant, he flashed on what being bludgeoned to death would be like—the shock, the pain, the froth of blood in his mouth, the slow oozing away of life. He saw his crushed body on the cold cement floor. Someone would find it and be horrified at the sight. Would anyone call the police? And who would call his parents? His stomach tightened at the grief this would cause them. He shook himself. This was crazy. He had to stop his mind from running wild.

To distract himself from his dreadful thoughts, he got up from the couch and started to pace. He willed himself back to reality. Who was behind this? Could it really be the Russians with the Great Dane? He fired up another cigarette and paused in his pacing long enough to take a deep calming drag. His mind scanned possibilities. Only the other day, someone had written ZILAIS, the Latvian equivalent of fagot, in the dust of his car windshield. He wondered at the time if it was skinheads. If it had happened in his old neighbourhood in Ottawa, that would have been a reasonable thought, but here in Latvia, Arnie's grasp of the local idiom was not as firm.

His thoughts started to wander. He had been surprised to find, in his first days in Riga, that his language skills were good enough to get by but where he found it frustrating was trying to make sense of the cultural undercurrents and contemporary slang. As his culture zone expanded, he learned that *zilais*, literally translated as 'the blue one', was a reference to Gainsborough's famous painting. Whereas the British had settled for a schoolboy term, Arnie noted the Latvians had chosen to exhibit their knowledge of European art.

Still, he hadn't seen any skinheads around the building, or anywhere else in Riga, for that matter. There were plenty of Russians, though. Probably willing to whack someone for a pack of American smokes. Come to think of it, he only knew of one or two non-Russians who lived in his building.

With a groan, Arnie dropped back down on his couch. Numbness trickled down through him like rain. The stress had made him go limp. He watched the smoke from his cigarette dissipate in the air. Then a new thought hit like a ton of bricks.

What if Mike had been in the garage being chased by somebody because of the photos he was supposed to be delivering? Mike could easily have thrown the breaker switch to alert Arnie that there was a problem. And it had certainly worked. Arnie had gone down as fast as he could and then seen a body. That's what it must be. Mike and his photos. Mike was lying on the garage floor in a pool of blood. Arnie kicked himself. Why hadn't he had a better look? And maybe he had still been alive at that point. Arnie should have called an ambulance even if he didn't want to call the police. And the photos. God, they must be dynamite!

After a few minutes, Arnie talked himself into changing his mind. He was on a roller coaster. It probably wasn't Mike after all. Why would Mike go through the garage? He usually buzzed at the ringer out on the street. Mike would turn up, fresh with some new wise guy talk, wearing his Air Jordans and if not, Arnie would call him later to make sure he was alright.

He felt calmer. The pressure in his chest was easing. He looked over at the table where he had left his drink and noticed that his glass was empty. As he bent over to crush out his cigarette, he decided to have just one more. Getting up, he made for the fridge and poured out a double straight vodka. No big deal about the double. He still wasn't up to Latvian proportions yet.

Firmly closing his mind to what he had seen in the basement, he went to his workstation. He gulped at his drink without tasting it while his free hand pawed through the debris he had let accumulate around his computer. How much had he lost? And where the hell was the manual with the *Retrieve* instructions? He found it. Stared in horror at the illegible hieroglyphics. *Christ! In Russian!* He threw the manual across the room. With a screech, Gerda disappeared under the couch.

Arnie could tell he was about to lose it. Time for desperate measures. With drink in hand, he marched to the bathroom and retrieved his pouch of pills. He shook out five milligrams of Atavan. Paused. It would make him drowsy. He put the pouch back. Thought for a moment, then dug out his headset and put on Celine Dion. He was in no state to endure the shriek of sirens, the commotion in the building, the cops banging on doors—all of which he expected to hear any minute.

He brought up the computer, checked the backup file. Thank God he had only lost the last bit about Father Gregory, and maybe that in itself was divine intervention. Maija Fischer was his IT girl for this issue and he knew he'd hardly scratched the surface. As for Father Gregory, the sooner he buried this latter day Rasputin underneath the classifieds where he needed some filler, the better. Father Gregory, no matter what his sins, just didn't fit in with the new Riga.

Arnie checked his watch. Twenty minutes left before he had to send his stories off electronically to the print-shop in Old Riga. And still no Mike. Worry about him later, Arnie said to himself. You can do it. Breathe deep. Think positive. Fortunately, he only had to replace two paragraphs. No sweat, thanks to Maija.

Arnie tapped on the keys as the room reverberated with a steady click click click breaking the silence of his concentration. The computer screen glowed an eerie green. It became the focus of Arnie's whole being. His fingers had taken on renewed urgency. Adrenaline pumping in his brain sending his body into fight or flight mode. It felt good. What an edition this would be!

Making his deadline, Arnie e-mailed the stories off with a big RUSH heading. Then he pushed back his chair and asked himself where the cops were. He imagined that they had already been at the scene and had started questioning the tenants. Soon, they'd make it up to the sixth floor. Arnie opened his door. All was quiet. From a distance, he made out the familiar mournful cry of one of the toms probably attracted by Gerda who was still in heat.

Arnie's nose for news twitched at the whiff of an in-house true crime story but he knew he would have to be careful this close to home. He had been warned many times to avoid the local police. In Latvia they were synonymous with corruption and brutality.

Stepping into the cold corridor still wearing his jacket, he locked up his apartment. He decided to investigate. At the lobby door, he checked for police cars. Nothing. Had he missed them or were they just slow to respond? Or maybe no one had called them. God, he didn't want to get involved. He *couldn't* get involved.

Almost against his will, Arnie opened the door to the garage. Old Mrs Klavins, wrapped in her shawl, was putting something into the locker room. Other than that, the basement was deserted. A few more parking places were filled. Tentatively Arnie approached the Lada. It had not been moved. He waited for the old lady to leave the garage before he got closer. A polite nod was his only interaction with most of the tenants. There was nothing to be culled from gossiping with someone like old Mrs Klavins. Or so he had always thought. Now, he paused to reconsider. He had been wrong before. Who knows what these old pussies could tell him. But this was not the time to find out.

Finally, the garage door shut behind the old lady. Anticipation gripped him and, underlying it, a building sense of dread. A warning voice whispered in his ears. *You shouldn't be doing this. You shouldn't get involved.*

Hesitating only for a few seconds, he moved closer to the Lada and crept around to the spot next to the wall where he had seen the body. Fear hit him like a bolt of lightning. Nothing! There was nothing! No body. No blood. He stood glued to the spot, stupefied. Again that feeling. Was there someone watching from the shadows? *Shit!* he finally yelled. It made him feel stronger. He was reacting. He was normal.

Still incredulous, Arnie reassured himself that he wasn't crazy. He had seen what he had seen. Could there be traces of blood still stuck to his loafers? There had been blood, lots of it. That would be proof of what he had seen. Proof that there had been blood with someone's DNA on it. Fear coursed through his body making his legs weak as he stumbled toward the door. Was someone behind him, ready to attack him with a tire iron? He held his breath, crept forward, reached the door, opened it. He was safe. He was out in the hallway making for the stairs.

Back in his apartment, Arnie removed his shoes and put them in a plastic bag. He wished he could call 911. Was there 911 in Latvia? Were there phone books? Yellow Pages? He'd never seen any. And where was Mike? No way could it be crazy ol' Mike's body that he had seen lying there on the garage floor. No way.

Feeling exhausted and alone, Arnie slumped down on his couch. He put his hand to his head and winced. A headache was forming at the back of his skull. Through the pain, he got a sudden glimpse of how hollow his life had become, how insubstantial it was. He had enemies, not friends. Oh, he knew people, lots of people but no one he could trust, no one who would listen to him, comfort him, care for him. He buried his face in his palms, tried to reassure himself, tried to figure out what to do.

He ran and re-ran scenarios—the police, the embassy. None of them worked. Suddenly a glimmer of hope flitted through his mind. There just might be someone he could talk to. What about that woman on the third floor? What was her name? Oh yeah, Vizma Gross. They had met at an expat function and always chatted a bit when they ran into each other in the hallway. They both happened to be Canadian. He knew he should have asked her out for a drink. Well, no time like the present. He almost smiled as he made up his mind. What was her phone number? He knew he had her card somewhere. But where? His hands wandered over his desk, through his pockets. He checked his wallet. Yes, thank God, there it was. He had slipped her card inside when he had given her one of his.

Bless you, Vizma Gross, Arnie breathed as he reached for the phone. He knew he couldn't just show up at her door. He had to call ahead, especially after nine. Holding the receiver and her card in his left hand, Arnie checked the number again as he positioned his right hand on the dial. Suddenly his heart slammed into overdrive. He remained rigid for a long moment as the adrenaline ran its course. For the second time that night, his world had gone black. He knew immediately that he wasn't going to make a phone call, wasn't going anywhere. There was no sound in his apartment. A shadow shifted slightly in the silence, wrapped itself around him. Arnie was scared stiff.

Chapter Three

He didn't have to think twice. There was no way he was going down to that basement again. He remembered the creepy feeling he had of being watched. No one was going to lure him out of his apartment tonight.

For the second time that night, Arnie lit the candle and poured himself a stiff drink of vodka. Already he could feel the temperature plummeting like a stone. It was going to be a cold night without the space heater. Still wearing his jacket, he wrapped himself in the blanket from his bed and lay down on the sofa. Gerda, declining the invitation to join him, made for her usual spot on the bed.

A few minutes later, the vodka had done its trick and Arnie's adrenaline surge had receded into the night. He began to doze off, only to wake up a short time later with a start. He sensed that there was something in the corner of the room. Something moving. A small tingle of anticipation sped through him as he stared hard into the cold gloom. A shadow stirred and he was finally able to make out the figure of a man dressed in old-fashioned clothes. "Hello," Arnie said out loud and smiled. It was one of his regulars.

Early on, Arnie had realized that he was sharing his apartment with the spirits of several former inhabitants. A little research and he had learned that one of them was probably Baron von Hahn. Arnie had observed that the prosperous Hanseatic League aristocrat always appeared in his apartment whenever Balzams was being served and had wondered what the Baron must think of his former apartment now.

Baron von Hahn had lived there at the end of the eighteenth century when the manorial six-storey house had been built. At that time, the apartment had been three times as large, with high majestic ceilings, ornamented doorways and parquet floors. And the furnishings had been splendid. Arnie's imagination luxuriated in the fabulous Biedermyer pieces, the sumptuous draperies, the rich Oriental rugs.

After the First World War, during the years of Latvia's independence, the lifestyle of the inhabitants had been more austere. Sometimes, when Arnie was lying awake at two or three in the morning, staring into the dark, an earnest well-to-do Latvian clergyman and his wife materialized. They never had much to say but Arnie felt that they didn't approve of his housekeeping. Often, he could hear soft clucking as tch...tch...tch sounds came to him from a corner of his bedroom.

Then the catastrophe. The Soviet occupation. Arnie had heard that all a Russian officer had to do to claim an apartment was nail a kopejka to the door. And so the magnificent building on Valdemara Street, like all others, had been desecrated, chopped up into tiny rat-holes, the Latvian owner and his family shipped off to Siberia. Their maid had been luckier. She had been allowed to stay but forced to share her cramped living quarters with strangers. There had been occasions when Arnie had seen her wearing her black uniform with the frilly white apron. She always wept and complained to him about the terrible conditions she had to live under. It had been better being a servant than a comrade.

Families from Mother Russia took over the house. Arnie could imagine the tension, the feuding, the squabbling in the decrepit warrens where a kitchen and bathroom had to be shared by a dozen people. No doubt there were homicides with secret burials deep in the woods. No one ever knew what had happened. People simply vanished. The Soviet regime revealed nothing, never admitted that there could be crime in the workers' paradise.

More change was to come. After Latvia regained its independence, the building was de-nationalised and a claim was made by a descendent of the last owner. This did not bring stability. Quite the contrary. Now Arnie's tenancy was in danger. Even though the apartment house still wore the patina of neglect, once the new landlord took possession, someone like Arnie would not be able to afford the rent. And local Latvians, who had even less money, had no chance at all of a decent apartment.

Arnie could hear the clonk clonk clonk of his new landlord coming to evict him and usually it was this that awakened him.

All night, Arnie had drifted in and out of sleep. At around four in the morning, he was up again and was so cold he decided to turn on the gas oven. As he felt his way to the kitchen, he almost jumped right out of his skin. A blast came from his radio. Seconds later he froze like a deer caught in the headlights. It took him almost a minute to realize that his power had just come on again. *What is going on!*

Arnie's head pounded with the beat of his pulse as he went around his apartment turning off lights. Finally, he got back into bed taking his short-wave radio with him. It was company.

When it was light, he got up. A hangover throbbed in his head, dread clenched at his stomach and his mind felt fuzzy from lack of sleep. Still, his thoughts immediately fixated on the scene in the basement. He had not imagined it. He was certain that he had found a dead body, that it was probably a murder and that quite possibly his breakers had been deliberately thrown, not once, but three times.

He reached for his pack of cigarettes, fingers clumsy with cold and with nerves. He took one out but didn't light it. Nausea swirled in his stomach. He couldn't stop his mind from bombarding him with the same old questions. What was going on? And what did it have to do with him? And where was Mike? He wished it had all been a nightmare. All of it. He wished he could just go back to his writing with nothing more serious than gossip to worry about.

Chapter Four

"Yuck!" Vizma Gross said to the person in the bathroom mirror. It was morning, the beginning of another grey lifeless day. She was depressed. "Damn," she continued snatching off her glasses. Without them she could barely see to put on her eye makeup. Mechanically, she stroked blue powder on her eyelids and made a scratchy attempt to outlined her eyes in black. Then the tricky part. Mascara. Her hand shook and she thrust a woolly gob straight into her eyeball. *Dammit. Dammit. Dammit.* She bit her lower lip as her eye teared and the sooty makeup ran down her cheek. Not a pretty sight, she thought and not for the first time. "Great. That's really great," she said out loud meaning just the opposite.

She was having another one of her bad expat moments. Her mascara stick would soon dry out and God only knows where she'd be able to replace it. Perhaps soon she wouldn't care. To her annoyance, the tears kept coming. Was she indulging in her most hated emotion? Self pity. No, she couldn't. She'd hate herself.

Even without her glasses she saw how puffy her face had become. Booze. That's what it was. Too many cocktails, too many bottles of wine sipped by the telly. The booze-bloat hit everyone. In her experience, every expat in Latvia fell victim to it sooner or later. The other day, she had caught sight of an acquaintance, Ingrida Brauns, and had sincerely wondered if the fifty year old woman, who looked ten years older then the first time they'd met the month before, was terminally pregnant. Why doesn't someone open up a Betty Ford franchise, she wondered. She'd be first in line.

To make matters even worse, she had started to smoke and there were days she felt one pack short of lung cancer. And she wasn't eating well, probably losing brain cells at high-speed with the drinking and smoking. But, for the moment, she didn't have the energy to do anything about it. She knew she looked older than her forty-two years. Older and harsher. Her hair was a bright yellow, no longer the pale ash frosting she was able to achieve in Ottawa. Still, could she really see herself back in Canada ever again? She had wanted a new beginning and had fantasized what Riga would be like. The fantasy had been a bummer but something still held her. Hope? Inertia? Perhaps a mixture of both.

She blinked away the tears, sprayed on some Tommy Girl cologne and straightened her shoulders. Time to wash up the morning dishes. Halfway through, she stopped. Held her breath. Was someone at her door? Or was the noise more like a rap or somebody accidentally hitting the door with a shopping bag? She waited. There it was again. She walked towards the door. Now what? Puzzlement flickered across her face. Thank God she had dressed, she thought as she smoothed down her hair. Her dirty white bathrobe was a disgrace. Natch, since there was no laundry room in the building. Approaching the door, she felt a twinge of alarm. Who could it be? She wasn't expecting anyone. After a year in Latvia, she had learned not to trust a soul. She had installed a steel door, a double deadbolt, a chain. Vizma opened the door a crack and peeked out. Arnie Damberg's face, round and soft as butter, eyes like goldfish swimming in a murky bowl, appeared in the inch-wide space.

"Hi. I'm Arnie Dambergs."

"Yes?" Vizma said peering at him over the security chain.

"I live on the sixth floor. Remember me?"

"Ah...Umm..." Vizma stared at him uncertainly, her lips tight with surprise.

"We met at the expat party about a month ago."

A slight frown played across her face. She cast an appraising glance over him. Yeah, it's him alright, she said to herself grimly. She had met him, had not really liked him but here he was.

"Ahhh, yes." She allowed her face to relax. "But it wasn't the expat party, was it? I remember now. It was that reception after the Finance Minister's speech at the Radisson. You're from Ottawa too, aren't you?" She slid the chain off, opened the door and smiled.

"Is this a bad time or could I come in for a minute?"

"Uh, sure. Come on in," Vizma said turning up the wattage on her smile just a little. "I was going to invite you over with some other people just arrived from Canada. But I haven't got around to it. Come in, come in," she said stepping back and holding the door open.

Arnie murmured a thank-you as he moved deeper into the room. His eyes darted around.

"Would you like coffee? Or something stronger perhaps?" Vizma chuckled to hear herself offering booze at this hour of the morning. In Canada, this would have been all wrong. She knew it was a measure of how interwoven she had become in the social fabric of her new life in Riga.

Arnie couldn't help but gape in envy. The apartment smelled pleasantly of coffee and Vizma's cologne. His gaze swept around the large room. Vizma watched him for a moment. How did her place look to him? she wondered not being able to read the envy in his eyes.

Her one bedroom apartment had been a real find. It was on the third floor. Never rent the first or last floor, she had been advised. There was a good probability of theft on the first. No water pressure on the sixth. And the elevator never worked. It was not a bad apartment. Correction. It was the best. Superb compared to the rat-holes most Latvians lived in. Newly renovated with its own hot water tank, it came equipped with a satellite dish on the balcony left by the previous tenant, also an expat. Vizma had heard that the tenant had to be air-ambulanced back to New York for reconstructive surgery after a fight with two Russians in a bar.

Arnie could see that Vizma's apartment had once been a part of a larger and grander apartment which, like many others, had been chopped up during the Soviet occupation to accommodate as many of the Russian proletariat as possible. He knew of only one Latvian, an author, who had lived in one of the few intact *belle époque* apartments. It had been his reward for all the propaganda he had written for the Soviet State. The place was now a mini museum and Arnie had no interest in seeing it.

Through the sheer curtains, a diffuse grey light was seeping into the room. The apartment was definitely superior to Arnie's dingy Soviet-style rat-hole with its Russian blue kitchen walls, no toilet seat and crumbling plaster. He had started to renovate his living room which doubled as workspace. He had even managed to buy a chandelier, a small coffee table and the sofa which lent his place a semblance of old-world elegance. And of course he had the space heater. But his apartment certainly couldn't compare to this.

"Nice place," Arnie said with a trace of indifference in his voice as he didn't want Vizma to know he was drooling. "I hope I'm not barging in at a bad time. I just had to talk to somebody."

Vizma smiled. She recognized a fellow stage-one expat. Loneliness and liquor.

"Coffee? A drink?" she smiled. "I'm having one. A nice hot drink, that is."

"That would be great," Arnie said with relief. Vizma motioned him further inside the room. She gestured at the couch.

"Make yourself at home."

Arnie flopped down and briefly closed his eyes while Vizma disappeared into the kitchen. He thought back to his first waking hours that morning. As soon as his eyes had opened, his head had started to throb, dread had clenched at his stomach and his mind had shot back to the scene in the garage. The early hours had passed in the dull haze of his hangover and dread. He had decided not to call ahead, not give Vizma a chance to find an excuse to put him off. He had gone straight to her door.

"Arnie!"

Roused from his half doze, Arnie bounced up.

"I'm making you a health drink," Vizma called from the kitchen. And she didn't mean tiger's milk or some yogurt-brewer's yeast cocktail. Humming to herself she smiled as she carefully poured two cups of black currant juice into a saucepan, added a few generous splashes of Balzams, a squirt of lemon juice and a tipple of Grenadine. Presto!

"Warms the insides and sets you up for the day," she announced. Arnie sighed with pleasure as he breathed in the fragrant aroma coming from the kitchen.

"Careful, it's very hot," Vizma warned as she deposited a steaming mug on the table.

"Mmm…" Arnie purred as he took a sip. Just what the doctor ordered. Cigarettes were lit and Vizma settled down in a chair opposite him.

"I think I saw a dead body in the garage last night," Arnie blurted out.

"What!"

"I know it sounds crazy but I just have to tell somebody."

"Well, of course you do. Where did you see it?"

"Well..." Arnie was suddenly speechless, fumbling for words, getting all upset at the thought of having to live through the whole thing again. "God! I don't know where to begin."

Frowning, Vizma waited as he stared into space. The sleepless night had dulled his mind and what was left of it was now being decked by the Balzams.

"Begin, already," she finally said, impatient to hear the story.

Arnie gulped on the drink now that it had cooled. He pulled on his cigarette. Leaning forward toward her, he began. He told her about the power failure, about what he had seen in the basement, about Mike, about how scared he was. As he talked, his anxiety lifted. Here was someone he could talk to. When he finished, he stared at Vizma with his watery blue eyes wondering how she would react. Vizma sighed, shrugged, finished her drink and lit another cigarette before speaking.

"Want coffee?"

"What!"

"Yeah, a real coffee. None of that ersatz crap. Real filter coffee."

Arnie frowned. Wasn't she going to say something? He nodded a yes to the coffee. Before going back into the kitchen, Vizma came to sit beside him. She looked at him earnestly and said in a low flat voice,

"You know, the best thing you could do is forget all about it. Like, what do you care? What's it to you? It could be anything. A mob hit, whatever. Forget about it. That's what I'm telling you."

Arnie stared at her. He couldn't believe his ears. Here she was sweeping a murder under her Art Nouveau carpet. His mind

29

protested but his body was giving in. Vizma's drink had almost made him comatose. His head lolled back and his mouth hung open. Lucky there aren't any flies around, he thought.

"You've had a terrible experience. Just take it easy." Vizma was soothing him. "Now, how do you like your coffee? Milk? Sugar?"

"Black," Arnie managed as he closed his eyes. Two minutes later, his mind became focused again. He'd kill for a bath. If he asked to use the bathroom, he could check out her hot water supply.

"May I use your bathroom?" Arnie said as loud as he could so that she could hear from the kitchen.

"Be my guest. Down the hall to your right. Don't mind the mess."

There was no mess as far as Arnie was concerned. He was impressed. A huge boiler hovered over an enormous tub. This must have cost, Arnie said to himself and wondered how long he should wait before asking if he could have a bath.

He used the toilet and returned to the living room as Vizma came out of the kitchen with two cups of steaming coffee. It was cold in the room. She switched on the space heater and lit another cigarette offering Arnie the pack.

"Thanks," Arnie sighed and managed a smile. It was an unguarded moment. Rare for him to smile but there it was. He wondered when the last time had been that he had smiled in a genuine way. Vizma noticed the smile, noticed the nice teeth.

"You're right," Arnie finally said in a stronger voice. "I'm going to forget all about yesterday." He glanced at his watch. A bit past one. His heart was starting to speed from the coffee.

"Have you had lunch?"

Vizma shrugged.

"I mean, would you like to go out for lunch with me?"

Vizma's face brightened. "Sure. I'd love to. Give me a few minutes."

Arnie got up. He was a tiny bit dizzy. He lurched forward a step or two but then managed to steady himself. He was alright. In fact, he felt much better than he had in days.

Chapter Five

A gust of wind scooped up the powdery snow and sprayed the air with a mist of tiny white crystals. How pretty, Vizma thought and how nice to be walking through the frozen streets with Arnie, going to a nice warm restaurant. Their hands were tucked into pockets, their shoulders hunched into the wind. Their words, when they spoke, puffed out like smoke in front of them. A few new snowflakes floated down from the sky and sprinkled over the grey stone buildings. The bare branches of trees, etched darkly against the light, rattled together in the wind. On the frozen ground eddies of snow danced across the pavement. In a couple of hours, there would be a thick white blanket softening the edges of everything underneath.

On each street corner, beggars stood with palms outstretched or squatted on torn dirty pieces of cardboard. Others, less hardy, huddled in doorways. Many bore placards telling of their misery—almost always in Russian. Thank God for that, Vizma muttered to herself. Mean as it was, she didn't want to know. Emaciated dogs roamed the streets looking for someone to bite and wounded cats dragged their bodies through the alleys, on the brink of losing their fight for survival. At the next street corner, as if to prove a point, Vizma and Arnie almost tripped over a cat with a broken leg inching itself away from the traffic. Vizma noticed that its eyes were covered in puss. She felt like screaming a plea of mercy for all these creatures. But how would that help? If she had money, she'd fund a Humane Society. But that would be a mere drop in the bottomless bucket.

In every way, the years of Soviet neglect had stripped Riga of its pre-war title. 'Paris of the North', Riga had been called in the days when the medieval cobblestone streets, elegant cafés, broad tree-lined avenues and picturesque architecture had made it an international travel destination. Both Vizma and Arnie's parents had filled them with stories of a charmed existence in the once splendid capital. But what they were seeing now were the remnants of the Soviet era which had had left its ugly pockmarks—derelict historic buildings, once elegant showcases, used as dumping grounds for garbage, their ornate wrought iron balconies filled with trash and their once magnificent avenues scarred wastelands in a damaged city.

In front of them as they walked, pedestrians lurched and stumbled on neglected sidewalks covered with ice. There was never any sand or salt to give some traction. And there was the constant danger from overhead. Huge icicles formed along the eves of the buildings and when the sun warmed them enough, they would crash down with no warning. Arnie had heard that dozens of people were killed every winter.

Cold vapour clouds billowed from passing cars as they picked their way across the ice. They passed a bookstore showing North American style Valentine's Day cards. They stopped to look at them and Arnie commented on the Latvian resentment of the growing trend to celebrate these foreign holidays. What did Halloween or Valentines Day mean to Latvians? A commercial ploy, that was all. Still, the cards were pretty and the jack-o'-lanterns were fun. Like all expats, Vizma and Arnie resented the American Chicken sign looming obscenely over the most prestigious square in Riga. While they acknowledged to each other that McDonalds was a resounding fast food success that created employment, they had not returned to Latvia to eat burgers or to stare at the eyesore ads marring the historic city. But money had to be made. Sadly, Riga, like the rest of the world, couldn't afford to be too proud.

They reached an easy decision about where to eat and headed for Osiris, almost a cliché in the expat community (although the place was not for the homophobic or for those short of cash). Still, if they could get the table near the wood burning stove, a good-natured waiter and the latest *International Herald Tribune*, they'd be as close to Nirvana as they could get in this cold and derelict part of the world.

Of course, there was always Riga's Bistro, the second best expat hangout in town. The owner of the newly renovated restaurant on Kaleju Street, Uldis Baltins, was trying to attract the artsy crowd by staging exhibits, poetry readings and discussion groups. He had even taken a shot at the newly emerging AA movement by offering to host a few meetings. Arnie had always thought that Uldis was trying too hard, that his prices were out of sight, not to mention that he was way too overtly gay.

Uldis had become enamoured with the expat community and wanted to become a player on the scene. In fact, he had even come up with the idea of holding a Young Miss Latvia contest. This had raised his profile another notch up the ladder. Arnie had heard that the American diplomatic corps were frequenting the Bistro on a regular basis and wondered who might be gay at the embassy. Perhaps he'd do an article on Uldis Baltins in one of his upcoming issues.

Arnie took off his coat and hung it on the rack next to the bathroom door. Vizma slipped hers off her shoulders but kept it close by. Today they were the lucky ones. The table by the wood burning stove was theirs. Now if only the friendly waiter would appear. But he didn't. As always, the staff looked as if they had been sucking lemons.

Vizma and Arnie continued to talk in English and even ordered their meal in English, which meant they'd get better service. They both ordered a beer, Latvia's own Aldaris. And a Greek salad. No surprises here. A few tired leaves of iceberg lettuce, a couple of tomato wedges, a chunk or two of cucumber, a sprinkling of olives, plus the occasional crumb of feta. This satisfied the expat craving for fresh greens but the ten dollar cost could be counted on to take their breath away. Thank God Arnie was paying. That suited Vizma just fine.

Casting an eye over the habitués, a few expats idling away the hours, a couple pouring over a map, Arnie decided there was no gossip to be had. He was beginning to feel his old self again. But with a difference. There was a nice lady sitting beside him. He would have to be nice. He laughed to himself wondering if he could manage it. Vizma caught the look of merriment in his eyes.

"What?"

"Just thinking," Arnie shook his head and cracked a grin.

"God, I just die for fresh greens over here, don't you? A couple of Americans pay a local farmer in Marupe to grow greenhouse lettuce. It retails for five dollars US a head."

"That's cheap," Arnie laughed. "Have you ever tried to find a thick juicy steak?"

"Well, no. I'm still hunting for dental floss and a stick of mascara."

Arnie grinned. "Luckily I don't have the mascara problem and I can't help you there. But I know where you can get dental floss. Go to the pharmacy on Brivibas Street right near the

Hotel Latvija. Now, for a change of topic, what brought you to Latvia?"

Vizma fell silent. For once, she felt like telling the truth.

Arnie noticed her hesitation. "Don't worry. I don't betray friends—the very few I have. No, let me correct that. The *only* one I have."

Vizma looked pleased. "It's nice of you to say that, especially as we've known each other for all of two hours. Umm, could I have another beer?"

"Sure. I'll have one too."

Arnie motioned to the gloomy waiter who looked like his best friend had just died. Vizma lit a fresh cigarette and closed her eyes for a moment holding in the smoke, then exhaled with a sigh. She reached across the tide of time. So long ago. It all seemed unreal to her now.

"Well, I got divorced. No kids. The job was nothing much. I thought before I'm too old... you know, for a new start."

"Before you're too old?" Arnie looked quizzically at her, ready with his well-honed schmooze.

"Yeah. Well, I *am* too old. I aged ten years in the first year I was here."

"Aw c'mon..." Arnie drawled. "You're only as old—"

"Sure, Arnie," Vizma interrupted. "Anyway, here I am. Doing the usual. Teaching English at the Art Academy and one course at the University. I was a legal secretary in Ottawa. The lawyer I worked for was a coke-head. Snorted all the profits from his practice up his nose. When I saw him using the funds from his trust account to pay his dealer, I got out."

It was nice to talk. It all seemed so simple when she said it. Somewhere along the way, the heartache had dissolved without leaving a trace. She didn't want a single thing back. Not the job, not the husband. Vizma shook her head as if shaking off any lingering regrets and turned the conversation back to Arnie.

"Now, about last night," she said lowering her voice. "As I said before, just forget what you saw in the garage. Killings are no big deal here. My advice is keep your head down and mind your own business. This is the Wild West Show, shootouts at high noon on Brivibas Street. Nobody sees a thing. It never happened. So, why should you care? This isn't your problem. Just mind your own business."

Yeah, I guess you're right," Arnie said slowly. He pushed the image of the heap of rags and the pool of blood out of his mind. Come to think of it, he'd hardly given it a thought over lunch. Now, his mind started to settle into its usual groove. He thought about work, about Mike and the photos he was supposed to have delivered. He was anxious to get a hold of Mike to find out what had happened to him. He had called in the morning but Mike hadn't picked up. Arnie still hadn't accepted that it was Mike's body that he had seen. He felt better about everything now. Quite possibly, once he was alone, the scene in the basement would start haunting him again but for now, he was fine. Checking his watch, Arnie gasped,

"Oh Lord! Look at the time! I'm sorry but I'm going to have to rush. I really appreciate being able to talk to you. I hope we can do it again."

Arnie pushed his chair back and stood up. Vizma felt jolted back to reality. He had thanked her and now he was leaving. And she would be alone again. This was not one of her afternoons of teaching classes and she felt a letdown. What would she do with the hours stretching ahead of her? She fought off a wave of depression as she reluctantly uncurled her legs from underneath the cozy banquette and slipped back into her coat. Hugging it around her, she braced herself for the outdoors.

"Ciao, Arnie. Now don't do anything silly and if something else comes up and you need to talk, you know where my door is."

Chapter Six

It wasn't until she reached Elizabetes Street that Vizma realized someone was following her. A few minutes before, she had noticed a heavy-set man standing at a street corner as she walked out of Osiris. At the time, she had thought nothing of it but she quickly changed her mind when the man started to shadow her the minute she walked away from Arnie. It was clear to her now that he had been lying in wait.

Stopping at a light, she casually glanced over her shoulder and scanned the pedestrians. Her eyes widened and a tingle of fear raced up her spine. There he was. For a split second she wanted to stop and confront him. Then she thought better of it and continued along. Trying to relax, she walked slowly, looking in shop windows.

A few minutes later, coming to a street corner, she stopped abruptly. Turned. He was there. Only a few feet away. The first thing that struck her was the long black coat. She thought that he looked like a Goth, like a thug with a rifle tucked beneath his arm, except that he wasn't a thug, he was more likely a hit-man.

As Vizma stared at him, a horrible realization swept over her. *He's after me*. She took in the cold expressionless face, the short-cropped hair. She knew instinctively that what lay beneath the blankness was the cunning mind of a killer. Abruptly, she looked away, turned back and picked up the pace.

Vizma usually loved walking through the streets of Riga. She would pick up her laundry or go on an errand and when she gave her name, there were no puzzled looks, no half smiles. She had a wonderful Latvian name and no one in Riga thought it was funny or weird. But now there was no enjoyment in her walk. She felt a creeping sense of dread. The Goth was definitely following her. But why? Nothing like this had ever happened to her before. She couldn't help thinking of what Arnie had told her. About the body in the garage. Panic started to build.

A few minutes later, she looked back again. She couldn't see him. The fact that she was in a relatively safe neighbourhood while it was still light made her feel a bit better. She had learned to avoid certain areas of Riga. Once, she had been kicked in the back by a child as she was walking home with her groceries. The boy looked about seven years old, only a child, Vizma had thought at the time. She had dropped her shopping bag but had managed to hang on to her purse. The Central Market area was particularly notorious for pickpockets and on any tiny side street, Vizma knew she would be easy pickings for the criminal urchins who had developed an almost genetic ability to sniff out an expat.

Keeping her guard up, Vizma walked along her favourite street, Elizabetes Street, which had been named before the Russian revolution, in honour of the wife of Czar Alexander I.

Somehow the broad avenue had managed to retain traces of its former grandeur. The buildings, which resembled the *hotels particuliers* of upper-class Paris, had been constructed of courses of stonework, wrought iron, stained glass, and Jugendstil ornamentation. Their magnificent black slate and terracotta roofs toped with golden spires and cupolas sparkled in the crystal northern light. This was the Riga of every expat's dreams.

The light was turning golden. By three it would be dusk. Vizma continued on her way, ignoring the signs of cracked foundations, leeching salt on masonry and garbage accumulating in doorways. Needing a beauty fix, she walked as far as the Fenikss House on the corner of Vilandes Street. The majestic nineteenth century apartment building had just been restored to its former splendour. For Vizma, this magical edifice was a sign of hope. It was the new Riga, rising out of the ashes of its Soviet past. Gazing up at the tower with its beautiful weather vane decorated with the inscription 1898, she realized that she had almost forgotten about the Goth.

Suddenly Vizma felt in a frivolous mood. Brushing aside any fears that remained, she started to play with the idea of getting her hair done. But her internal voice had a mind of its own, telling her that the smart thing to do would be to go straight home. Seeing Arnie at lunch looking at her from across the table had made her self conscious about her looks. The hairdo won out.

Having made up her mind, she turned away from the Fenikss House and walked back along the way she had come. She headed for the Hotel Latvija. For her, the hotel was the ultimate Soviet-built eyesore. Why don't they just tear it down, she muttered to herself. She was sure there were other monstrosities out there but this hotel was *it* as far as she was concerned.

Her thoughts turned to the hairdresser. Maybe she could find the Latvian word for highlights. A few weeks ago she had tried. *Šķipsniņas?* her hairdresser had asked. *Jā, jā,* Vizma had replied. You got it. Let's do *šķipsniņas*. But things had not gone well.

Coming out from under the dryer, Vizma had looked as if her hair had just exploded. And, as if that wasn't enough, the hairdresser still had more tricks up her sleeve. Bunching and shaping most of the hair with vigorous back combing, she had swirled the whole mess up into a pile on top of Vizma's head.

Mortified, Vizma had walked out of the salon looking like an over-the-hill Russian streetwalker with her orange hair teased up into a monstrous sixties beehive. Four inch heels and a pimp were the only things missing. And she couldn't believe how much the do had aged her. On top of it all, she discovered that the metal spikes used to hold the rollers in place had burned her scalp which, by the next day, had become covered with thick itchy scabs. It had taken about a week before she could put a comb through the whole mess. Come to think of it, why was she going back to this hairdresser? She shrugged. Creature of habit, she guessed.

With a brisk pace, she approached the hotel. Grey concrete led into the grey foyer of the ugly grey high-rise. Vizma averted her eyes from the toughs that always congregated in the hotel lobby. The place had all the atmosphere of an airport passenger lounge. Clusters of dark haired Hulk Hogan types with cell phones attached to their ears mingled with tourists. To the left, by the windows, was an oasis—a tiny bar complete with the usual tired sad-eyed waiter. Vizma decided on a quick pick-me-up before heading upstairs to the hair salon.

Janis, the barman, had his usual tale of woe. Vizma had heard it all before, many many times before. No one had money. Tourism was down. Janis was about to lose his job. She tried not to get too depressed. Very soon her head fuzzed over with the booze. She had gulped too fast. She thought to herself, you think you've got problems, I'm about to be made over into a Russian beehive.

Idly she examined the hand that was holding the drink. Should she have a manicure while she was at it? She laughed as she though about her favourite scene where James Bond in *From Russia with Love* was being attacked by the female general whose army brogues had suddenly sprouted six-inch daggers which were aimed at his crotch. Maybe the hairdresser could fit up each of her fingernails as weapons to use on the Goth. The thought made her laugh out loud. Janis gave her a quizzical look. What was it she was drinking? A Cinzano with a twist, no ice. The salad at Osiris hadn't been much of a lunch and the Cinzano was going to her head. She declined a second drink, quickly munched down a packet of peanuts and left the bar.

As she walked through the hotel lobby toward the staircase that led to the beauty salon, she cast a quick glance over her shoulder. All of a sudden, her mellow mood evaporated. There was the Goth, pretend reading at the newspaper kiosk. Fear made her entire body jerk. Without thinking, she did a quick side step and ducked into the nearest door. Luckily for her, it happened to be the ladies room.

Once inside, she gripped the sides of the sink and tried to get rid of the fear with a furious shake of her head. Her image stared back at her, vague and pale in the dusty mirror. Was she being ultraparanoid? No. The Goth was clearly after her. She tried to plan. She'd wait till one of the counter girls came in for a smoke and then ask if there was a back door nearby. She hoped they'd speak Latvian or English. Until then, she decided to go into one of the four stalls and squat on the toilet. A bolted door made her feel safer and she managed to calm herself. She waited, listened to the footsteps in the hall. There was no click clack of high heels. No brisk female walk.

Just as she settled to wait, panic hit. She heard the door open. Who was coming in? She held her breath. Listened. Didn't hear any of the usual sounds. No purse being opened. No running water. Heavy footfalls echoed on the cement floor. Then stopped. Somebody was standing outside her stall. She could smell him. Taste the danger. The moment was interminable. It was both real and surreal. *I don't want to die sitting on a toilet,* she cried to herself. Seconds before, she had instinctively pulled her legs up towards her body. Not daring to breathe, she kept still as a mouse, her stomach cramping, her throat aching with silent screams. After what felt like an eternity but was not more than a minute, she heard a shifting of feet. Then footfalls. A few seconds later, she heard the door of the ladies room close.

Vizma felt such relief that she almost keeled over. She dropped her legs to the floor, put her head in her hands and lurched against the flimsy stall divider. She steadied herself, got up and cautiously unbolted the cubicle door. There in front of her she saw a scrawl in black marker on the dusty mirror. Three words. *Go home fockyou.* The word *fockyou* had been corrected a few times. Vizma's only thought was to get the hell out of there. She pulled hard on the door. It was locked from the outside.

Chapter Seven

From time to time, Arnie reached for his glass of Balzams on the antique table next to him. This particular evening, he was drinking Balzams straight, much as he would an after-dinner liqueur. But Arnie was flexible. For him, it had become an all-purpose drink. He had a generous shot of it with strong black coffee and lots of sugar for his mid-morning pick-me-up, a liberal splash with blackcurrant juice and lemon as a hot toddy, or cut with Coke or vodka as a happy hour drink. Some of his acquaintances had tried it with Sprite but Arnie had passed. He was a traditionalist. At one point, he had thought of publishing a recipe book. The ingredients of Balzams could easily fill a chapter: herbs, ginger, oak bark, bitter orange peels, linden blossoms, iris roots, nutmeg, peppermint, valerian, cognac, and sugar. He was amazed that someone would take all that trouble but he was delighted that they had.

But as much as Arnie loved his Balzams, he always knew when to stop. A little while longer and he'd have had too much to drink, the candles would burn out, the mood would pass. And the snow would melt in the morning sunshine revealing once again the grit and grime of post-Soviet Riga.

Arnie was pleased with what he had managed to do with the apartment's limited space. He had made a work area along the back wall of the larger room. His personal computer, his printer and stacks of papers and books crowded a long wooden table. At the opposite end, he had made himself a living room.

Arnie noticed that his glass was almost empty again. His glazed eyes focused for a long time on the rich amber colour staining the bottom of the wine glass. He didn't need any more. He lit a cigarette, took a big drag and blew a fine stream of smoke towards the ceiling. Images floated past the inside of his eyelids. Pictures from the past gave way to a series of high gloss clips of the success waiting for him just around the corner. It was time for a fantasy fix.

He re-ran an old favourite. The saga of Arnie Dambergs, the years of poverty, struggle, neglect, the *sturm und drang* of the life of an unknown young writer. But wait. Fame was just around the corner and when it came, after years of hard work, Arnie would still be young enough to savour it.

Smiling to himself, he envisaged the scenario. There he was at the 'Reporter of the Year' bash, Arnie Dambergs, the newcomer, the *ārzemnieks*, crowned czar of Riga's investigative journalists. Latvia had never seen anything like it before.

There he was again descending from a limo at the snow-capped entrance of Riga Castle, sweeping nonchalantly up the grand staircase, invitation in hand. He paused, his coat resting on his shoulders, just long enough to allow the assembled glitterati to stare in envy and admiration. A short moment later, it was open two-lip season with cheeks swivelling from side to side, tongues wagging and eyes throwing meaningful glances across the crowded room.

Even though he often indulged in daydreams, Arnie still had a good grip on reality. He never confused his fantasies with real life. As a professional journalist, he never made anything up and he never disclosed his sources. Arnie had principles.

The other week, someone had offered him five hundred dollars not to do a story. Arnie had turned it down flat. Money isn't everything, he had said to himself, smelling the desperation behind the five hundred dollars. He knew that every politico, every sort-of celebrity, sheltered a pile of dirty little secrets just ripe and ready for an exposé. Still, Arnie was an expert at picking his way through the flotsam and jetsam. He usually managed to get a handle on the really important issues that would impact the social fabric of the post-Soviet nation—or so he believed.

Even though, to some of his readers, Arnie was a bottom-feeding scavenger, in his own mind he saw himself as a cultural anthropologist examining the inner workings of Riga's new social scene.

Arnie put his heart and soul into his job. The tiniest tip-off, a snippet of gossip, and he'd be hotfooting it out to the nearest dumpster, snuffling and digging, like a pig hunting for truffles. Arnie put it differently. He was doing research, investigating, keeping the public informed. He was proud of the fact that he only did high-class sleaze, never touched street crime, unless, of course, there were big players involved.

Sleaze, scandal, disgrace—it was all good stuff for the Czar of Gossip. But there also had to be a glamour component. And fun. Popular culture was entertainment, as far as Arnie was concerned and nothing entertained like a full-page spread detailing the downfall of some power obsessed Johnny-come-lately.

Sleaze had traction. It got him places, places he couldn't have imagined in his wildest fantasies.

*   *   *

In the fall of 1995, Arnie had arrived at Riga International Airport with copies of *Time* magazine and the *National Enquirer* tucked under his arm. His fear of in-transit boredom during the long stopover in Frankfurt had made him pick up the magazines left on a seat by a fellow traveller. Later, he would ask himself how it was that he had thrown out the copy of *Time* but had kept the *National Enquirer*. Was it simply jet lag, or a deeper sense of his destiny?

Once Arnie got to his room at the Hotel de Rome, he turned on CNN. This was the day that the verdict came down in the O. J. Simpson trial. He had been hooked that whole summer and had decided to splurge on the most expensive hotel in Riga just so that he could be in the courtroom for the verdict. The coverage was riveting. Then came the shocker. Like the majority, Arnie was flabbergasted at the news that O.J. had got away with murder.

An era had ended for Arnie. Another had begun. He was in a strange new land, looking for a nebulous beginning, one last chance to be someone, to do something special. At the end of the evening, Arnie couldn't help but feel let down that the trial had come to an end. He knew he'd miss Larry King with all the excitement of Bronco-chase witnesses, legal expert testimonials and sobbing relatives. It had been a true-life soap opera, a *TV verité* special full of glamour and suspense. There'd be nothing like it ever again.

The next morning, Arnie phoned room service for coffee and, while he waited for it to arrive, turned on the television. Having a feeling of disgust about the O.J. verdict, he didn't linger on the endless post-mortems. Clicking the remote, he stopped when he saw American soap opera royalty, speaking in Russian with Latvian subtitles at the bottom of the screen. He couldn't believe it. It was Dynasty! There was American starlet, Linda Evans, in silk peignoir descending the circular staircase, every platinum blond hair in place. "Hold me, Blake," softly filtered through the heavy Russian dubbing. Arnie found out later that every secretary and lots of others higher up on the socio-economic ladder stayed away from work every Monday morning, gluing themselves to their Soviet-made televisions to watch Dynasty.

When his coffee arrived, he clicked off the TV. Not having his usual copy of *The Ottawa Citizen* to read with his first cup, he made do with his rescued copy of the *National Enquirer*. And so it happened that during his first waking hour on his first day in the home of his ancestors, Arnie saw a need and knew he could fill it. His attention had fixated on the *Enquirer* and he had found himself asking, why not? Why not create his very own Latvian tabloid?

The start-up of Arnie's enterprise had come easily enough. He took ten thousand dollars from his retirement fund and bought a computer, desk-top publishing software and a printer. Arnie would have loved a fleet of motor-scooter paparazzi but his only employee to date was a cool-ass fine arts student he'd met at a local café who took pictures with a telephoto lens and charged him a modest fee. Shortly after Arnie met Mike, he had purchased a scanner to add to his professional set-up. Pictures were his meat and potatoes. He had learned that there was a bottomless pit of interest in captioned glossies depicting the darker side of the new upper class wannabes. Everyone read his stories, gaped at the pictures, wanted more—although no one liked to admit it.

"I'm going to tell you a secret I never told anybody before," old Mrs Norvils breathed. Arnie perked up his ears. He could almost taste the delicious gossip about to come from the other end of the phone. "Have you heard?" the old lady went on, her voice taking on an intimate excited tone. She slowly expelled a rush of air and paused. Making him wait was the good part. Arnie was in heaven. He loved the anticipation. A scandalous tidbit was about to drop into his lap. Leaning back on his sofa, he inhaled the secret as if it was a narcotic. Then, like a cat playing with a mouse, he kept the story alive, juggling it in the airy spaces of his brain until it was ripe and juicy and ready for one of his well timed exposés. Arnie stroked with a reassuring easy tone. Old Mrs Norvils didn't feel a thing, didn't have a clue, had no idea that Arnie was already laying out a headline.

Slipping out of the shadows Gerda came snaking over. She looked up with her yellow eyes, started to purr and rubbed herself up and down on his ankles. It was dinnertime. Arnie smiled, ended his conversation and reached down to pick up the cat.

Arnie's apartment was a nest, a perch high above the streets of central Riga. Arnie put his cat on the sofa by the window. It was Gerda's favourite spot from which to watch the birds and wait for her dinner. Gerda's excited chattering and the flapping noise from the birds as they came and went sometimes got on Arnie's nerves. But there was nothing he could do about it. It was simply the dance between predator and prey.

Arnie had often thought that he should have one of those La-Z-Boys shipped over. His sofa was elegant but uncomfortable. Thinking of all those poor bastard neighbours who couldn't afford it, Arnie set his space heater on high. For added heat, he took a final gulp of Balzams. Finally, he was ready to write up his stories. Squeezing his eyes shut for a moment, he sharpened his metaphoric nib, dipped it into his own lethal brew and set to work. In moments, gossip started to flow like poisonous lava as his chubby fingers pecked at the keys as fast as they could.

Years before, Arnie had chosen Truman Capote as his spiritual mentor. He admired Truman's style, his panache and his ability to convert everyday gossip into art. But Arnie knew that what he himself produced was far from being on a level with Truman Capote. To date, he had only managed to eke out a modest living recycling the waste from other people's lives. All he did was write it up and peddle it each month in his very own *WOW!* magazine. He was no artist, no alchemist of the ordinary, just a somewhat malicious tabloid reporter. The comparison with a real writer always depressed him.

Shortly after his arrival in Riga, when Arnie had his first glass Balzams, he took to the national drink as if his genetic code had been pre-programmed. He found it really did calm his nerves. And fortunately, it was not the same taste he remembered from his childhood when his grandmother had given him a tablespoon for a cough. At least, she had told him it was Balzams. Someone must have sent her a gift, how else would she have got it? Could she have brought it with her when she had to flee Latvia in 1944? It didn't really matter. Arnie felt it was a family tradition spanning the generations. Last year, he included a few bottles in his Christmas package to his parents in Ottawa. Usually, after the second drink, Arnie felt a surge of creative energy and, at moments, even thought that perhaps he was ready to write his memoirs.

Although, by any stretch of the imagination, it would be hard to count Arnie as one of the beautiful people, as middle aged men went, he wasn't bad. His round childlike face and ruddy complexion made him look younger than his forty-five years. He was almost six feet tall and carried his somewhat flabby body with a certain panache. In fact, compared to his age group in Latvia, he could even be called dishy. He had all his teeth, a good head of hair, and a dapper air of prosperity. Who was to know he had only a few thousand dollars left in his pension fund back in Canada? All the same, in the bleak and impoverished post-Soviet era, a North American bachelor was a trophy, a catch, a promise of a new and better life. Arnie now basked in his new-found popularity.

On those three-drink soirées, in his Balzams induced bliss after a deadline had been completed, it came to Arnie that he still aspired to great writing. Being in this mood, he would fantasize about winning a Pulitzer. He could see it clearly in his mind's eye. In Canada, he had had a hack job as copy editor at *The Ottawa*

Citizen. In Riga, lolling on his sofa with his third drink, Arnie knew he was worth more than that.

He wrote his *WOW!* stories in English, then had them translated into Latvian. He knew that the bilingual aspect of his publication would attract both expats and locals and do better than any other run-of-the mill tab. So far, Arnie had no real competition—in fact, no competition at all.

Arnie had favourites. At the moment, Maija Fischer was his special target. Not only was he entertained by Maija's audacity to offer herself as the Martha Stewart of Latvia but also he was amazed at the circles in which she travelled. Maija had married up. Her American husband was part of the delegation at the US embassy on Raina Boulevard. Maija had met the diplomat at a New Year's Eve ball given by President Guntis Ulmanis. Arnie had managed to get himself invited and had witnessed the sensation Maija had made in her rhinestone belly button dress which showed off her breasts to full advantage. Only a few intimates (maybe not so few) knew about the silicone implants. Maija was a novelty. She had come to a world where cosmetic surgery was almost unheard of.

On that evening, at Riga Castle, along with every other heterosexual male in the ballroom, fifty-eight year old Donald Fischer had jostled in line to be introduced. The cognoscenti shook their heads. They were doubtful. The American diplomat had a past. But, after three short and intense months of courtship, Maija became Mrs. Donald C. Fischer and made a seamless transition to the inner circles of the diplomatic world.

Few in Latvia knew the details of Don Fischer's background. What they did know was that he was a former businessman, not a career diplomat. And it was through his political connections that he had won his appointment as Commercial Attaché in Riga. At the time of his recent appointment, there were rumours of impropriety and insider trading. And worse. A cloud of suspicion had been cast over him by the sudden death of his wife of twenty-five years. The death had been deemed a suicide. His wife was supposed to have died from carbon monoxide. There had been unanswered questions at the time. Calling in a few favours, Don Fischer had been able to get out of Chicago and make a fresh start in the diplomatic corps. Now his life was going great and he had found himself a sexy new wife. Still, there were those who said that he had got away with murder. Behind his back, they called him Teflon Don.

Arnie chuckled to himself as his fingers raced from word to word. He knew that if his stories weren't dead-on, if they weren't filled with the right mix of salacious details, he risked getting raped by the likes of one of those up-start copycats coming down the tube.

After an hour and a half at his computer, Arnie took a breather. He sat back in his chair and lit a cigarette. There was no easy way to describe Arnie Dambergs at this point in his life. He was a talented bitter man, aware that he had failed to achieve what his immigrant parents had expected from him and sacrificed so much for. They had made sure that their son had the best education money could buy, while they themselves struggled with poverty in the new country.

Sometimes, Arnie felt that he was seeing his lifelong ambitions fade before him faster than the morning mist over the Daugava River. He felt he had failed his parents. And in doing so, he had failed himself. Arnie had grown up in Ottawa. At university, against his parents' wishes, he had decided to become a writer. Upon graduation, he got a job at *The Ottawa Citizen*, the premier (and one and only) newspaper of Canada's capital city. But there had been no promotions, and grappling with a midlife crisis, he had decided it was time for a drastic change.

Arnie had discovered his patriotism late in life—in 1991 when Latvia regained its independence from Soviet rule. For many expats like himself, Latvia represented new territory, new adventure, new hope. Arnie didn't think for a moment that going back to his roots made him a fugitive from his own life. He was simply re-inventing himself. In Riga, the world was seeing him with new eyes. He was no longer stuck in a dead-end job in west end Ottawa. The possibilities were limitless, and so were the risks.

Chapter Eight

Fear and disgust overwhelmed her. Vizma held her breath, tried not to feel her body trembling all over. The smell of the public toilet nauseated her. Somewhere in the back of her mind a voice was screaming: *You'll never get out! Never! Never!* Her fear was just seconds away from terror. She rattled the doorknob, pounded on the door, pounded until her hands ached. She knew she could die of fear, have a heart attack, an aneurysm. She opened her mouth, yelled *help, help*. Then, she yelled in Latvian until her feeble cries sputtered into a coughing fit. No response.

Finally, exhausted, she closed her eyes and leaned against the rusty sink. The only sounds came from the trickle of water escaping from the faucet and a running toilet somewhere behind her. When her eyes popped back open, there she was, staring from the mirror at the tiled walls of the empty bathroom. Her hair, for heaven's sake! It didn't even look that bad and it was what had got her into this mess. How vain, how stupid she had been, but there was no point in beating up on herself now. She needed to save her energy.

How could it be that there was no one around? The creep had probably bribed someone to put an out-of-order sign on the door, or even closed the whole goddamn hotel. It was a conspiracy. She looked at her hands. Awful, swollen. Her knuckles bleeding and an ugly bruise about to surface.

Vizma's mind kept running from one extreme to the other. She'd go nuts if she didn't get out. Giving up on her fists, she took off her shoe and pounded. Nothing. No footsteps approached. She clenched her teeth against the urge to cry. She couldn't let this break her. She opened one of the faucets and let the rusty water splash into the sink. It was freezing cold. She let it run over her hands and then scooped it up and put her face in it. She dried herself with her scarf and felt a tiny bit better.

Checking her watch, she saw that it was a little past four. Would there still be daylight? Maybe a bit. She turned her eyes back to the mirror. Suddenly, she smiled. The stupid ass couldn't even spell English. Vizma started to giggle. The thought of some dumb asshole struggling with the most common English obscenity made her laugh out loud. Of course, it had to be the Goth. Who else could be so stupid? But what had she done to attract his attention? Maybe it was a case of mistaken identity. Maybe not. Maybe being with Arnie had got her into trouble. Her brain puzzled over the events of the day, from eleven in the morning when Arnie had knocked on her door to their meal in Osiris and to her walk to the hotel. At what point had things started to go wrong?

To rest a bit, Vizma slumped down on the floor, holding her head in her hands. As often happened when she was about to give up, her unconscious mind came to her rescue. It threw up a valuable memory. Vizma suddenly remembered her landlord in Ottawa fixing the lobby door to prevent it being jimmied. Hey, maybe...

With determination she pulled herself off the floor, and brushed down her coat. Feeling a lot better, she started a detailed study of the lock. Soviet built, just as she'd hoped. She located the pin on her side of the deadbolt. Rummaging in her purse, she pulled out her VISA card, then started to work it in between the doorjamb and the pin. Luckily there was lots of room to manoeuvre the card. After a couple of tries, Vizma saw with relief that the pin had slipped back away from the jamb, exposing the bolt. Quickly but deliberately, she turned the cheap hardware knob. Presto, the door opened.

With the stealth of a cat, she slipped out into the lobby and took a long deep breath savouring her triumph. A chatter of voices reached her. Thank God it was crowded. It looked as if a tour group was just booking in at reception.

Vizma quickly scanned the room. The schmuck who had locked her in didn't seem to be around. She could see no grubby black overcoat prowling around, only beige raincoats and tweed standing in knots of threes and fours. She wondered idly where they were from. No way was she going to hang around to find out. On the other hand, it would be better to leave the hotel surrounded by one of those knots.

Within minutes, Vizma was able to relax enough to walk normally. But her hands still throbbed from the pounding and she felt a headache creep over her skull. All she wanted was a hot bath, some soothing chicken soup, a good film on the telly, and then, blessed oblivion. Thank God for the satellite dish. She had said this to herself many times before. Her one point of pride was that she hadn't lost her head. Hadn't gone screaming for help from some hotel security guard, or worse, from the police. She was smarter than that.

In a casual manner, she glued herself to a foursome of chatting tourists. Stood around smiling for a bit, then walked along with them through the lobby. Pausing for a moment just outside the front door, she reached into her purse and pulled out a pack of cigarettes.

"Would you like a light?"

Vizma whirled around. Heard the click of a lighter. Saw the flame. Clutched at her chest as if to stop her heart from popping out.

"I didn't mean to frighten you," a gruff male voice said politely.

Vizma's shoulders slumped with relief. God she was a nervous wreck! Her eyes focused on a well-dressed man who had been standing a few inches behind her. His face was pleasant and his cheeks were flushed pink with the cold.

"Are you alright?"

"Oh, yes," she breathed nodding her head. Recovering, she offered him a half smile and her cigarette. "I've had such a bad day… It's all right. It's just that I…" Vizma sucked in smoke then peered into the face. She knew that face. "We've met, haven't we?"

"Yes, we have. Last Friday, at the US Embassy TGIF? Beer and chicken wings?"

"How could I forget!" Vizma laughed. "You're Paul Stivirins. You had just come back from the US, newly divorced and so in demand that I really didn't get a chance to chat."

"Yeah, that's right."

Paul visibly grew an inch and puffed out his chest as he smiled. Vizma was laughing to herself knowing that the local Latvian twenty-somethings were already discussing how much his pension was in lats. She had heard the rumour that his ex had taken him to the cleaners and that was why he'd come back to Riga. Vizma wondered which of the local lovelies would catch this silver fox from Ohio. She knew they were all hoping to find themselves in a lifetime episode in a mansion in Boulder, Colorado or, better still, in LA. She wished them nothing but luck.

"If I'd known how popular I'd be here, I'd have divorced that woman years ago. Would you believe that I turned sixty-five a month ago?"

"No way, Paul. You're putting me on. You don't look a day over...um...fifty?" Vizma was enjoying this.

Paul gave his head a youthful toss.

"I'd better rush now," she said, adding her standard parting line. "I'm expecting a long distance call." Then realized that Paul Stivrins was already half way down the block.

She shrugged. Must be rushing to his current twenty-something. But he did stop and turn. "See you next Friday," he called after her as she set out along Brivibas Boulevard.

"Not if I see you first," Vizma muttered under her breath.

Her opinion was that expat men were very uninteresting. Besides, they always went for local girls half her age. Latvian homeboys could be enticed by the perceived wealth of expat women, although not many of the local men lived past fifty as smoking, drinking, rough living, and poor nutrition took its toll. And she was sure none of them had heard of Viagra.

That left the US military. Vizma sometimes met them at the American Embassy TGIF cocktail hour. But even from this pool no one had really attracted her. "Fish or get off the pier," a female friend had admonished her at one of the expat gatherings. Vizma had laughed. By now, she was well off the pier and had no intention of ever going back.

Life had certainly changed. She was a different lady now. No longer the trim well-groomed legal secretary with a halo of frosted hair and manicured nails. It was amazing how much weight she had gained in a single year. Well, yes, the booze-bloat, that's what it was. And the smoking didn't help.

Vizma sighed, took a quick drag on her cigarette and pitched the butt into a snow bank. She felt a hint of the old loneliness steal over her but vowed not to give in. Gotta quit smoking, she muttered under her breath knowing full well that she wouldn't. Instinctively, she looked over her shoulder to make sure no one was trailing her. No satanic Goth or street urchin or pickpocket.

She was almost home. The people on Gertrudes Street looked ordinary. Women rushing to do their evening shopping, some leaving work early. Conditions had improved to the point that people rarely had to wait in long line-ups but still buying groceries took time. Every store was a liquor store, the booze section always prominent at the front. It wasn't fair. They were making it too easy. Yep, it was all their fault.

Tonight, Vizma knew what she wanted. She wanted one of those big fat smoked chicken thighs. Yes, that's what she'd have for her dinner. Maybe she'd have two. And some grapes and cheese and delicious black bread. It would be a feast.

As she turned on Valdemara Street, Vizma felt she was approaching Nirvana. Her apartment promised warmth, peace, enjoyment. In the next blink of an eye, she'd be curled up on her couch with a golden oldie on the box, the space heater turned high, her mind fuzzing over from the nightcap. It would be bliss.

But, as she unlocked her front door, she realized that she could not just wipe everything from her mind, the way someone would surely wipe the grotesque message from the bathroom mirror. She knew that the go-home-fuck-you message would be replaying in her head, echoing through the busy streets, the corner store, her kitchen, her bedroom. It would be there as she was falling asleep alone in her narrow Soviet-era bed. Closing her eyes, she would try to will a dreamless sleep. But she would not succeed.

Chapter Nine

The morning had been really busy, just the way Arnie liked it. He had switched over to work mode. The events of the past few days skulked around somewhere in the far recesses of his mind and he intended to keep them there. He spent an hour answering Internet inquiries and going down his list of household chores. From time to time, his resolve weakened and his thoughts perversely slipped back to the body in the basement. Each time he had to spend a lot of energy pushing them away. Life had to go on, his next issue of *WOW!* had to be produced, he had to put one foot in front of the other.

It was thinking about Mike that bothered him more than anything else. Arnie had called him before going to bed but Mike had not picked up. Arnie would try again. He felt worried and guilty remembering that he owed Mike some fifteen lats and Mike was always complaining that he was short of money. Even at that, Arnie felt doubly guilty because he knew he wasn't paying Mike very much. The Maija shots were priceless. Arnie decided to add another five lats. That would make it sixty bucks Canadian. A good deal for them both.

What Arnie now needed was some up-to-date shots for the March issue—a super-sized Maija in the famous belly button dress which she liked to wear on formal occasions. He knew he was becoming fixated on Maija. And there was a good reason for that. It was more than just wanting to spoof her. He sensed that something lurked beneath the glitz and glamour of Maija's persona, something very wrong and that both Maija and her husband hid it well, whatever it was.

Arnie knew there was a dark side to the diplomat—besides the stuff in Chicago. It would take time to dig it all up and he would have to do it as quietly as possible. The Fischers could prove to be dangerous. He knew they were connected. To what, he wasn't sure. Arnie wasn't reckless. He could live with a certain amount of danger but if the mob was involved, he'd split. He had no doubt about that.

Arnie scowled as he picked up the phone to call Mike's cellular. The cell was Mike's pride and joy, the ultimate status symbol in Riga. Arnie had wondered how Mike could afford it but had never questioned him about it. Likewise, the car that Mike had recently acquired. There was a lot Arnie didn't know about this guy. But then, all he really needed to know was that his pictures were sensational. He'd be lost without Mike.

His call went unanswered. *Where the hell was Mike?* In some fifteen minutes, Arnie called again. No answer. No way was he going to give up. *Pick up, you bastard!* Angrily chain-smoking, Arnie punched in Mike's number every fifteen minutes. Picking up a pen, he drummed it against a stack of papers on his worktable as resentment and frustration grew. Mike had a cell while he himself had to make do with a Soviet-era phone which lacked a redial button. At least there was voice mail. He left urgent messages. Got nothing back.

"Son of a bitch!" Arnie muttered as he banged the phone into its cradle for the umpteenth time. The kid was never around when you wanted him. Arnie was stuck. Mike did good work and Arnie had planned more photo pages in the March issue. He couldn't help wondering about the photos Mike had promised him. Had the kid been high when he had called? Drunk? With him, it was hard to tell. He got into this wise guy shtick and Arnie had no idea where he was going or where he was coming from.

Arnie wondered how Mike managed to get himself included in high society events. Bribes? Connections? Drugs? Sex? All or any of the above, Arnie concluded and let his mind wander. He shook his head at some of Mike's idiosyncrasies. Mike was certainly a strange duck. The deal was that Arnie speak English with him, call him Mike. His real name was probably Miķelis, or maybe Mikhael. Understandable, Arnie thought. He himself had changed his name from Arnis to Arnie years ago. But the moniker would make it harder to find the guy. He was no-surname Mike as far as Arnie knew.

Two hours later, Arnie finally gave up calling. Putting down the phone, he tried to remember their last conversation. They had met at the Irish Pub a week before. What had they talked about? This and that. There had been the usual gangster banter with Mike trying out phrases he had picked up from some pirated video and he had done the look—cigarette stuck to his lower lip, eye squinting through the smoke—and had practised talking with a toothpick hanging from his bottom lip. Arnie had to admit that Mike was getting good.

Mike had talked a bit about his girlfriend, Anda, whom he insisted on calling Andy, thinking it was an Americanization of her name. He had laughed telling Arnie that she preferred being called Cupcake or Sugar or Sweetie Pie. Arnie hadn't paid much attention. Then they had talked about the Young Miss Latvia contest and Arnie had ordered shots of the girls for the upcoming issue. Mike had mentioned the Young Mr Latvia contest which would be held the following month and Arnie had grimaced in distaste. He saw the whole thing as underage sexploitation. Still, he had decided to do a short, yet cynical, reportage debunking the contests, exposing them for what they really were. It had struck Arnie that Mike would flunk out of any Mr Latvia contest with his tall gangly build, thick glasses and bad teeth. But looks weren't everything. The kid had talent, that was for sure. And ambition. For what, Arnie wasn't sure.

Arnie stubbed out his cigarette. He'd have to quit. Instead of calming him, smoking seemed to be making him more agitated. He had decided to buy some nicotine gum or the patch but then had realized that there was no way he'd find any of that in Riga. He'd have to go cold turkey. Now he needed some fresh air to clear is head. A good time to check out some of the places he'd been to with Mike.

A half-hour later, Arnie arrived at the Irish Pub in Old Riga. As he walked into the darkened room, he scoped out the scene. It had an eerie kind of quiet about it. A hard-nosed bouncer type, slumping at one of the tables, nailed him with an unfriendly stare. A few daytime drinkers sat at the bar. Mike wasn't one of them. A sullen bartender looked up as Arnie approached and asked if he knew someone called Mike.

"Mike? What Mike?"

Arnie described him.

"No Mike," the bartender responded in a fuck-off tone and shrugged. Not a single smiley-face in sight. No one to cut him a break. Arnie had already been pegged as a nosy expat and his colloquial Latvian wasn't good enough to make casual conversation. Still, he felt he should order a drink.

"The crazy American gangster?" The bartender suddenly remembered as Arnie put a five lats note on the counter.

"Yes. Yes, that Mike."

"Haven't seen him," the bartender said as he snatched up the money.

Looking around again, Arnie changed his mind about the drink. He didn't need to get into a fight with anybody. The bar was crowded and friendly at night—a favourite with expats, but during the day it was seedy and forlorn. Without a word, he turned away and walked out the door hoping no one would follow him.

Arnie now worried that his search would be fruitless. He didn't even have a picture of Mike. He would have to make a sketch himself from memory if he wanted to track down his ace photographer. What did he remember from high school art? Artful graffiti, doodles, that was about it. But he'd give it a shot. Arnie remembered that Mike was taking some classes at the Art Academy. He'd try that place too. And perhaps there'd be a call-back from Mike on his answering machine when he got home. Arnie didn't want to be negative but he doubted there'd be any message.

The sky was a depressing grey. It matched Arnie's mood perfectly. Not a glimmer of sunshine pierced the damp semi-darkness. All around him were grey stone buildings, grey pavements, dull gloomy squares, alleys and parks with a few forlorn benches, scrawny pigeons scratching around for something to eat and a couple of plump, bundled-up babushkas whisking their brooms around, earning their fifty cents an hour.

Arnie soldiered on. He was stubborn when it came to Mike. He wouldn't be easy to replace, certainly not at such short notice. With determination, he set out to the famed Art Academy just off the Esplanade. Unexpectedly, a sudden ray of light escaped from the clouds and the sky shimmered an iridescent pink, like a mirage. Arnie's mood lifted.

Walking through the city from Old Riga to the centre of town had always seemed like stepping through the pages of a book on European architecture. Arnie passed buildings reminiscent of every period in history—English Gothic, Romanesque, German,

Swedish, Renaissance Venetian. In Riga all styles of architecture coexisted and created the most fascinating urban environment. He never got tired of admiring the fantasies and excesses of Jugendstil, his favourite art movement, which coincided with the time of Riga's greatest prosperity. He loved the decorative arts of this period, the painting, the architecture, the fashion, the over-the-top ornamentation and the spirit of freedom and abandon.

Picking his way carefully over the ice-crusted pavements, he came to the place in central Riga where the canal gently winds its way through the ancient parks and the empty flower gardens. Arnie had chosen as his own special spot the picturesque stone footbridge which linked the National Opera and Latvia's University. From here, he would look around and feel the great heart of Riga beating its eternal tempo. He could feel its past, its ancient soil and take in the meaning of all that surrounded him.

Arriving at the Art Academy, Arnie braced himself and pushed open the heavy front door. Darkness wrapped itself around him. He adjusted his eyes for night vision and breathed in the smell of artists at work—a heady mix of oil paint, turpentine, wet plaster, coffee, cigarette smoke, and booze. A dim light from the magnificent leaded-glass windows illuminated the spacious foyer which led to the grand central staircase. Arnie had learned that the Gothic-style red brick edifice had been built in 1902 as a College for Commerce. It later became a German high school. Now, it was Latvia's most prestigious art school, as it had been during the Soviet era.

Freezing air swirled around him. An old lady, the custodian, stared at Arnie from her cubbyhole without moving. He looked over at her with curiosity but couldn't tell if she was still breathing since there was no vapour trail coming from her mouth or nose. Arnie approached, caught a strong odour of alcohol mixed with a faint hint of Cologne 4711.

He understood all too well. Boring job, bottle at her feet, or at least somewhere tucked away in the recesses of her dark little cubicle. Feeling completely out of his element, Arnie apologized in his best Latvian and asked if he could look around. The custodian kept staring, her rheumy eyes giving him no sign that she had understood what he was saying. Could his Latvian be that bad? Suddenly, a convulsive movement, with which she pulled her sweater tighter around her bosom, betrayed the first signs of life.

Arnie noticed a space heater at her feet and a small bowl of milk. He recognized a fellow cat lover. He would have loved to start up a cat conversation, maybe glean some information from her but the tired old eyes looked down. Time for another tipple, no doubt. And Arnie was keeping her from it.

Turning away, he slowly began to wander along the dark hallway. Some doors were open. He peeked into the studios. Everybody was busy at work. Large canvases blocked his view. No nude models in sight. Thank God, Arnie breathed. He was prudish and wouldn't know how to react.

Suddenly, a rush of young bodies poured out of a doorway and made for the grand central staircase. Without thinking, Arnie followed. They could be going on a break. In fact, he was sure of it as the aroma of freshly brewed coffee grew stronger. Minutes later, he found himself in the basement moving along with the laughing students past the cloakroom and into a tiny café where they formed a line. Arnie glanced at a hand-written menu. Coffee, beer, *pīragi*. He had learned not to trust local *pīragi* (nothing but lard) and bought himself an Aldaris which he drank standing up. Students clustered around the four small tables, enjoying close quarters with each other.

For all his expertise at prying out information from unsuspecting informants, Arnie felt very self-conscious. This wasn't his milieu. The students looked serious and respectable. No weirdo punks with nose rings or mohawks. No androgynous types. Girls were girls and boys were boys, although the girls far outnumbered the boys. Arnie's gaze settled on a foursome of attractive young women, sipping coffee and smoking. He had rehearsed his opening line.

"Excuse me, ladies. I'm looking for a student who does photography. He calls himself Mike."

The girls giggled. Shrugged.

"No, Mister," a jolly looking girl with short red hair said in English.

A giggling fit erupted from her companions. Arnie looked away, feeling the flush of embarrassment warming his cheeks. A table became vacant. He sat down and pulled out his pack of cigarettes, only to find that he already had one in his mouth. How the hell was he going to get anywhere? Maybe they all thought he was some kind of weirdo predator hitting on girls. No one joined him at his table. Students slouched against the walls, smoking and talking. They gave him a quick look then ignored him. Arnie lost his nerve. He got up, went to deposit his empty beer bottle on the counter, turned to wave at the four girls who burst out in peels of laughter and called bye-bye as Arnie left. What a waste of time, he muttered under his breath. He had zilch.

Snow was falling as he pushed open the heavy front door. For a moment, he stood still before descending the steps to the sidewalk. It was such a lovely scene with the fresh snow, the magnificent buildings and the wide expanse of the Esplanade. Arnie lifted his coat collar, stuck his hands in his pockets and started to walk. Well, so much for finding Mike. He'd try calling him again. And there was still the hope that Mike had called him back.

As he walked, Arnie hugged himself against a stiff gust of wind which sent snow flying down his collar. For some reason, he suddenly felt very uneasy, as if he was slipping into a strange, uncharted darkness. So many bizarre things had happened. He had been forced to veer off his predictable path. It was ironic that just as his magazine was really taking off, all these things were happening—the power outages, the body in the garage and now Mike disappearing.

He breathed in the cold moist air. His fingers and toes felt numb; his nose and throat raw and achy. Was he getting the flu? No, not that on top of everything else! He had to think, had to plan what to do next. He decided to come back later that evening and put up a notice on the bulletin board. He would be looking for a photographer. Flexible hours, good pay.

Out of nowhere, the image of the body in the basement flashed before his eyes. Fear rushed in. He was being haunted. He knew he had to do *something* or go insane. But what would that something be? The police. The only logical thing.

Arnie steeled himself. He knew where the closest police station was. As he approached the building, he thought of Vizma's warning to forget all about it. But he just couldn't.

With trepidation, he stepped into a decrepit bunker. Must be Soviet built, he muttered under his breath. It was dark and cold. Behind a counter sat a youngish officer. The officer looked up and gave Arnie a quizzical look. Arnie started his story. Unresponsive, the officer shrugged, said something in Russian and picked up the phone. To his amazement Arnie realized that he had been dismissed. He tried again but the officer didn't look up. Shaking his head, Arnie walked out the door. Was everyone expected to speak Russian in Riga? Arnie should have known that the answer was a resounding yes.

For a moment, Arnie wondered if he would make it home. He was exhausted from the lack of sleep, from smoking too much, from not eating well and from stress. He could see himself collapsing in a snow bank, freezing to death. By now it was early evening and the pavement had a hidden layer of ice under loose snow. Several times, he lost his balance and fell. Still, he had to keep moving.

He thought about food. What was in his freezer? Nothing much. What he wouldn't give for a big bloody steak and mashed potatoes right now. In his dreams! He had heard that the better cuts of meat were routinely stolen off the delivery trucks even before they reached the stores.

The light was gone and fatigue had settled over him like a dark wet shroud. He clenched his teeth as he moved laboriously over the last few meters to his front door. At last, he was home. He unlocked his door, flipped on the lights. With a high-pitched yowl, Gerda jumped down from the top of the windowsill, came running towards him, hackles on edge. Shock went through him like a gunshot.

A moment later, he let out a hoarse gasp and remained standing motionless in the doorway. His apartment had been ransacked. He scooped up the cat, stepped inside, closed the door and locked it. His apartment looked like a war zone. As if in a trance, he stumbled around, clutching the captive feline. Gerda's body was tense, her eyes wide. She was ready to spring away but Arnie was holding on for dear life, not allowing himself to be swallowed up by fear.

His world had been destroyed. Drawers had been spilled out on the floor, closets emptied. He stared at his sofa. A huge gash had been cut in the leather. Insanity, sheer insanity. His heart was pounding like some huge heavy sack in his chest. He pressed the cat closer for comfort. Gerda protested, let out a shriek and finally managed escape. Fear knotting his stomach, Arnie stood staring at the shambles around him. Maybe if he had never gone down to the basement, this wouldn't have happened. Maybe if he had never left Ottawa. Maybe, maybe, maybe…

Chapter Ten

Sunlight on her face forced Anda awake. As she opened her eyes, she had the feeling that she had lost something, or someone. She didn't need to stretch out her hand or feel the other side of the bed to know that Mike wasn't there. She lifted her head and frowned, remembering that she had waited for him to come over all last night but he hadn't even called. She tried to think if they had been quarrelling. But no, they hadn't been. He had called her Cutie Pie the last time they had been together. Cupcake, Sugar, Honey, Cookie were some other English love-words Mike liked to use. Saccharine overload, she thought. Nevertheless, food she could understand but not the meaning of Hootchie-mamma or Hotstuff.

She shifted in the chilled sheets, searched with her right foot for the hot water bottle. Then she remembered she had decided not to fill it expecting her bed to get hot enough when Mike got there. But he hadn't come. She wondered what had happened. Maybe he had work to do. Maybe he hadn't been able to call her because he had lost his cell phone.

As Anda closed her eyes wanting to doze for a few more minutes, her cat jumped off the pillow and scooted under the bed. He knew what was coming. The doorbell was about to shriek. Anda jolted upright. God! It couldn't be Mike. He knocked, knowing that the doorbell drove her crazy. She glanced at the clock on her bedside table. Five past eight. Who in the world could it be?

Smoothing down her hair, she hurriedly draped a shawl over her most glamorous night-gown that she had worn in anticipation of Mike's visit. Shivering, she padded through the kitchen to the door. God, was the floor ever cold on her bare feet! Her jaw tense, she picked up her canister of Mace which she always kept by the door. Just in case. She had bought it a month ago when she had been mugged on her way home from a movie and vowed that would never happen again.

She opened the door a crack, unlatched the chain and pulled the door wide open. Silvia, her sister, stood there, her face tear streaked. She was holding her six year old son, Vilnis, by the hand.

"My God, Silvia! What is it?"

"Ahh..." Silvia let out a sigh. Vilnis began to whine.

"Come. Come in. Take off your coat. Sit down."

Frigid air had rushed in through the open door, leaching out the precious warmth from the apartment. Still wearing her overcoat, Silvia flopped into Anda's frayed old armchair and closed her eyes. Anda noticed that before Silvia sat down, she had wrapped her coat even more tightly around herself, hugging it against her thin body. She looked very pale, her face at rest was lined. Her hair was limp and uncombed and there were dark circles under her eyes. Anda was glad that Vilnis ran off to look for the cat.

It was clear that Silvia needed to talk. Anda was alarmed at the pathetic moan that came from her sister. She had never seen her this low. She walked to the chair and lent over to touch her sister gently on the shoulder.

"What can I get you, Silvia? Some Coffee?"

Silvia opened her eyes and Anda saw how desperate she looked.

"No, nothing," Silvia replied.

"Is it Sasha?"

"Ye-es. But no. That's not why I'm here."

"Well, tell me. What is it?"

Silvia sat up straight and her eyes finally focused on Anda. With one shaking hand she twisted her hair behind her ear. She rocked forward in the chair.

"It's Daina!"

"Daina? What about her?" Anda watched her sister struggle with her emotions. She felt helpless.

"Daina's disappeared," Silvia whispered, her voice catching in her throat.

"What are you talking about?"

"What am I talking about? I'm talking about Daina. Daina's disappeared. She's gone," Silvia burst out, exasperated. How could Anda not understand?

Anda's eyes widened in alarm.

"Oh, Silvia…"

Anda sat down opposite her sister, the two faces at the same level only a foot apart. Silvia took a deep breath, gathering her strength to tell her story.

"Did you read about the Young Miss Latvia contest in *Diena*?"

Anda shook her head. "I haven't had much time to read."

"Well, someone at work cut out this article. It looked interesting and I told Daina about it. I thought she might have a chance to win it. She's so pretty and the prizes were unbelievable. Daina was really excited about it and so was one of her friends. They were going to go together to the audition. That was yesterday."

"Yesterday?"

"No, wait. It was the day before. I've lost a day."

Silvia put her head in her hands. She seemed to be at the end of her rope. Then, she looked up at Anda.

"Could I have a drink now?"

Anda knew Silvia didn't want coffee. Her sister needed a boost and there was no point in Anda lecturing her, knowing how upset she was about Daina. She wondered what she had in her cupboard. Then she remembered Mike's bottle of vodka in the freezer. Getting up to go to the kitchen, she said, "I'll be right back."

Two minutes later, coming into the living room, she saw that Silvia looked brighter and was quick to reach out for the glass, taking a couple of short sips at once. Leaning toward Anda again, holding her glass with both hands in her lap, she went on with her story explaining how her fourteen-year-old daughter had gone to the audition and had not returned home.

"Where did she go? I mean, to what address?"

Silvia looked embarrassed. "Well, I was at work. She told me the night before that she was going with a friend. Her friend's father was supposed to drive them. She told me the friend's name but I wasn't paying attention. I can't remember who it was."

Anda's shoulders slumped. She despaired of her sister. Everything was too much for her. She was barely hanging on.

"So, what did you do?" Anda asked, trying to appear calm.

"I telephoned the number in the paper. No one had seen her."

Silvia took a prolonged sip of her drink, looked at the glass and saw that there wasn't very much left.

"No one knows anything. No one cares."

"What does Sasha say?"

Anda noticed that when Sasha's name was mentioned, Silvia downed the rest of her drink in one gulp.

"Sasha! Don't make me laugh. He doesn't know. He's driving a car to Germany for some client. Probably a stolen car."

Silvia held out her empty glass to Anda, a gesture that plainly indicated that she would like a refill. But Anda, taking the glass, put it down on a table beside her indicating no intention of providing more.

"He doesn't tell me anything about his business. I never even know when he's going to be away. Sometimes I wait for hours with his dinner and then he doesn't show up and I just never know. But if he comes home and I don't have his dinner ready, he hits me."

Anda's face registered shock. She clenched her fists. *The bastard!* She had heard this before but each time it affected her. *The bastard*, she had wanted to scream over and over but she knew that wouldn't do any good. It would only make her sister want to defend him.

"Besides, you know how he feels about Daina. She's not his daughter, so…" Silvia's voice faded. She pulled a handkerchief from her purse and blew her nose.

"Did you talk to any of Daina's friends? Did you…" Anda's words were interrupted by a screech coming from the bedroom.

"Vilnis, leave kitty alone!" Silvia's voice took on new energy. Screaming at her kids always made her feel involved in their upbringing.

"Just let him be, Silvia. No-name cat knows how to defend himself. I'm worried more about Vilnis."

"Oh, I don't know…" Silvia said feebly slumping back in the chair.

"I asked you about Daina's friends. Did you talk to any of them?"

"Oh, her friends…" Silvia stammered. "Yes, well, I looked for Daina's telephone book but she must have had it in her purse when she disappeared. I'll have to wait till one of them calls."

Anda's heart sank. She saw that Silvia was overwhelmed. She would have to take charge. But how? Silence descended between the two sisters. Each was thinking her own thoughts. Silvia had closed her eyes and leaned her head back against the armchair. She seemed more relaxed and had loosened the grip on her coat. Anda noticed how pretty she could be when she was peaceful. Silvia was the older of the two. She was thirty-five. Anda was five years younger. But she had always been the big sister, the caregiver.

Both women had fine light brown hair, grey eyes set deep in a delicate pale face. Anda bleached her hair a subtle blonde but Silvia made no effort to look glamorous. She pulled her hair back and usually wore it in a skinny braid that fell down her back. She rarely had a moment to herself with two kids, a job as cashier in an electronics store and a husband who never helped with household chores.

Anda was the first to break the silence. She took a deep breath.

"Did you go to the police?"

Silvia let out a sardonic laugh. "What's the point? They'd only laugh at me. Young Miss Latvia means nothing to them. They'd write down a report but do nothing. Sometimes it's worse if you go to the police. We handle things ourselves. At least, that's what Sasha says."

At the mention of Sasha's name Anda rose. She didn't want to hear another word about that bastard.

"I'm making coffee. Want some?" she asked as she went to the kitchen.

Silvia's answer came out as a sigh. "Yes, please," she said, lit a cigarette and remained in the chair staring into space.

Before going into the kitchen, Anda checked on Vilnis who was in her bedroom. She was worried that he might be cold, took his little hand and found it was a lump of ice. She rummaged beside her bed in a pile of clothes and found one of her sweaters that had shrunk. She put it on him. His hands disappeared but she found them somewhere around the elbows of the sleeves and quickly rolled them up. Vilnis protested for a minute, then went back to his magazine. Anda touched the radiators. They were only slightly warm. Thank God for the sun, she breathed. Otherwise the cold would be unbearable.

Still in her nightie, she decided to take two minutes to dress and, as she rummaged through her cupboard for a pair of wool socks, her mind turned to the Young Miss Latvia contest. How ridiculous, she thought. Something new, something American. She was ashamed at how everyone was grabbing for prizes and money and some sort of fame. She had heard that the promoters of these contests even offered a trip to Hollywood for the winner. Hollywood indeed, Anda let out a cynical snort. More likely a trip to some Arab country for a stint as a sex slave. How naïve people were, how hungry and deluded. Finally she shrugged. There was nothing she could do about it and her sister was waiting for her in the living room. She shook off her annoyance and quickly ran a brush through her hair before going into the kitchen.

The kettle was boiling. Anda poured the hot water into the filter cone and, before replacing the kettle, she leaned over the hot burner to trap the heat and warm her hands. Pouring out the coffee, she suddenly thought about Mike. Where had he gone? Why hadn't he told her? Anda passed her hand over her forehead. A headache was threatening. She sighed. Life was an endless series of heartaches and complications. But for Silvia it was worse. Why have those kids, Anda had often thought and then she would always feel guilty. She was fond of her nephew and niece but was sorry that Silvia was trapped. Her latest worry had been that Silvia was drinking too heavily, probably also on the job. Many people did but that was no excuse.

Anda gave her sister a smile as she came back into the tiny living room.

"Vilnis is alright. I turned on the radio for him and he's looking at magazines. Mike left a copy of *WOW!*. What a scandal sheet! But it does makes me laugh."

"I wouldn't mind a laugh right now," Silvia said in a weary voice.

"Oh, you're just out of practice. I'm sure things will get better. Daina will turn up, I promise you. I've made some real coffee for us today. Want a shot of Balzams in it to really warm you up?"

Silvia eyes brightened.

"You read my mind," she said and smiled.

Anda knew there was nothing she could do about her sister's drinking. And it was at moments like this that she herself needed a shot.

"Thank God it's my day off. Mike and I were going to spend it together but, when I woke up this morning, he wasn't there. I don't know what to think. It's not like him."

Silvia took the proffered mug and warmed her hands on it. The coffee was divine.

"Have you eaten anything today, Silvia?"

With a wave of her hand Silvia brushed off the question. "Oh, I'm not hungry."

"Well, drinking on an empty stomach…" Anda knew a lecture would do no good. "What about Vilnis?"

"He's alright. He's never hungry in the morning." Again, Anda bit her tongue. Vilnis was too thin. In fact, they were both too thin.

As if trying to even the score, Silvia put in her two santimes worth.

"You know, Mike doesn't sound reliable," she said stiffly. "I don't think he's really the guy for you. You're so young and pretty and smart. Don't get trapped with a man who will only drag you down." Silvia didn't add *like I did* but both sisters knew that's what she meant.

"Yeah, well, that's life," Anda said grimly. "And speaking of Mike, I'm calling him right now. He'll tell us what to do about Daina."

Anda punched in the number. No answer. Her face creased in worry.

"I'm calling his cell. He's compulsive about taking calls. Even when he's in the bathroom. Even when we're in bed together. I remember he had it the other night." Anda stifled a chuckle.

Silvia blinked. "He talks on the phone when you're in bed?"

Anda didn't bother to answer and went on, "You know, I've though of someone. The guy Mike does some work for. He knows all about everything."

"Who's that?"

"Arnis Dambergs. The guy calls himself Arnie. He's an American or something. He puts out *WOW!* magazine."

"Oh, that's just gossip."

"Sure, but the guy knows a lot of people. I bet he could help. Are you sure you don't want to go to the police?"

Silvia scowled. "Anda, sometimes you don't listen. Have you ever gone to the police? Remember that time you were mugged? You didn't go to the police, did you?"

Anda shrugged. She noticed that a tiny bit of colour was coming back into her sister's cheeks. Anger always energized her.

Silvia continued. "So where's this *dude* of yours? He calls everyone *dude*, or *man*. Even when he's speaking to a woman. What kind of English is that? He's not a very serious person. Not reliable."

Silvia was scolding. Anda suppressed a grin. She preferred Silvia the bitch to Silvia the sad sack.

"So, call Mike again."

As much as Silvia didn't trust Mike, she trusted foreigners even less.

"Tch," Anda made a sound of annoyance. "Okay. I'll try one more time."

No answer. Even the voice mail recording was off.

"God knows where he's gone. Maybe he lost the phone. Maybe it got stolen. Maybe he sold it. Maybe he couldn't keep up with the bills. Maybe…" Anda rattled on.

"Maybe he's not reliable. Maybe he's crazy. Maybe he's in jail," her sister joined in.

"Alright. I'm going to find this Arnie Dambergs. I'm going to track him down and I'm going to make him listen," Anda announced slamming her fist down on the table so hard that the coffee cup jumped.

Silvia made the sign of the cross. She knew her sister meant business.

Chapter Eleven

If someone were to read her aura, what would they see? They'd probably see a jagged angry red instead of the soothing blue that nice people were supposed to have. Above her bathroom mirror Vizma could see the flashing neon sign: WASHOUT LOSER IDIOT. She sniffed and swiped a hand beneath her nose. She wasn't going to give in.

Lately, it seemed as if every morning she experienced this same deadly mixture of self-pity and despair. Surely, she wasn't about to crack. Her reflection told her she couldn't afford another bad night. Her eyes were bloodshot and burned with fatigue, her complexion was pasty. She frowned with impatience coming to the end of her dental floss. It had taken several trips to find the stuff in Riga. She splashed cold water on her face, determined to fight her depression. She could start running. Although, no one did. Well, no. That wasn't quite true.

One day, a month ago, she had seen an old guy in a gym suit running through Vermane Park. Pigeons scattered, dogs started to bark and the babushkas sweeping the park dropped their brooms. What a sight that had been! The runner had been wearing some sort of weird headband, had himself plugged into a CD player and was brandishing a bottle of Perrier water. He might as well have been stark naked for all the commotion he had created.

Just as he was rounding a corner, from somewhere out of the bushes stumbled an elderly drunk. Before Vizma's startled eyes the two collided, falling down into what looked like a lovers' embrace. Only one of them got up. The runner just lay there, his eyes closed. Babushkas had swarmed around him examining the CD player and his Adidas. To them, he might as well have been roadkill wearing a Rolex. They'd never seen anything like this before. He didn't look drunk. Obviously, a wealthy foreigner and they hadn't seen many of those close up.

As Vizma watched, the jogger slowly started to get up and one of the babushka's stretched out her hand. Vizma didn't wait to see if this was to help him up or to slip off the watch. Feeling a little guilty, she had slunk away.

After a shower and coffee, Vizma felt a bit better. Maybe she'd get a dog. People had told her it was a great way to meet locals. Pet owners always had a lot to talk about. Then the sun came out from behind a cloud and her apartment was flooded in light. The day looked a little brighter and Vizma decided that she would reconsider the dog.

She looked out the window at the blue morning sky and was glad that she had an English class to teach at the Art Academy that day. It would help keep her mind off the Goth and the toilet lockup of the day before. And she always got a surge of energy from being with her students.

As she dressed, Vizma even hummed to herself. She looked forward to her walk, enjoyed feeling like a professional as she made her way to the school, swinging her briefcase.

The light was behind her as she walked up Valdemara Street. From a distance she could see the delicate spire of the Academy through the bare tree branches. Old, majestic, dreamy, the building had an air of poetic tranquillity about it and shone in the shadowy air like some enchanted castle in a long-ago fairy tale. Her first sight of the building never failed to lift her spirits. At that instant, she knew why she was here. She belonged here among all this beauty and history.

As she got closer, she waved to a couple of rosy cheeked girls who were coming from another class. Vizma experienced a surge of happy anticipation as she walked in the front door. Her mind left behind all its worries and she thought of the fun there would be. Certainly, she wasn't doing it for the money. What did her salary come to? She figured three dollars an hour.

As usual, she started the session going around the room with what-did-you-do-yesterday. One of her students told her about this weirdo who had approached her in the café.

"Well, describe him," Vizma said hoping to teach some new vocabulary.

"Sure. Foreigner, tall, fat, old, no glasses."

Vizma asked for details. "*Very* tall, *very* fat, *very* old?"

"No. Just, you know…weird."

Having milked the foreigner incident, Vizma turned to the blackboard. The conditional tense. "Today, if I *had* money, I *would* buy a car. Last year, if I *had had* money, I *would have* bought a car."

Confusion followed. Vizma was no English teacher. She was winging it, hoping something would rub off. If nothing else, she thought, they'd be left with the impression that learning English was fun. Fun. She had tried to explain what this important word meant in Latvian. It wasn't easy but she felt that they had caught the gist of it.

As her students were copying grammar rules from the black board, her thoughts slipped back to Arnie. It would be nice to see him again. Perhaps she'd drop in after her class. It would be close to lunchtime. She knew that Arnie worked out of his apartment. Maybe he'd welcome a break. Would she kiss him lightly on the cheek when they met again? She imagined herself cooking for him. A cheese omelette and some sort of salad. Maybe something heartier. Maybe what she called her signature dish, Beef Stroganoff. Then dessert. A fruit salad or—

The scraping of chairs brought her back to the present. She shook her head, let out a soft snort of laughter. How silly she was.

As always at the end of the class, Vizma assigned homework and handed out reading material. She spent more money photocopying than she made but it was for a good cause. The truth was that her part time job kept her sane. She was very popular with the students, although the staff resented her. Her fellow teacher in the language department taught from a dusty old manual which still extolled the selfless deeds of Soviet workers.

Vizma, on the other hand, used the living language method. Each class, she would come in as a soap opera diva and the students had to guess who she was—Crystal, Alexis, Dana, or some other glamour puss. She only had one strict rule: no Latvian spoken. Only English. If anyone got stuck for a word, they had to put up their hand and ask 'how do you say…in English?' Vizma would always express mock horror as the hands went up and used the eenie-meenie-miny-mo method for choosing which hand she'd pick first. The students loved the playfulness, although Vizma had heard complaints from the classroom next to hers about the distracting roars of laughter.

But there were surprises. Vizma had discovered that cheating on exams was tolerated. After marking her mid-terms, she had noticed identical answers and had learned who the cheaters were. She had stormed into the Dean's office only to be laughed at. This was all part of student life. She had also been surprised to find that university level students in Latvia worked less than they had in grade school. Their attitude seemed to be that, if they had made it to university level, their futures were assured.

It worried her, like it worried everyone else, that Art Academy life was being threatened. All the students were on State scholarships and the State's coffers were empty. Quite frequently, teachers weren't paid on time. Vizma always managed but wondered how the rest of the staff could survive without their salaries. They were always paid in cash. Cheques and banking were still new concepts. Now, there was talk of closing the Academy. The arts didn't seem important in a country where many people had nowhere to live and were on the brink of starvation.

Vizma learned first hand that independence brought freedom but also chaos. Housing was being privatized. Many expats were reclaiming family property and the people who had been paying practically no rent were in danger of finding themselves out on the streets. Pensions for the elderly had been dramatically decreased. Crime had risen. Corruption was rampant. Vizma was shocked when she heard people say it was better in the old days. But she could also see why.

It was close to noon. The students had left. Vizma remained behind. She looked around the shabby room. The desks were old and in disrepair. There was never chalk or erasers and it was always cold but she loved the atmosphere. She loved every minute of her time in the Academy. The charm of the historic building and everything about it erased all the negatives.

Vizma sat down at her desk and, as she looked through the tall leaded glass windows, her imagination flew back in time to pre-Soviet days when the elegance and character of these grand buildings reflected the style of the population. In her mind, the thirties were a charmed era. Her parents had told her wonderful stories of their own student days, the semi-annual shopping expeditions to Paris, the vacations in Venice and the marvellous extended family get-togethers by the seashore.

Vizma was decades away, back in an era where students dressed to come to class, deposited their overcoats in the *garderobe*, met for coffee at Schwartz afterwards and planned their evening festivities. Her eyes misted over as she stared into the amber glow of her candle. She loved the Latvian custom of lighting candles during the day in these dark winter months. She had noticed that the office workers had candles on their desks and often in shops there were candles next to the cashier. Leaning back in her chair she let her mind wander and contemplated what she'd do with the rest of the day.

There was someone in the sculpture department, a prof, a tall craggy arty type who had caught her eye. She had heard that he was quite famous. His class next door to hers ended in another few minutes and, even though she had not yet managed to break the ice, perhaps this time she might bump into him in the hall. After all, there wasn't much for her to do back at her apartment.

She had finally admitted to herself that she was staying late on purpose because she was afraid that she would frighten Arnie off if she knocked on his door, offered to make him lunch and told him about the incident at the Hotel Latvija. And she didn't want to have to tell him that she had gone straight from their lunch at Osiris to have her hair done. He might get suspicious. She saw that she would have to work her way around that detail.

Fifteen minutes later, there was no sound of students leaving the sculpture studio. Curious about the silence in the corridor, she went to investigate. There on the door of the studio was a notice announcing that the class had been cancelled. Another victim of the flu, she murmured to herself. So much for that. Standing in the cold dark hallway, staring at the locked studio door, Vizma suddenly felt old and very tired. Truth is, she was relieved. What a silly thing to do, she said to herself and went back to blow out the candle.

She put on her down coat brought from Canada, her hat and gloves and knotted a scarf around her neck. She was out of there in a minute. A few polite nods to her colleagues and she walked down the dark hallway to the front door.

Stepping out from the darkness of the Academy into the light, she squinted and turned her face up to the sun. The day had brightened considerably and the sky glowed a luminous light blue. As she looked across the Esplanade, she saw the pavements and the trees all silvery, shimmering in the soft sunlight as pale and delicate as an ancient watercolour.

She was glad of her thick rubber boots and heavy socks as she strode briskly along Valdemara Street. She knew she looked like the Michelin Man in her puffy down-filled coat but there was no one to impress. She stopped to admire The National Museum of Art. The ornate old building was magnificent, one of the jewels of historic Riga. She had never been inside. Going through museums made her think of loneliness. She wasn't sure why.

Even though the sun was shining, the air was still damp, still cold for February. The moisture in her breath froze and puffed out white. She snuggled her scarf close to her face and was glad she hadn't forgotten her fur lined gloves. She thought back to the month before when she had put down her gloves to pay for her groceries in a neighbourhood store. A scruffy looking boy had snatched them and had been making for the door. The eagle-eyed security guard had spotted the theft and her gloves had been returned. Ever since then, they never left her sight.

As she waited to cross Elizabetes Street, she looked back at the Esplanade and the bare branches of the Linden trees. She couldn't wait till spring when the air would be perfumed with their blooms and the flower stalls would be overflowing.

It was still dark at eight in the morning when she headed out to her morning class and it was dark again at three when she left for home. Initially, she had liked it. The mysterious darkness that crept over the city during the winter months shrouded everyone, made it spooky and mystical and strangely wonderful. But now, there was nothing she craved as much as the hot blazing sun.

Vizma was amazed to see so many cars on the streets. In Soviet days, cars were scarce and only the upper echelon Communists would have one. Now there were Mercedes and Volkswagens and Hondas and Citroens. The car market was booming. People would pile into cars or buses and drive to Germany to buy used cars. Then, they would drive them back, fix them up and make a profit. Most people turned their noses up at the tinny Ladas and Zhigulis. Still, all the staff at the Art Academy took the trolley-bus to work. Gas was very expensive and cars were kept for special excursions.

She remembered Arnie telling her that he had an old car that he kept in the garage. It needed some work and he himself didn't know where to begin. She had made inquiries at the Academy about a mechanic. Everyone was anxious to make a little money and Vizma thought that she could get Arnie's car repaired before the good weather hit. She couldn't help daydreaming about the two of them driving to the seaside some hot summer day or maybe even up to Kolka, the westernmost tip on the Baltic Sea.

On an impulse, she slipped into her favourite grocery shop on the corner of Dzirnavu Street. She would get a bottle of wine for Arnie. Her decision not to call on him had dissolved. Sunshine made everything seem possible.

As she made her way to the store, she looked up at the street sign. It was fascinating. She had been told that the streets of Central Riga had undergone recent name changes. Since Latvia's renewed independence, all Russian signage had been blotted out and pre-war Latvian names revived. Vizma was glad of that. She couldn't imagine the foreign looking Cyrillic signage on the beautiful streets of Riga. In places, on some street signs, she could still see splotchy scabs of Cyrillic letters, scars that were not so easy to cover up and impossible to forget. No matter what, her Riga was always going to be the Riga her parents had told her so much about.

Before she knew it, Vizma was at her front door. How lucky she was to live in this part of town! She knew plenty of people who had to take a bus out to the suburbs to one of those hideous Soviet-built concrete slabs. In fact, that's where most local Latvians lived as it was Russians who had been awarded apartments in the elegant historic buildings in central Riga. Most of them were determined to hang on.

As Vizma climbed the stairs, anticipation overtook her. She clutched her briefcase in one hand and the expensive bottle of wine in the other. She didn't even stop at her own apartment but climbed straight up to the sixth floor. What did all this excitement mean? Oh, she was just being neighbourly. Nothing more. And she was glad that she had a purpose for the rest of the day or at least, she hoped, for a few hours. Neighbourly, my foot. If she were perfectly honest with herself, which she wasn't, Vizma would have to admit right then and there that she liked Arnie and wanted to spend some more time with him.

Nearing his door, Vizma felt a slight knot in her stomach and, as she prepared to knock on Arnie's door, she saw that her hand was trembling.

Chapter Twelve

Vizma hesitated before she knocked a second time. Was she losing her nerve? After no response again, she felt like turning away and going back downstairs. Just then, a door opened down the hall and a monstrous panting dog shot out, dragging a man at the other end of a chain.

Foo! Foo! Vizma heard him shout and she knew that was Russian for 'bad dog'. God! That must be Bambi, she thought, Arnie's nemesis. Not being a dog person, she pulled back, thinking that a monster like Bambi would be turned on by any smell of fear and would go for the throat. To her surprise, Bambi ignored her, as did the owner. Nature called. Bambi stopped pulling and hunched over. Vizma could smell it and didn't see a poop bag in the owner's hands. As she pinched her nostrils closed, she decided then and there to become an activist for poop and scoop laws in Latvia.

Holding her breath, she turned back to Arnie's door. Time to feel insecure again. The thought occurred to her that this could be a bad moment, that she had been foolishly impulsive, silly to think that they'd have a cozy *tête à tête* over her bottle of wine. She had even thought of suggesting that he might like to take a bath in her apartment and had already planned a way of doing it without sounding as if she was coming on to him. She could offer him her key and say she had to go out for groceries and would he stay for lunch. She'd put her space heater on high, crack open a bottle of Riga's Champagne, light candles, and turn on the cassette player.

Standing there at his door, clutching her briefcase and bottle of wine, she suddenly felt absolutely ridiculous. Why was it taking him ages to come to the door? Perhaps he wasn't home, or maybe he had a lady friend with him. How mortifying! She pictured Arnie coming to the door, dishevelled and annoyed at being disturbed in his love nest.

But she didn't turn away. After a few minutes which seemed like hours, she finally heard his footsteps, then the rattling of the safety chain and the click of the dead bolt. Arnie peered out.

"Phew! Was that damn dog just out here?"

He looked awful, pale and glum and in need of a shave. In an instant the scenario changed. Vizma took three mental giant steps back. Forget the wine, not to mention the lunch, and the bath was simply out of the question. Peeking around him without appearing to be nosy, she could see that the apartment was a mess. She wondered to herself if this was how he lived.

"Yeah, the dog was out here and couldn't wait to get to the park."

"Oh, hi," Arnie blinked at her.

Vizma expected the door to be thrown open but instead, he just stared as if he had never seen her before.

"Oh! Is this a bad moment?" she asked, taken aback. Why was she acting like this, for heaven's sake? "Or maybe I've got the wrong door," she added more forcefully. Her cocky grin was back. "How soon they forget. Should I introduce myself?" she asked facetiously.

Arnie's face relaxed. The corners of his lips flicked up in a reluctant smile.

"Sorry, Vizma. Look, it's good to see you. Come on in. It's just that..."

"Well, if you're busy, I won't interrupt."

"Hell no, Vizma. I'm not busy and you're not interrupting." Arnie raised his hands in mock surrender. "Wait till I tell you..."

Her eyes widened as he opened the door all the way and gestured for her to come in. She had never been in his apartment before. Jeez, how can someone live like this? she asked herself again.

As she stepped inside, Arnie peered into the hallway, closed the door and locked it. Vizma noticed that his feet were bare and that he was wearing a t-shirt with the Moosehead Beer logo and a pair of faded jeans.

"I'll tell you in a minute. Just don't mind the mess."

"Mess? What mess?"

A sardonic smile came across her face. Still, she was relieved that there was no woman around, and that Arnie wanted to talk to her. They'd be having their *tête à tête* after all, even if the wine and the bath would have to wait for another day.

She took off her coat and slipped her purse over the back of a chair. She rammed the wine bottle into her briefcase, hoping that Arnie hadn't noticed it.

"Come on through to the kitchen and I'll make coffee. And what did you say your name was?"

"Don't push it, Arnie."

Vizma grinned and followed him into the kitchen, eager to hear what had happened. And she had news of her own. After picking up and discarding a few mugs, Arnie found two that looked mostly clean. He filled them, plunked them down on the splintered kitchen table and added an ashtray.

"Have a seat," he said lighting a cigarette.

He inhaled deeply, breathed out a puff of smoke and squinted at her. Vizma helped herself to a cigarette from his pack and sat down.

"So, are you finally going to tell me or is it written in the stars for me to read?"

Arnie gave a snort. "Well, hey. Let me call my astrologer."

"Come on, Arnie. Spit it out."

"Yeah. Okay."

Combing his hand through his hair, sighing with exhaustion and exasperation, Arnie leaned back in the chair and started his story.

The day after their lunch at Osiris, he had gone out looking for Mike. When he hadn't been able to find him after a couple of hours, feeling worried and dejected, he had come home only to get the shock of his life. His apartment had been ransacked. The door had not been forced open. Arnie had knocked at his neighbours, but the people hadn't even opened the door calling *nyet nyet* from inside.

Vizma grimaced. The apartment was a wreck, but nothing looked destroyed.

"They probably planted a bug. We shouldn't be talking," she said softy.

Arnie shrugged. He went on cataloguing.

Someone had rifled through all his possessions. His papers, books and briefcase had been searched. His rug in the bedroom had been turned up. His bedding all messed, the trap in the ceiling of the bathroom askew, the sofa pulled away from the wall and turned over and cut open in a search of the upholstery.

Pillows in his bedroom had been thrown off and cases removed. In his closet, suitcases had been pulled out and emptied, bureau drawers spilled out the floor. They had searched his computer. He never left it on, but when he came home, he saw that someone had been through it. He saw the crude *Go Home Fockyou* typed on his screen.

"The *Go Home Fockyou* sounds familiar, Arnie. This character must have learned English from a specialist. Now, let me tell you what happened to me."

Arnie sat there, looking dazed. "Yes, tell me, but before you do that, give me a hand with this mess. I really can't stand it any more."

They moved through the apartment putting things in order. Arnie stopped for a minute, lit a cigarette and gazed off into space. At first, he had thought that they had taken the topless picture of Maija Fischer from his briefcase which they had emptied on the floor but he had found it propped up in front of his computer screen. They had turned on his computer but he wasn't sophisticated enough to be able to tell if they had copied his hard drive. The most frightening thing was that they obviously had a key to his front door. What had these goons been looking for?

Vizma was shuddering inwardly. She couldn't fend off the thought that her apartment might be next. Even when she was inside, there was only the chain to prevent someone with a key from walking in on her. She made a mental note to change her lock the very next day.

An hour later, they took a break. After brewing some more coffee, Arnie kept the gas stove on low. They had to think. They both felt under siege. Vizma told her story about the Goth and the incident at the Hotel Latvija. Someone was using scare tactics on them both and the level of intimidation was escalating.

*   *   *

Their coffee break stretched to an hour. They sat sipping coffee and smoking as they examined possibilities and motives. They tried out different theories, searched for a pattern. Maybe they hadn't been paying attention, looking but overlooking, missing something. They both knew that there was resentment against expats, jealousy mainly but this was scary stuff. Maybe they had unwittingly witnessed some sort of crime. Did Arnie know something that he didn't know he knew, something that threatened someone? Every theory they tried led to a dead end, a fast track to nowhere.

For a change of scene, they adjourned to Arnie's work area and computer and their investigation bogged down with a hundred questions. Who was Arnie on the outs with? Who had been his most recent journalistic target? Arnie let out a snort. The sexpot Maija Fischer, for heaven's sake! Utterly harmless. Or was she? Maybe Don Fischer wasn't happy with her plastic surgeon.

Arnie looked away from Maija's topless portrait and turned beet red when he caught Vizma's eye. He'd been thinking that there was nothing wrong with them pair of knockers. In fact, he'd become quite fond of the photo. He saw Vizma roll her eyes. Never mind, he knew it would be a sensational cover for the next issue of *WOW!*. Thank God, it hadn't been stolen.

Before he knew it, Arnie's mind became caught up with his magazine. Now, where was that cocktail waitress photo, the one he needed for the March issue? Arnie felt a sharp jab in his ribs and saw Vizma do a face scrunch. He picked up the topless and put it in a folder.

Who else was there? He had stayed away from Mafia related exposés or so he thought. He should have known that almost everything that went on was somehow Mafia related. Arnie thought back to some of the people he had featured recently in *WOW!*.

There was the high-ranking police officer who had made a present of a stolen Mercedes to his wife's brother, the Minister of Agriculture. The Minister had filled his gigantic freezer with the best cuts of meat from the prize winning pig at the Fall Agricultural Exhibition. Not to mention the Ambassador of Australia. The Ambassador had packed a shipping container of Latvian national treasures only to be ratted out by an anonymous tipster. Mike had taken a great photo showing the diplomat in handcuffs at dockside standing beside the container. Neither of these stories had done anything for his popularity in government or diplomatic circles. And he hadn't even published the stuff about Maija yet. Maybe she and her husband had somehow got wind of it. But how? Could that be why Mike had disappeared, or worse, been murdered?

There were horror stories galore and one led to another as Vizma and Arnie turned their attention to the bottle of wine she just happened to have stashed away in her briefcase. As things were going, pretty soon they'd both land up in her bath, Vizma thought to herself and chuckled.

Arnie was caught up in his war stories. Just a few days ago a judge, returning home from the Courthouse, had been shot dead on Brivibas Street. Arnie tried to imagine what would happen to him if he were attacked on the street. How long would it take the police to get to the scene? How would the crime be investigated? Would the press be able to report freely on the events and the reasons behind the crime? A lone gunman, in a car with a driver, had shot the judge in the back. A shot could come from anywhere, an apartment house window, a passer-by. The murder was probably not going to be solved. Too much fear, too much corruption. Arnie shuddered at the thought that one day it might happen to him. The press had written that the judge's murder was a warning from the Mafia. Stay off our turf! An expat had seen the whole thing from the door of her apartment house and had suffered a nervous breakdown.

Vizma and Arnie looked at each other, both thinking the same thing. Going back to Ottawa didn't seem like such a bad idea.

Chapter Thirteen

Even though the day had been a disaster, Vizma and Arnie decided to go together to the expat dinner being held at the Muzikas Klubs in Old Riga. Arnie found these events to be a source for stories and didn't like to miss any. Besides, he and Vizma had almost got the apartment right side up and neither of them had ever been to this club. And boy, could they use a little distraction! They felt the price was steep, eight lats a piece, drinks extra. It had probably been organized by one of the expats whose salary was paid in American dollars. Vizma had always felt ambivalent about these gatherings but this time she thought that the evening might be a success. Sharing it with Arnie made all the difference.

As if fuelled by a new purpose, both Vizma and Arnie felt re-energized. The rest of the day passed quickly. Arnie went back to the Art Academy to put up his ad for a photographer and Vizma prepared for her evening class. She had completely forgotten the English conversation about the fat old man who had accosted a student in the café. She had no reason to remember. In her eyes, Arnie couldn't possibly fit any such adjective.

Earlier, they had talked about Mike and Vizma wondered if she had seen him around the Academy. She knew he wasn't in any of her English classes. Mike was much too advanced, Arnie had said. In any event, she decided to ask around but the thought had already occurred to her that Mike wasn't a fine arts student at all. He sounded to her like some peeping tom, selling pictures to the highest bidder. She had chosen to overlook Arnie's role in the peeping tom business. Arnie was a serious journalist and no one was going to tell her any different.

They arranged to meet at Laima's Clock at six o'clock after Vizma's evening class. Vizma had always wanted to meet someone under this Riga landmark. Unofficially, the Laima Clock marked the division between Old Riga, the cobblestone pedestrian-only section, and Central Riga. There was something chic and romantic about choosing this meeting place.

Vizma imagined hundreds of young women, perhaps her own mother in her youth, meeting some dashing officer at the Laima clock and then strolling into the fashionable Otto Schwartz Café, *the* place to see and be seen. The café had always been filled with fascinating people—politicians, artists, writers and members of the *haute bourgeoisie.*

In her mind's eye, Vizma could see elegant ladies wearing magnificent hats and silk stockings, gentlemen sleek and groomed, poets reciting their verse while the *crème de la crème* of Riga's café society cheered them on. On opulent trays rested the finest Sacher Torte, Napoleon Torte, Alexander Cake, all served up with delicate cups of steaming hot chocolate or deluxe coffee topped with mountains of whipped cream.

Vizma's own youth had been nothing like that. She had worked her way through high school waitressing in a deli and then had gone to secretarial school. Still, there had always been a yearning for the finer things in life. As a young woman, she felt that she had somehow been cheated of an old world style courtship which she had so often heard her mother describe.

She had imagined a more beautiful way of life as she listened to her mother's voice painting her pictures of Riga in her own salad days. She was transported to the romantic dances, to the refined afternoon teas, sleek young women wearing little white kid gloves. She longed to finger the lace-edged hankies, try on the hats with veils, the blouses with hand-faggoting and flowers embroidered on the points of each collar. She had wished to experience this gentler world first hand and that was partly what had called her name across the Atlantic. To date, it had been a far cry from what she expected but she still hadn't given up hope.

As Arnie and Vizma walked along the narrow winding streets, they could see glimpses of Riga's turbulent history in the thick walls that had at one time surrounded the medieval town. They both loved Old Riga with its romantic spires, gables and turrets blending Romanesque, Gothic, Renaissance and Baroque styles of architecture and never failed to turn up their nose at the Soviet-built uglies which marred the picture-postcard facades of the ancient streets.

It was already very dark and they had to spend some time poking around the narrow streets before they found the restaurant. Relieved to finally get there, they stamped the snow off their boots and stepped inside. Immediately, a rush of warm smoky air greeted them along with the sound of gabbling voices of the people at the bar.

"Oh, thank God. This place has plenty of heat. I found it really cold out there tonight. My feet are freezing," Vizma burbled as she pulled off her boots and put on the pair of pumps which she had tucked into her briefcase.

She squared her shoulders and steeled herself for the meaningless chit chat that was *de rigeur* at these gatherings. She knew Arnie would be off working the crowd to glean the latest expat news for his magazine.

She hoped she looked alright wearing her clingy red angora dress and reminded herself to suck in her stomach on account of all the weight she'd gained. The red angora was all she had. Feeling self-conscious in the dress while teaching her evening class, she had kept her coat on, claiming to have a cold. She glanced at Arnie as he was checking their coats and noticed that he looked quite dashing in his business suit. She was about to make some remark but Arnie was already half way to the bar.

The restaurant was lit with low table lamps and candles and the ambiance was friendly and warm. The who's who of expat society had assembled for their weekly reunion. Nice-to-meetchas' were exchanged at the door with the organizer. Vizma was ready to make her entrance. Luckily no one was paying attention and she quickly slid over to the bar. She ordered a martini and drank it quickly. As she was always nervous walking into a crowd, she decided to order another before daring to mingle.

Layers of cigarette smoke drifted around the room as Vizma, glass in hand, smiled, nodded her head this way and that. She caught snatches of conversations and bursts of laughter which peppered the steady undercurrent of gossip. She waved at somebody she knew halfway across the room and then, after the second martini, swaying slightly, she worked her way through the crowd to say hello.

Networking was going on full force, taking the form of ritual business card exchange, schmoozing, bragging, complaining, swapping stories and sharing tips on available apartments. Clusters of blue blazers, their waists and hairlines showing the years, clapped each other on the shoulder and women dressed in casual luxury, sleek and frosted blond, gossiped and made luncheon dates they wouldn't keep.

Vizma knew many of the regulars, more or less. She knew that these encounters, however meaningless and superficial, were necessary to keep the herd together. For some reason, she hadn't gone out of her way to cultivate the women of the expat community, even less so, the men. In fact, to date she had made few friends.

There was Linda whose gossip rating was high. A female lawyer, Linda from Detroit, who regularly came to troll for business and cruise for men, was complaining in a loud voice about the price of the drinks. Linda invariably arrived at these gatherings in a black pinstripe business suit but, within minutes, always put the jacket on the back of a chair revealing her ample bosom which tested the limits of her white Lycra shell top. Rumours circulated that she had been sanctioned by the Judicial Dress Code Committee in Detroit for her excessive décolleté but Vizma suspected that Linda might have started the rumour herself.

As soon as Arnie saw Vizma talking to Linda, he elbowed his way to her side.

"I hope they don't serve eel stew or pig's feet. And I hope they bring on the food, whatever it is, very soon. I'm starving," Vizma was saying.

"From my experience at these dinners, they try to hold back the meal so that they sell the maximum amount of booze. I'm told that's where they make most of the profit," Linda responded. She was clearly already on her third.

Arnie greeted her and when Linda realized that Arnie wasn't going to buy her a drink, she bent over towards him ostensibly to brush some ash off her skirt and straightened up just in time to catch his reaction. Arnie had quickly averted his gaze and was now staring hard at the toes of his shoes. Vizma gave him a sharp nudge in the ribs. But Linda interrupted the mood by saying,

"Oh look. There's Don Fischer. I must go and say hello."

"Ah, yes. Teflon Don," Arnie said unkindly. "So where's Maija?"

Vizma gave him a look. "Arnie, the waiters are starting to bring in the first course. Let's go and sit down."

"Okay, Vizma. You find us two seats and I'll join you in a minute."

There he goes, off to see how the real Maija compares to the photo, Vizma said to herself and smiled a sardonic smile. Oh yeah! Good luck, Arnie. Vizma had already heard that Mrs Fischer would not be attending. She had heard rumours about Maija and some Russian. Taking a closer look at Don, Vizma hoped that, for Maija's sake, the rumour about the Russian was true.

There were other things on Vizma's mind. Apart from being hungry, she was interested in finding out where these lovelies got their hair done. Not a brassy blonde among them. Well, this evening won't be a total loss if I get the name of a good hairdresser who knows about frosting, she said to herself.

Just as she had thought, this time she was enjoying herself. She had come for an evening out, for a chance to walk through the streets of Old Riga with Arnie and not be terrified of being mugged—although being a couple was no guarantee. A colleague and her husband had been mugged in broad daylight as they were coming back from a dental appointment on one of the top floors of the Universal Department Store. There were only a few santimes and a bus pass in her colleagues purse but losing her keys and her address book had been devastating.

Arnie was still talking to someone at the bar and Vizma decided not to sit down alone at the long table. She continued to circulate through the crowd. A few moments later, she glanced across the room and saw Arnie shouldering his way through the clots of people, possibly looking for the men's room. She saw that his mission was cut short as a clearly non expat young woman approached him.

Arnie stopped, surprised by the pale slip of a girl. It was certainly not her milieu.

"Hello," he said in a pleasant voice.

"I'm looking for Mr Dambergs," the girl replied quietly in Latvian.

"*I'm* Arnie Dambergs. How can I help you?"

Anda had heard about the expat dinners from Mike who had gone once with Arnie to take some photos.

"Would you like something to drink?"

The girl accepted an orange juice. They sat down at the bar, leaned towards each other and kept their voices low. There were a few more minutes before everyone was expected to sit down. A number of lethargic waiters were filling water goblets and setting out baskets of bread.

"My name is Anda Andersona. My friend, Mike, told me about you," she clarified.

"Mike? Good God! You know Mike! Where is he?" Arnie was so excited he toppled over his glass of beer. "I've been trying to reach him on his cell phone for the last three days. He's disappeared off the face of the earth. It's not like him. He always calls back, especially when I owe him some money for photographs."

"Yes, I'm looking for Mike too. I came to ask *you* where he is. He said he was going to see you Monday night. He told you owed him a payment and he really needed the money."

Anda saw the flicker of alarm register on Arnie's face. She realized that Arnie hadn't seen Mike either. A waiter was walking behind them on his way to set out more places at the long table. They both stopped talking. Instinctively, neither of them wanted to be overheard. For a long moment, they just sat and stared at each other. Arnie couldn't help admiring Mike's choice of girlfriend and Anda was trying to decide if Arnie could be trusted. What had Mike told her about Arnie? All she knew was that Arnie paid Mike good money. Could she trust him enough to mention Mike's package?

In the background, Arnie heard the shuffle of feet moving toward the long banquet table and realized that the dinner was about to begin. He turned, looked behind him for Vizma and had no trouble finding her in that red angora dress. She beckoned him to come and join her at the table. He signalled that he would be there in a minute and turned his attention back to the young woman sitting beside him. Anda, realizing that she would have to leave, suddenly blurted out,

"Mike gave me a package to keep. I don't know what's in it."

"A package?" Arnie's eyes widened.

"Well, a large thick envelope."

"Where is it?" Arnie shot back. He was really excited now.

"I brought it to my parents' house. Mike seemed nervous that someone could find it. He didn't tell me what was in it. Maybe a book."

Or maybe photographs, Arnie said to himself.

"But I have another problem. My niece, Daina, didn't come home last night or the night before. We haven't heard from her for three days. Silvia is really frantic. Daina's only fourteen and she's never done anything like this."

"Who's Silvia?" Arnie asked wanting to get back to the package.

"Silvia is my sister. She's going through a hard time. No money, husband who neglects her, drinks—I don't think you want to know…" Anda's eyes became bright with tears.

You read my mind, Arnie wanted to say but then he felt guilty. Anda was his only link to Mike. And he liked her, felt sorry for her. There were times, yes, that the milk of human kindness welled up in Arnie's chest.

"What do you know about Latvian beauty contests?" Anda asked.

Arnie shrugged. "Not much."

"Well, Daina went off to try out for this beauty contest and never came back. Silvia doesn't know what to do. We were hoping you'd help us."

"How long has she been missing?"

"Like I said, we haven't heard from her in three days," Anda replied impatiently. She hoped that Arnie Dambergs wasn't getting drunk.

Arnie made a decision. He would sit through the dinner but he had to see this girl again. He stubbed out his cigarette and finished his beer.

"Anda, I'd like to help you but now I must go join the others. I hope you don't mind. But I definitely want to see you tomorrow. Where can we meet?"

"I'm working until six at Roze's Bookstore on Barona Street."

"Fine. I'll pick you up there. And listen, don't say a word to anyone about this."

Anda nodded, smiled and was gone.

Chapter Fourteen

Arnie had slept a scant three hours. Horrible thoughts festered in his mind as he drifted from one dream to another. At five in the morning, he awoke with a hang-over but couldn't remember if he had been moderately drunk the night before or full-out drunk.

He scarcely remembered the dinner—scarfing down food, not knowing what it was, walking home, talking to Vizma but all the time thinking, thinking, thinking. *The body in the garage.* His mind hadn't dared to come to a conclusion. But a part of him knew. It *was* Mike's body lying there in that filthy garage. And it had been Arnie's fault. Arnie had owed him money, had made him work for a pittance. Mike had been hurting for cash and he had been on his way to deliver more photos. Now Mike was dead.

Arnie had never been the sentimental type. He was surprised at the guilt and remorse that was now torturing him.

He put in a few hours at his computer but most of it was spent just staring at the monitor thinking about Mike and the meeting with Anda that evening. Surely, she would have news. Maybe he was wrong about the body. Maybe Mike had finally shown up or, at least, had called. Arnie thought of phoning Anda at the bookstore, or maybe he could rush over right now. Or maybe he would have to be patient.

Ennui. Today, Arnie knew what the word really meant. The French existential stuff had never been clear to him until now as the inexorable passage of minutes turned into hours and crept along like a tired snail going up a very steep hill. He lost count of the number of times he checked his wristwatch and stared at the minute hand creeping around the dial. Hurry up, snail!

At five o'clock he could wait no longer. He'd walk to Barona Street. He had already planned the route he was going to take five times.

When he got to Elizabetes Street he had to push his way through a small knot of women who were staring intently at the display window of the newly opened Christian Dior cosmetic boutique. Arnie couldn't help laughing out loud. What in the world was this all about? Then the light went on in his head and he gave a derisive snort. Another money laundrette, of course. Beautiful sad-looking young saleswomen stared out the window knowing full well that there wouldn't be much of a rush on the luscious lipsticks and gilded, bronzed and pearled eye-shadows in a multitude of tints and shades. What a depressing way to spend the day, Arnie thought and then he remembered that these girls were only bored, not cold and hungry like so many others.

He arrived at the bookstore early, didn't see Anda anywhere in sight and decided he might as well kill some more time, having done nothing else all day. He examined the tables of American best-seller translations, boxes of stationary, European travel books. His eyes scanned the aisles between the rows of bookshelves as he worked his way from table to table. There were a few shoppers, a cashier behind a counter. But he didn't see Anda.

After a few minutes of skulking around, he decided to make a direct approach to the male cashier who had been eyeing him suspiciously. He asked for Anda. A non-committal shrug was all he got in response. Arnie insisted by telling the cashier that he had arranged to meet Anda at the end of her shift. The cashier grimaced an I don't care. Arnie felt his blood pressure rise, hands start to ache wanting to throttle the guy. Another one in need of some Wal-Mart service training, he thought. Sometimes he longed for the greeter at the door and a friendly have-a-nice-day.

The cashier, sensing Arnie's frustration, picked up a phone. Was he calling the cops? Arnie knew he wasn't going to get anywhere. Perhaps Anda would rush in at the very last minute to meet him, or maybe she'd be outside the store waiting. He had to maintain his cool. He didn't want to be arrested for causing a disturbance.

Closing time arrived and Arnie swallowed his disappointment. There was no Anda. He decided to come back the next morning. He kicked himself for not having asked Anda for her phone number last night.

The following morning, Arnie had Anda's telephone number in two minutes. Twenty dollars worked magic. He lit up a cigarette, headed for a public phone in a nearby café and made the call. A feeble voice answered on the third ring.

"Anda?"

"Yes."

"It's Arnie. Arnie Dambergs. I…"

"My sister's dead."

"What!" Arnie exclaimed in horror not able to say anything else.

"Silvia, my sister, died. She froze to death."

Arnie was still speechless. Clichés welled up in his mind along with a couple of other thoughts. Could this have anything to do with Mike?

"I'm so sorry," he groaned. After a short pause he went on. "Tell me what happened."

"Remember last night I told you I'd taken Mike's package to my parents? Well, Silvia went to our parents' house to pick up her little boy and somehow found Mike's package and opened it."

Arnie gasped. The package!

"After she saw what was in it, she went straight to the tavern. On her way home, she fell into a snow bank and couldn't get up. She froze to death."

There was a minute's silence after which Anda started to sob.

"Please, Anda. Please talk to me. I want to know what happened."

Drawing in her breath, Anda started to speak in a soft voice.

"They found her in the morning, frozen to death near the back steps of her apartment building. She wasn't wearing a coat or boots. The police said that she must have passed out from the drink and had died of the cold."

Arnie heard Anda blow her nose. In a steadier voice, she continued,

"Now, I have Vilnis to look after. He doesn't want to stay with my parents. He's afraid of his grandfather. My father drinks all the time with his friends and he's no help at all. My mother has no one but me and now I've got Vilnis to look after."

"Anda, where's the package? Do you have the package?"

"Looking ahead, I can see so many changes now. Every morning, I'll have to get up an hour earlier just to dress him and take him to daycare before I go to work. He keeps asking me 'Where's my mother?'"

"Mike's package, Anda! Do you have it? Is it still…"

"Yes, yes. I have it. It's here in my apartment now. I don't want my mother to see it."

"You stay there. I'll take a cab. I'll be right over. What's the address?"

Arnie was insistent. He wanted that package more than ever. Whatever it was that Mike had been bringing him had become really important, especially if Mike had been killed because of it.

Anda let out a long sigh. Arnie could hear a child wailing in the background.

"Okay. I live on Marijas Street. 61. First floor. The front door is broken. Come right in and knock on number three."

Arnie wasn't sure exactly at what moment the warning light had come on in his head but it had made him use a pay phone to call Anda. He had decided against taking a cab since it would be as easy to walk. He crossed Barona Street and headed down to Marijas Street, an area infamous for prostitutes. He saw no one who could pass as a hooker. Only a few bundled-up people waiting at bus stops or waiting for trash pickup or waiting for life to get better. Around him were peeling wooden buildings, grey concrete blocks and streets cracked and pocked with potholes.

He walked hurriedly, searching for 61. Half a block down, Arnie found the derelict three-story house. The place looked abandoned. The front door hung half open. As his eyes moved upwards, they settled on the large dormer windows of the roof. For him, the windows of a building were like the eyes of a face. He saw right away that these windows belonged to a corpse. No life left in them—not a plant, not a cat, not a milk bottle, not even curtains. As he stared at the building, a babushka waddled up the sidewalk and started sweeping the pavement which was broken and badly discoloured by dirt and pollution.

The building loomed dark and silent in the dim daylight. Even before Arnie walked in the front door, he could smell the damp plaster mixed with an overlay of greasy cooking, unwashed diapers, dog and cat poop, decay and alcohol. He imagined that sunlight never quite reached this place.

As he pushed open the door, roaches as big as rats scurried for cover. Like so many times before, Arnie thanked his lucky stars that he lived on upper Valdemara Street in his sixth floor walk-up. Even without hot water, it was a world away from this roach haven.

He hesitated for a moment, thinking he could hear the scurry of rats. It was terribly cold and dark in the small space which passed as a foyer. Arnie stopped to let his eyes adjust. Turning to his left, he saw a door, stuck on it a piece of paper with the number three. He knocked. A minute later, the door cracked open and Anda's face appeared behind the security chain. Seeing Arnie, she unlatched the door and opened it. There was no rush of warm air from inside the apartment. Perhaps it was warmer outside but Arnie couldn't tell.

Anda's face was pale and miserable. Arnie could see that she had been crying. She was wearing a scruffy pair of jeans and a heavy navy blue sweater that looked as if it was unravelling at a steady pace. On her feet, she wore heavy wool socks. Arnie realized that these houses probably had wood burning furnaces but, if the caretaker ran out of wood, there would be no heat. If, indeed, there was such a thing as a caretaker. Maybe the tenants had to do it themselves or maybe the wood was wet or newly cut. Or maybe there was simply no wood.

From the cold depths of the apartment, a snotty looking child rushed forward calling *"kožene, kožene"*.

"He wants chewing gum," Anda explained raising her eyes heavenward. "Don't mind him."

A pair of velvet pads came scurrying over, a tail raised in anticipation.

"And what do *you* want?" Arnie said fondly as he bent down to stroke the cat.

An instant later, a sudden enraged screech made him spring back. "Shit!" he exclaimed and sucked the blood that was trickling down the back of his hand.

"Don't mind the cat," Anda said in a weary voice. "It has no manners."

Oh great, just great! Now she tells me, Arnie thought as he searched his pockets for a tissue. Perched on a table by the window, the cat was busy licking the spot of Arnie's blood on its paw. Arnie suppressed a *frisson* of dislike.

Let's cut to the chase, he thought.

"The package," he said gruffly. The bleeding had stopped but he noticed that the cuff of his shirtsleeve was in shreds. It happened to be his best Hathaway. *Get that fucker put down*, he muttered under his breath as he rolled up the torn shirtsleeve and tucked it up under his coat.

"The package Mike left you," Arnie repeated enunciating every word between his clenched teeth.

Silently, he made himself count to ten, fighting the urge to go tearing through the apartment in search of the package so he could leave.

"Yes, yes. The package. It's somewhere," Anda said picking up her wailing nephew.

Arnie rolled his eyes, stepping across a pile of clothing, cardboard boxes, magazines, newspapers. Making sure the cat was not about to pounce, he positioned himself gingerly on a rickety old chair.

From the bedroom, he heard Anda coaxing her nephew to lie down on her bed and look at a magazine. There had to be some children's books at this store Anda was working at but then Arnie realized that the poor girl had just been struck by a tragedy. He bet there was no washing machine on the premises and he wondered where the closest grocery store was located.

Anda came out of her bedroom still carting Vilnis on her hip. He had refused to stay in the bedroom. In her free hand, she was holding a large brown envelope. She looked at Arnie with a level gaze. He could tell that she was hiding her emotions, not daring to give in to her grief and anger in front of Vilnis.

She handed Arnie the envelope. He opened it. Took a sharp breath. Instinctively, he knew he had stumbled on something horrible. Photos spilled out. Photos of young girls and boys, in suggestive poses, scantily clad.

Anda turned the child's head away and pointed out the shot of her niece Daina. The pretty teenager looked scared but had struck an awkward come-hither pose wearing a skimpy black teddy and sucking her thumb. Arnie frowned and clenched his lips together, searched for the right words. He looked at Anda and saw that she was shaking.

"Daina's still missing," Anda said with a sob. "Tell me what I should do."

Arnie tried to look thoughtful as he raised his gaze away from the photographs but his eyes were distracted by the squirming body of Vilnis who looked as if he might prove to be even more vicious than the cat. Arnie decided against reaching out to hold him.

"Look here," he said in a low voice, pulling out some pocket change. "For you."

Vilnis smiled and reached for the shiny coins. Getting down, he took the coins and tottered back into the bedroom, counting his loot.

Arnie knew that he should walk away fast. But he couldn't. He felt immobilized as if bitten by a spider just before his entrails were to be sucked away. Anda moved some items of clothing off her couch and slumped down in one corner.

"We'll get to the bottom of this, Anda. I promise."

The words brought a smidgen of a smile to Anda's face. Foreigners could do anything. Everyone knew that.

"Didn't Mike say anything to you, Anda? About the photos, I mean."

"No, nothing." Anda gave a shake of her head. The smile had vanished and she was staring fixedly into space twisting a strand of hair in her hand.

Arnie pulled his chair closer to her.

"Tell me exactly what was said when Mike gave you the package."

"Well, he just handed it to me. That was last week. He said to keep it for him in a safe place. I could tell that he didn't want to talk about it, so I didn't ask him any questions. Later that evening, I walked over to my parents' apartment and put it in the bookshelf. That's where my parents keep any extra money when they have some. No one trusts the banks around here."

"Do you have any idea where these photos were taken?"

Anda looked at him with surprise, her eyes angry, her voice loud and shrill.

"Yes! Yes, I do! It's this Young Miss Latvia contest. I can bet it's that."

"What makes you say that?"

"Oh, I just know it. How else could there be a photo of Daina?" Anda paused, her mouth open. "Unless…"

"Unless what, Anda?"

"Oh, I don't know. I've always worried about Daina. The way men look at her…"

"Could Mike have done something like that?"

"What a horrible thought! I still think it's the beauty contest. It has to be that."

"You're probably right," Arnie said in a weary tone.

He had heard that his old friend Maija Fischer was one of the judges in the Miss Latvia contest. Arnie couldn't help but wonder in what other way she could be involved. But God, it was cold in here! He saw that Anda had grabbed one of the pillows and was hugging it to herself. The bloodhound in him rose to the surface.

Time to roll, Sherlock, he said to himself as he got up from the chair.

"Anda, trust me. Give me one of the photos. The one of Daina. It will help find her."

"No!" Anda's mouth was tight with anger. Her eyes blazed.

"Please. It's the only way I can help you. Daina's a missing person. This photo will help."

Anda bit on her lower lip, then let out her breath in a long sigh. "Ahhh… What can I do? Oh God, help me!"

"With your permission I'll take this," Arnie said reaching for the photo of Daina. "Trust me, Anda."

Anda's face was expressionless. She didn't move. Arnie took the photo and carefully positioned it inside his jacket breast pocket, underneath his coat. Mike would probably be back for his package. Or would he?

"Hide those photographs, Anda. Hide them where no one will find them, and I don't mean in your parents' bookshelf," he said sternly.

There was silence. Anda had dropped her head into one hand while the other kept clutching the cushion. He hoped she wasn't crying.

"Yes, yes, I will," she said finally looking up.

Her eyes were dry. A look of steely determination crossed her face. She picked up the envelope.

"When Mike comes back, I'll give him this. And I'm going to ask questions."

"Be very careful, Anda. And call me the minute you see him."

Anda nodded. "I'm sorry I didn't offer you coffee."

"Oh, no. Please, that's all right. I should have brought you something."

Anda got up and smiled at him. She had to trust someone. He was the only one who could find Daina. She was sure of it.

"Here's my phone number but, when you call, be very careful what you say. I've had the feeling for the past couple of days that I'm being followed. My apartment was ransacked. There's probably a listening device on my phone."

Anda looked at him with alarm. She didn't say anything, only shook her head. She listened as Arnie continued,

"It could be that these photos are what they were looking for. Mike was to bring them to me. He never turned up but no one knows that. I might have been followed to your apartment. You'd better be very careful."

Arnie wondered silently if Silvia's death could be related to Daina's disappearance. All Arnie's senses were in overdrive and he was taking nothing for granted. He was smart enough to be good and scared. He didn't know if Anda was thinking along the same lines and didn't want to alarm her any more. Before Arnie turned to go, he said softly,

"Is there anything I can do for you right now?"

Anda shook her head.

"This is the money I owe Mike. You might as well have it."

Arnie pulled out the money, added ten lats and handed it to her.

"Call me later tonight or I'll call you. I want to know how you're doing. Maybe I'll have news for you."

Then he shook Anda's hand and walked towards the door. The cat looked restless and Arnie was anxious to beat it.

Chapter Fifteen

It was the *r* that would give him away. The expat *r*. The locals rolled it while Arnie, like most expats, used the soft English *r*. He practised his lines a few times hoping that he would sound like a native.

"My daughter is only twelve but she looks older. I want to bring her over to fill out an application for the Young Miss Latvia contest. I'd like to come right now."

Arnie thought he sounded quite good. It had taken him half the morning using a variety of phone booths to finally get through and now there was silence at the other end.

Come on, come on, my phone card's running out, he muttered and thought for a moment that he had been disconnected. But then, he realized that maybe he wasn't as good as he thought. Something must have aroused suspicion.

"We apologize but the contest is now closed. We have too many applicants," came a frosty voice.

"Assholes," Arnie muttered and slammed down the phone.

He would have to try another tack. He didn't have the nerve to ask Anda to make the call. It would be a five-dollar favour, he figured. Whom to approach? He didn't want to waste time. Well, this was ridiculous but the only person he could think of was the lady who folded his wash at the Laundromat on Terbatas Street.

Here goes, Arnie said to himself as he rushed home to gather up a load of wash.

"No problemo," came the answer to Arnie's request. Arnie laughed. Mrs Skuja had picked up a vital word or two from her mainly expat clientele.

Her telephone inquiry about her young daughter received a warm reply.

"Oh, yes, yes. Send her to our studio on Brivibas Street. Just have her take the bus down to Matisa Street. Our studio is one flight down. She can come alone. She doesn't need an appointment. We will take photographs. As you know, the first prize is a modelling job in New York City. So we have many candidates."

The good lady frowned. Arnie's five-dollar bill was slightly torn.

"No, no. I don't want that one." She shook her head and, gesturing, explained to Arnie that torn or marked bills were refused in Riga.

Arnie had five lats on him. He handed over the money. Mrs Skuja beamed. She had just scored fifteen Canadian dollars for a two minute call.

"Any time," she called cheerfully as Arnie walked out.

Back in his apartment, Arnie grabbed a beer, lit a cigarette and chuckled. He was finally getting somewhere. Now he had an address for the contest headquarters and evidence that they were taking kids as young as twelve. And he had nice hot stuff to look at. The photo of Ms Cleavage herself. Arnie just couldn't wait to tackle her. He gave the famous photo an appraising look and wondered if Maija would live up to it.

As he pecked away at his keyboard, he knew that nothing was going to deter him from his story. Not the cats in the hall, not a power failure, nothing. He was throwing caution to the wind. If this didn't flush them out, nothing would. He was already on somebody's hit list. He might as well go for broke.

This time, Arnie saved every few sentences. An hour later, the March issue of *WOW!* was in the can. The headline was dynamite. KIDDY PORN IN HIGH PLACES. Now, *that* was going to bring the vermin scurrying out of hiding. Arnie grinned as he pressed the save button for the last time. He just hoped it didn't pull the roof down around his head.

As he sat back, the thought occurred to him that he should move. Just vanish into the suburbs of Riga, melt in with the locals. He wondered what Vizma was doing. He had seen her the other night at the garbage stop. As was the custom, people came down with their pails at five o'clock each evening and waited for the truck. Then they'd scurry forward and dump out their waste. The process was a sure-fire way of meeting the neighbours, better than the Welcome Wagon.

Startled at seeing him there with his pail, Vizma had waved but had not approached, probably embarrassed by the less than romantic setting. What an opportunity for a hit, Arnie had reflected as he looked up and down the street waiting for the garbage truck. It was so predictable. The truck was seldom late. Drive by at five, fire a shot, create mayhem, then gun down the target.

Arnie shuddered as he pictured himself diving into the dumpster and burrowing deep into the garbage. Dumpster diving! Arnie laughed out loud at the thought. That's exactly what he had been doing. But now everything had changed. He had a real story. A social issue. A crime. And somebody was threatened enough to come after him. He knew he wasn't paranoid. He just had to hang in there. One great international exposé and he'd be a big shot. He'd be on television, perhaps even CNN.

An hour later, Arnie got the call. The chicken-shit printer had refused the job! But then, on second thought, Arnie realized what a fool he had been to send the issue to an outside printer. No matter how well he knew the print-shop, this thing was too hot to be handled by anyone but himself.

Twitching with excitement, Arnie smoked non-stop as he paced around his room. All he needed was a small edition. He'd get it out on the streets then wait for all hell to break loose. Doing the job on his desktop printer would be an all-nighter but he knew it could be done. He quickly reviewed the layout. He had emphasized the missing child story and had buried Maija Fischer's name on the back page. Most readers could put two and two together. There was a ton of work to do. He needed help and he knew where to turn.

Without losing any time, he walked briskly down three flights of stairs and stood at Vizma's door preparing to knock. He paused, hearing footsteps on the landing below. Vizma appeared in the hallway lugging two enormous shopping bags. Arnie rushed toward her to help.

"I was hoping you'd be home. I really need to talk." Arnie's voice was urgent. Vizma could tell he needed something.

"Yes, sure," she replied as she unbolted the door. "Come on in."

Once inside, Arnie remained standing.

"Sit. Would you like coffee?"

"No. Actually, I'm in a hurry," Arnie said starting to pace.

"Let's go into the kitchen. I need some coffee and I want to put this stuff away."

Arnie waited until Vizma had settled herself across from him at the kitchen table, had lit a cigarette.

"I went to see Anda," he said.

"Anda?"

"Yes. You know the girl who came looking for me at the dinner?"

"Oh yes," Vizma said coldly. She felt a moment's annoyance. Was Arnie chasing young girls? And why should she have to hear about it?

"Her sister died."

Vizma gave him a puzzled look.

"Let me explain. I'll tell you the whole story." Arnie lit a cigarette, inhaled deeply and tying Anda and her sister together with what Vizma already knew, he gave her more details. He told her about Mike and about the beauty contest and Maija Fischer.

Vizma exploded. "For God's sake, Arnie! That's dangerous stuff. Do you want to get yourself killed?"

Ignoring her, Arnie continued,

"I'm going to force the local papers to pick up the story. And that'll get the police to investigate. They certainly wouldn't listen to me if I simply went to the station with this."

"But is it worth the risk?"

Arnie looked her straight in the eyes. "Yes, Vizma. Yes, it is. Now, I'll tell you what I need from you."

To her own surprise, Vizma felt swept away by Arnie's conviction and sense of urgency. His excitement was contagious.

Arnie got up from the table and started to pace again.

"I have to produce this issue myself. I need ink, I need paper, I need someone to help put it together. Then distribution."

"Shouldn't you check this out? See Maija Fischer?"

"No. I want the element of surprise. I want to see the reaction."

"Yeah, you want a bullet through your heart!"

"Don't talk like that, Vizma. Listen, I'm not stupid. I mean, I'm not *that* stupid. I'm the one with access to the photos. Killing me won't do anyone any good. Perhaps someone will offer to buy them. Or bribe me to just go away."

Looking up at him, Vizma could sense that nothing would make Arnie turn back.

"When can you come upstairs and get to work?"

It took her exactly two seconds to answer.

"Give me twenty minutes."

Chapter Sixteen

The snow had wrapped the city in clean cotton wool, turning the grime and grit into a make-believe fairyland. But the temperature had dropped suddenly, making the footing on the sidewalk godawful and Vizma almost broke her neck a couple of times rushing down Valdemara Street. When she turned off on Elizabetes Street, where Buro's was located, the walking was even worse. She wondered at how the new snow could make everything look so beautiful but could also make it hell to get around the city.

It was very dark and the street was like an icy tunnel in front of her. She had to get to the office supply store before the six o'clock closing. As she cautiously shuffled her feet as fast as she could through the loose snow, she kept her right hand curled around the can of Mace deep in her coat pocket. The can had become a familiar presence in her hand, a talisman against evil. She had bought it right after her encounter with the Goth.

From time to time, she tested herself by placing her finger on the push button, ready to repel any assailant. She was alert, on guard, always looking, ready to react. Around her, shadowy figures moved slowly through the darkness. Anyone could be a predator. Stumbling over the icy pavement, she kept her hands jammed into her pockets, her eyes scanning for trouble—a runaway kid ready to rob her, a stray dog jumping for her throat, the Goth. It could be anything.

Her pulse was racing and she wished she could make her feet move faster. She felt the urgency and the responsibility weight on her. She knew that Arnie had a tiger by the tail with this story. He just had to hang on to the tail. One slip and the tiger would get loose and devour them both.

Finally reaching Buro's, Vizma panicked when she saw there was no one inside. Was it closed? In her haste to reach the doorknob, she forgot to inspect the icy steps. Her heart stumbled in her chest as, with a mighty *whump*, she fell to the ground. As she struggled for air, a pair of boots entered her field of vision. She looked up and saw they were attached to a heavy-set man who was exiting with a shopping bag. In a burst of energy, Vizma pulled herself up and rushed at the door, seconds before the clerk got there to lock it for the night.

"Oops," she breathed pushing herself through the door. She was in. The clerk looked sour but gave her two minutes to make her purchases—copy paper, ink cartridges for the printer, a legal size stapler and several boxes of staples.

Mission accomplished, Vizma breathed as she rushed back as fast as she could to Arnie's apartment, almost going ass over tea kettle a couple of times on the treacherous layer of ice. Climbing up the six flights of stairs, lugging all her parcels, winded her and she thought momentarily about giving up cigarettes for good. By the fourth floor, she was sure she had broken her kneecap when she had landed on it trying to save herself from one of the spills she had taken. By the fifth floor, she decided that she was just too old for all this excitement and maybe Arnie just wasn't worth it.

Using the spare key Arnie had given her, Vizma let herself back into his apartment. She said hi but there was no reply. Jerk, she said under her breath. Arnie was still hunched over the computer, putting the finishing touches on the story.

She took off her coat and sat down to look at her knee. There was a hole in her good wool slacks and a dark spot of blood. She pulled up the pant leg and saw that a large bruise had started but it was no longer bleeding. At that moment, Arnie asked if she'd managed to get everything on his list and added, without waiting for her reply, "Put on a pot of coffee, would you."

When pigs fly, Arnie! she said to herself but something about seeing him working so intensely over his computer made her willing to be a part of this project again. She was smart enough to realize that it was going to be easier just to fall in with his demands until this job was done.

Vizma put on coffee and then quickly unwrapped the new cartridge for the printer and set about extracting the old one. When she finished, she washed her hands before refilling the paper tray with legal size paper. Fanning the stack of clean white sheets, she loaded the paper tray and made sure that there was space on the table to stack each edition. This would be a home-office job, slow and tedious. She wondered if she was up for the long haul; she hadn't had an all-nighter for ages.

Still, she couldn't help laughing when Arnie told her where he had hidden the photograph. You never know, he had said. Anything's possible. He had wrapped it carefully in plastic and had slipped it into Gerda's litter box. This was one of those expat moments when he wished he had some North American clumping kitty litter since Gerda had immediately done an excellent job making her contribution on top of her box. Now, she came and watched Arnie with her head cocked on one side as he extracted the hidden envelope.

The change of plan for the production had made a lot of extra work for him. He had to reformat the layout to be able to reproduce it on his own copier. Then he scanned the photo, saved the document and put it back into its hiding place.

Arnie and Vizma made quite a team. Talk was scarce and hurried as Arnie, completely in control, issued orders to Vizma who executed each command efficiently. As he worked, Arnie prayed the power wouldn't fail, that there was no hacker at work, that no goon with a crowbar was camped out on his doorstep. As he worked, he felt sweat start to warm his scalp despite the cold air in his apartment. Vizma had found her groove. She slowly felt the pain leach out of her knee as she caught Arnie's excitement.

As production kicked into high gear, Vizma marvelled at how efficient she was. She realized that she liked hard work. Liked the adrenaline rush. It made her feel alive. The two of them were on a mission.

Finally, the big moment arrived. Arnie positioned the photo on the front page. A bit of cut and paste, a bit of editing and the layout was done. He held his breath as the first page came out of the printer. Ta daaa! It looked great! Then out came the second and third. Arnie beamed as Vizma meticulously placed the printouts in a pile. This would be a limited edition. Very limited. And very lethal.

Arnie stopped a few minutes for another fix of Vizma's coffee. The story had been written in a hurry but he liked the breathy quality of his work. He was searching for a missing child, warning the public to safeguard their children. The steady hum and clack of the printer was reassuring. Arnie topped up his mug and took Vizma hers. Even though he probably hadn't remembered, Vizma was pleased that he had left it black, the way she liked it.

Sipping her coffee, Vizma continued to keep her eyes on the printer. It was eating up the copy-paper and keeping her busy refilling the bin. She had to focus on what she was doing as she piled the finished copies on Arnie's leather couch. Arnie had started to talk to her but she lost her concentration and mixed up some of the finished sheets so she had shushed him up by saying, "Later, not now."

It was a little past eleven when they finished fifty copies. Arnie wanted the news to hit first thing in the morning. He knew that the news-stands in hotel lobbies were open all night. Then, there was the airport, the Internet, the TV stations, the radio, the dailies.

The coffee gave them both a new surge of energy. They forgot about being tired. By eleven-thirty, they were ready for distribution.

"I have a suitcase with wheels," Vizma volunteered.

"Great. Why don't you go get it while I package all this stuff up."

"Yeah, sure but we're going to need a car."

"Right. Bloody hell! I've got a car in the garage downstairs and it doesn't work. Do you know anyone?"

She blew out a sigh. "No. Don't you?"

"No. No one I can trust. So, what are we going to do? I don't have any Yellow Pages or anything like that."

"Wait. I think I've saved a number from a cab I used the other week. I think I know where it is."

"Okay. I'll wait till you get the suitcase and we'll call the cab. Wake the driver up if we have to. Twenty lats would probably do it. It'll clean me out but we can't stop now."

"No, no, Arnie. I'm really spooked. I don't want to go near my apartment alone at this time of night. And my knee is starting to hurt again. You come with me."

"Jeez, Vizma. Do you need a bodyguard?"

Vizma narrowed her eyes. "No, Arnie. What I need is protective headgear and a stun gun. But right now, you're all I've got."

Arnie's eyebrows rose. This was no time for a spat.

"Okay, okay. Let's carry all this stuff downstairs and pack it in your apartment. That way we don't have to come back up here. We'll call the cab from there."

Luckily, when they called, the cab driver hadn't gone to bed and was eager to drive them when he heard about the extra money. Things were going their way. They hoped the good Karma would hold and that no dark-haired gypsy woman would cross their path and throw them the evil eye.

Valdemara Street was silent and deserted as Vizma and Arnie stood at the front door waiting for the cab. Snow was falling again, gently and gracefully through the still air. Arnie gripped the suitcase and Vizma held her hand curled around her lucky charm.

They had a plan. First the news media and then hotel lobbies. Vizma relaxed. She felt like the pretty blond in Mission Impossible. She loosened her grip on the Mace. She was one of the good guys, and good guys always won.

Chapter Seventeen

It was three in the morning when Vizma and Arnie, fuzzy headed from lack of sleep, too much coffee and not enough food, slipped back into their dark apartment building. Wearily climbing the stairs, they parted company at Vizma's door agreeing to meet again at eight o'clock at Arnie's. Vizma didn't want to miss a thing. Like a star waiting for early morning reviews, she had to be there to see the reaction.

The minute she walked in the door of her apartment, Vizma gave up all thoughts of anything but sleep. She staggered into her room, flopped on the bed and, within minutes, was dead to the world.

Next morning, she woke up at quarter to seven. Her knee still ached and so did her head. She washed, dressed, had breakfast and climbed back up the three flights of stairs to arrive at Arnie's door at eight on the dot. Letting herself in, she found Arnie glued to the Internet. The TV and the radio played softly in the background. No grass growing here, she muttered. The air was still thick with smoke and the smell of burned coffee but it was too cold to open windows. Vizma walked up to Arnie's workspace. Arnie looked up at her with his nobody's-home eyes.

"Yo!" Vizma said loudly.

"Yo, yourself," Arnie replied.

"What's new, Arnie?"

"Nothing."

"Nothing? How come?"

Arnie shrugged. He didn't feel like chatting and went back on the Internet. Vizma scrunched her mouth up into a pout. It wasn't going to be much of a conversation. A minute later, Arnie swivelled around in his computer chair long enough to pull his shoulders up and down in a 'don't know' gesture. Vizma rolled her eyes, collapsed on the couch and closed her eyes.

They were both on automatic pilot. Their brains were half-asleep. The adrenaline rush was over. The hardest part was doing nothing, waiting and wondering when the phone would begin to ring.

Vizma dozed, from time to time struggling to open her heavy eyelids, not wanting to miss a thing. Arnie was in full workaholic mode. His head throbbed, his eyes ached, even his teeth ached but he couldn't stop. He kept staring at his computer, surfing the news, then staring some more.

The first call came at nine-ten. Arnie grabbed the phone. Vizma sat up, wide-awake.

"A missing child. I want to help," came the soft intimate voice. Arnie had bagged a biggie. It was Maija Fischer.

And he was ready for her. He glued the phone to one shoulder and reached for a notepad.

"Mrs Fischer? Maija? I was hoping you'd call. Can I call you Maija? You don't mind?"

"No, no. That's fine. Please do."

"You certainly will be able to help. Would you be willing to do an interview with me about the Young Miss Latvia beauty contest? Perhaps at their headquarter on Brivibas Street?"

"But why there?" Sweet and manipulative, Maija was at her best. "I have so little to do with the contest. I simply agreed to be a judge. They wouldn't take no for an answer. The judging is still two weeks away. It's going to be a big deal—television, prizes..."

"I know, I know," Arnie spoke over her words. "Right now, I'm only interested in the missing girl."

"Ah, yes. The missing girl. Just before calling you, I spoke to the co-ordinator. No one has seen this girl. She never came to the studio. They have no record that she signed up."

"No record?" Arnie echoed. The picture of Daina itself was a record and he certainly wasn't going to tell Maija about the other photos. He had to play this close to his chest.

"You've implied in your article that there's something illicit going on at the beauty contest but what proof do you have? Don't you think you're going too far? I know you like to stir the pot, Arnie, but don't you think it's a stretch to link this girl's disappearance to the Young Miss Latvia pageant? Surely, you don't think that in my position I would have anything to do with it if there was anything illicit going on?"

This was Maija at her best, in full flight, and Arnie was too tired to interrupt.

"O.K. Maija, you may be right. But how about doing the interview with me anyway? It's good publicity for you and the beauty contest."

The bubble in his head said: And if I'm right, it just might shake up somebody enough to make a mistake so that we can find this missing teenager.

"Now, where would you like to meet for the interview?"

"Will there be photos?"

Arnie almost laughed out loud. Photos? He still had the topless. He had used the nipple-skimmer in the February issue and Maija had not objected. Oh, that was Halloween, she had quipped. I dressed up as a waitress. He was glad he had saved the topless. Publishing it would have alienated Maija completely and he wouldn't have got a word out of her.

Before he could answer, Maija continued,

"Alright Arnie, come to my office this morning. I'll be here till noon."

Smiling, Arnie put down the phone and reached for his briefcase underneath the desk.

"What did she say? Will she meet you?" Vizma was breathless with excitement.

Arnie was already half way out the door when he called back over his shoulder,

"I'll tell you later when I get back. Cover the phone. And make sure you bolt the door behind me."

Arnie knew the address on Gertrudes Street and had often wished he could afford to rent an office in one of the prestigious modernized buildings. After a fifteen minute walk, he turned into a tiny courtyard. Fresh sparkling snow had covered the trees and the bushes and the newly restored fountain. For a few moments, he stood still and soaked up the old world charm. The coffee shop on the ground floor looked inviting, its window filled with Swiss pastries which made his mouth water. It was brightly lit, clean and attractive. Inside, he could see some business types and imagined they were entertaining their clients.

Light poured from the large glass windows of the offices on the upper floors. Business must be good, Arnie thought to himself. Nobody in Latvia left the lights on during the day if they could help it because electricity cost a fortune.

He had heard that there was an expat travel agency on the first floor. As he walked toward the front door, which was beautifully maintained with polished brass hardware, he admired the travel agency's shingle—a toucan with its yellow beak peeking around the word LIDO. The poor bird looked frozen and lost with a blob of snow on its head. Lido, indeed. Why didn't the stupid bird fly south, thought Arnie as he stepped into the lobby shaking the snow from his shoulders and stamping the sludge from his boots.

Maija's *Deco-Rama* was on the third floor accessed by an outside staircase at the side of the building. The snow had not been cleared and Arnie noticed that his weren't the first steps on the stairs. Inside the entranceway, slumped over on a desk, was a security guard, snoring away, his head resting on a magazine. The top of a thermos jug half filled with coffee was next to it and Arnie thought he could smell booze. The radio was playing. Arnie wondered how the guard could sleep through the noise. As the door banged closed behind him, the guard lifted his head, gave Arnie a quick look, lit a fresh cigarette and went back to his magazine.

After a short walk down a hallway, Arnie came upon a steel door. *Deco-Rama* printed in an ornate script announced Maija's place of business. A motion detector had discretely blinked its tiny red light at him as he approached the door. What's this broad got in here? Arnie wondered, impressed by the high tech security.

Maija opened the door, a vision of ditzy loveliness. A Martha Stewart clone—the working man's version, that is. Her hair was not quite as pale, her skin not as fine and the outfit just a little too ornate. It was not Martha but Maija herself in all her garish splendour, wearing a tight red skirt and a black turtleneck with lots of heavy gold jewellery. Her hair fell over her right eye in a Martha peekaboo and partly hid her face. Arnie noticed that she was wearing heavy makeup and wondered for a moment if he could detect a bruise under one eye. Suddenly, for some reason,

Maija and Martha flashed on his mindscreen. They were both wearing matching orange jumpsuits but Arnie wondered if Maija would be up to the challenge of decorating a jail cell.

"Hi, Arnie. Come in. Is it still snowing outside? Let me take your coat. Before we start the interview, would you like a cup of coffee?"

"No thanks."

While Maija watched, he peeled off his rubbers and then followed her into her office. She gestured him to the loveseat.

"Cigarette?" Maija proffered a silver box.

How elegant, Arnie thought to himself. And how pretentious. Smoking was no longer as glamorous as it once was. He took a cigarette, stepped close to Maija to light hers. Smelled her Opium perfume.

With a sigh, Maija sank into her couch. She took a studied drag sending a cloud of smoke into the air then looked around for the ashtray.

The high-ceilinged room contained the ubiquitous wall unit that Arnie had noticed in every apartment and in every office he had visited in Riga. In it was an arrangement of artefacts, a few books, a framed photo of Maija and her husband and loads and loads of decormags—*Architectural Digest, House and Garden, Shöner Wohnen.*

Arnie's eyes did a quick inventory of the room, its ferny green wallpaper, computer at a workstation, deep modern couch plus loveseat, coffee table stacked with more magazines and tons of colour swatches. He noticed right away that there was no need of a space heater. The room was toasty warm and there was probably hot water in the bathroom.

"My secretary isn't here right now. We'll be able to chat. And the phone is off the ringer so let's get started right away."

Like two old pros in the ring, each probing for the other's weaknesses, they started off the interview. Maija wanted free publicity for her business and Arnie wanted to find out about the pageant. Each knew they would have to give in order to get. The question was: how little for how much?

"I can give you the next hour but I have appointments all afternoon. You have no idea how demanding the diplomatic circuit can be. They all want the job done yesterday. They just don't understand that, in the new Latvia, they'll be lucky to get it by next *year*. Now, which of my recent commissions would you like to highlight in your next issue?"

Arnie received Maija message that there would be a quid pro quo for any information about the Young Miss Latvia contest. He quickly signalled his interest in *Deco-Rama* for next month or perhaps the month after. Having settled that issue, he turned back to Daina and the reason for his visit.

"At the moment, I'm interested in this beauty contest. When I got off the plane, I couldn't get over the number of gorgeous tall blondes. I rated them even higher than the standard Swedish girls we see in North America."

Agreeing with him, Maija went on.

"This beauty contest is a great idea to promote them around the world and give them access to the fashion scene in Europe and New York. But lots of these young teenagers aren't very sophisticated and their parents probably don't know the lifestyle to which their children will be exposed. Drugs, booze and pimps feeding off the mega bucks these girls can earn in the early days of their careers."

"Now, Maija, tell me if this trip to New York with a fashion shoot for the winner is for real?"

Maija gave him a humourless smile and said, "Where did you hear that? There is to be a fashion shoot but it's to be in Milan and it will be very well chaperoned. Milan is such a fabulous city. It's the heart of the Italian design industry and I just love going there for the shows each year."

Arnie was puzzled when Maija went off on this tangent to Milan. He definitely remembered seeing the New York trip mentioned in the blurb in the paper that Anda had shown him.

"Maybe I got it wrong. But any trip like that is a big adventure for a young impressionable girl."

"Well, we're all thrilled to death about this competition. It will put Latvian women on the world stage. God knows, they deserve it. And it might even give the Latvian fashion industry a boost."

"Yes, yes. But just how young are these girls?"

"It's not the *Little* Miss Latvia contest, Arnie. We don't take children."

"Yes, but thirteen is still a child."

"Correction, Arnie. A *teen*ager," Maija said tersely, waving her cigarette in the air.

"Do they have to provide some sort of proof of their age? Anyway, I think thirteen is pretty young, still a child."

"Well, they probably do. I don't know every little detail. I'm involved in judging, as I told you before."

"Are there any as young as twelve?"

Arnie wouldn't leave the topic alone. He was thinking of the call Mrs Skuja had made about her phoney twelve-year-old daughter.

"No, certainly not," Maija sniffed as she stubbed out her cigarette in a crystal ashtray.

Arnie noticed that her eyes suddenly appeared wary. She had drawn back into the corner of her couch, hiding in the pile of designer pillows. He found it reassuring that his instincts about this woman were proving to be right. He could swear that she was bullshitting him about the winner's trip and possibly the age thing as well. Maybe he could get her to talk about the other judges and the people who were organizing the whole thing. But just as he started to ask the next question, the doorbell shrieked. Arnie jumped. He felt a surge of fear. Paranoia in overdrive.

135

"Oh, it must be my husband!" Maija trilled. "I forgot we're having lunch."

With a gasp, Maija extricated herself from the depths of the couch. High heels clicking, she made for the door. Opened it. The trim middle-aged figure of Don Fischer walked in with his usual air of self-importance. Giving Maija a brief patronizing smile, he looked at his watch. He ignored Arnie, apart from a quick nod of recognition. Arrogant rude bastard, thought Arnie.

Nothing was going to faze this dude. Don Fischer stood stone-faced near the door and said,

"Ready, Maija?"

Arnie could see why he fitted in so well with the other dips. His shirt was stuffed like all the rest of them. Tall, thin, almost bald. Snazzy dresser, though, Arnie noted with a twinge of envy. That Burberry's expensive. Arnie had met him at parties and they had met for lunch recently. Don had wanted something. What was it? Oh yes, a retraction of a rumour he'd published in *WOW!*. Arnie hadn't been forthcoming and Don, for a diplomat, hadn't been very diplomatic.

Arnie stared at the diplomat. Donald Fischer wore rimless glasses through which he stared back at Arnie with as much condescension as he could generate. Clearly, Don Fischer was not the forgiving type. Arnie wondered what his problem was—alcohol, drugs, some Russian hooker blackmailing him, being married to Maija? It could be anything. Of course Arnie had heard about Chicago.

Maija came to the rescue.

"Oh dear, we were just finishing the interview. Don, you know Arnie Dambergs?"

"We've met," her husband replied icily, turning to go.

For a moment, Arnie felt that Maija was afraid of Fischer. The story in *WOW!* must have unnerved them both. Still, despite the tension, Maija managed a slight nervous giggle but hubby didn't crack a smile. Although all three of them were observing the formalities, Arnie could smell a trickle of blood in the water. One whiff of the scent and Arnie was going for broke. Nothing was going to shake him loose from the trail he was on, even if it led to some very dangerous people.

He said goodbye to Maija, inclined his head in Don Fischer's direction and walked out the door. He was anxious to get back to his apartment. Anxious to hear what Vizma had to report.

Outside in the courtyard, Arnie suddenly realized how hungry he was. He could duck into the café for a snack, or perhaps detour a little further and pick up some extra-crispy Buffalo wings from American Chicken on Brivibas Boulevard. Vizma was probably starving too.

Within seconds, his attention shifted away from food. Suddenly his breath caught in his throat. An orange Lada pulled out of a parking spot, waited till Arnie was out on Gertrudes Street, then slowly moved alongside.

Arnie quickened his pace as shivers of fear raced across his shoulder blades and down his spine. The car kept coming. He didn't dare stop, didn't dare turn his head and look to see who was inside. He thought of the photo lining Gerda's litter box, remembered the judge who was gunned down in this very same neighbourhood. Seeing a doorway to a café, Arnie darted inside. A minute later, he cautiously looked out the window. The car was gone.

Chapter Eighteen

The parking lot of Meža Kapi Cemetery was a well known haunt for car thieves so Anda had been very relieved when Sasha offered to drive them all. She was surprised that he didn't even leave a sentry to watch the car when they left it in the parking lot. Perhaps he had contacts. No, *for sure* he had contacts.

The last couple of days had been a living hell. Sasha had gone to Moscow and Anda had to make Silvia's funeral arrangements all by herself. She broke down and cried when she had picked out the dress for the undertaker. It was the smell that had brought her sister so vividly back to life. And then, there was the anxiety about Daina who was still missing. Anda imagined Daina's naked body lying face up in the snow, blue and battered, bones broken, teeth smashed.

She knew her imagination was running wild but she couldn't help it. And why was Sasha leaving all this to her? After all, it was *his* family—his wife and stepdaughter and son, Vilnis, that Anda now worried about. Her mother was too old and too ill to help and Anda had to shoulder the burden all by herself. At the same time, she had to hold on to her job. She needed the money. Through it all, she clung to the hope that Arnie would help her and prayed that he would find Daina.

Being surrounded by beautiful woods was the perfect natural setting for her sister's funeral and Anda hoped it would all go off without a hitch. As they walked towards the chapel, they became part of the throng of people moving in and out of the cemetery. Even in February, it was a beautiful place but still very, very cold.

From far away, Anda could hear the bullhorn voice of a babushka warning mourners somewhere up ahead that they had to move because they only had fifteen minutes in the chapel. As they got closer, the voice got louder. Anda noticed that there were three other funerals which all seemed to be taking place at the same time. Two were ahead and one was forming up behind. Again, she heard the grating noise of the babushka issuing her orders to move up and keep out of the way.

Anda closed her eyes and took a deep breath. She was lulled into a trance by the slow procession of people shuffling quietly up the avenue in their grey and black coats. There was a constant shuffle of feet punctuated by stamping every now and then, all of this accompanied by a chorus from the babushka who suddenly appeared waddling her way down one side of the row of mourners. On her head was a neon blue kerchief round which whirled large red mittened hands beckoning some and stopping others while she bellowed instructions with no respect for the dead. Anda was revolted by this comic character who had taken over her sister's final event and ignored her completely.

Inside the chapel, she paid little attention to the pastor's sermon. She was too exhausted to listen and her mind was far away with memories of Silvia. Her thoughts leapt to the painful moment of the past few days when her mother had first seen Daina's picture on TV. Anda had thought her mother was having a seizure. All she could think of was the weight of her mother's body when she had caught her. Now, she found herself looking over at her mother and she was struck by how frail and old she seemed, shrunken into her black cloth coat.

Two minutes later, it was over. Vilnis, who had been so silent and well behaved, was now skipping ahead of them on the way back to the car. He knew that his grandmother had made cakes and cookies for his tea.

Anda's new routine, always with her nephew in tow, seemed like an endless dance between her own apartment, her parents' and finally Silvia and Sasha's apartment. Vilnis got crankier at each stop and she found that dressing him in his winter clothes took at least an extra half-hour.

Anda hoped that Daina's friends would telephone or drop by Sasha and Silvia's apartment. Maybe she could learn from them what had happened the day Daina disappeared. Now, sitting by the phone in the empty apartment, her gaze settled on her sister's wedding picture. It had been such a happy day for Silvia. Sasha even managed to look protective with his arm around his bride.

It was shocking but really no surprise that Sasha had taken the news of Silvia's death in stride. His business deals always came first. Sasha and his friend who had just returned from Moscow went back right after the funeral. Anda had overheard them talking in Russian and she had tried not to listen. The less she knew the better. They were probably getting ready to drive another hot Mercedes to sell in Moscow. Car culture was a man's world and it seemed to Anda that it always involved some illegal transaction.

Even before her sister's death, Sasha's modus operandi had always been emotional detachment when it came to Silvia's family. It had been the same thing when he had learned of Daina's disappearance. Russians were an emotional people and Anda couldn't understand Sasha's coldness. Perhaps he was in shock. Perhaps he really didn't care. Perhaps he was glad to be free. He hadn't seemed to worry about Vilnis either and was relieved when Anda offered to look after the child.

Looking at Sasha in the photo, Anda saw his cold eyes staring out at her and she remembered how desperately in love Silvia had been. Yes, Sasha was an unusually good-looking man—tall, muscular with dark wavy hair only slightly tinged with grey, brilliant blue eyes and high Slavic cheekbones.

Silvia had wanted to make a life with him, a good life with books and music and friends and good food, and an education for Daina and Vilnis. Instead, there had been boisterous drinking and a constant flow of buddies talking business deals and get-rich schemes.

Sasha had moved in with Silvia and Daina a few months before Vilnis was born. For some reason, Anda was sure he had a wife somewhere else and probably children as well but there had been no stopping Silvia. Vilnis was born and Sasha's passion cooled. Silvia had gained weight, had become depressed, had started to drink. Sasha threatened to leave but, after a few days absence, he always turned up and things went on as before.

There were other things too. Anda worried because it seemed to her that Sasha had a weird relationship with his stepdaughter. Anda remembered how often he had commented on how pretty Daina was and how much he had flirted with her whenever his friends were about. She could be a model, he had said. Over and over, Sasha had asked her to pose for a photograph next to one of his cars, like they did in America.

Finally, the phone rang. Anda snatched up the receiver and let out a sigh of relief. It was Ilona, Daina's best friend. Anda tried to keep the panic out of her voice. Speaking calmly and in a friendly voice, Anda learned that the two girls were supposed to have met up at the studio on Brivibas Street. But Ilona said that she hadn't seen Daina there and had come home, disappointed that she had not been given an interview. She was sorry now that she hadn't waited for Daina. At the time, she had been jealous. Daina was prettier but Ilona had felt that she too should have had a chance to become Young Miss Latvia.

Anda put down the receiver, hoping that other friends who had gone to the studio would call as well. She hadn't learned much from Ilona. As she gathered up her things and started to bundle up Vilnis for the trek back to her own apartment, she sighed with relief at the thought that she still had a couple of days off from her job. She needed a doctor's certificate for more. Not a problem. Doctors were glad to help out. Doctors' pay was abysmal, almost as bad as teachers'. Anda's friend, a paediatrician, would give her one. Her friend, even though she was a doctor, had to take in children to baby-sit on her day off just to survive.

It would be much simpler for Anda if Vilnis would stay with his grandparents. But he had dug in his heels. Vilnis was afraid of his grandfather Ivan. Once, Vilnis had seen him skin a rabbit and, since then, didn't want to go near him. No one knew much about Sasha's family, except that his parents had moved back to Russia a few years ago.

Late that night, Anda realized with a pang that she had totally forgotten that she was in love. She hadn't given Mike a thought for days. Funny how quickly her feelings had changed. She remembered the first time she had met Mike. A friend had invited her to a party. She had been lonely then and Mike was with a group of friends doing his American gangster impersonations. Everyone had laughed, even Anda, although she was usually very serious. That evening seemed many lifetimes ago. She didn't feel like laughing now and she certainly didn't have any time to be lonely.

Anda had often wondered what it was about the women in her family that made them get involved with Russian men. Ivan, her own father, was Russian, though he had come to Latvia as a teenager. For some reason, he had chosen to take his bride's name. He was known as Ivan Andersons. Anda always found it strange that her father didn't get along with Sasha but had found an instant friend in her boyfriend Mike. Attractions and connections were hard to figure out but Ivan treated Mike as if he were a part of the family.

When her sister had finally married Sasha, she hadn't bothered to take his name. Anda wasn't even sure if Vilnis went by Atnikoff or her own family name. Sometimes Anda even had doubts about Mike. He and Ivan rattled on in Russian even though Anda's mother preferred hearing Latvian spoken in her home. Was Mike Latvian or had he changed his name from Mikhael? He spoke perfect Latvian but that didn't mean he wasn't Russian.

Anda shivered. Cold air was bleeding into the room from the windows that didn't close properly. She had tried to tape them but still the chill invaded her apartment no matter what she did. She hurried to get ready for bed, quickly washing her face and brushing her teeth. As she climbed into bed, she thought about her missing niece, Daina. She had never liked the way men looked at Daina, least of all Sasha. Daina was only a child, a tall, skinny, girl with a wide expressive face, milk white skin and a wild mass of reddish hair. Anda had never trusted Sasha around Daina and when she had mentioned it to Silvia a few times, her sister had only shrugged, lost in her own apathy and fatigue.

Anda's bed was now a refuge, the only place she found for introspection and rest. She could hear Vilnis cough and wondered if she should get up and make him a cup of hot herb tea with honey. She decided to wait a few more minutes to see if the coughing would stop. Besides, the apartment was now very cold and she was just beginning to feel warm and cosy in bed. As she drifted into sleep, her ear remained tuned to the little boy in the bedroom next door and she felt a tenderness that she had never experienced before.

Chapter Nineteen

Arnie's heart kept beating with sickening thuds. Maybe it was a trick of the light or his own mind playing games with him but he still felt sure the Lada was after him. It wasn't paranoia. The coincidences just couldn't be reasoned away. Instinctively he knew he was in danger.

He slid up to the front of the café, peered out the window. The coast looked clear. So why was he hesitating? Could the Lada be parked in a shadow just beyond his field of vision? He was sure it had been trailing him along Gertrudes Street. Gritting his teeth, he looked around and saw that his only chance of getting away safely was to duck through the kitchen and scoot out the back door.

In seconds, he was outside. He scuttled up the lane and speed-walked out to the next street. He was taking the long way home, moving suspiciously, checking the traffic as he waited at each corner. For a split second, he felt foolish as if acting out a scene in a spy movie. Then he shivered. Truth was stranger than fiction. He knew he couldn't afford to feel foolish. He had to keep his brain on high alert to get home without being killed.

Progress was slow as Arnie lingered in the shadows of buildings, watched for any sign of the orange car before he went near the curb to cross the street, watched everything—cars, bikes, people near him, people in the flow of pedestrians.

Slowly his pulse rate eased back to normal. He was almost home. He saw at a distance the garbage truck rumble to a stop in front of his house. A few people were out with their pails. No one he knew enough to nod his head at.

As he pushed open the front door leading to the dim vestibule, he tried to shake off the jitters he had been feeling all the way home. For a moment, he wondered if he was smart enough to keep one step ahead of his pursuers. In his mind the Young Miss Latvia contest was like Pandora's box full of writhing snakes. He had opened the box and now the snakes were loose. He could sense them slithering after him, ready to strike.

Glancing uneasily over his shoulder, Arnie went down a flight of stairs to the basement of his apartment building. Just as he thought. No orange Lada in the parking space. He released the breath he'd been holding and stumbled back up the stairs. The hallways were dark and gloomy, lit by only the occasional bare bulb and, as always, filled with the familiar scent of cigarette smoke, cat urine, mildew and decay. He hadn't encountered a soul.

As he unlocked his front door, he was surprised at the smell coming from his apartment. Food? He had almost forgotten about Vizma and here she was cooking his lunch. Her excited voice reached him before he could say a word.

"Tell me all about it. How did the interview go? Did she throw you out or, better yet, did she seduce you? I want to hear all about every last detail."

Not waiting for a reply, Vizma hurried on.

"I had some frozen *karbonades* in my freezer. We need to eat. I don't know about you but I am just ravenous."

"What's been happening?" Arnie interrupted. He took off his coat and dropping it on the chair beside the door, went to his computer still wearing his scarf and boots.

"There's been a slew of calls. I took messages. They're right by the phone."

Arnie got on line. Sure enough, his story was on every site. He checked his e-mail. Twenty messages. He picked up his phone.

"Come eat while the food's hot," Vizma called as she came out of the kitchen to get him.

"We're about to be killed and you think about eating," Arnie said with a smile as he put the phone down and followed her back to the kitchen.

The *karbonade* was crispy, just the way he liked it. The potatoes were thinly sliced and pan fried. Delicious.

"Enjoy it. Especially if you think it's going to be your last meal," Vizma said raising a forkful of pork cutlet to her mouth.

"I haven't had a change to tell you this and I wish I didn't have to but, coming out of Maija Fischer's office building, I discovered I was being tailed by an orange Lada. Remember I told you that the car in the garage the night I saw the dead body was an orange Lada? Well, it isn't there any more. I checked just now before I came upstairs. Somebody's moved it."

Vizma stared at him thoughtfully, then said, "Well, this city is full of orange Ladas. Maybe it's a coincidence."

"It's too damn many coincidences if you ask me. And I can't risk being complacent right now. Neither should you. I can see I'm going to have worry for both of us. Surely, you haven't forgotten your Goth."

"Don't call him *my* Goth, Arnie. I hope I never run into that creep again." Vizma sighed, pushed her empty plate to one side and propped her head up in her hands.

Arnie looked over at her. "I robbed you of some beauty sleep last night. You'd better go downstairs and have a nap. I can handle things at this end. I don't want to put you in any more danger than necessary."

With a jolt Vizma realized that she was being got out of the way. Well, she could take a hint. God knows, she certainly could do with a nap.

"Forty winks sounds good to me but I made us a fresh pot of coffee and it smells so good. Can I take time to have a cup while you tell me about the interview with Maija? Do you want one too?"

"Sure," Arnie said but already his mind was focusing on checking his phone messages. Still, he wasn't going to be rude to Vizma. While they were having coffee, Arnie told her about the meeting and about Donald Fischer's rudeness.

"Yeah, I've heard things about him. Ordinarily, I don't have a lot of time for the expat girls' club but they do have a pretty good networking system and, after what you've just told me, you might be interested in this."

"What's that?"

"Well, the word is that Donald Fischer cheats on his beautiful new wife. And guess what? He shows up next morning and Maija gets a beating. I guess their honeymoon was short and sweet and is *definitely* over."

"Hmm... I've heard the rumours too. About someone stashed away at the Radisson. He probably screws under-age girls like Daina."

Vizma grimaced.

With only her apartment to go back to and no hurry to get there, she drank her coffee slowly. She thought about her evening class at the Academy. Perhaps she'd cancel. The thought of being out after dark scared her now. She'd see. Arnie had kept her up all night and a nap sounded tempting after all. She tidied up a bit but left the dishes in the sink. Arnie was already back on the Internet when she waved goodbye. He got up, bolted the door behind her and went back to his e-mails.

The next few hours were nerve-racking but exciting. His magazine article was the hottest news in Riga. Even the North American press had picked it up. His old alma mater, *The Ottawa Citizen,* published a short paragraph about Arnie's exposé. This was a first.

Three death threats had come in. Two as e-mails and one on his voice mail. Twice, Arnie had picked up the phone to hear an angry voice yell at him in broken English. A Latvian voice or a Russian voice? He couldn't tell.

None of that spooked him. He was on a roll, already planning a second run of the March issue. He was adding a supplement to include more of Mike's photographs. There were too many questions that he still couldn't answer. He would have to throw caution to the wind and ask these questions directly. What is the intent of these photos? Is the fix in at some level of government? Where are these kids now? Have any others gone missing? Did they enter beauty contests? Young Miss Latvia? The questions would be out there. He only hoped he'd be around to hear the answers.

This time, Arnie would have to use a professional print shop and he would risk doubling his normal run. He would look for a smaller operation off the main street, one that didn't do government jobs.

At around four o'clock, Arnie went downstairs to the nearest phone booth and called Anda. He asked to meet her later that evening. She sounded exhausted but agreed. He wanted to know about Daina and about Mike. But most of all he needed the rest of the photos. Believing that Mike meant them for him, Arnie dipped into his dwindling savings. He would give Anda some more money. He knew she could use every penny. They didn't say much on the phone. Arnie knew he had to be careful.

Half way through his return climb up the dark smelly stairs, he stopped. He heard noises on the landing above. His heart felt fluttery. He stood still, listening but could only hear his own heavy breathing. He shrunk back into a shadow, waiting for what was coming next. Suddenly, a black form launched itself past him. He could feel his heart stop beating, then go wild with fear. And there it was again, the shuffling of heavy feet on the stairs above. Someone's up there. Waiting for me. The thought sent shivers sprinting up his spine.

More shuffling then a voice. Arnie almost keeled over as he exhaled a tremendous sigh. "Min...min...min," he heard again. For God's sake! It was the great she-cat herself. The Cat Lady, looking for one of her scrags. As tension drained from his body, Arnie realized he was drenched with perspiration. Gritting his teeth, he continued up the remaining stairs, hoping she hadn't noticed his bizarre behaviour. But she had. Arnie could hear her soft clucking. "Tch, tch, tch..." she went on, shaking her head in his direction as she disappeared down the hallway.

Back in his apartment, Arnie slumped down on his couch to recover. He knew he couldn't afford to waste time being scared. It was only nerves still, with everything that had happened, he dreaded going out after dark. This time, he decided to take a cab.

At eight o'clock, he stood in front of Anda's apartment door on Marijas Street. He knocked. Waited. Called her name. Knocked again. There was no light under the door. As he stood still listening, he could hear a mournful meowling coming from inside. Anda's no-name killer cat. How long had it been alone? With dread he imagined a crime scene. Anda murdered with Vilnis in her arms. Her throat cut. Vilnis suffocated. The cat padding through pools of blood and then licking each drop carefully off each paw. And Mike's photos gone.

Chapter Twenty

Arnie scowled into the darkness. At one in the morning, he was still awake, reviewing his finances, wondered where he'd put his will. Was it in his suitcase, briefcase, or the bank box back in Canada? If he died in Latvia, would his parents be able to inherit? First thing in the morning, he'd wire his bank manager in Ottawa and cash out his retirement saving fund. He needed the money. The moment had come for serious measures.

As sleep stole over him, Anda's face materialized. She was floating up above him, shrouded by mist, holding Mike's photographs out towards him. With her other hand she held on to Vilnis. She smiled. Then suddenly a streak of orange shot through the air. The next instant, Anda was dead. Vinis was dead. The photographs were gone. But the noise was still there. It went on and on. Arnie gasped as he realized it was the phone ringing. He fumbled around on his night table and picked up.

"You're dead, asshole."

"Who's this?" Arnie was wide awake now.

"None of your fucking business. Keep your trap shut or you're dead. You and your lady friends."

The words came in perfect English. Then the click. Arnie wished he had call-display. He knew of no way to trace the number. He couldn't place the accent. American? Canadian? Australian? He unplugged the phone. Sat up in bed. Turned on the light and looked over at Gerda. She looked back at him with her yellow stare, then yawned and closed her eyes. So much for companionship.

Arnie lit a cigarette. Up to now, he had been dealing with threats quite well. But at night, things were different. He needed some nerve pills and padded to the bathroom giving Gerda's litter box a worried look. He reached for his medicine pouch. Two Atavans should do it. He took a glass of water back to bed. Looked at the clock on his night table. Almost two. He decided he'd have to move. Not use the phone again. In fact, were it not for the fast-acting Atavan, he would have checked straight into a hotel.

A few hours later, Arnie was awakened by banging on his door. He looked at his watch. Just a little past eight. He stumbled to the door with Gerda pitty-patting behind him and peered through the peephole. Police. Two of them. Not the regulars but the security militia, armed with handguns and decked out in camouflage. Arnie had been warned about them. He had heard these guys were mainly volunteers committed to protecting state security and roughing people up. Unlike the weedy kids who passed as policemen, these guys were solid thick-necked toughs. They could keep him locked up someplace with his mouth taped. Torture him till he talked about the photographs. If it wasn't for the Atavan fix of the night before Arnie would have lost it then and there.

He knew he had about another minute before they'd kick in the door. What the hell! No fire escape and no back door. He might as well let them in and get it over with.

The minute he pulled the bolt back, he was hit in the face as the door was slammed against him. The two militiamen barged inside, not waiting for an invitation. Arnie felt foolish in his pyjamas but there was nothing he could do about it. This was not a social call.

"Passport!" the older of the two hurled at him.

Arnie kept his cool. He had two. Latvian and Canadian. He knew the thugs would kill for a Canadian passport. He didn't produce it. They examined his Latvian passport which had been issued in Ottawa. Scratched their heads. Arnie lit up and offered each of them a cigarette. Hey, take the whole pack.

"We have information you possess narcotics," the older of the two stated as he pocketed Arnie's smokes. Arnie stared. Not sure he heard right.

"What! Certainly not. You won't find any drugs here. I don't even drink anymore," he lied as he opened his liquor cabinet door knowing that it contained an unopened bottle of Metaxa brandy. He knew this was high up on the bribery list. Holding it out to the older one, Arnie said,

"Do me a favour and dispose of it."

The younger of the two took the bottle, crammed it into the pocket of his camouflage jacket. Taking turns, Arnie thought.

They weren't through yet.

"We'll have a look around," they said in unison. Heels clunking on the bare floor they marched through the apartment.

By some miracle, not a single copy of his magazine was lying around and his computer had been turned off.

"I'm a writer," Arnie said glancing at his desk. "I'm writing my memoirs now that I'm an old man." Arnie tried some humour. No one laughed. No one smiled either.

"Yeuggh…" a sound of disgust came from both guards as they neared the kitchen. Gerda was scratching in her box, working her way right through to the bottom.

Arnie stared in horror as the plastic lining came into full view. If she went on she'd shred the photograph. He felt sweat beading his forehead. Fucking cat, he muttered under his breath as he kept watching her in horrified fascination. The men had probably never seen a litter box.

"You feed her too much," one of the guards said turning away.

"That's true," Arnie replied, beginning to breathe again. He couldn't remember the last time he'd cleaned the litter box. "She likes her privacy," he continued ushering the men out of the kitchen.

"Well, you will have to leave. We have orders to tell you that this rental is illegal. Three days. You have three days."

Arnie's mouth hung open in shock. First shock, then relief. He had got off easy—a pack of smokes, a bottle of booze. Realizing that Arnie wasn't going to offer them money, the guards strode to the door. They were leaving. Arnie felt weak with relief. His photo was safe. His computer had not been searched.

The minute the door closed, he sprung into action. Immediately he made two disk copies of the March issue. One he hid in Gerda's box, the other he'd stuff in his pocket when he was ready to go. No matter what, he had to get the story out. He knew he had a window of opportunity. No one would expect a supplement. He'd run Mike's photos on the front page. Line up all the kiddie porn photos. WHERE ARE THEY? his headline would scream. Then, he'd go into hiding. Money? First thing he did was e-mail his bank manager in Ottawa. It would take a few days, but the money would be wired to him. Western Union was reliable.

Arnie scribbled down a plan of action.

Day 1: Get photos from Anda. (Where the hell is Anda?) Put together new issue. Find printer. Distribute copies.

Day 2: Money. Cash advance on Visa card.

Day 3: Pack and find a deep hole to hide in.

A few minutes later, as if in answer to his wish list, the phone rang.

"Hello. My name is Lilita Andersona," came a soft voice speaking in Latvian. "Meet me at the Universal Store, by the front door, in one hour. I know what you look like. I will approach you."

Without waiting for an answer, the woman hung up. He was sure it was Anda's mother. Arnie rushed through his morning routine. Cold water. Quick shave. Coffee. The Atavan had left him groggy but the coffee managed to revive him a bit. That and a jog to the Universal Department Store in Old Riga would do it. It would take over a half an hour to get there. He looked at his watch, didn't dare be late. No. He had to rush. No time to jog. He called a cab even though he was running out of money fast.

As he sat in the cab his legs jiggled up and down. The Atavan had definitely worn off. He was a bundle of nerves again. His heart raced but it couldn't catch up with his mind. The photos! God bless Anda! And where was Anda? But what if this was a trap? Maybe it wasn't Anda's mother. What if the phone was bugged? What if he was abducted, tortured, made to talk? He knew he had really rattled somebody over those damn porno photos but he hadn't realized that it would lead to murder. He felt pretty sure that this is was why Mike had been killed and maybe Daina too and now, there was Anda on the list as well.

Goosebumps prickled on his forearms. He passed a hand over his eyes. God, is all this really happening to me? Maybe I had a stroke and fell down and hit my head and I'm actually in the hospital dreaming all this. And maybe, when I wake up, I'll have indigestion and have to rush to get to the *Ottawa Citizen* for my boring dead-end job.

Arnie shook himself. There was nothing imaginary about those ugly photographs. He had to plan carefully. If he could get his layout done this afternoon and delivered to the printer by four o'clock, the supplement would be out on the street by tomorrow and then there was no chance of this story being swept under the carpet. Maybe he'd even find a Zippy Print somewhere in Riga. Then he'd get the hell out of town before it all hit the fan.

It was only now that he remembered his parents asking him to look up a cousin living in Jurmala. Arnie had spoken to him and they had invited him to visit. Now might be the perfect time.

A few minutes later, the cab pulled up at the edge of Old Riga. It was only a short distance through the cobblestone street to the Universal Department Store, the K-mart of Riga. Arnie ran. He had to get there on time.

As he rounded a corner, he could see the massive department store which rose like a dark monolith among the historic buildings of Old Riga. His heart hammered against his chest wall. God he was out of shape! Leaning against the entranceway, Arnie panted as he tried to get back his breath. Exactly one hour had gone by since the phone call. He looked around. He had never been inside the Universal Department Store. He knew that it had recently been renovated in an attempt to cast off its Soviet label but still the expat community shunned it. There was a depressing air about the place. Even from the outside, Arnie could understand why he hadn't heard a good word about it.

He shivered and this time it wasn't from the cold. He double-checked his watch. He was on time but where was Anda's mother? Uncertainty gripped him. Could this be a set-up? As he debated how long he should wait, his eyes started to follow the progress of an elderly woman walking along Ridzenes Street. Like almost everyone else, she was carrying a loaded shopping bag which must have been heavy, as she listed to one side. Arnie observed her as she approached the entranceway, walked towards him, paused for a second, and without turning her head, said, "follow me" in a low voice.

As he moved forward Arnie felt as if he had walked into the pages of *James Bond in Riga*. But where was Octopussy? And he wished he had a watch that shot bullets from the winder stem or hurled steel cables across chasms. Suddenly, the image of Bond's Aston Martin appeared in his mind and he longed for an ejection seat. He would even have settled for a Lada.

Arnie knew that Latvia's population had spent a lifetime under surveillance. Eluding detection and fooling Big Brother had become second nature. But to him, it was very unusual, very cloak and dagger—and very dangerous. Dodging in and out among the other shoppers, Arnie had to work hard to keep the woman in sight. She had cleverly chosen the noon hour. There were lots of other people shopping and both of them were able to melt into the busy throng.

Without looking around, she stopped at the café, bought herself a cup of coffee and sat down. Next she pulled a newspaper from her bag. It was the usual heavy plastic bag that all shoppers carried in Latvia, strong enough and roomy enough to carry ten pounds of groceries home on the train. On its side was a garish ad for cigarettes. She started to read the newspaper.

Trying to appear nonchalant and preoccupied, Arnie did the same. He bought himself a cup of coffee and sat down at the table nearest her. A few minutes later, leaving the newspaper on the table, she got up. Arnie noticed that her hands were empty. Shifting in his chair for a better view, Arnie was able to see she had left the shopping bag on the floor. He waited a minute. Waited until she had left. Then he took his coffee, slid over to her table and started to leaf through the paper. With his feet he felt for the shopping bag. He lit a cigarette. Looked around. Nothing unusual. Only shoppers. No men in dark raincoats, no militia. Just ordinary folk, mainly middle aged women, plainly dressed, looking for bargains, then stopping in for coffee before the trip home.

Casually, he folded the newspaper and reached down to put it inside the bag. He took a last sip of coffee, stubbed out his cigarette. Picking up the bag, he was caught off guard by its weight and almost fell backward onto the chair. God! What does she have in here? He didn't dare stop to look inside. He browsed for a few minutes, observed the passers-by, then quickly left the store. Clutching the bag tightly, he headed straight for the nearest taxi stand.

It would be another all-nighter. As Arnie closed the door behind him he had to bend down to pick up a piece of paper. A casual glance told him it was from Vizma. 'How are things going?' He let his eyes scan the note before absentmindedly letting it slip from his fingers onto the hall table. No time for chit-chat. There wasn't a moment to lose. He dropped his coat on the nearest chair and, knowing he'd need refuelling, he went into the kitchen to check on his coffee supply. Thank God there was enough.

The minute he had walked into the kitchen, his nose had wrinkled at the smell. Gerda had abandoned the dirty litter box and had started doing her business on the floor. Still clutching the shopping bag, Arnie grabbed the box and headed for the bathroom. He locked the door. Didn't turn on the light. A tiny window gave out on the courtyard. He was six flights up but paranoia had taken hold. He opened the bag. There under a head of cabbage and some carrots nestled the brown paper envelope. He reached for the photos. One by one he took them out, went to the computer, scanned each photo. Then brought them back. There were eight in all. He made copies on two diskettes and was careful to delete them from his hard drive.

A half hour later, Mike's photos were all wrapped in plastic and buried in Gerda's box. Arnie took a few minutes to clean out the cat clumps and added fresh litter. Here in Riga, it cost a fortune. Then, he quickly cleaned up Gerda's mess in the kitchen and set to work on his copy. It was well past one. Halfway through his article, it occurred to Arnie that he should be sending Vizma out to dig up a printer. He needed some obscure hole-in-the-wall, preferably not in central Riga. In Pardaugava. He would pay extra for no questions asked and a rush job. Arnie picked up the phone.

"Hi, Vizma. Am I glad you're home! Can you meet me on the fourth floor landing right now?"

The urgency in his voice convinced her. Whatever it was, she wanted to be part of it.

"I'm on my way," she said, without hesitation.

Two minutes later, their faces inches apart, they continued the conversation on the landing.

"Now, don't interrupt me. Just listen. Things are moving really fast. I've been given three days to get out of my apartment."

Vizma drew in her breath with the shock.

"It could be a hoax but I've decided it's a damn good idea. I got hold of Mike's photos this morning. I've got to get more copies of this edition of *WOW!* printed. I'm thinking at least two thousand copies. And fast. I need to find an obscure print shop that can handle it. What I wouldn't give for Yellow Pages right now. I realize how hard this must be for you. This is dangerous stuff. But I've got to shake things loose."

Just then, they saw a couple of men who were coming up the stairs. Neither looked familiar and didn't look like the run of the mill tenants.

"This isn't good," Arnie muttered.

Vizma nodded and said quietly,

"We can't talk out here. I'll come upstairs in ten minutes."

"Fine by me."

Seconds later, Arnie was back in his apartment reediting his story. The photos were in place, the headline looked good and the rest of the stuff flowed like hot lava. Arnie was satisfied. And Vizma was right on time. Ten minutes, she had said. The first page of *WOW!* was just coming off the printer. They took a second to admire it.

"I had a brainstorm while I…" Vizma started to say.

Arnie interrupted her with a hard look. Putting his finger to his lips, he guided her to the bathroom, flushed the toilet and turned the taps on.

"You want to share that brainstorm?"

"Okay," Vizma said exhaling a deep breath. Arnie was making her nervous. "I've been thinking of how to get this job done. I can go to the graphic design department at the Art Academy. I know the department head. Those guys are cool. I bet they'd know where to send me."

"Wait a minute. If the Art Academy has a graphics department then maybe they must have a good size copy machine. Do you know what they're using?"

"No, but I can find out. That would be a good solution if they did. It would be ideal if we could do it ourselves."

So as not to lose any time, they decided that Vizma would take the hardcopy with her to the Academy. She had to get her coat and boots and briefcase. Without skipping a beat, they were on their way. Vizma, with Arnie right behind her holding a large envelope, went down the three flights to her apartment.

"This is what we'll do. We'll put the copy into a plastic bag and I'll pin it to the underside of the lining of my coat. I'll carry my briefcase stuffed with last term's book reports. If anyone grabs it, no harm done. Just wait a minute. I'll get my safety pins."

"Good. Anyone watching will think you're just going off to a class. "

Arnie was relieved. He thought this could work. Vizma spread her navy duffel coat open on the sofa and then sprinkled the safety pins into Arnie's outstretched palm. Working quickly, she pinned all four sides to the underside of the lining. Picking it up she gave it a quick shake to make sure nothing was going to drop out. She put on her boots, the coat and picked up her briefcase.

"You scared?"

"Yeah. A little. But I've got the Mace and it won't be dark for another hour. Oh, no! The Mace is in my other coat pocket. I can't leave home without it. It's my lucky charm. And we've got to arrange a signal. I don't trust the phone."

"Nor do I. Whatever you do, don't use the phone. I'm going to trail you over to the Academy just in case. And then I'll wait for you at the Clock."

"Alright. I'll meet you there. I'll hurry."

"You'll be able to tell me if you can do the print job or not. And don't let me forget. You'll need some money."

"Yes. We won't get anywhere if we don't offer him cash. A hundred US. That should certainly do it."

Taking the money from Arnie, Vizma stuffed it into her small shoulder bag which she wore under her coat. She put her coat back on, picked up the briefcase and stepped out the door.

"Break a leg, Vizma," Arnie called after her.

"Break a leg, yourself," she said looking back. "Don't wish that on either of us. The streets are a nightmare and I hope you aren't expecting me to give you a piggyback."

Chapter Twenty-One

Vizma tried to ignore the tremble in her legs. She could feel the plastic bag, which rested against her back, shifting slightly with ever step. Taking long deep breaths she picked her way carefully down the sidewalk, trying to avoid any spot that looked the least bit icy. The last thing she wanted was to dislodge the hardcopy pinned to her lining. Her eyes darted in every direction to check for the Goth, the orange Lada or anyone who looked the least bit suspicious. One hand was curled around the Mace, the other gripped the briefcase. She didn't dare turn around completely to check that Arnie was following until she was right at the doorway of the Academy. But when she turned to look, she couldn't see him.

At a little after five, Vizma walked through the door of the staff room. She had always admired the room with its high stained-glass windows and dark heavy walnut furnishings. Stale smoke and the faint smell of alcohol permeated the air. Here, between classes, profs found a refuge. Many never made it back to their students but nodded away until the night cleaner shooed them out.

This late afternoon, the room was as still as a morgue and at first, Vizma thought she had it all to herself. But no. She was lucky, very lucky. There was the very person she was looking for. Arnolds Goba, the head of the graphic design department, was slumped over in his usual chair, staring out the window, a cup of coffee hanging mid way to his lips. Most of the time, he seemed to be in some sort of trance, perhaps a symptom of his genius, an integral part of his creative process. Or perhaps it was drugs.

How perfect does it get, Vizma thought as her spirits soared into the stratosphere. The coffee cup had still not moved and Vizma approached as quietly as she could, extricating her cigarettes from the shoulder-bag under her coat. Arnold shifted the cup slightly as if to say he was still there and would accept the offer of a smoke. Vizma shook one out from her pack and moved it between his outstretched fingers. Slowly, she saw him apply pressure around the cigarette and it slipped silently out into the air on its way to his lips. Quickly she clicked on her lighter and held it against the free end until it glowed. Moving slowly and deliberately, she pulled up a chair beside him, pushed an ashtray in his direction to catch the long ash that had already formed and then lit her own.

Trying to establish rapport with Arnolds, Vizma let out a long sigh, groaned a few times and saying nothing, quietly puffed away for several minutes. She sighed again trying hard to get Arnolds to bite on the hook. She thought to herself, come on you bastard, I'm in such a rush. Speak to me. Finally the words came. With a sad knowing nodding of his head Arnolds started to speak.

"Ah uh, I knew the day would come. You've finally realized that we're all in the same shit hole here. You superior expats! You think you're so superior but sooner or later..." Arnolds' voice trailed off.

Looking carefully around to make sure they were alone, Vizma opened her purse and took out five crisp new American twenties. She fanned them under Arnolds' nose. His sleepy eyes widened as he reached for the money.

"I've got a job for you," she said, quickly putting the cash beyond his reach while looking straight at him. "I need to run some photocopies so I want the use of the print room. All night. All you have to do is give me the key and show me how to run the copier. That's it. Easy money. When I'm finished, I'll leave the keys in your mailbox together with the rest of the cash."

Arnolds was fully awake. At this point, Vizma pulled out one of the twenties and said,

"You get the rest when the job is done."

Pocketing the bill, Arnolds got up on his feet and gestured with his head toward the door.

Ten minutes later, after a crash course, Vizma was alone and in charge of the print room. She soared to the moon. It was all coming together like clockwork. With a happy sigh she looked at her watch and saw that she still had time to set up the copier and start outputting before meeting Arnie at the Laima Clock.

Arnie kept glancing over his shoulder. He felt that people were staring at him as they went by. That's normal, a normal part of the paranoia, Arnie reassured himself. For the first time, he noticed that his clothes were loose. He had lost weight. He couldn't remember the last real meal he had eaten. Yes, there had been Vizma's *karbonade* and a scattering of fried potatoes but he had eaten in a hurry and probably not enough.

He had tailed Vizma until she safely disappeared into the Academy and then decided to go down to the bar in Hotel Latvija. He would have a drink with the barman who usually fed him some bit of news that he had occasionally been able to use in *WOW!*. This time he was interested in just getting warm. Time flew by. This barman was right up there in the gossip ratings. Arnie was on his second cup of coffee when he realized he would have to hurry to meet Vizma on time.

A few minutes later, he saw her rushing along Aspazijas Boulevard. She ran up to him and grabbed him by the arm. She was excited and out of breath.

"It's O.K." she exclaimed. "I've got the print room. The machine is running. But you've got to come help."

"I'm right behind you."

Vizma could feel him smile. This was it. They were so close to getting the story out. No way was anything going to go wrong.

With hurried steps, they made their way back along Kalpaka Street, past the snow covered Esplanade Park. As they approached the Academy they saw students leaving. Vizma said a hurried hello to a few of them. A group of girls stared at Arnie, exchanged glances with each other. One of the girls recognized him from the café encounter. She giggled and whispered something to her companions.

"Silly girls," Vizma said to Arnie as they walked up the steps and entered the darkness inside. Without a glance at the custodian's cage, Vizma led Arnie downstairs and through the narrow dimly lit basement hallway. She stopped at a door. Reached for the key. The key? Vizma fumbled in her purse. She made a choking sound. *The key*. She could feel the colour drain from her face. She went through her pockets.

"For God's sake, Vizma!" Arnie raised his voice. "Open the door so we can get out of sight."

"Shut up, Arnie," Vizma shot back. She was doing all this for him. For his magazine. For his career. But where the hell had she put that key? The blood wasn't reaching her brain. She couldn't think.

Arnie pressed the tips of his fingers against his forehead wishing he had some extra-strength Atavan. He turned away from her. Didn't want to look at her. Was afraid he would hit her.

In one quick gesture, Vizma dumped the contents of her purse out on the floor and pawed through the loose change, gum wrappers, nail file, hairpins, stamps and assorted flotsam that always accumulated. There was her change purse but no key.

Arnie wanted to scream. All he had was his Swiss army knife if they were attacked. Vizma picked up her change purse. Something rattled inside. She let out a gasp. Something had slipped through a hole in the lining. She tore at the lining. A few coins spilled out. And the key!

Within seconds, two enormous gasps of relief resonated through the hallway. The anger drained out of them as quickly as it had exploded. Vizma slotted the key into the lock and opened the door. Then closed it carefully behind her. It locked automatically.

The room was chilly. No space heater. There was a long beat-up table with several large boxes of copy paper sitting underneath. On top, at one end, was an extra ink cartridge in a silver plastic bag. At the far end of the room, against the wall, was a large pale grey copy machine, its tiny red and green control lights glowing reassuringly while the low drone of its engine announced that it was out of paper. At one end of the machine, Arnie and Vizma could see the neat stack of finished output.

Arnie carried the copies to the near end of the table and started to fold and stack each one as Vizma refilled the paper tray. Soon the noise of the machine changed to a reassuring PUT PUT PUT as it spat out more and more copies. The stack of papers on the floor was already three feet high.

"So far so good," Arnie breathed.

"Yeah. I think we're into the home stretch now."

Vizma was pleased with herself for having come up with the idea of the Academy. She was the one that had found the photocopier. It was clear that Arnie couldn't do without her.

Every iota of their concentration was fixed on the job. Except for a few bathroom breaks, they worked all night. Vizma thought she might have dropped off while sitting in the chair but she wasn't sure. Towards morning, they were both in a daze, eyes red, muscles aching.

Next came distribution.

"How much money do you have, Arnie? In lats, I mean."

"Maybe thirty. Why?"

"I think we'll have to trust someone. I can barely stand up."

"Well, who?"

"I know one of the cleaners here. He spends most nights snoozing in the staff lounge. Does the bare minimum but puts in the hours. He's got an old wreck of a car he parks by the back door."

"It's a risk, Vizma. If I had more energy, I'd say no."

With that, Vizma carefully opened the door. Looked around. Still too early for students or staff.

Luck was with her. She walked into the staff room and found Guntis slumped in a chair, snoring loudly. Vizma banged the door behind her, then approached the blinking caretaker.

"Gunti, wake up! I have an important job for you. And lots of money. More than you make in a week."

Guntis' eyes shot open. He sat up. Recognized Vizma and gave her a toothless grin.

"What?"

"We load up your car with newspapers. We give you the addresses. You deliver them. My friend will come with you."

Guntis shrugged. "Well…"

"Basically, we're renting your car for a few hours. What do you say?" Vizma pulled out the twenty lats she had in her purse. "My friend will give you ten more when the job is finished."

Guntis brightened. It was ages since he had seen so much money.

"Let's go," he said getting out of the chair.

Chapter Twenty-Two

It was five forty-three in the morning. Arnie hadn't eaten for the past twelve hours and couldn't wait to brush his skuzzy teeth. His mouth tasted sour from all the coffee and cigarettes. He and Guntis had just finished distributing *WOW!* from one end of the city to the other. At the end of their run Guntis had let him out of the car a block from his door.

Dragging himself inside his building, Arnie sighed before setting off to climb the six flights of Mount Everest. Where were those Sherpas to chair him up? His legs felt leaden and had turned to jelly by the second floor.

Rounding the landing, he lurched forward almost losing his balance. "Excuse me," came out of him automatically. He had bumped into a wall. Looking up, he saw that it wasn't the wall but the stolid form of the Cat Lady. She immediately drew in her breath and then launched herself into rapid-fire Latvian so that the only words he caught were drinking, foreigners, cats, dogs, drugs, cats, and drink. Arnie got the gist but was too tired to laugh. Turning away with a final 'excuse me', this time in Latvian, he continued to drag himself upwards towards his apartment.

Finally, he was there. He leaned against his door for support and, catching his breath, he searched in his pockets for the keys. Finding them, he let himself in and noted with relief that his apartment had not been trashed again.

Without losing a moment, he went straight to Gerda's litter box, stuck his finger through the three inches of grott and felt the edge of Mike's photographs in their plastic envelope. Relieved, he straightened up, washed his hands in the sink and set about putting his plan into motion. In a fluid dance, he moved here and there organizing what he needed to take with him. He made sure all his work was on floppy disks. He tucked them into his money belt with some lats, his VISA card, both his passports and of course, the photographs. Then he buckled it around his waist, next to his skin. Tucking his shirt into his pants, he looked around thinking about what else he would need in the next few days.

To keep himself awake, he did some out-loud questioning. Would he have to leave the country suddenly? What to do with Gerda? Would the police do anything if he were to disappear? Would the Canadian Embassy be able to help? Now that *WOW!* was on the street with new pointed questions and photographs of children, his next move was to jump into a fox-hole. No way would he survive the fallout if he didn't.

Still, one thing was clear, Gerda was a top priority. He called Vizma, woke her up out of a deep sleep.

"Look after my cat," he said. "You still have my key. I'll be in touch."

He didn't get an answer, didn't wait for one.

Time to bail. Arnie put on an extra sweater to hide his bulge and to keep himself warm in case of trouble. He had already phoned his cousin in Jurmala. He was expected. Not welcomed. But expected. And that would have to do. They had lots to catch up on but the only catching up he wanted to do right now was sleep for at least twenty-four hours.

Standing by the open door, Arnie took one last look around. He hadn't realized how attached he had become to all his treasures—his antique table, his leather couch, his collection of books and even the old lacy curtains moving subtly in the drafty window. History was attached to everything and it had brought Arnie a sense of home that he had never experienced so completely before. He had only realized this a few minutes before. Now came the most painful part. He had to say goodbye to Gerda. She instinctively knew he was abandoning her and had hidden herself under his bed. It made him feel awful.

Everything else felt as if he were walking in his sleep. He managed to get to the train station. Got on the train. Got off at the right stop. Said hello to his cousin Janis who was there in his beat-up old Toyota.

First thing Arnie did was to sleep for twelve hours.

Chapter Twenty-Three

He got away, thought Vizma, with a tug at her heart as she listened to the ringing of the phone that wasn't being picked up. An unanswered phone must be the loneliest sound in the world, she thought to herself. She was still in bed, recovering and was sipping on her first cup of coffee. She missed him already.

Do you really think he cares about you? she asked herself. Her inner voice was wise beyond years but optimistic too. Maybe. Maybe he cares. The last words Arnie had said to her were about Gerda. She couldn't believe how she felt about that. How could she be jealous of a cat?

Fed up with lolling around in bed, Vizma suddenly threw off her duvet and jumped out of bed. God it was cold! After rubbing her hands together, she found her bed socks at the foot of her bed, put them on and padded out to the kitchen for coffee.

She wasn't going to hang around to wait for some creep to gun her down. She had plans. Major plans. Arnie was gone and she was going to drag her ass out of there too. Hell, she'd cut her hair. Dye it black. Dress like a local. In short, Vizma Gross was history. Hello Natasha!

She decided to go to a hotel for a day or two till things cooled down. The next call she made was to the administrator at the Academy. Lucky she still had her gravely smokers' morning voice.

"I have the flu," she whispered.

"I'll put a notice on the door. Call me when you feel better," the office worker who answered the phone said as if this was routine.

"Yes, I will. Thank you…very…" Vizma spluttered between coughing, letting the sentence stop in a loud blowing of her nose. Before she had taken her nose out of the Kleenex, she heard the click disconnecting the phone.

In a fit of guilty conscience she thought, this is the first time I've done this but promised herself she wouldn't make a habit if it. It was just too easy. Of course she wouldn't be getting paid but what did that matter in the whole scheme of things? Vizma was going under cover. She had no idea when she would see Arnie next. It didn't matter. She could wait.

Arnie hadn't given her a chance to say anything when he had called asking her to look after Gerda. He knew she couldn't refuse even though cats gave her the willies. When she was a child, her grandmother had told her a story about a cat suffocating an old lady who had spent her entire pension feeding it all kinds of delicacies. In the end, the cat ate the old lady.

Grudgingly, Vizma went up the three flights of stairs to Arnie's apartment. As she unlocked the door, she heard a plaintive mew from inside. Thinking Vizma had come to feed her, Gerda trotted over and rubbed herself against the intruder's shin. It paid to be friendly, Gerda had learned, even with strangers and she was so hungry she'd even allow herself to be petted. But no, the intruder didn't bend down and coo and scratch behind her ears. She just opened the door and said, *shoo!* Gerda's eyes widened dramatically. She had never heard that word before. She glared up at the intruder with her amber eyes, her back arching with displeasure.

"There you go, Sweetums. Get lost!"

Vizma picked up Gerda and put her down again just as the cat was about to deliver one of her Cuisinart slashes. Before she knew it, Gerda was out in the hall, on the cold marble floor. She shivered, first from the cold, then from something else. She suddenly remembered the raucous love calls of the handsome tomcat who patrolled the hallways. Her spirits lifted. Now she was free to check out the action.

Without giving the intruder a backward glance, Gerda set off. Vizma grinned. She had heard that the Cat Lady kept a very good table—cream, sardines and chicken livers, just for starters. God only knows how that poor Cat Lady will end up, Vizma thought to herself, remembering her grandmother's stories. She shook her head and called, "have fun" as Gerda, tail high, padded eagerly down the hall, ready to start her brand new life.

Back in her own apartment, Vizma hurriedly packed an overnight bag. She looked at herself in the mirror. Not a pretty picture. Her dark roots were showing, something that would have been a definite no-no back in Ottawa. No way was she going back to the salon in the Hotel Latvija. Why not dye it brown? Cut it short? Anyway, she was too old to wear it below her shoulders.

An hour later, after a trip to the drugstore, she admired her handiwork as she tied a scarf around her short dark brown hair. Leaving behind the expat golden ghetto, she stuffed her overnight necessities into two local-style shopping bags and, presto, she was ready for the real world. She could be Natasha Maslova, shlepping bag-loads of brassieres to sell at the market. She could fake a limp, fake being deaf and mute, fake any number of disabilities. She could go around talking to herself and no one would raise an eyebrow. More to the point, no one would gun her down or push her under a bus.

This time, fatigue worked in her favour. But who the hell would rent *her* a room? Well, money talks and no one should be fooled by appearances. After all, she wasn't heading for the Hotel de Rome. Or the Hotel Latvija, God forbid. Vizma thumbed quickly through her tourist guide. There was Hotel Valeria on Marijas Street. Not quite a roach motel but almost. She'd take a category three room with a communal toilet and showers. She'd keep speech to a minimum. Fake having a sore throat. She knew her expat accent would give her away no matter what she wore.

Sitting on the tram, she tried out her new persona. To her relief, there were no second looks or stares from the other passengers. She fitted right in. A few minutes later, she arrived at Hotel Valeria and walked into the lobby. The guy behind the reception desk looked fixedly at her. His eyes said, no-hookers-allowed. Was her babushka slipping? This hotel has a rodent problem, she remembered reading in *The Ultimate City Guide.* And the guy certainly did look a bit like a rodent with his small dark eyes and sharp pointed nose. Vizma thought of the box of industrial strength *rodent cafeteria* tucked away under her kitchen sink and wished that she'd put it in her overnight bag.

Looking at the clerk, she flashed a quick smile. Her first mistake. She did a mental eye roll. No babushka-head flashes quick smiles. Uh oh, this is going to cost me, she said to herself as she took two steps backwards. Why in the world did I flash him my Julia Roberts mega-mouth? This guy only deserves an energy efficient fifteen watts. Why is it that when I get overtired, I revert to Canadian ways? How could I be so *stupid*? You'd think by now I would know the local idiom. No chitchat, no pleasantries, straight business talk only.

Vizma shifted gears. Using her no-nonsense voice she asked for the category three weekly rate. She wasn't going to crack a smile, no matter what. The clerk eyed her up and down having decided the moment she stepped in the door that she was a foreigner. She hadn't fooled *him* with her disguise. He had trained himself to smell a foreigner from miles away. He could figuratively smell the money. To him, all foreigners smelled of dollars. He liked the smell and he definitely liked this woman, quite apart from that one cheesy smile.

Vizma reached into her purse and took out a wad of cash. The smell was divine. But *who* was this woman? And *how* could he get his mitts on her wad? Clicking his fingers he started to roll his shoulders. Vizma's eyes widened as he let out a breathy but unmusical *Pretty woman, dum dum dum doody doo dum...*

God! A Roy Orbiston fan. Heaven help me! The crooner reached for the cash and then for a key. He pushed out his lips and continued, *Walkin' down the street...*

This was not going to stop. Ducking her head down to control an attack of hysterical laughter, Vizma jerked her hand forward and held it out for the key. She tried to regain control. The guy must have just seen the latest Julia Roberts video. She had heard that Latvian men were crazy about Julia Roberts and thought that all American hookers looked just like her. Go figure, Vizma muttered as she took the key. Oh, what the hell, she said to herself. Before turning away, she gave him a big wink.

Vizma was amazed that her life had gone from boring to terrifying to absurd in a few short days. She looked at herself in the mirror. She was in one of the communal bathrooms where the light was on a timer. The dark hair wasn't bad. And she liked it short. She brushed her teeth. Flossed. She knew she'd be reusing the same piece of string over and over. God knows where she'd find dental floss. She didn't even know how to say it in Latvian.

Back in the room, Vizma lay down on the bed. She was just going to rest but, before she knew it, she had clonked off to dreamland.

Chapter Twenty-Four

Vizma's hair stood up on the back of her neck. Her stomach muscles clenched. Struck dumb with horror, she stared at the front page of *Diena*. The headline screamed, EXPLOSION ON VALDEMARA STREET!

Lower down, she saw two words, CHILD PORN. She refocused on the photograph under the top headline. It was her apartment building with a large gaping hole on the top floor where Arnie's apartment used to be. No mention of anyone injured. Gas leak suspected.

There but for the grace of God, she muttered under her breath and felt sick at the thought of how close Arnie had come to certain death. She'd make sure to watch the news on Panorama that night. There was a television in the lounge and hotel guests assembled for the news, sitting in rows just like being back in school. She knew there'd be comments. And she knew she couldn't show her reaction. She had to keep her eye on the bigger picture.

Arnie's Missing Porno Children piece was everywhere—front-page news in the evening editions as well as right after the explosion on Valdemara Street in *Diena*. Most readers could put two and two together.

The best thing to do was lie low, Vizma decided. Just put on her babushka clothes and shuffle through the streets. No makeup and as little interaction with people as possible. No trendy cafés or areas near the Academy. Parks were okay and the market too was a great place to melt in. No pickpocket would target her. She looked too pathetic.

It was a blessing that the weather was milder now. Maybe spring would be early this year. Vizma hoped it would. During the day she window shopped, strolled through parks, watched old timers playing chess and grandmothers chatting on park benches while babies slept in prams. She even went to a movie dubbed in Russia. It was Pulp Fiction. She didn't understand a word. Saw the brutal aggression but couldn't figure out what was going on. Still, she loved John Travolta, even in Russian.

Once, against her better judgement, she struck up a conversation with a Russian woman in Vermana Park. It turned out that the woman was a doctor who had lived her whole life in Riga but who didn't speak a word of Latvian. And no English. They both spoke a smattering of German. She saw the same woman an hour later, walking a short distance behind her on Brivibas Street. A coincidence or was she being followed? Vizma realized that there could be no more striking up of conversations.

The days went by slowly and the inactivity was starting to drive her crazy. But at least, no Goth was shadowing her—or so she thought. She felt confident that she had managed to stay under cover.

Then it rained. Vizma had no rain boots and she returned from wandering through the streets of Riga earlier than usual.

She felt very cold, shivery even. Her feet felt like lumps of ice. Her leather winter boots leaked and her socks had been wet all day. Her fingers were numb inside her gloves, her nose dripped. She used the same old hanky over and over and washed it out every night drying it out flattened against the windowpane where it froze until morning when she retrieved it. She was always amazed that it looked as if it had been carefully ironed.

Back in her room, she wrapped herself up in blankets and prayed she wasn't getting the flu.

The next evening, coming back into the hotel after another day of terminal boredom, Vizma noticed the same clerk who had been working the reception desk when she had arrived three days before. Why was he smiling at her like an idiot? Okay, so she had winked. And there had been the Julia Roberts smile. Clearly that had been encouragement enough for this guy.

"Come have a beer with me," he said, as she walked past the desk.

Vizma saw that his dark rodent eyes were bright with anticipation and his nose almost twitched. She imagined she could see a couple of long whiskers on each side of his nose.

For a moment, she hesitated. Then she shrugged. Perhaps she should feel flattered. The guy seemed nice enough, didn't look like a wacko. And, there she was, alone, no cable TV to flop down in front of, no good book to read, no one to telephone.

The day had been miserable and she was feeling more tired and dejected than usual. This could be part of the Latvia experience no expat woman should be without, she said to herself and decided to give it a shot. Perhaps he had noticed that she was on her own, that she was lonely, perhaps he wanted to practice his English, or perhaps he was a gold-digger—or perhaps, came a sinister whisper from the back of her mind, someone had bribed him to lure her into danger. She firmly pushed the thought away and accepted the invitation.

Within an hour, Juris was showing her his version of a night on the town. He was definitely trying to impress her by taking her to the newly opened Staburags, a ye olde Latvian restaurant, with long rustic wooden tables, alcoves with open fireplaces and traditional Latvian food. Vizma thought that the atmosphere was phoney and the staff more moribund than usual but it was close to the hotel and Juris plainly loved it.

As soon as they sat down, Juris began,

"What are you up to?"

"Up to?"

"Well, what are you doing here? Tell me about yourself."

"There's nothing much to say," Vizma replied. "I dreamed of the Motherland. Did the tourist thing. Ran out of money, and here I am."

"Running out of money is relative," Juris said dryly.

Inwardly, Vizma rolled her eyes. Here it comes, she said to herself. The long-pent-up grudges, the resentment, the jealousy. She knew she spent more on most days than a pensioner had to live on for a week. She knew all that and there was nothing she could do about it. The whole topic was a mood killer. Bottom line, she didn't care. She had enough problems of her own. And a sick headachy feeling was beginning to creep over her.

She stifled a sigh and realized that she didn't feel like having a drink with this man after all. It would be a struggle to find something to talk about. The chasm between them was insurmountable. She wanted nothing more than a soft warm bed to sink into and a long dreamless sleep. Just then, the waiter brought them the beer and Vizma felt she couldn't walk out.

She wasn't sure just at what moment the sensation of being watched started creeping over her. As she sipped on her beer, the feeling intensified until she almost felt daggers in her back. She twisted around and her stomach did a back-flip. The coldest eyes she had ever seen were staring right at her. It was the Goth. She stared back. Was it really the Goth? For a moment she wasn't so sure. There was no long black coat. The man was wearing a tan windbreaker. She dropped her eyes and turned back to Juris. Still, if it wasn't the Goth, who was it? When she looked back again, the starer was gone. Is this a set-up? she asked herself, frowning at Juris.

"A friend?" Juris asked with a hint of irony. Vizma though she detected a smirk.

"I've never seen him before in my life," she replied fighting to sound as off-hand as she could even though every hair on the back of her neck was standing on end. She knew she had to get out of there.

Juris watched her for a moment, then finished his beer and motioned for the waiter.

"Are you hungry? The food's great. Would you like to have dinner with me?"

"Sorry, I can't but thanks for the beer. Maybe some other time," Vizma said as casually as she could muster, glad to have a chance to make her escape. Would the man be waiting outside for her? Had she been lured away from the safety of her hotel? What a fool she had been. She checked her watch. Dropped her get-away line.

"I'm expecting a phone call. I have to go."

There was a tiny hesitation. Juris stood up.

"It was nice meeting you," he said as he bent down over her hand.

"Yes," Vizma said and gave him a tight little smile in return for this quaint but out-of-place gesture. Then she turned and made a beeline for the exit. At the door she waited, hoping she could melt in with other people leaving the restaurant. But no one was coming out. She would have to make it on her own.

As quickly as she could, she walked down the street heading back to the hotel. Suddenly she was drag-ass tired. Stumbling, she felt as if a weight had been tied to her legs. Had Juris slipped something in her beer while she had turned her head? The thought chilled her to the bone. Where would she go for help? At the door to her hotel, she glanced back. There was no one following her.

Once inside, all she could manage to do was unlock the door to her room and flop down on the bed. She closed her eyes. She felt nauseous and sweat began to trickle down her arms. Paranoia tugged at her brain. The Goth, Juris, the Russians—they were all after her.

As she started to undress, there was a knock on the door. She froze. "*Who...*" she croaked. Her mouth was dry. She tried to swallow and struggled to call out again. "*Who...*" The word came out as a strangled sob. Thank goodness she had remembered to lock the door behind her.

With hands that wouldn't obey she fumbled into her coat pocket for the Mace. Her hand came to rest around the canister but she couldn't make her muscles curl her fingers around it. How odd, she thought to herself. What's happening to me? Her eyes wouldn't stay open but she thought she saw the door moving inward. It opened. With a groan she slumped down on her bed. The next instant she was dead to the world.

Chapter Twenty-Five

Arnie cut the outboard motor and just drifted for a while. Beyond the horizon of fir trees, the sky was turning a pearly grey and clouds were rolling in. He stared out at the sea as if answers to all his problems lay somewhere within its undulating blue surface. The vast expanse of water and the glorious sky lulled him as the boat moved gently up and down. He began to see himself and his plight as just a tiny speck bobbing on the limitless waves of the universe.

Then the silence was broken as Arnie pulled the starter cord bringing the engine to life and sending the boat gently put-putting along the shore. His exhaustion gradually faded and his problems seemed less urgent, less frightening. He passed huddles of picturesque cottages slumbering peacefully in the twilight and thought how wonderful it would be to have a little hideaway in this tranquil wilderness. In summer, the beaches would be packed but now, very few visitors disturbed the serenity. With five coastal villages stretching along the Gulf of Riga like bright amber beads on a silver necklace, Jurmala was perfect. It made him feel safe.

Arnie wished he had been able to see it when it had been known as the Baltic Riviera. But now, the Gulf of Riga had become so polluted with gobs of tar and oily guck that swimming had become a health hazard.

He knew that Jurmala had been a favourite spa for the Czar and Russian aristocracy who were drawn by the sulphur springs, the mineral water and the peat and mud. During the more recent occupation, the top brass of the Soviet military had emulated their political predecessors. Now that they had been sent packing, a new generation of Latvian artists had discovered the area and were helping it regain its seaside charm.

Once again, the birch-lined avenues with shops, cafés and outdoor markets had begun to thrive. Even though it was the off-season, the larger hotels that catered to the spa clientele were still open but Arnie wasn't tempted. At this time of year, most of the guests were pensioners, some hobbled by arthritis with the occasional wheelchair or pair of crutches in evidence. Arnie had never been to Lourdes but thought that this must be a northern version. He had been hoping to find the bathing suit calendar bodies which always gravitated to the world's destination beaches. What a let down!

The *WOW!* story had outraged his cousin but he was also proud that Arnie had risked speaking out. Arnie was now a celebrity. The snag was that they weren't allowed to say anything to anyone. It was killing Liga not to be able to brag about their famous cousin from America.

Janis' weathered old cottage was tucked behind a dune, sheltered by a row of majestic pines with white birches standing straight and silent among them. Janis and his wife had welcomed Arnie and hadn't been offended that only now, when he needed to hide, was he looking them up. Arnie had not even brought with him the gift packages which were standard when an expat called on relatives. Arnie had only brought trouble. Having no children, they were less worried about taking him in.

The next day, Arnie set out on foot for his walk through the village of Majori. It was a desolate day and the cold wind was making him wish he had something warmer to wear. He looked up at the overcast sky and saw that it was about to rain. As he let the first drops fall on his face, he wondered how long he could stand it here. The first day was enchanting but then the weather turned and it looked as if they were in for a long spell. He had been told that Jurmala was great in summer but now it was morbid. Arnie muttered to himself as he headed back to the cottage. He had decided against the spas and there was nothing else to do but walk from village to village.

He was dripping wet by the time he reached the main street. About to cross, he looked both ways. The traffic was thin, a car every three minutes or so. Suddenly he blinked several times and shook his head. Was he seeing right? His mouth dropped open. Halfway across the street, he stopped dead in his tracks. An orange Lada had just pulled out of a parking spot and was starting slowly toward him. Within seconds, it would be positioned so that a hand could reach out and fire a shot. In a flash, he visualized the bumper pining him to the ground, the bullet entering his forehead, his brains spilling out and then the blood. Instinctively he spun around. Weaving in and out to avoid being shot, he ran back the way he had come. Turning a corner, he looked frantically for a shop or café to disappear into. There was nothing.

Calm down, think rationally, for heaven's sake, he muttered to himself as he kept running. There must be hundreds of orange Ladas in this country. Thoughts buzzed in his mind like angry bees. *It's them. They've found me. I'm lost.* Someone could have followed him from the apartment to the train station. Then followed him to Jurmala, driving in the shadows, stalking him, waiting for a chance to gun him down.

He was almost at the cottage when he glanced back and saw that the Lada was still trailing him. He switched to plan B, turned away from the cottage and started to run down to the beach. The rain had stopped. He could see a couple walking with a dog, a jogger running in the sand, a boat that was about to moor. There were just a few yards to go.

He threw a quick glance over his shoulder and saw that the car was pulling off the road. He heard the squeal of tires, a car door being opened, then slammed closed. Terrified, he doubled back to the edge of the forest and ducked into a thick clump of evergreens, scrunching down close to the ground. He held his breath and closed his eyes trying to will the car away. A few minutes later, he peered out. It was gone.

The first thing Arnie did when he got back to the cottage was ask Janis if he knew anyone with an orange Lada. Cars come and cars go, Janis told him but no, he hadn't noticed an orange Lada. He promised to ask around.

Feeling edgy, Arnie didn't go walking after that. He spent the next day alone in the cottage, sitting in a chair by the radio and mumbling to himself, *I'm going nuts...nuts.* Janis, who worked in an auto repair shop and Liga, who ran the local bookstore on Jomas Street, were away all day. After an hour of sitting, Arnie moved to the bed and stared up at the ceiling.

So much for his safe hiding place. Frightening thoughts tormented him. What if they knew he was at the cottage? What if they torch the place? Arnie had read about the explosion in his apartment building on Valdemara Street. Thank God Vizma had taken his cat. And where was Vizma? And Anda? And Mike? And Daina? His computer and all his other possessions were destroyed. Thank God he had cleaned out the litter box. All the photographs and discs were safely stashed under the floorboards of his cousin's outhouse. From one shit-box to another, he had quipped as he and Janis had pried open the boards.

Arnie sighed, closed his eyes and managed to fall asleep. He dreamed of being on a deserted beach with miles and miles of sand dunes around him. Ahead, across the water, a circle of light appeared from which a creature was emerging—a mermaid, a water sprite, a beautiful young sea goddess. Her eyes were soft and welcoming, her arms reaching out for him. Just as he touched her, the sky turned black. The waters churned angrily around him as the undertow carried him away from the safety of the shore and pulled him down to the bottom of the sea.

When Arnie woke, he knew he had to do something. He had to make plans. His mind worked better when he was moving and he decided to leave the cottage for some fresh air. This was Friday. Before leaving Riga, he had worked out a pre-arranged signal with Vizma. The following Saturday, at exactly three in the afternoon, the phone would ring in Sam's café. Vizma would be sitting at the bar, drinking a beer. Arnie would ask for Natasha. The barman would call out the name. Vizma would take the call, get a number and call him back on a payphone. Arnie wondered if she had taken the cat with her. He surprised himself by worrying so much about Gerda. The thought of her blown up in the apartment made him feel sick.

He turned and started to walk back to the cottage. The sun came out for a moment and gold threads glistened in the dark treetops. A fresh white cloud was skating across the sky. It was a breathtaking sight but Arnie knew he couldn't stay.

Chapter Twenty-Six

Vizma was reluctant to go to Sam's. She had barely recovered from the horrible flu that had hit her like a ton of bricks and had forced her to spend two entire days in bed, delirious from the fever. The motherly housekeeper had brought her soup and bread and some Russian cold remedy that had made her sleep for hours. She could remember thinking, just before the fever sent her loopy, that Juris must have spiked her beer. Poor guy, maybe she'd give him a nod next time he was on duty at the desk. But she'd keep it curt and business like. No more winking.

Vizma knew Sam's was a favourite with expats and worried that she might be recognized. But there was nothing she could do about it. She and Arnie had agreed. She would have to risk it, *sans* babushka disguise. Vizma knew that if she appeared at Sam's wearing a babushka, she'd be tossed out on her ear.

Sam's catered to an upscale clientele. Arnie had chosen Sam's because he had been there before and noticed that the barman took calls for patrons. And he was one of the few in Riga who actually smiled and had a personality. Somebody had said that the barman was running an escort service. It was said as a joke but still the suspicion lingered and it suited Arnie's purpose well.

It was ten to three. Vizma had ordered a Tuborg and was sitting at the bar trying to look relaxed, even bored. She examined her nails, consulted her watch. She took out a cigarette and, in a flash, the barman was leaning towards her with a light. Ah, European men, Vizma sighed as she let out a plume of smoke and watched as it disappeared into the air. She prayed that no one she knew from the expat community would come sauntering in. It was a safe time of day. Too late for lunch and happy hour for the expats didn't start till after five.

Vizma didn't want to let her anxiety show and so she started a casual conversation with the barman who said his name was Jo. When a lull came in their conversation, Vizma looked around. She saw immediately that there was no danger of being picked up. A bevy of Russian cuties were weaving back and forth from their table to the ladies' room, their haughty butts and large breasts creating a stir with the male population.

She focused back on the phone beside the cash register. The minutes ticked by. Her life was in limbo, her nerves were a wreck. Goddam it! Ring! she shrieked inwardly. Outwardly, she remained a study in nonchalance. She toyed with her cigarette, idly sipped on her beer. Gimme the phone, for God's sake! she almost hollered when it finally rang.

"Natasha? A call for Natasha," the barman announced and winked at her. She was the only female sitting at the bar, the most likely person to be Natasha. With perfect control, Vizma turned her eyes heavenward, shrugged and lazily picked up the receiver.

"My husband," she said, dripping contempt as she nodded a thank-you.

A minute later, she handed the phone back to the bartender.

"He wants me home. I gotta go."

With the slightest smirk, the barman exchanged a glance with one of the other regulars. Then, looking down at the glass he was polishing, he turned his back.

Muttering the number Arnie had given her so as not to forget it, Vizma got up, left Sam's and headed for the nearest phone booth to make her call.

"How's Gerda?" were the first words she heard from Arnie.

Goddam the cat! Don't worry. I stuck her in the freezer, Vizma wanted to say.

Instead she said, "Fine, Arnie. She's fine." He didn't have to know everything.

Arnie let out a sigh of relief. Then continued, "Guess what I saw?"

"What?"

"The orange Lada."

"No kidding, Arnie. Are you absolutely sure it wasn't just any old orange Lada. Did you see who was driving? Did you get the license number this time?" Not waiting for his answer, she continued,

"Guess who *I* saw?"

"Who?"

"Well, guess."

"Just tell me who you saw."

"Yes, Arnie," Vizma said evenly. "I'm sure I saw the Goth. In a restaurant. He was staring at me."

"What were you thinking of, going out to a restaurant? For God sake, you're supposed to be undercover. Were you alone?" Panic sounded in Arnie's voice and Vizma liked hearing it. He was worried about her, maybe even cared.

"Arnie, every morning since I saw you last, I get out of my lumpy bed, eat a crust of bread, drink a cup of lukewarm coffee and tie on my black flowered babushka. Then I'm ready to hit the streets of Riga with a fluttering heart. Barely able to contain my excitement, I drag my shopping bag from one park bench to another. I guess the babushka doesn't fool everyone because some psychic street urchins have tried to mug me for the shopping bag. Now I have to find another area of town where they don't know me. I was thinking maybe today I'd try the train station. And if anyone tries to pick me up, I'll go."

"Vizma, you didn't answer my question. Who were you with when you saw the Goth in the restaurant?"

"Oh, I was alone," Vizma said, a smile in her voice. Arnie must know that this was a lie.

"Listen, Vizma. This isn't a game. You have to take it seriously a bit longer."

"Arnie, I'm dying of boredom. I need a little fun. You, on the other hand, are now famous and are probably signing autographs wherever you are. I see you on the news and in the paper all the time."

"So what are they saying? I mean, the people we know."

"Well, it's not as if I hang out with *them* any more, Arnie. I'm a refugee from the golden ghetto." Vizma's voice was getting shrill. "All I've done for the past few days, which feel more like months, is trail around Riga, window shop, sit on park benches, walk some more, then go home to my empty room. Where would I meet the people we know? I'm Natasha, remember? I've got brown hair and I've put on some weight."

"A fat brunette, huh? Okay, enough joking. I want to get serious. Now, listen to me. Here's the plan."

After arranging a coded message as the 'I'm okay' signal, Arnie rang off.

Chapter Twenty-Seven

On her way to leave Vilnis at his day-care, Anda caught a glimpse of the headline in *Diena*. It was something about Jurmala. She was behind and didn't dare stop. She had been warned about being late for work and couldn't risk it again this week. She would have to wait until her lunch hour to buy a copy of the paper and read the article.

After dropping off Vilnis, she had to wait for the tram. Standing at the stop, she put her face up to enjoy the soft caress of the late winter sun. It was getting warm enough to melt the icicles hanging from every building. It was also that time of year when she had to pay special attention and remember to walk on the outside of the sidewalks so as to avoid being hit by sheets of ice that occasionally would drop from the eaves on the unsuspecting pedestrians hurrying along below. She couldn't risk being injured now that she had a child to look after.

Arriving at her destination with five minutes to spare, Anda hurried down the street to the nearest news kiosk and bought herself a copy of the paper. As she focused her eyes on the print, her knees almost buckled and she had to back up against the wall of a nearby office building for support. A wave of heat rose in her neck and she felt perspiration trickling down her face. Taking off her patterned white mittens, she tugged at the knotted scarf which Silvia had made for her just that past Christmas. Finally, managing to get it undone, she felt a rush of cool air revive her. She retrieved the newspaper which she had folded and tucked under her arm.

Her eyes popped. The first time she had read the article, the type had dissolved into a grey blur. Now, it had come back into focus as her initial shock had receded. Just underneath the headline, in smaller typeface, she read ARNIE DAMBERGS DROWNED AT JURMALA.

Anda was stunned. What could have made Arnie Dambergs go near the sea at this time of year? It didn't take her long to decide that Arnie had been murdered. Quickly, she scanned the rest of the story, sighed, refolded the newspaper and tucking it into her shopping bag, she hurried the last few metres to the bookstore. Ducking inside, she quickly looked up at the clock and was relieved to see that she was on time.

Anda had gone back to work because she was desperate for the money, especially after putting Vilnis in day-care. Sasha had disappeared right after Silvia's funeral leaving her no money with which to take care of the boy. How had her sister put up with Sasha all these years? No wonder she had started drinking to blot him out. If only Anda could have helped Silvia turn her life around. And now it was too late. She would have to take on Vilnis as if she were his mother. And the realization of what this meant frightened her. To her amazement, she had hardly thought about Mike in the last few days. She had been too busy with Silvia's funeral arrangements, Vilnis, and her mother, who was not taking it well. And now this! Arnie Dambergs. Dead.

Right from the start, Anda had put Arnie on the expat pedestal. When she had told him about Mike's disappearance, he had made her feel that he would take care of everything, that Mike and Daina would magically reappear. Now, Arnie was dead and she was back to square one.

Anda looked at her watch. She would only take a half-hour for lunch hoping that her boss would let her leave early to pick up Vilnis. She was saving money by bringing her lunch from home. Today, she had a hard-boiled egg and an apple. As she brushed the eggshells off the table into her cupped hand and dropped them into her shopping bag, she looked around reflexively. She wasn't supposed to eat in the stockroom. Suddenly, she noticed that a piece of shell had landed on the floor and bent over to retrieve it. Her eyes saw something move. It was a roach. She smiled. She had no fear as she had lived with them all her life. She decided that even a roach needed to do what it had to for survival and left the tiny piece of eggshell hoping that there was still some egg stuck to it.

Still smiling, she picked up the newspaper. Seconds later, a frown creased her face as she stared at the by-line about Arnie's death written by Rihards Plavins. Then a thought occurred. Maybe this journalist could help her. Would he be interested in hearing her story? She had nothing to lose.

Checking her watch, Anda saw that she still had a few minutes left on her lunch hour. Visions of Daina held captive somewhere spurred her on as she threw on her coat and hurried out of the bookstore. Scarcely looking either way, she crossed Barona Street and ran to the phone booth. Holding her copy of *Diena*, she dialled the number and waited to be connected with the journalist. To her surprise, he answered almost immediately and said that he would be able to meet her at four o'clock. How would she know him? She was told to watch for a tall young man with glasses wearing a brown leather jacket and a plaid scarf. He would be waiting outside the bookstore.

How slowly the afternoon passed! For the umpteenth time she found herself looking at her watch, convinced that four o'clock would never come. But it did. And then she was out the door like a shot.

He was waiting for her. She knew right away that the pleasant looking man was Rihards Plavins. They walked quickly down the block and ducked into the first café they came to. Finding an empty table, they settled themselves and Anda quickly began to tell her story. The journalist listened intently without making too many interruptions.

When Anda had finished, Rihards acknowledged that he had followed Arnie's exposé in *WOW!* magazine. He told her he was researching a story on human trafficking himself and that was why he had been assigned to Arnie's story. In spite of the suicide note that had been found, he echoed Anda's fears that Arnie's death had not been an accident. Forgetting that Anda's sister had died, insensitive to Anda's feelings about Daina's disappearance, he rattled on about his research. His eyes narrowed as he speculated that a young tall attractive girl like Daina would be worth a fortunate. With revulsion caught in her throat, it took all Anda's willpower to remain silent as the journalist continued his story.

Showing no consideration, Rihards went on to tell her that, if someone had kidnapped Daina, she had probably been sold by now to some pimp in Moscow for five thousand US to be kept as a sex slave in a brothel. Cold and callous, lost in his own story, he added that Daina would be snuffed if she opened her mouth to the authorities or tried to escape.

Anda's knuckles turned white as she clenched her hands together in her lap. Her body involuntarily contracted, her knees locked together and her shoulders hunched forward as if to protect

Daina's vulnerability and her own. She had to get away from this man and from what he was telling her.

Earlier, Anda had telephoned the day-care to ask them to keep Vilnis an extra hour. She would have to pay, of course. Parting company with Rihards, after agreeing to stay in touch, she rushed to the tram stop worrying that she would be paying for two hours instead of one. As the tram slowly worked its way across the city back to her stop, she couldn't help going over and over what Rihards had told her. She was horrified. And that hadn't even been the reason she had called him. She had wanted to find out more about Arnie Dambergs' death and all he had talked about was his upcoming article. Her mind had immediately pictured Daina bound and gagged in some hellhole in Moscow.

No matter what she did, Anda couldn't get rid of the images that Rihards had drawn for her. She knew they would haunt her dreams. He had certainly seemed interested in Daina's disappearance in connection with the Young Miss Latvia Competition and asked herself what he'd do about it, if anything. Also, she felt there was something about Arnie's death he hadn't told her. As she got off the tram, she wondered what it was.

Chapter Twenty-Eight

The scene unfolded before his eyes. A capsized boat in the dark of night. The cold ocean swallowing him up.

Arnie stared at the blank sheet of paper resting on the table in front of him. But his mind refused to go there. Instead, it travelled to a knot in the wood that was raised slightly above the grain of the surface of the desk. He ran his fingertip across it to make sure he could still feel it.

What would he say in the suicide note? Where would he leave it? It had to be found soon after the event. And his will. Should he make any changes? Should he include Vizma? A legacy to look after Gerda? He picked up his Mont Blanc pen admiring the black case with its white star at the top and though how silly to spend all that money at the duty free on something so transient. What poor decisions he had made based on want rather than need.

After all, what was wrong with a disposable ballpoint? Silly brain, where was it going? Got to get it down on paper. Focus. Date it first. *When you find this, I will be gone,* Arnie wrote. And then he thought, who will really give a damn?

God! Was he going to live through this? He was paralyzed. Every muscle was frozen as he went down. Slowly, his brain came to life with the overriding thought that he must kick his legs to start his body moving up to the surface. Adjusting to the water temperature, he could feel the change in direction. Slowly, slowly, he was able to get his legs in motion. Kick, you bastard, kick! After what seemed like ages, Arnie broke the surface gasping for air. *Thank you God, thank you, thank you.*

Opening his eyes, he searched for the boat. It was only a dark blob visible from the crest of the waves. Already the current had taken it beyond his reach. So this is really it, he thought. Coughing as he caught a mouthful of salty water, he craned his neck to keep his head above a large swell. Sculling with his hands, he turned around trying to find some lights on shore to check how far out he was. On the crest of the second wave, he spotted a cluster, but it was tiny. Panic. Had he drifted that far out? The lights were very far away. Or were they from those cottages further back from the shore? That must be it. Still, no time to lose. He had always been a strong swimmer. In fact, it had been the only sport he had ever done regularly. But never in the sea at night and in winter. The grease he had slathered all over his body and head must be helping, but still the cold was numbing him.

Slowly, he forced himself to raise his right arm first, swing it out in front, cup his hand and *pull*. He could feel the resistance of the water as his body moved forward. When his arm was down below at a ninety-degree angle to his trunk, he bent his left elbow until he could feel the cold air on the skin of his raised left arm.

He was underway. He was moving forward toward the shore. Deliberate, steady strokes. No heroic sprints. Just hit that rhythm that had powered him up and down at the Y. But would it be good enough for this? Gulp of air. Breathe out slowly under water. Splutter. Caught a mouthful. Spit out. Wait for the wave to hit and move on before each breath. He hadn't been paying attention. The waves weren't regular so he would have to adjust his stroke to their rhythms. Go with them. Don't fight against them.

He was pleased with this new strategy. It seemed to be working better. No mouthfuls for what Arnie thought must be a few minutes. He hadn't bothered to check his watch. No time to waste. Later maybe. Pull. Breathe. Another arm. Breathe. Pull. Keep the same stroke. He felt warmer, he thought. Could he really be able to generate heat from his exertions? Impossible. His legs felt like wooden logs. He willed them to kick. But they dragged out behind him. He would focus on his kick for a few minutes and see if that helped. After what seemed like an hour alone with his body, he decided to take a short break to check on his progress.

He couldn't help worrying about Janis and the phone calls he had promised Arnie he would make. The first was to Arnie's parents in Ottawa before any word of his suicide appeared in the Latvian press. That was to let them know what was going on. But now, Arnie wasn't so sure that it wouldn't be a phone call to announce the real thing. He imagined his parents sitting in the living room of their Ottawa bungalow, getting a second call to say his body had washed up on shore in Jurmala and that he really had drowned. Just thinking about it made him screw up his eyes. He had to get these thoughts out of his brain and concentrate on the swim. He got back into his stroke, breathing and pulling down as hard as he could. No time for bad thoughts.

On the crest of the next wave, he would make sure he was still moving straight for the shore. No lights. What's wrong? Direction wrong? Panic. On the next crest, to his left, a pinpoint of light. Check right. More lights. Good. He would keep them as his landfalls and check every five minutes to make sure he was going straight toward them. He didn't want to be pushed sideways wasting his efforts going parallel to the shore. His jaw was clenched shut to stop his body from shivering. He would have to get it open to breathe when he got under way again. No time to waste. Get the stroke back. Steady. Pull. Pull. Pull. Kick. More Kick. Damn it.

Five minutes later, Arnie checked his landfall again. He was disappointed he didn't seem to be any closer. He'd worked hard. Maybe a little closer. Get started again. He must have done this a dozen times before he saw a definite improvement.

Another half an hour later, Arnie could make out some buildings on shore. But he knew he was swimming more slowly and he was losing his drive. The cold was unbelievable and it was going to win if he didn't get out really soon. Where were those car headlights? Go straight in. No zigzags. Pull. Lift. Cup the hand more. Pull. Better. Kick. Crest of the next wave. Lights. Car lights. Beautiful car head lights. Why were they called headlights? Heavenly lights.

Pull. Pull. Faster. Harder. Now. Now. Kick. Now. Wait for the wave to swallow you. Pull down in the trough. The waves were bigger now. Why was that? Why were they coming closer together? Is it my imagination? Pull. Pull. Yes, they're closer. Different rhythm. Don't fight them. Go with the flow. Open your eyes and check again for the lights. God, that salt water stings! Why hadn't he used goggles? Poor decision. Oh, well, too late now. Noise. Louder. Could it be the surf? Was he that close? Check again. Yes. White caps up ahead. Pull. Pull. Harder. He was feeling desperate. What if he got this close and then ran out of steam? Steam heat. Where was the steam heat? A warm bath. He longed to soak in a warm bathtub. To see the steam on the mirror. Feel the roughness of the towel on his back. Suddenly, he felt a knife in his leg as his calf muscle bunched up into a knot. He cried out with the pain. He rolled over on his back and managed to massage it away.

God, the night air felt warm compared to the water! But he knew it was just an illusion. A rogue wave pushed him under just as he was taking a mouthful of air. He started to choke, tasting the cold salt water in his mouth. Momentarily forgetting the pain in his leg, he trashed his arms reaching for the surface. Where was it? Air! Air! He needed to find the air. Suddenly, there he was back on the crest of a wave and he could see the flashing headlights of the car. It was Janis, he was sure of that. He spat out salt water, coughed a couple of times, clearing his throat and then struck out for shore as hard as he could. Next time he checked, he was able to see the outline of the car slightly raised above the level of the beach. His crawl was rhythmic and smooth beating out a comfortable tattoo.

What was that? Did I hit bottom? Kick. Kick. Yes, there it is again. Try to stand. Nothing. Noise. Kick. Pull. Yes, that's sand. There it is. I've made it! I've done it! A handful of sand. God! How good that feels! On all fours, Arnie dragged himself up the slight incline of the beach until he was completely out of the water and collapsed.

Janis' voice was calling his name. A towel. Thank God. A blanket. A swig of Metaxa. God bless the Greeks. Metaxa. More. Searing heat going down, down through his frozen body. He tried to stand, but couldn't. Janis grabbed his arm through the layers and said,

"Can you make it to the car? I can't drive it onto the beach. It'll get stuck in the sand. Come on. You don't want anybody to see you here now that you're good and dead."

"Hah!" Arnie managed a snort of laughter.

With Janis' help, Arnie made it to the passenger seat of the car. He leaned back, pulling the blanket closer around him waiting for Janis to get behind the wheel. As they both sat there, Arnie, his lips blue, his teeth still chattering uncontrollably, grinned at Janis and sputtered out between clenched teeth,

"Where's my knapsack? I can't wait to change into some warm dry clothes. How far is it to this farmhouse where I'm going to lay low? I hope they have their sauna heated up when I get there. I don't think I'll ever be warm again. Now, lets put the suicide note into circulation. And don't forget to send Vizma a Happy Birthday telegram. That's the signal to let her know I'm OK."

"What did that salt water do to your brain? I've never heard you talk so much. Here's the Metaxa. That'll warm you up and I'll have you there before you know it."

Chapter Twenty-Nine

Vizma had lonely girl written all over her. Awful hair, no makeup, lousy wardrobe. All that plus a get-lost attitude if anyone approached her.

The sun was in and out of the clouds all day. Towards evening it started to rain, a heavy insistent rain that pounded through umbrellas and sent commuters running for shelter. Vizma had come back to the hotel just before the downpour started. There was nothing to do but sit staring out the window of her solitary room as darkness closed in around the city.

She worried about her classes at the Academy. Would she still have them when she returned? She knew there was Svetlana, a Russian woman, gunning for her job. Svetlana had a PhD in English from Moscow University but persisted in using her own brand of the Queen's English. Vizma had snorted at Svetlana's pronunciation of the word divorce. I'm *die*-vorced she would insist. For those who learn languages phonetically, English was indeed a challenge. At times, it seemed that Svetlana's undergraduate degree had come from Dynasty. In a trashy way, she even looked like Joan Collins—short, big breasts, big hair and a big hungry smile. Still, however badly Svetlana spoke English, it was not half as bad as her Latvian.

It amazed Vizma to learn that Latvian had not been considered a real language under Soviet rule. *Suņu valoda*, the language of dogs, Russians had called the language of their occupied territories. Apparently, since 1991, things had changed a bit but not much. Some Russians still refused to learn Latvian, considered themselves to be indispensable and whined about discrimination and ethnic cleansing.

Vizma had plenty of time to ruminate. She sat by the window spinning her wheels. Going a little crazy. There was nothing for her to do. The heavy rain kept her inside. She started to listen to footsteps travelling up and down the hallway. She was familiar with the heavy tread of the housekeeper and knew when she was about to enter without knocking to change the sheets or to sweep. Suddenly, a knock sounded at her door. Vizma jumped. Who could that be? Perhaps it was one of the other guests with whom she had developed a nodding acquaintance. The interruption didn't alarm her but came as a genuine relief for her waterlogged mood of gloomy boredom.

Catching her breath, Vizma almost ran to answer the knock. Didn't even think of the Mace. As the door swung open, playing its usual symphony of metal squeaking on metal, she found herself face to face with her front desk suitor. It was Juris.

My God! A genuine Latvian Harlequin moment! Pushed out in front was a large bouquet of red carnations which rustled gently in their cellophane wrapper. Vizma's mouth flapped open. She was caught completely off guard. She tried to think of something to say while she wondered if he had had an accident with his after-shave. And why was his hair plastered down like that, all greasy and shiny? And then the minty smell on his breath gave it all away. He was going to try to suck her face!

For a minute, she remained frozen to the spot. Seizing his opportunity, Juris smiled, exposing his sharp little teeth and followed the flowers over the threshold.

"Happy Birthday!" he exclaimed beaming the two English words at her. From somewhere in his clenched hand, he produced a telegram, *sans* envelope. Still caught somewhere between surprise and alarm, Vizma read the two words that she and Arnie had agreed to use as their 'All's well' signal. Back in control, she accepted his flowers and said, "Thank you," with more meaning than Juris could possibly have understood. Blithely, she stepped toward the door, opening it wider and with a gracious gesture, motioned him out with a firm "Goodbye!"

She saw his face register surprise. "Goodbye? No, goodbye. Hello!"

Vizma took a step forward. "Out! Now! Go!"

Juris grinned as she took him by the elbow and ushered him back over the threshold.

"Thank you for the flowers," she said primly as she closed the door and locked it.

Minutes later, seated on her bed, she wanted more words to read. Why couldn't the signal have been longer, in fact, a whole page? But she would have to be satisfied. Make do with what she had.

Vizma's routine continued its endless monotony. She set out in the mornings to walk around Riga, lunched in a cheap restaurant or picnicked as she browsed through the market. She had discovered *Rama* on Barona Street. The place offered a full vegetarian meal for one lats, courtesy of the Hare Krishna, with chanting at no extra charge. She noticed the free soup kitchen downstairs and kept it in mind. Her expenses were mounting. She had no income and was paying for the hotel room as well as rent on Valdemara Street.

From time to time, she longed for a big juicy hamburger and took herself to McDonald's on Basteja Boulevard. Vizma would order a *komplekts*—one *Bigs Maks*, *fri*, and *kokteilis*. She had heard that the place had the cleanest public toilets in town and, after doing her own research, discovered this was true. In fact, it was the main draw. She was also dying for seafood and that didn't mean lamprey or eel. She hoped Red Lobster would make its way to Riga soon. And turkey—she had missed it at Thanksgiving and again at Christmas. It had come as a shock when she had been confronted by a whole hog clenching a red apple in its teeth at her first New Year's celebration in Riga.

Vizma fought boredom as best she could. Each evening, she sat in the hotel lounge and watched TV. She had not made friends with the other guests, preferring to keep them at a safe distance and made herself scarce whenever Juris was on duty. She had got into the habit of buying beer and drinking it in her room. It lifted her spirits for a short time then always put her to sleep.

Desperate for reading material, Vizma was training herself to read Latvian. Since she spoke the language and Latvian was phonetic, it would only be a matter of time before she could read without making an effort. That was one good thing that had come out of all of this. Latvia had a rich cultural tradition and many masterpieces her parents had told her about but which she had never read.

She picked up *Annele* by Anna Brigadere. She remembered her father reading her the book when she was a child. Her father had been a stern unsentimental man but for some reason had enjoyed reading over and over the passage where Annele's own father dies. And Vizma and her little sister had cried. In her memory, it was the saddest most beautiful book. Before she knew it, she was once again caught up in the story of Annele.

After reading about the explosion, Vizma decided to risk walking by the apartment house to see the damage for herself. She was horrified to see that Arnie's apartment had been blown to smithereens and was now a gaping hole in the wall of the sixth floor of the otherwise undamaged building. The police called it a gas explosion but everyone knew what it really was. A hit. A grenade thrown in deliberately.

Vizma's conscience kept nagging her about Gerda. She shuddered at the thought of Arnie's cat caught in the explosion and tried to reassure herself by thinking that the Cat Lady had probably adopted it. God bless the Cat Lady, Vizma murmured, crossing herself even though she wasn't Catholic.

Not daring to go near her own apartment, Vizma was going crazy walking the streets of Riga looking like a Russian tramp. She longed for the comfort of satellite TV and her own surroundings. Even though her money was running low, she had decided that the hotel was a safer option. It was clear that the bad guys were playing for keeps and, in Riga, it was hard to tell who they were—Latvian Mafia, Russian Mafia, the underbelly of the black market, the bottom feeders of the political scene, not to mention the local police. They were all options in the pick and mix bin.

Vizma had heard that the mob had infiltrated all levels of government as well as the police. They bribed and intimidated— and killed anyone they couldn't bribe and intimidate. She would bet her sweet bippy that the mob was taking care of the police chief and knew that any expat who got in the way would be taken to the Daugava River for a midnight swim—with a cement block chained around the neck.

Chapter Thirty

Finally it was spring and spring always made Vizma want to wear something pretty. She couldn't wait to trade in her leaky winter boots for the pair of Aerosoles stashed away in her apartment cupboard. On this first Saturday in April, Vizma was fed up and tired. Her clothes felt dirty. She had no money, no friends, nowhere to go.

The constant question loomed, making her more depressed as time went on. What was she to do with her day? How would she pass the empty hours? The fact that she could feel the warmth of the sun, the return of the light and the buds on the Linden trees did little to change her mood.

She decided to be a creature of habit after all. On one of her walks across town, she had noticed a sort of bomb shelter like place in a nearby basement. The sign on the doorway said

Dynasty. Laughing out loud, she had decided to go down the crumbling cement steps and take a closer look. It appeared to be a no-frills hairdressing salon. Surely more affordable than the Hotel Latvija and she hadn't seen any Goths lurking around.

The time had come to try it out. Vizma couldn't help smiling as she glanced at the sign. The interior promised more. And she wasn't disappointed. The minute she opened the door she was assailed by a powerful whiff of garlic. Taking two steps inside, she found herself being greeted by a plus-size Alexis who was in the process of chewing on a bologna sandwich. Vizma's eyes widened. Wow! And there was Crystal under the dryer, blowing on her dark purple nails. But there was a snag. The women were gabbling in Russian.

Making with the smiley face, Vizma tried a tentative *labdien*. Alexis shook her head. Another Russian only place. Still, Vizma was fascinated. Having finished the sandwich, Alexis lipsticked her mouth, then shrugged her shoulders in Vizma's direction. Vizma decided that she would have to play deaf mute. She picked up a magazine and, putting it under Alexis' nose, she pointed to a young beauty with curly black hair. As she removed her babushka, she noted Alexis' eyes pop in horror.

Not wasting a second, Alexis bolted out of her chair, grabbed Vizma's arm and steered her to the sink. Shoving Vizma's head back unceremoniously, she ran cold water from the tap through a rubber shower attachment. *"That's too cold!"* Vizma exploded in a shriek. For a moment, Alexis' eyebrows knitted together in puzzlement, then her face took on an expression of delight.

"Oh, English! American?" she said as her eyes flashed dollar signs at the thought of having a member of the expat community in her clutches. Vizma started to reach for her babushka, preparing for a speedy exit. But it was too late. Her head by now was dripping wet.

Minutes later, Alexis was busy dabbing on a revolting smelly lotion to each skinny roller she had installed on Vizma's head.

Mixed with the garlic of the bologna and Alexis' dime-store perfume, it formed an overpowering potpourri. Vizma was on the verge of passing out. Alexis sunk two teeth into her heavily lipsticked lower lip and, with determination, set the timer for forty minutes, then walked away, leaving Vizma under the dryer. Holding her otherwise unoccupied babushka to her nose in a vain hope that it would filter out the smell, Vizma doubted she would last forty minutes.

After what felt like an eternity, the timer went off, bringing Alexis to her side. Expert fingers removed each roller, leaving a stinging sensation on Vizma's scalp. Her eyes began to run and she daubed at them with the babushka.

"Beautiful! Beautiful!" Alexis crowed in English, holding a hand mirror up to Vizma's face. Vizma was speechless. *That's not me! No, not me!* But when she reached out to touch the Afro with her hand, she realized that it really was her face staring back at her. A large clump of greenish tinged hair came away and stuck to her fingers. Vizma examined it with a mixture of fascination and horror. It felt like an abused Brillo pad and, as if to give confirmation, it crumbled to nothing and disappeared into a small smudge of dust on her slacks. She looked back in the mirror and had to accept that the strange finger-in-the-light-socket head staring back at her was what she now looked like.

A minute later, Alexis reappeared at her elbow, shoving forward a small piece of paper. The bill. *"How much!"* Vizma screamed. It must have sobered Alexis, because she quickly produced a pencil and changed what she had first written.

Minutes later, as Vizma fled up the stairs, her head invisible under her babushka, she was followed from below by Alexis screaming in heavy Russian. Vizma had no trouble understanding every word. Having left half her hair behind and seeing the other half falling out in large clumps, it was a no-brainer. No tip for Alexis.

*   *   *

The next day, Vizma left the hotel and stepped into the spring air. She paused for a moment, trying to decide whether to turn left or right, not really caring which direction she set off in. She knew she really should be out looking for a wig but had no idea where she could find one. Maybe a larger babushka would do the trick or maybe she could go whole hog and get a chador. Surely, there must be some orthodox Muslims in Riga.

With a shrug of her shoulders, she turned right and slowly sauntered up Marijas Street. Suddenly her head started to spin as if she were halfway drunk. She couldn't believe her eyes. There, at the tram stop, was the outline of a familiar figure. Could that be Arnie? For a moment, she didn't know what to do. Her first reaction was to turn and go in the opposite direction. She looked awful and she didn't want Arnie to see her like this. Then she realized Arnie wouldn't even recognize her the way she looked now. Another thought occurred. Perhaps Arnie didn't want to be recognized, even if it was Arnie. What an idiot she was being! Turning, she saw that he was still in the same spot and, as she got closer, could see he had lost weight, grown a moustache and was wearing glasses. In spite of the weird cap he was wearing, she knew without doubt it was Arnie.

Now she was glad that she hadn't rushed up to him. As she sauntered up the block, pausing to look in shop windows, she saw that he was following her at a discrete distance. Trust Arnie. She hadn't been able to fool him with her disguise. Where could she go so that they could talk without being spotted together? She had wandered through this area every day for weeks but couldn't think of any place that would be safe. Suddenly, picking up her pace and swinging her ever-present shopping bag, she decided on a destination.

She knew that the Central Market would be teeming with shoppers and she and Arnie would easily disappear into the crowd. Lucky for them it was a Saturday. Even more important, their conversation would be lost in the general din.

Vizma had read in one of the tourist guides that the five halls of the market were former Zeppelin hangars, leftovers from the 1930s. At the head of Merkela Street, she could see the train station on the other side of Marijas Street and knew she would have to get across by using the pedestrian tunnel. She didn't hesitate. On a Saturday, with so many people around, there would be less risk of being mugged. Up to now she hadn't dared look behind to check that Arnie was still following but now she decided that she would. She turned, their eyes made contact and she even thought she saw a wink.

Moving forward again, she ducked into the entrance and down the stairs to the underground passageway. Walking quickly through the assortment of beggars, baby carriages, crutches, blind people, dogs and the occasional accordion player, she left this scene from Dante and was glad to re-emerge into daylight. Without hesitation, she plunged into the crowd and quickly became one with the stream of shoppers milling around.

The tables in the halls groaned with mountains of food, each category having its own hall: farm and garden produce, meat, fish, dairy products and bread. Vendors overflowed the crowded buildings at stalls set up outside. Pickpockets thrived. Outside, in front of the halls, colourful and crowded flea markets had been set up. Babushkas swarmed all over the place, selling vodka, selling cigarettes, selling puppies from shopping bags. Vendors displayed piles of brassieres, underpants, jeans, pirated videos. Gypsies sold booze, smokes and everyone's fortune. Small time merchants displayed rows of goods at their feet—a couple of old handbags, a pair of running shoes, a few t-shirts, mangled pieces of fur which perhaps had been a collar or a pair of cuffs and, dotted here and there, small piles of used books and magazines.

Vizma stopped at a stall that was selling baked goods. There was rich dark rye bread, sourdough bread, white bread, rolls, and assorted pastries. She picked up a loaf and paid for it and saw that Arnie was right next to her. Casually, they started a conversation about the heavenly aroma of fresh bread. They spoke to each other in Latvian. There they were, if anyone was observing them, two ordinary strangers, chatting about nothing much. Suddenly, Vizma felt Arnie jostle her with his elbow and realized that his hand was fumbling at her coat pocket. She pretended to pay no attention and slipped the loaf she had just bought into her shopping bag. Before she knew it, Arnie was gone, swept up in the flow of anonymous faces and scuffing feet.

The sun came out from behind a cloud and Vizma tilted her head up, closed her eyes for a moment and revelled in the light which warmed her face. Oh blessed sunshine, she murmured to herself, fingering the note Arnie had dropped in her pocket. She knew she had to find a quiet corner before she could look at it. And she had to put distance between herself and one particularly sinister-looking vendor who seemed to be selling bags of road-kill and other hijacked merchandize stacked on a small cart.

She moved away from the bread stall and walked past several other vendors until her progress was halted by two women having a tug of war over a spandex animal-print jumpsuit. She carefully worked her way around the cluster of shoppers who had stopped to watch in hopes of honing their own technique. The one that gets the jumpsuit is the real loser, Vizma murmured as she veered out of the way.

Leaning against the counter of a coffee stand, she put her hand into her coat pocket and felt the metallic can of Mace. Her fingers searched through the other debris—bits of Kleenex, some loose change, a bic lighter and a pen. Suddenly she froze. Stifled a scream. From behind, a hand had gripped her shoulder. Was it the sinister-looking vendor trying to sell her his road-kill? Or was she going to end up in his shopping bag? Clutching the Mace, she twisted around.

"Here madam, you left your shopping bag. It is yours, isn't it? I saw you buying a loaf of bread. You were with a friend."

Vizma turned red. God! He'd given her a fright! Here was a decent senior citizen with a ruddy face holding out her shopping bag.

"Oh, thank you, thank you!"

She saw a puzzled expression cross the man's face as she spoke in Latvian. She realized that he expected her to have a Russian accent. Without saying anything more, she waved goodbye and beat a hasty retreat, grateful that her shopping bag was back in the crook of her elbow.

Finding an empty bench a little further along, Vizma sat down and placed the shopping bag between her knees. She found the unfamiliar piece of folded paper in her pocket, pulled it out and consulted it as if it was her shopping list. On it, in Arnie's handwriting, was scrawled *call at eight tonight from a payphone* followed by the number.

Mission accomplished. Vizma suddenly felt light as air and very hungry. Admiring the rich array of cheese, she decided to spend a little of what money she had left. She had learned from experience not to buy the local Latvian cheese. It was delicious but the smell was overpowering. She opted for Gouda to go with her loaf of rye bread. Next, she bought some Aldaris beer, found a park bench and ate her picnic in the gorgeous midday sunshine. She broke off large chunks of the rich bread and nibbled on the cheese. The moment was perfect. Birds flapped around her and trotted after the crumbs she threw for them.

Vizma was gnawing her cuticles, waiting for eight o'clock. What else could she do to make the day pass quickly? A movie? The film playing closest to her was Waterworld, a dud if there ever was one. But beggars couldn't be choosers.

She walked into the Daile and bought her ticket. She sat down on the hard wooden chair and was glad no one was in front of her as the level floor made it hard to see the screen. Snorting in disgust and stifling groans, she wished someone would throw rotten eggs at Kevin Costner and the rest of the crew. Instead, they lapped it up.

At least Kevin got me to four o'clock, she thought as she re-emerged into the late afternoon. Another four hours to kill. What would she do now? Some more walking around was a likely option. She made a mental note that when she got back to her apartment, whenever that might be, she would do a number on the boots she was wearing. She would never put them on her feet again, that was for sure. She would take those boots and bronze them or burn them or bury them—or boil them à la Charlie Chaplin and serve them up to Arnie *au gratin*.

At this point she really needed a smoke. She knew that some bars and cafés sold cigarettes one by one. Even though she had decided to quit, this wasn't the moment. With determination, she walked into *Bitite* to buy herself three cigarettes. Next, she stopped in at the grocery store beside the café and bought supplies for the evening. Salami, apples and more beer to go with the bread she still had left over from lunch.

This was proving to be a day without end. The slow moving arms of her watch taunted her. Boy, could she use a smoke! She covered three blocks looking for an acceptable hole-in-the-wall café to sit in. It wasn't until she was half way down the fourth block that she found what she was looking for. She walked into an obscure little eatery and ordered a bowl of cabbage soup.

Smoking her second cigarette, she whiled away some more time and wondered if Arnie was up to date with everything that had happened since they put out the story. Did he know about the public outcry? Did he know about the accusations being volleyed back and forth between members of parliament? Had he heard the news that the Prime Minister promised a thorough investigation of the scandal? Mentally, she made a list of what she was going to tell Arnie and forced herself to save her third cigarette for after the phone call.

ILZE BERZINS

She had already chosen the phone booth from which she was going to make her call. She knew from painful experience that the old phones were useless with their metal tokens. So she looked instead for one of the new modern Lattelekom booths. She was glad that she already had a phone card. Eight o'clock was drawing near. There was just a little over an hour to wait and she went back to her hotel room to rest.

She must have dozed off. She woke with a start and looked at her watch. It was seven forty. God! She had to run. She had wanted to get there early to make sure that nobody else was using the phone at eight o'clock.

Throwing herself into the dark clutches of the gusting wind and rain, Vizma made for the phone booth on Barona Street. Good. Good. Good. It was empty and, as the door swung closed behind her, the light came on. Even better. She stamped her feet and shook off as much of the rain as she could from her coat, curled her fingers around the phone card and repeated the phone number Arnie had given her which she knew by heart even though she had kept the slip of paper.

Finally, she was ready to make her call. She checked her watch and saw that she was still early. She decided to pick up the receiver and pretend to be listening to a conversation to put off anyone else who might want to use the phone. Once in a while, she moved her lips. Her mind drifted. She though of her friend Mara who had met one of the English telephone engineers brought to Riga by Lattelekom. The last time Vizma had seen her, her friend had told her that she was about to leave to visit him now that he was back in England. Was it a surprise visit? What a shock it would be for Mara to find Mr Lattelekom in the bosom of his family.

Still, Vizma felt a twinge of jealousy. When this was all behind her, she would make a decided effort to get out of her apartment and take part in the social possibilities now available

216

in Riga because of the influx of interest being shown by the rest of the world.

She looked back at her watch. Had it stopped? There were still five minutes to go. She clutched her card in one hand and Arnie's number in the other and prayed that no one would thump on the door and get her even more nervous than she already was.

The minutes ticked by, stubbornly slow. Her heart thumped painfully as she paced the floor in her mind. Finally, to release tension, she let out a snort of laughter at herself. Get a grip, for heaven's sake! What a fool she was. She shivered as a gust of wind sent rain slashing against the Plexiglas booth. At last, the slow moving hand reached eight. Thank God, she muttered and was about to slip her card into the slot when a sharp tattoo of raps on the door made it fly out of her hand. God! She grabbed at the card that had landed at her feet. Then without turning, she motioned to whoever was rapping on the door to get away. Immediately, she returned her hand to her pocket and curled her fingers around the can of Mace. She would take no chances.

As if by magic, the phone worked perfectly. Vizma heard the musical beep-beep of the dial tone and punched in the number. It rang three times before Arnie answered.

Chapter Thirty-One

Maija Fischer was wearing dark glasses and was not having a good day. Her Martha Stewart dream was crashing down all around her. Her husband was on the warpath. He had refused to pay her rent in the office building on Gertrudes Street. He was cutting her off and all because she had agreed to give an interview to that Arnie Dambergs. Right after their honeymoon, Don had had no trouble adopting the local attitude toward domestic violence. In fact, he took to it like a local and the proof this morning was Maija's black eye hidden behind her dark glasses in spite of the overcast sky.

There was no question of her going to the police. They would simply laugh at her and leak the story to the press. She decided to roll with the punches and patted herself on the back for being a survivor. She had survived this kind of abuse before and she'd survive it again. Very soon after her marriage, she realized that Don had married her just for the window dressing. He rarely showed any interest in her but beat up on her at the least suspicion of infidelity.

There was a lot going on in Riga and she wanted to be part of it. Riga's nightlife set a frenetic pace, a pace Maija loved. She was in synch with it and felt that the city was trying to make up for the time it had lost during the dark cheerless suppression of the Soviet regime.

Maija had met Sasha Atnikov quite by chance on one of her visits to the Bimini, a swinging nightclub with disco dancing and a karaoke bar. A rhinoceros on the façade made it conspicuous on the otherwise shabby Marijas Street. Maija had heard that it was the *in* place with locals and expats. No way was she going to drag boring old Don along. Instead she had gone with one of her women friends.

On that fateful night, Maija's well-tuned sexual antenna had signalled an alert before she even entered the club. As she walked into the room, she immediately saw two remarkably good-looking men. As luck would have it, the table next to them had just become vacant. Maija pounced. Bending down low in a practised move as she seated herself, she exposed her famous cleavage. As soon as she had ordered a vodka martini, she craned her neck in the direction of the next table. Maija noted that the two lookers were smoking, drinking and holding an animated conversation—and it was in Russian.

Quite a challenge. Maija felt reckless. She rummaged in her purse, pulled out a cigarette, stopped, looked around. Damn, where were her matches? Within moments, a light appeared. Maija cupped her hand around the proffered flame, lightly grazing a masculine fist. Cheap plastic lighter, she said to herself, having hoped for a silver monograph. Her girlfriend giggled.

Before they knew it *champanski* had appeared in front of them. To hell with the language barrier, Maija muttered. The men, who had now joined them, spoke a smattering of English. They were Sasha and Dimitri. Sasha was by far the better looking of the two. Tall, broad shoulders, intense blue eyes and the Russian curly black hair. His smile was flawless. Maija held her breath as the man bent over her hand, kissed it and looked at her with his killer smile. He lifted the *champanski* out of its bucket, water dripping and refilled the glasses.

And that's how it had all started. Maija laughed when anyone mentioned the language barrier. That night at Bimini there were no barriers, just four attractive people, laughing and joking as the *champanski* flowed.

Maija's girlfriend had been more guarded. She was not ready for the Russian experience. Maija was. For her, it was major chemistry. She threw caution to the wind. Before they parted, she gave Sasha her business number at *Décor-Rama.*

She hadn't really expected him to phone. But he did, the very next day. Why do they say women fall in love and men fall in lust, Maija wondered and wanted to tell everyone that she knew better. She was in lust, head over heels. Since it wasn't in her genetic code to turn her back on pleasure, she threw herself into an affair with Sasha Atnikov that rivalled anything any film producer could invent. Last Tango in Riga was how she thought of this steamy week of sex.

Early in February, she had seen Sasha on Terbatas Street. He was talking to a stunning young girl. Maija judged her to be about fifteen with a mop of Titian red hair, an innocent beauty, not yet aware of her power over men. Maija surprised herself. She felt a stab of jealousy, a feeling she was totally unfamiliar with. She had always exuded a raw sexual energy that men found irresistible but she had never been beautiful and wasn't getting any younger.

Mesmerized, Maija had stepped into the grocery store on the corner of Blaumana Street and through its glass door, stared at the girl Sasha was talking to. No woman, no matter how sexy, could compete with youth. Maija forced herself to pay attention to the couple. They appeared to be quarrelling. Suddenly Sasha grabbed the girl by the arm and propelled her to a car parked just a few yards away. He opened the door, pushed her into the back seat and drove away.

After that, Maija had not seen Sasha for almost a month. Then he called her again and came over. They had made love on Maija's couch in her office and later, over a cigarette, Maija casually mentioned seeing him with a very beautiful young girl a month ago on Terbatas Street. Sasha equally casually replied, "Oh, that was my stepdaughter. What a handful!"

Chapter Thirty-Two

When Anda woke up on the living room couch, she didn't open her eyes right away. She wanted to sink back into sleep, reluctant to face the overwhelming effort the day demanded of her. She had awakened earlier than usual. It was still dark outside, not yet time to get Vilnis up and make breakfast. She looked over at the small coffee table where she kept a framed picture of Silvia which Mike had taken. Next to it, she had placed a bud vase in which she always had a fresh flower. She wanted Vilnis to remember his mother and often, before going to bed, the two of them would sit on the couch and talk about her.

Lately, mornings always brought anxiety. Anxiety about work, anxiety about her family. And also, a certain clarity. Something important had dawned on her just before she had opened her eyes.

As she sat up, she tried to figure out what to do. What she suspected couldn't be right. The more she thought about it, the angrier she got at herself. Perhaps, it was this subconscious anger which had awakened her. She should have seen it sooner, much sooner. The story that Rihards Plavins had told her about young teens sold into the sex trade haunted her. Could Daina have fallen victim to a sex slave trafficker? Fear erupted. And where was Sasha?

A part of her must have known all along but she had been reluctant to worry her sister. She had nothing concrete to go on. Just feelings and the memory of the way Sasha had looked at his stepdaughter and she was terrified that Daina could be locked up in some brothel, perhaps still in Latvia. Anda knew nothing at all about the sex trade and had no idea what part of Riga could house such horrors. But if Sasha was involved, it was more likely she was somewhere in Moscow. Anda's eyes teared over because she simply didn't know how she was going to cope. Why hadn't she insisted that Silvia do something to protect Daina from Sasha? And now, it was all up to her—if it wasn't already too late. Her heart was heavy like a boat anchor unable to find the ocean floor. Her spirits spiralled down into the darkness. She understood why her sister had reached for the bottle and oblivion. Sometimes, there seemed to be nothing else. No one to comfort her, no one to put an arm around her.

There had been Mike. A lover, a friend but never particularly supportive or reliable. And Arnie. She had trusted him. What had really happened to him? Murder? Suicide? An accident? She wished she could believe the rumours that he was still alive.

Then everything went black. Anda had fallen asleep again. The next thing she knew, Vilnis had crawled into bed with her and was tickling her awake.

She always made porridge for them both but this time she was late. She gave Vilnis a banana and grabbed some coffee for herself. Coffee was her only luxury. It was filter, not the ersatz powder that many of her friends drank. She made it in the evening and reheated it in the morning.

A quick wash and she was out the door with Vilnis in tow. Day-care started at eight. That gave her a few minutes to sit in a café before heading for work. She always chose a table by the window and just stared with unfocused eyes out on the street as she sipped on her second cup of the day. Time alone was precious now. Her mother called every night and Anda did her best to comfort her. There was Vilnis in the evenings and, during the day, demanding customers to satisfy.

Often during the night, she'd be awakened by the sound of Vilnis crying. She would get off the couch where she now made her bed and tip toe into the bedroom. She would rub his thin little back and tell him stories until she heard his regular breathing. She would kiss him and softly shut the bedroom door as she made her way back to the couch.

As she sat at the table by the restaurant window, her eyes alighted on a familiar figure moving along Brivibas Street, a camera bag over his shoulder. Could that be Mike? The walk was exactly the same, the shoulders rolled from side to side because of the long strides of his legs. It had to be Mike.

Anda leapt up, hitting the table leg and upsetting her cup of coffee. Her heart pounding, she shrugged herself into her coat, slung her plastic shopping bag over her arm and dashed for the door.

Once out on Brivibas Street, she turned in the same direction Mike had been walking but he had disappeared. Damn! Just for a second, she wondered if her mind was playing tricks on her. Still, she was sure that it had been Mike. How had he disappeared so quickly? Right before her eyes, he had been swallowed up by the morning pedestrian crush.

Anda hesitated for a moment, trying to decide whether she would risk being late for work. To hell with work, she decided and raced down Brivibas Street in the hope of catching him.

Three blocks later, panting for breath, she still couldn't see him. Had he turned off onto a side street or hopped on a tram? Or perhaps he had left his car parked in the neighbourhood. Anda remembered that, when Mike had purchased the beat-up Opel, she had asked him where he had found the money. He had been evasive and had never come clean. At the time, Anda hadn't pushed him about it but now she wished she had. She had let him live off her wages, staying over at her apartment and eating up her food. In all the time he had the car, he had only picked her up from work twice and both times had been payday.

Anda turned back, her disappointment showing in the way she dragged her feet. As she walked into the bookstore, she was startled by the angry look in the manager's eyes as he checked his watch. To hell with you, to hell with everyone! her eyes shouted back.

Chapter Thirty-Three

"I owe you for the cat," were the first words that Arnie said when they finally met face to face.

"The cat?" Vizma mumbled blankly. It took her a full thirty seconds to figure out what he was talking about. She risked a lie.

"Sure. No problem." She expertly slid over the cat and quickly steered him around to what really mattered. "You made the front page three days in a row. That's great, isn't it?"

"Yeah, but I wish to God, I'd been able to enjoy my fifteen minutes of fame. Spending an hour in that freezing Baltic water was a bloody hard way to go about getting it. A couple of times, I really thought it was going to turn into the real thing. That water is cold beyond belief. If I'd know what it was going to be like,

I doubt if I'd have had the guts to try it. Now, where's Gerda? How's she doing?"

"Oh, I gave her to a friend for safekeeping. They don't allow animals in my hotel." Well, that wasn't a lie, Vizma said to herself, thinking of the Cat Lady. "And about the fifteen minutes, it's not over till it's over. I'm sure you'll get your chance to bask in the limelight. And how come they didn't mention *me* in any of the stories?"

"They will. You know I couldn't have put out the magazine without you. You'll get your fifteen minutes. Don't worry your pretty head about that."

Vizma smiled. "You say the silliest things, Arnie. Are you making fun of this dreadful Russian perm? And to think, I did it all for you."

Without missing a beat, Arnie shot back, "You shouldn't have." And they both broke up laughing. It felt good.

The countryside glowed gold as the sun settled into pools of light on fields fresh with their newly sprouted crop of winter wheat. Vizma and Arnie were sitting on the stoop of the farmhouse, sipping beer. Peteris and Marta, friends of his cousin, had taken Arnie in. Vizma turned her face upward to enjoy the amber sunshine. Spring on a farm. What could be more delightful! She thought of the poor animals cooped up in the barn. Any day now, they'll be out again, bouncing through the fresh sunlit meadows.

Vizma had taken the train to Madona to see Arnie. At the end of that suspenseful eight o'clock Lattelekom conversation, he had invited her to come for a visit. Going to the train station, Vizma had made sure no one had been following her. Once on the train, she felt relatively safe and was dying for a change of scenery from her old overused stomping grounds of downtown Riga.

Arnie was pleased to see her and she was over the moon. He looked fit and was pleased with himself. He had been helping with the planting and this outdoor work had done him a lot of

227

good. Peteris and Marta had a small dairy farm and Arnie was learning a lot about country life. Vizma thought to herself that both she and Arnie had lost their expat patina and looked better for it. Arnie's face took on a more earnest expression as he turned to Vizma.

"I want you to go see Anda for me."

"Anda? What for?"

"Well, you remember that niece of hers, Daina, who had disappeared? I'm really worried about her and I'm worried about Mike. My gut feeling is that his disappearance may somehow be connected to Daina's disappearance. Can you do it for me? You'll have to be careful. Someone may be watching her. Call her first, arrange to meet somewhere quiet. Use a phone booth."

"Oh Arnie, suppose you call her yourself."

"I'm supposed to be dead, *comprende*?"

"Yeah, brain-dead," Vizma said with a laugh. "What am I supposed to say to this Anda?"

"I want you to tell her about me. I promised to help her. She has no one."

"No one? What about her family? Her parents?"

"God, Vizma. You're heartless. Anda's mother must be at least eighty and overwhelmed with grief. Remember, I told you that Anda's sister froze to death on the street."

There was nothing Vizma could say to that. She was ashamed at her resentment of Anda. The pretty young Latvian damsel in distress made Vizma feel old and mean spirited.

"Okay. You win, Arnie. Let's figure out how I'm supposed to meet her. Do I just walk up to her in the bookstore?"

"Well, yeah. Make sure no one else is around. Go early in the morning. Ask about a book. Talk a bit and then tell her you'd like to have coffee with her after work. Tell her you have something from me. You'll pull it off."

"So, basically, all you want is for me to tell her you're alive?"

"Yes. And ask her about Daina. Maybe the girl has turned up. And Mike."

"And what're you going to be doing?"

"Oh, I'll just hang out with these folk. Learn to milk cows, slaughter pigs, watch the daisies, you know…farm stuff."

"And I have to go back to my lonely girl life on the streets of Riga?"

"You can do it, babe," Arnie said and got up to stretch his legs.

Vizma looked out at the serene beauty of the mist rising from the rolling pasturelands. Dusk was approaching, with the kind of dreamy light that would glimmer all night when midsummer came. She could see the last vestiges of snow in the ploughed furrows on the shady side of the closest field and wondered when the farmer would be ready to put in the potato plants. She didn't need to ask what would be planted because a large percentage of arable land around Riga was used to grow potatoes which in turn would be made into *fri*. No doubt, Peteris dreamed of a long-term contract with Macdonald's, the one smack-dab in the middle of central Riga. Good luck!

Vizma was startled back to the present by a large stork which had landed on a nearby fence-post. Maybe she'd been too hasty. She had bought into the local folklore and took the presence of the stork to mean that the farmer was in for a streak of good fortune. Maybe even a contract with McDonald's!

The stork flew off to join its companions high up in the treetops. Vizma closed her eyes and imagined what it had been like in her grandmother's time when the meadows were full of daisies and wild flowers, when wedding feasts lasted three full days and tables groaned with home cooked delicacies and everyday life came to a standstill.

There would be cups of bouillon accompanied by tiny delicate *pīragi*, platters bearing whole poached salmon, their delicate pink flesh decorated by overlapping slivers of cucumbers, heaping bowls of cold creamy potato salad, glass jars of herring nestled in with thinly sliced carrots, onion and pickles, a whole side of roasted meat, home-made cheeses, some white and soft, others hard and brown in their skins of rind.

There'd be jugs of home-made beer to quench the dancers' thirst and speed the feast on its way. Nearby, an army of helpers kept their eyes alert for any empty dish or jug. Then, just when everyone would be slowing down, compotes, cakes, cookies, sweet wine and urns of freshly made coffee with heavy cream would appear. All this, punctuated by laughter, songs, and toasts. Over the meadow she could hear the voices of children playing, couples dancing to accordion music. She remembered a song her grandmother had taught her:

> *Thrice the sunrise, thrice the sunset*
> *At my sister's wedding feast.*
> *The table groaned and broke it's legs*
> *And I broke my shoes while dancing.*

Vizma had been jealous of Arnie's new found life as she listened to his description of his daily routine, especially when he told her about the *pirts* sauna that he enjoyed at the end of each day. Some of the wood that Arnie had cut himself would be used to heat the boulders, later to be doused with water when the heat had reached such a temperature as to make everyone sweat. Arnie could still only stand the steam for a few minutes. He'd been told that in winter, the men rubbed down with snow afterwards. When Vizma suggested that they try it together, he had to tell her that the women took their saunas separately. What a disappointment!

Arnie's description made Vizma decide that she wanted to join him to experience this first hand for herself. She felt she had been denied a side of Latvian life that few of the expats ever experienced.

Arnie had told her about his visit to one of the neighbour's farms. It was a relic from the Soviet era of collective farming which had left the land in ruins with soil erosion, derelict farm buildings and drainage systems beyond repair. Under Communism, survival had depended entirely on the small private plots where each worker was allowed to grow vegetables for his own family. Most farmers had been able to grow enough to sell at the local markets and so a tiny bit of money had come in.

As they talked, Arnie and Vizma had been sitting in the grove of tall white birch trees that encircled the farmhouse of their hosts. Nearby, was the small greenhouse which was filled with carnations for the flower market—the very carnations that had allowed Marta and Peteris small luxuries like coffee and oranges.

After their harrowing experience in Riga, both Vizma and Arnie had revelled in the sense of peace and security which their new surroundings had given them. Like true Latvians, they had inherited a love of nature from their parents who had never stopped telling them about their memories of country life. As Latvians, they were inextricably tied to the natural world around them. Folk songs, poetry and the ancient nature-centred religion still spoke to them.

Even though she had agreed to Arnie's request, Vizma was reluctant to go back to Riga so soon. She could go native very easily. Rise with the sun each morning, milk the cows, feed the pigs and chickens, work in the potato fields, then the sauna and hours by the bonfire, drinking beer and singing all night.

She had been listening to the birds chirping in the trees, feeling better than she had in months.

"I'm really enjoying this, Arnie. The air is just so fresh and clean after Riga. Why don't I stay over tonight and go back to town on the first train tomorrow morning? Would you mind?"

"I suppose that would be alright," Arnie said, not being able to think of an excuse. "I'll have to talk to Peteris and Marta."

"Come on. Let's go and ask him. There he is coming out of the carnation house."

Before Arnie could ask, Peteris announced,

"Marta is cooking dinner for all of us and she thinks you'd better stay overnight."

Vizma gave Arnie a playful little hip check.

"You read my mind, Peteris. That would be great!"

When they walked through the door, it was really nice to feel the warmth of the wood fire burning in the huge cast iron stove that dominated the large kitchen. The long wooden table by the window was covered with a white linen tablecloth on which sat a ceramic pitcher filled with red carnations. Plain wooden chairs surrounded the table. Vizma saw that two doors led off the kitchen and decided these were the bedrooms. The floor was bare wood, scrubbed clean every day.

Before supper, Vizma and Marta went to the *pirts*. Fresh and rosy, they ran back to the house. Peteris had set the table and lit candles. Everything was home-made and produced on the farm. Delicious cabbage soup, bread, pickles, butter churned by hand, cured ham, cheese and plenty of wonderful dark home-brewed ale. For dessert they had *kompots* of stewed fruit. They ended the evening with Vizma's gift—a bottle of Metaxa brandy.

Vizma was happy, truly happy, as she sunk her clean well-fed body into the soft mattress and pulled the enormous eiderdown up around her. She smiled and stretched luxuriously. Snoring peacefully just a few feet away lay Arnie, off in his own little la-la land. In a strange way, Vizma found his snoring mysteriously erotic. She sighed happily as a sliver of moon peeked into the window. Then one of the glittering crystals up in the velvety sky winked down at her. There really *is* a God, she said to herself as exhaustion swept over her like a warm blanket. Still smiling, she closed her eyes and fell instantly fast asleep.

Chapter Thirty-Four

Vizma liked Arnie, liked him a lot. He pushed all her buttons without even trying. Still, she wondered how far she could safely allow herself to be drawn into the spider's web of bizarre connections that seemed to centre on Anda. Anda and her missing boyfriend, her missing niece, her dead sister. She wasn't sure that Arnie's interest in Anda was just professional. But Vizma could understand why Arnie was hooked on this story. Even she was, even though she sensed the danger. She realized from the tone of Arnie's voice while they were waiting for the train to appear how desperate he was to connect with Anda.

How would she approach Anda? And when? Well, not the lunch hour because she might not be there. After thinking about the various possibilities, Vizma settled on the plan of going to the bookstore straight from the train station. It would be about ten thirty.

Vizma wiggled on the wooden banquette, hipbone aching from the rough ride on the un-upholstered seat. Across from her sat an older man. His eyes were bleary and he smelled of beer. So early in the morning, the smell suffocated her.

Vizma reached over and tried to get the window open. It didn't budge. From the corner of her eye she saw that the old man was pulling himself up to help her. At the next lurch of the train, she drew back, instinctively sensing what was about to happen. With a loud 'Oy!' the man pitched forward, falling on top of her while his out-stretched hand landed on her breast. For a minute, she wondered if he'd done it deliberately. Giving him the benefit of doubt, she gently pushed him back.

Recovering from her contact with the beer-logged passenger, Vizma settled herself and checked her watch. She saw that it was only ten passed eight. Arnie had insisted that she catch the first train back to Riga. Stifling a yawn, she concentrated her gaze on the countryside flying past outside.

The train stopped at every village, gradually filling up with country people. Between each stop, the clickity-clack of the metal wheels rolling over the joins in the ties below created a symphony of background noise that freed Vizma's thoughts, if only temporarily, from worrying about what lay ahead. Her focus settled on the scenery passing by, pretty fields being readied for spring, little streams, bridges, clusters of children waving and dogs barking as they ran alongside. Then, slowly, the countryside gave way to urban sprawl and cottages were replaced by dilapidated concrete Russian apartment blocks. Here and there, a few remnants of beautiful but crumbling pre-Soviet stone buildings rolled by. The train slowed more and more, finally bumping to a stop. Moments later there she was. Back in Riga.

Even if she had wanted to, and she didn't, Vizma had no time to go back to her hotel before going to see Anda. She didn't feel like wandering through downtown Riga. She'd done enough of that. Would she go back to the apartment house to check up on Gerda? Vizma now knew Arnie well enough to have realized that she would be in the doghouse if anything happened to Gerda. She would buy some tinned shrimps from Norway. She could knock at the Cat Lady's door. Quickly, she decided that this plan was too dangerous. She wasn't about to blow her cover over a cat.

Thinking of those tinned Norway shrimps had made Vizma realize that she had eaten her breakfast at the ungodly hour of five in the morning before having her first lesson on how to milk cows. Walking slowly through the station, she decided to have a cup of coffee and a shot of brandy at a stand-up counter. This was standard fare for the Latvian commuter on his way to work and, luckily, they had all passed by an hour before. She had the counter all to herself. Already she missed the country air, the good food, the sauna, the carnations and the open fire. All too soon, her coffee cup was empty. It was time go.

The day was cloudy with a pewter-coloured sky. Feeling on edge, Vizma walked into the bookstore and saw that a few customers were browsing. A grouchy looking older man stood behind the cash register. Vizma let out a breath she hadn't even known she was holding. There she was. The girl that Vizma had been jealous of when she had monopolized Arnie before the expat dinner. She was stacking books on a table by the window. Up close, she was even prettier.

Vizma approached. She noticed that the man behind the cash had sat down and had picked up a newspaper.

"Hello," Vizma said softly. "Would you be able to help me?"

The girl turned towards Vizma, fixed wide eyes on her, recognizing the expat accent. Vizma leaned forward close to Anda and lowered her voice even more.

"I'd like to talk with you in private."

Anda's face tensed. This must be Arnie Dambergs' friend. She remembered the woman in the red dress.

"Yes, I'll show you," Anda said leading Vizma away from the cashier. They stopped at the other end of the store and looked through a rack of greeting cards.

"I have a message for you," Vizma said in a hushed tone.

"A message?"

"Yes. A message from Arnie Dambergs."

The shock on Anda's face was instant.

"What!"

"Shush." Vizma put a finger to her lips. She looked around and dropped her voice to a whisper.

"Arnie's all right. He's in hiding. He wanted you to know that he's still trying to help you."

Vizma picked up a book and moved away as other customers approached.

"Please wait for me outside," Anda whispered. "I'm going to tell the cashier I'm taking my coffee break now." She couldn't lose her chance to talk to Vizma some more.

Two minutes later, the women were together again.

"How long have you got, Anda?"

"Just fifteen minutes. Let's go next door. I need to sit down."

"Good idea."

Once they were settled at a table, Vizma noticed that Anda had slipped her feet out of her shoes and was rubbing at her ankles. Straightening up, she said to Vizma,

"My feet are always sore. I wish I had the cashier's job and could sit all day in a little booth."

They smiled at each other. Vizma decided she would stick to business and asked,

"Has Daina come back? Or have you heard from her?"

"No. No, I haven't. Daina hasn't come back. I filled out a report at the police headquarters. They told me someone would be calling me but no one has."

"Mmm," Vizma made a soothing sound. She beckoned the waiter and ordered pastries, hot chocolate for Anda and tea for herself.

There were no words Vizma could think of. She didn't know what to say about the missing girl. Anything would sound banal. She could probably come up with some hackneyed phrase about everything working out in the end. But Vizma was no Pollyanna. The girl could well have been kidnapped, raped and killed. And the police would take their sweet time doing nothing about it.

Vizma moved on to Mike.

"How about Mike? Have you heard from him? Any idea where he is? Arnie really wants to get in touch with him."

Suddenly Anda became more animated, opened up, glad to talk to someone. In a low trusting voice she told Vizma that she thought she had seen Mike with a camera bag over his shoulder on Brivibas Street two days before. Vizma could see that he really meant something to Anda as she talked about him. But Anda had rushed on, telling Vizma that she suspected Sasha was involved in Daina's disappearance.

"Slow down, Anda," Vizma said. "I don't know who Sasha is."

Anda turned down the corners of her mouth and did an eye-roll.

"I'm sorry to say, he's my brother-in-law. And he's Daina's stepfather. He had the nerve to leave everything to me and took off for Moscow again right after my sister's funeral."

"Sounds like a real jerk," Vizma said contemptuously.

"And my sister put up with that. For years."

"Well, I couldn't. And I bet you wouldn't tolerate a moment of abuse. You look too smart for that."

"But listen to this. A few days after the funeral, when I started to think more clearly, I realized that Sasha went off to Moscow the same day Daina disappeared."

Vizma shook her head in amazement. "Is Daina the sort of girl who would go off like that without saying something to her mother?"

Anda sighed. "Anything's possible. Sasha could have told her some story."

Anda finished up with a description of her daily grind with Vilnis without any financial support from her rotten brother-in-law who had only shown interest in Daina.

Vizma kept thinking about Sasha and Daina.

"Did you confront Sasha? Did you ask him about Daina? Did you tell the police about this?"

Anda replied with a typical Latvian shrug, as if to say, what's to be done by going to the police and Vizma realized it was a cultural lapse on her part to have even mention it.

"Did you confront Sasha directly? What does your father say?"

"I tried to…but you don't understand. If I accused him, he'd have his friends take me out to the woods and shoot me."

Vizma's eyebrows shot up. "God!" she stared at the girl. "Answer me, Anda. Did you tell your father?"

Embarrassed, Anda continued,

"My father and his friends are secretive, doing things on the Internet all the time and they stop talking when I come into the room. I don't understand when I do hear them talking. It's all computer talk. I don't know computers. Then they switch to video cameras. Once, one of my father's friends made a joke about Daina being such a pretty girl and my father laughed but told him to shut up."

After a pause, Anda said a hard tone,

"My father didn't have anything to do with Daina's disappearance."

Vizma pinched her lips together and said nothing. But if she had, the words would have been, "Listen, you say that with so much conviction but I know you're not sure. I don't like the sound of what you're not telling me."

Chapter Thirty-Five

Usually, when Anda was told to unpack a shipment of new books, she found that time passed slowly alone in the stockroom. But today, she was glad to be on her own. She was still reeling from the news she had got from Vizma.

Arnie Dambergs was alive! She felt a new surge of hope. He would help her find Daina. But his friend, Vizma, looked much less glamorous than when Anda had first seen her. Her hair was so ugly. Why had she dyed it and permed it?

These two were the only expats she had ever met. They were quite ordinary, spoke Latvian quite well, even though they had a funny accent and often had to search for words. But they didn't fit her mental image. In her mind, expats or foreigners, as they were called, were like birds of paradise, free to fly wherever they wanted, free to do whatever they wished. She realized that these two were different. They had clearly become involved in something dangerous and had been touched with the reality of Latvian life. Vizma had warned her not to say a word about Arnie. No matter how glad she felt, Anda knew she had to be careful.

That evening, she decided to call her parents and see if they would take Vilnis with them to the cottage. A neighbour had offered to drive them. Anda needed a break and her nephew needed to blow off steam in the fresh air. There were moments during her new life with Vilnis when she felt absolutely desperate for some time to herself. It was more of an adjustment than she had imagined. Besides, this was a special day for her.

Early in the morning, she had packed a bag for Vilnis with a change of clothes, his teddy bear and a tiny chocolate surprise. He had been excited that he was going to the cottage even if it meant having to put up with his grandfather. But when she told him that she wasn't going with them, he had been disappointed. He startled Anda by kicking at his back-pack and threatening to run away. It took her almost an hour to calm him down. The pain in his voice tugged at her heart and she wanted to hug him. But Vilnis pushed her away. His emotional outburst made her realize how hurt he was and how they had bonded with each other.

She ached for Vilnis even though she was glad to see him go for the weekend.

At the end, he had been persuaded to go with his grandparents. Anda had bribed him with the promise of a new kitten since her no-name slasher cat had been run over by a car tearing out of a parking spot in the courtyard.

As the two of them walked slowly down to Matisa Street, something chilling and horrible shifted inside her. She was still going over her meeting with Vizma the day before and wondered if she had been wrong to talk about the conversation between her father and his drunken friends. Even though they had been drinking, she knew they were deadly serious about people making money by showing pictures of their kids on the Internet.

The men had guffawed, made some stupid comments and the conversation had quickly veered back to cars and hunting. At the time, Anda hadn't fully taken in what the men were talking about but now she felt a chill. Did people really do things like that? She knew that desperately poor people could be driven to almost anything in order to survive. And a picture was just a picture, would be how they would justify it in their own mind. But the way the men had laughed had given her the creeps. Stupid old men. They didn't have a clue about computers.

Anda had never got along with her father. There were times, she wondered if Ivan even was her father. Now she felt sympathy for Vilnis. What was it about the women in her family that made them choose Russian husbands? She wondered if it was some kind of negative attraction. Were they looking for punishment? Was their self-esteem so low? Her sister Silvia had married Sasha. Her mother had married Ivan. And, oddly enough, her Russian father had chosen to take the name of his Latvian bride, perhaps having an intimation that Latvia would once again be independent and that a Latvian name would make life easier. She promised herself that she would never marry a Russian. Now, Anda revelled in the thought of having a weekend to herself. She'd catch up on sleep, phone a friend and maybe go to a movie.

Anda and Vilnis had come to the end of their journey. After saying goodbye, she stood alone in the courtyard as four old people, a dog and a child piled into the beat-up old Japanese sardine can. It coughed a few times, managed to turn over, then bleated at the pedestrians who refused to get out of the way. After several minutes, the wreck managed to pull out of the courtyard and onto Matisa Street. From there, it would lumber its way across Riga and on to Saulkrasti. Anda blew Vilnis a kiss and hoped that the car wouldn't break down half way there and that it wouldn't rain cats and dogs all weekend long.

To comfort herself, Anda pictured Vilnis running on the beach with the neighbour's dog, then sitting by a bonfire at night and toasting sausages. At least, that's what she hoped for, providing that the men didn't get drunk or that the dog didn't run away or that it didn't rain.

When Anda had finished her housework, she sat down to read the Saturday edition of *Diena* that she had bought at a kiosk on her way back to the apartment. She hadn't realized how quiet it would be without Vilnis and was glad to have the distraction of reading the paper. She had seen the headline on the front page. The article that Rihards Plavins had written about the sex slave trade was on the second page. She started to read it but found it so disgusting that she couldn't finish. She remembered that at the end of their meeting, Rihards had suggested that Anda call him when the article appeared. Anda decided that this was as good a time as ever. Just like the first time when she had called, she was surprised to find him at his office. And even more surprised when he suggested lunch.

Anda was thrilled at the invitation. Since waking up she had known something good would happen this day. And, for once, she didn't have to hurry. They had agreed to meet at the Bistro at one o'clock.

Anda arrived first, took a table by the window, ordered a beer and enjoyed the anticipation of company and a good lunch. She felt comfortable in the warm cocoon of the restaurant and noticed how pretty the embroidered tablecloth was. She sniffed at the small bouquet of carnations in the ceramic vase. They were real but had no perfume. She fingered the cloth napkins and examined the pictures on the wall. She supposed that the pictures were art and tried to understand how a few triangles floating in a sea of murky grey deserved to be put in a frame and on a wall. She shrugged. There were many things she didn't understand.

Anda sighed. Her sigh went unnoticed. A comforting hum came from the other tables while Vivaldi played softly in the background. The Bistro was almost full and she felt lucky to get a table by the window. She probably should have waited to be shown to a table but not today. She wanted the best.

From her vantage-point, he could see people passing by. It was almost as good as she imagined it would be to sit at a sidewalk café on the Left Bank in Paris. She could hear *La Vie En Rose* on the accordion. It was spring. Love was in the air. But Anda was miles and aeons away from Paris. The street she was looking at was grey and drab and the people walking by looked gloomy and worried, except for the few tourists who stuck out from the crowd with their well kept appearance and superior air.

Anda thought of Arnie Dambergs and smiled. He was different. He didn't make her feel inferior. Arnie was real. And he was alive! But now she had to remind herself not to let it slip out.

Her thoughts slid back to romance. Was she interested in Rihards? Well, she was alive wasn't she? She liked to dream a little. The two of them walking along the banks of the Seine with Notre Dame resplendent in the background. They would stop at the Quai Aux Fleurs and he would buy her a bouquet of lily of the valley.

And here he was, coming towards the restaurant. Tall, light brown hair, grey eyes. She liked the way he looked, natural, healthy and full of life. It wasn't hard to pretend that he was her lover.

Her daydream vanished in a heartbeat as Uldis Baltins rushed up to greet Rihards at the door. She knew that he was the owner of the restaurant but hadn't expected the effusive personal greeting that he gave Rihards. Wearing a dazzling unwrinkled white shirt closed at the neck and buttons pulled taut over his protruding gut, he put one arm over Rihards shoulder while he shook his hand with the other. Anda found it bizarre and disturbing that Rihards Plavins, who had just written an article about sex slaves, was on such good terms with Baltins, one of the organizers of the Young Miss Latvia contest. She shuddered as she thought of Daina locked up in some dark dank hole in Pardaugava.

Rihards approached and, as he pulled out the chair opposite her, flashed a smile, apologizing for being late. Although he wasn't. Once seated, he handed Anda his article.

Pushing the sheets of paper away, Anda said quietly, "This is sickening. I've already looked at your story. I couldn't finish it. It was too horrible. That part about those poor women selling meat out of plastic bags and then finding out that the meat was human."

Anda grimaced, pinched her nose while covering her mouth. The very idea was repugnant.

"That's right. The flesh came from a cancer ward," Rihards continued.

Anda didn't respond. She was speechless with horror.

"It's hard to take but people have to know what's happening in the world around them. The worst of this goes on in the Balkans."

"Well, probably in Russia too, don't you think?"

"Yes, I'm afraid so. There's an AIDS epidemic in Russia."

"Could you get AIDS by eating infected human flesh?" Anda was drawn in by the horror. "Could you get cancer that way?"

Rihards gave her an odd look. Then he shrugged. That wasn't his field. He couldn't say. Anda continued.

"What about here? What's going on in Latvia?"

"It's not that bad here, I don't think. I'm sure there are brothels. But no NATO soldiers to pay for the girls. No American military installations. It's always money that drives the market."

Anda leaned closer to Rihards and whispered, "I've heard that there are people who create pedophile bulletin boards on computers. Sell pictures of their own children."

"That goes on everywhere now. It's horrible too," Rihards said with a shake of his head.

The conversation was starting to make him feel slightly sick. He looked up at the waiter hovering by his elbow and asked Anda if she was ready to order. They both turned silent as they read the menu. Anda looked up first and announced that she would like a *karbonade* and some noodles. No meat for Rihards. The thought of meat after what they had talked about made him queasy. He ordered an omelette.

Anda changed the conversation like a frustrated person flipping TV channels.

"It's my birthday today!" she blurted out. "I'm another year older, an old lady."

Rihards looked surprised, then delighted.

"Well, this calls for champagne, Anda. Aren't you going to tell me which birthday it is? I'm going to take an extra hour for lunch to help you celebrate."

Anda blushed. She stared down at the tablecloth and, before she knew it, the embroidered flowers melted in a blurry pool. She had decided earlier not to talk about it being her birthday but it had just come out. Today there had been no gifts and even her mother had forgotten, grieving for Silvia and worried about Daina.

When the champagne arrived, Anda felt happy again, totally relaxed. She drank a glass. Then another. Thoughts were running slow-motion through her head as she sipped the bubbly liquid. She mused out loud,

"This is so nice and when I see Arnie Dambergs again I..." she blinked a few times. Didn't finish the sentence.

Rihards' eyes widened. Anda's words caught him like an elbow in the ribs. He leaned over and refilled her glass. Anda had compressed her lips. Her face was flushed.

"I'm asking you to trust me, Anda. Can you do that?" Rihards' voice was warm, his eyes sincere.

"What do you mean?" Anda looked at him, disconcerted. "I'm only just babbling. I'm not used to drinking."

"Arnie Dambergs is alive, isn't he?" Rihards tried to sound casual, not overly interested, even though his journalist's instincts had already sounded the *achtung* alarm.

Anda shook her head.

"Oh, I don't know. I'm not sure if he is or isn't. But I hope you won't write anything in the paper about him." Anda lowered her voice. "It could put many people in danger."

"Of course not," Rihards said, dying to get back to his office. Within moments, he had composed the article in his head. What a pity he couldn't just run off. To be decent, he would give the birthday girl another twenty minutes. But not a moment longer. Rihards felt sure he was going places with this one. A few scoops like this and they would have to hire him for that TV newscaster job he was after. Why else had he spent all that money getting his teeth capped?

Anda was a nice enough girl but his career meant everything to him. He used people. And in turn, they used him, to plant stories, to get publicity. That was the name of the game. Besides, he owed it to his readers to keep them up-dated. To hell with Arnie Dambergs.

The same sour-puss waiter who had brought the meal approached their table and picked up their plates. Would they like coffee? A pastry? More wine?

Rihards looked at Anda. She looked uncertain. He felt he needed to cajole her. Maybe she had more information. Exactly where was this famous Arnie Dambergs hiding? For a second, he felt guilty and felt that buying Anda a good dessert would somehow get him off the hook.

"Yes, why not," he said hiding his impatience. He hadn't had a cigarette in four years. He felt a surge of adrenaline coursing through his blood. He was dying for a smoke. But he would have to wait.

Chapter Thirty-Six

Surprise, motherfuckers! Bang! Bang! Bang! Don Fischer's mind was in high gear. *Bang!* He shot again with his make-believe gun, which happened to be one of his shoe-horns. Nothing of the distinguished diplomat remained. His face was contorted and he was laughing wildly imagining the look on Maija's face. He would burst in on her décor love nest, blow them both out of the water. She and that Russian of hers had done the unthinkable, had insulted his masculinity.

Don was standing in his shirttails, pantless with suspenders still holding up his socks. He had just taken off his shoes, having tiptoed across the broadloom rug of the master bedroom that he shared, for the time being, with his wife. He was very late returning from yet another reception at the Embassy and he had found Maija asleep in their king-size bed.

Real guns were hard to get in Latvia, not that he didn't have contacts. With his money and his connections, he could easily order a hit. One thousand US would probably do it. But he needed the satisfaction of hands-on. He could strangle her, haul her into the bath, drown her. Still, the sudden death of two wives in a row could prove to be a problem. He knew that the case was still open in Chicago. He would have to think carefully. Maybe he'd let someone else do the heavy work after all. Get someone to kidnap her, chain her up, blindfold her, then not pay the ransom. Humiliate her, make her suffer, then have her dumped somewhere.

As soon as he opened the cupboard door to hang up his suit, he heard her voice.

"Is that you, Don?"

"Who do you think, Princess," he muttered under his breath adding more quietly, "Were you hoping for Sasha? Sorry to disappoint you."

Maija propped herself up on her pillows and turned on her bedside lamp. She had been crying. Sasha had let her down again. More than anything, she was mad at herself, horrified that she had fallen for a Russian hustler. For an instant, she wondered if Don knew. Surely not, she said to herself.

"Could you bring me some Tylenol, honey. I've got a terrible headache."

Don grimaced. A headache is nothing compared to what's coming, slut-face, he muttered under his breath as he rummaged in the medicine cabinet. If he could give her an overdose, he would.

"Bad day, darling? I missed you at the reception. Everyone asked where you were. Where were you, by the way?"

Don came toward her carrying a glass of water and the Tylenol. As she raised her gaze to him, sudden fear gripped her. Her husband loomed over her, his face partly hidden in the shadows. Without seeing his eyes, she could sense that something was wrong. *He knows.* So what! She gave an inner shrug. She had been through this scene a couple of times before.

"Yes. It was hectic. The beauty contest scandal is draining. I don't really know what's going on because their office has been shut down and the phones have been disconnected. It's all Arnie Dambergs' doing. He's nuts. I just don't believe any of his story."

Maija knew she was a good actress but this time she surpassed herself. She knew that bringing up Arnie Dambergs was like putting out a false scent that would throw Don off her trail. The mere mention of Arnie's name made Don scrunch up his face as if he was smelling a pig farm. He had rolled his eyes up so far that he was seeing stars.

"Well, if you'd been there tonight, you'd realize that there are people who actually believe every word that Arnie Dambergs writes in that rag of his. The Ambassador has personally warned me to stay away from anything to do with that damn Miss Latvia Contest and I advise you to do the same. If not on your own account, then think about me and the position you've put me in. Now, I'll thank you to never mention that Dambergs man to me again."

Don's face took on a sinister look. He knew he had to extinguish the porno story before things got completely out of control.

"By the way, Don dear, and I hate to bring this up just now, but you haven't paid the rent on Gertrudes Street this month. If you write the cheque first thing tomorrow before you go to the office, then I can take it with me and give it to the property manager. You won't forget will you, even if I'm not up when you leave?"

"Yes, dear," Don replied smiling to himself at the thought of the fireworks to come knowing full well that hell would have to freeze over first.

Fifteen minutes later, Don was snoring gently from the far side of their bed. Maija had not gone back to sleep. In fact, she was feeling queasy. In fact, she'd been feeling queasy all day. But now, holding her arms across her stomach, she hurried to the bathroom. Taking care to close the door behind her, she threw up into the toilet. For the first time in her life, she wondered if she could be pregnant.

Chapter Thirty-Seven

Don Fischer was a neat freak. Everyone at the embassy knew that. Countless times, he had chewed out a secretary for moving his papers an inch or two on his desk or messing with the way he arranged his pens in a little glass holder, tips down, colours lined up in his own special order. It didn't take a genius to know that men who were that neat liked to be in control of everything and everyone around them. His staff certainly knew that.

Don had exploded with all the fury of a bomb when he learned that some files had been displaced at the office on Brivibas Street. He had offered to give Maija a hand with some of the paperwork at the Young Miss Latvia contest. She had been making a mess of things because she was short of time and Don, who uncharacteristically kept saying, "Here, let me help you," insisted that everything be done right. But his good will toward Maija had run its course. Today, he was furious at her.

Don Fischer had just turned sixty but he looked eighty. His white pasty skin was bloated and blotchy. His eyes were sunken into his white skull and underneath were puffy yellowish bags of excess body fluid which were always worse in the morning.

He knew exactly what was going on. Wifey dearest was a slut. She and that Russian scumbag of hers were having an affair, out in the open, for everyone to see. No fool like an old fool, he said to himself bitterly, the corners of his mouth scowling downwards. He was probably the last to know. It was *one thing* for him to have something on the side. He was discreet about it. It was *quite another thing* for Maija to cuckold him in public and he was damned if he would go on funding her. As well as feeling public humiliation, he was furious that he had lost his control over her.

But what got to him even more was Arnie Dambergs' sex trade exposé. Maija had whetted Arnie's appetite with that free-wheeling interview she'd done with him, blabbing her head off from that chinzy overdone pad that she called her office and that *he* was paying for. He knew she was using to have it off with some Russian. He had decided that this was going to come to end so fast it would make Maija's head spin. He almost smiled imaging the snit-fit he knew he could expect. He knew Maija would go ballistic and he almost looked forward to it.

There had been rumours that Don's first wife's death had been disguised as suicide. The fifty year old woman had been found in her car, the motor running, the garage door closed, a garden hose hooked up to the exhaust pipe. There had been no suicide note. There had been suspicion that she had been murdered and then her body moved to the car.

Don knew he was vulnerable. After all, this was why he had been only too glad to get this posting to Latvia. He had wanted to re-establish a low profile and now, because of Maija, here he was right back on front-page news.

He was going to be late if he didn't hurry. This was one time he did not want to make an entrance. Better to get to this lunch in time to blend in with the other guests. But he would make sure he was immaculately groomed, up to his usual performance. He'd been nicknamed the Teflon Man back in Chicago, hadn't he? Well, he'd make sure he earned the title here in Riga as well. He'd be his usual debonair charming self but he'd have to be careful not to overdo it.

He thanked God that Maija hadn't shown up. She was just too unpredictable and might lose it completely if somebody asked directly about the article in *WOW!*. Still, things weren't looking too good. He wasn't sure, but he thought the Ambassador had cut him from next month's social calendar at the embassy.

Maija had been at her office since nine o'clock. That was early for her. There was work to do. She really needed this contract because she realized that she might have to pay the rent herself.

With her coffee close at hand, she was at her computer fine-tuning her decorating proposal when she got an email alert. She checked at once and saw that it was from a name she didn't recognize. She looked at her watch. Email always took up more time that she allotted it but today, she couldn't be late. She saw that she still would have plenty of time to go home to dress and then drive to the US Ambassador's residence for his wife's birthday party, a private affair for two hundred.

Maija felt self-satisfied at being included in this event. She'd been dieting for a week and couldn't wait to pig out on all the freebie food. She'd tried on the to-die-for little black sheath she'd picked up in Milan on her last trip. God! That had been fun! No Don, just his credit card. The dress had been too tight for her then but, this morning, she had managed to do up the zipper.

She knew she'd get admiring glances from all the men and would upstage the Ambassador's birthday girl who was a perfect career diplomat's wife, not a hair out of place, a firm handshake and a good grasp of protocol. Maija knew this lady wouldn't say shit if her life depended on it.

Maija had been waiting for Hotmail to pop up on her screen and just then it did. She ran her eyes down the list of unread mail and saw a couple of names she recognized. Glad to see that the North Carolina supplier had answered her inquiry about the delivery date for the fabric she was waiting for, she hoping that it would be good news. Then she saw a name she didn't recognize. Probably could wait. But then her curiosity got the better of her. She opened it.

Dear Mrs. Fischer, There's something you should know about your husband. I have to warn you about him because he killed my sister.

When Maija had finished reading it, she sat back in her swivel chair, lost in her own thoughts which started with a brief nod to serendipity, perfect timing, divine intervention and ended with how she would screw Don for every penny. She had certainly earned it.

Chapter Thirty-Eight

The gloves were off.

"You killed her and I can prove it." Maija's voice was soft and deadly. Her eyes were cold as she stood by the writing-table a few feet away from her husband.

Don looked up from his paperwork. His face suddenly turned a greenish shade of pale.

"What!" He was confronted by a stranger. He had never seen her like this.

"What!" he shot out again, this time louder. His mouth flapped open. He gaped like a fish. "What the hell are you talking about?"

She was ready for this. Her eyes were slits.

"You *know* what I'm talking about. I'm talking about Chicago."

Don struggled to speak, his jaw nearly cracking with the effort.

"You're fishing…just fishing," he spat out. He could feel his nerves drawing tighter and tighter. He was ready to explode.

"No, I'm not," she said calmly her mouth curving into a nasty smile. "And you know it."

The smile infuriated him. He had to clamp down on the urge to grab her and rip it off her face.

"You crazy bitch!" The fury that surged through him was volcanic. Fighting for control, he took a couple of deep breaths and clenched his fists at his side. He could feel himself getting closer and closer to a major eruption. But he had to hold on. He had to find out what she really knew.

Maija was shaken but managed to stand her ground. She was pleased to see that his face had turned beet red and that the large knotty vein on his forehead was standing out.

"Calm down, Don. We can work this out."

"Work what out?" Hatred rose up like molten lava, coursed through his chest to the base of his throat.

Maija kept smiling. It took all of Don's strength to resist the urge to smash his fist into that face. His molars were sore from gritting his teeth. In a hoarse voice, he managed to say,

"Blackmail? Is that what you're up to? Do *you* really think you can shake *me* down?"

"Well…" Her tone was almost playful now.

"So, that's it. So, you think you're going to blackmail me? Let's have it. What do you think you've got to hold over my head?"

"Oh…let me see now. Ah yes, there was that call from… guess where? From *Chicago*, Don! A very interesting call. And it gets better. I have some info from your former sister-in-law. Remember her?"

Her words hit their mark like bullets.

"You bitch! How in the world…"

" I told you, calm down and never mind how. So, do you want to talk?" She looked straight at him, still with a glint of a smile in her eyes. She wasn't afraid.

"How much do you think I'm good for, Maija?"

"I don't want much. You keep up the payments on Gertrudes Street. Leave me alone. That's all. It's really so simple." She felt a rush of pleasure. It was working.

"I'll think about it."

"The rent is due tomorrow. I don't want to lose the place."

"I'm sure you don't." Patience, he told himself. His mind was already planning how he was going to get rid of this millstone.

"Oh, you can't possibly be jealous," she laughed in his face. "The ball's in your court, Don. If you can't see this as a good deal for you, you're really in trouble."

"Fine," he said flatly. The back of his shirt was sweat-drenched. He was trying not to wonder about what she knew. What could she possibly know? But he couldn't take any chances. There were too many problems right now. He'd have to deal with them one by one.

"Thanks," Maija said with haughty indifference. She turned very slowly, very deliberately and sauntered out the door. That was the joy of being Maija. She always won.

Chapter Thirty-Nine

Anda struggled with her keys without removing her heavy shopping bag from her arm. It was awkward but she managed to get the door open and quickly dumped out the groceries she had bought on her way home from work. She checked the clock and saw that she still had a few minutes before her mother was to arrive bringing Vilnis home. She would just be able to get the dinner on the stove. She wanted to sit down and read Rihard Plavins' most recent article in the paper but it would have to wait until Vilnis had been put to bed. She glanced at the headline.

CHILD PORN WHISTLEBLOWER ALIVE!

Anda gasped, struggled for composure. Rihards had betrayed her and it hadn't taken him long. Rage and shame washed over her. She had botched up everything. And what a naïve ninny she had been. A bit of flattery, a glass of champagne and she had started to babble, trusting a complete stranger.

She paced furiously through her apartment, using her excess energy to clean the bathroom, dust in the living room and set the small table in the kitchen. But first, she had put a pot of her home-made chicken soup on the stove and plunked a bunch of bananas into a bowl. Twice, she had gone to the phone and, holding his business card, had started to punch in Rihards Plavins' office number. But both times, she had stopped midway. What's the use of giving him a piece of her mind? It wasn't going to change anything now. Her mother would be delivering Vilnis soon. She had to get a hold of herself. She couldn't take her anger out on the child.

She couldn't forgive herself. She had put them all in danger— Arnie, Vizma, Daina. What could she do now? Write to the editor about the false story? Tell him she had seen Arnie's body wash up on the shores of Jurmala? They needed a body. For one insane moment, she thought of talking to Sasha. Hell, he'd know how to get his hands on a body.

It was at times like this that Anda felt that her world was falling apart, the people in it disappearing. She forced herself to stop thinking about Daina. She looked at her watch. Her mother had said that Vilnis would be back before supper. She started to worry about one of her father's Internet predators. Could someone have got to Vilnis?

Hearing noises outside, she hurried to the door. She was looking forward to hearing Vilnis' excited chatter about the events of his day. Suddenly, she stopped. There was dead silence behind the door. She knew Vilnis was a chatterbox. Who was this? For a moment, she debated whether to go back and get her Mace. But no. She couldn't live with fear in her own home. She went to the door. Latched on the chain. Unlocked the door. Through the tiny wedge she saw him.

"Anda, it's me, Mike. Let me in," he hissed through the crack in the door. His voice was ragged and tired. Anda saw his teeth, nicotine-stained, broken. His hands were jammed into his pockets. He looked as if he hadn't changed his clothes in weeks.

For a wild moment, she wondered if he had a gun or maybe a knife. She stood frozen, staring at him, not knowing what to do. So much had happened. Mike seemed like a stranger to her now, not coming to her like the lover she had waited for a lifetime ago. She was almost afraid of him. He looked like a *bomžik*. Anda couldn't imagine how Mike could do that to himself, live on the street like a bum. He smelled and his appearance repelled her.

"Please, Anda." Mike lowered his head, took a rag out of his pocket and blew his nose.

She continued to stare at him for just an instant before quickly slipping back the chain. She was startled by the way Mike pushed past her. After closing the door, she leaned against it for support, feeling her heart hammering in her chest, her legs trembling.

"I have to talk to you, Anda." Mike was still whispering.

The light glinted off his glasses and she couldn't make out the expression in his eyes. Anda's gaze slid over the torn jacket, the rumpled jeans, the boots which were worn and dirty. A stubbly beard and unkempt hair covered most of his face. His voice pleaded with her, his hands clasped so tightly that his knuckles were white.

"Sit down," Anda said evenly. "I could make us some coffee."

Mike shook his head. "Anda, where are the photos?" He tapped a cigarette loose from his pack and clamped it between his lips.

From the kitchen, the telephone sounded its high pitched ring. Oh God! What now! Anda got up and rushed to answer it. She heard her mother's voice.

"Vilnis has a fever. We're keeping him here for the night."

Anda drew in her breath. "Have you called the doctor?"

261

"There's a paediatrician who lives on the third floor. She gets home at nine. I'll ask her to come see him. Don't worry."

But Anda did worry. She put the phone down, sighed and walked back into the living room. Her anxious inner voice nagged her to run see Vilnis. But, looking over at Mike, she knew she had to deal with him first.

"The photos. Where are they?" His voice was gruff, angry.

"They're safe, Mike. You have to trust me. Where have you been?"

Mike hesitated. He shot a stream of smoke up at the ceiling.

"I would like coffee after all," he said inhaling deeply.

Anda fanned the air and opened a window on her way to the kitchen.

"It'll have to be instant this time," she called back.

Mike looked up at her as she brought in a tray. She had prepared two mugs of coffee and had scattered some biscuits on a small dish.

"I'm listening, Mike," she said grimly, settling herself on the couch. Whatever his story, she could hardly wait till he left. She was exhausted and her mind kept meandering back to Vilnis and back to Daina and back to all the horrors that Rihards had told her about. She hoped that she was wrong about her father and his weird friends with their pervy interest in the Internet.

As if to shield herself, Anda picked up a pillow to hug, still expecting a soft bit of fluff to leap up into her lap, settle down and start to purr. She missed her no-name cat, still shuddered remembering the moment she had seen the lifeless body in the courtyard. She shook her head and forced her mind back to Mike.

"I was in an alcohol treatment clinic in Jelgava."

"Heavens, Mike! I didn't know your drinking was so bad."

"Well, to be honest, it wasn't. I drank myself crazy one night. The cops picked me up and somehow I managed to talk them into referring me to a doctor. That's how I got into the clinic."

"Are you cured?"

"Cured? I'm alive, that's the main thing. I'd better tell you what happened before I got to the clinic."

Anda's eyes widened. She was all ears.

"You know that I was working for this Arnie Dambergs, right?"

Anda nodded.

"I had to see him one night. I had to show him the photographs I had found while I was doing a shoot at the Young Miss Latvia office."

"You mean, those horrible pictures? The picture of Daina too?"

"Yes. I was looking for my folder of negatives when I glanced into this envelope and just couldn't believe my eyes."

"I'm glad it wasn't you that took those pictures. At first I thought..."

"God! I'd never get into that! This Don Fischer guy was there to see his wife. I heard them arguing in the next room. Just as I stuck the envelope under my jacket, Don Fischer came in and asked me what I was doing there. I told him that I was on my way to an appointment and I got the hell out."

Anda sucked in air. "Go on," she urged. She forgot all about Vilnis and Rihards Plavins and couldn't wait to hear what had happened next.

"But, before I reached Arnie's house, I realized that I was being followed. I tried to lose my shadow and decided to duck in through the garage. The door was easy to open. Once inside in the dark, I heard footsteps behind me. I turned just as a hammer was about to land on my head. I pushed the guy away as hard as I could. I think he must have caught his heel in a crack in the cement floor. He fell backwards and hit his head. It happened so fast. All I wanted to do was protect myself. The guy just lay there on the floor. He didn't move."

Anda placed a hand over her heart.

"You killed him!"

Mike's face darkened. "I didn't mean to. It was self-defence, Anda. He would have killed me, I'm sure of that. He had this hammer and was trying to hit me. I didn't know he would fall."

"Then what happened?" Anda felt a flicker of fear. She could be serving coffee to a murderer. Don't be silly, she said to herself realizing the danger Mike had put himself in by making off with the photographs.

"I dragged him into a corner of the garage. Then I went to get my car. I put him into the trunk, drove a few miles and dumped him into the Daugava. He's fish food now."

Anda's mouth hung open in shock.

"You didn't think of going to the police?"

"Hah!" Mike let out a bitter laugh. "That would have make everything worse."

"But you still had the photos?"

"Yes. That's when I came over and asked you to look after them. I tried very hard to appear normal that night."

"Well, you succeeded. Nothing told me you had just killed someone."

"Anda, it was an accident. I was trying to defend myself. You have to believe me."

"So, why didn't you go upstairs and give Arnie Dambergs the photos as you planned?"

"I didn't want to lead them straight to Arnie and I was really scared. There may have been other guys lurking around and, don't forget, I still had to hide the photos."

"So you put me and my family in danger instead?"

"Anda, I had no choice."

Anda knew they both needed a break from the intensity of the conversation.

"Listen, I'm going to pour myself a drop of vodka. How about you?"

"Yes. Yes, please. When you've poured your drop, bring me the bottle," Mike said lighting up his last cigarette. He had smoked almost a half pack.

As Anda opened the window a little more, a chill breeze rushed through the room. Within moments, she reappeared with two glasses and a half bottle of *Kristal Dzidrais*.

"*Priekā*," she said and they clinked glasses.

"After I dropped off the photos here with you, I kept thinking about where I could hide. I was getting desperate and it was damn cold outside that night. Well, anyway, I was standing outside this bar when I saw the police pick up this vagrant. That gave me the idea. What better protection than to be in police custody? But I never guessed I'd be sentenced to a detox centre. I was lucky. It was a good holiday. Nice people. Good food."

"But what made you steal those awful photos in the first place? What were you going to do with them?"

Breaking eye contact with Anda, he looked away and hesitated for a brief moment. But the moment was long enough to make Anda think that whatever he said next could be a lie.

"I *had* to take them. Don't you understand? Those photographs are illegal and whoever took them should be exposed. I guess it was finding a photograph of Daina that really did it. I didn't want to leave it there. I didn't want anybody to see her like that. Besides, these were only photos, not the negatives. They could always print another set. I needed them as proof that there was exploitation going on at the Young Miss Latvia Contest and I knew Arnie Dambergs would pay me good money for them."

Anda stared at him, not being sure at all. Had Mike really done a public service or had he wanted to sell Arnie a scoop? Or was he covering up the fact that he himself was involved in the sex cartel? She thought about the car that Mike had been able to buy. Where had he got the money?

"Do you still have your car?" she asked warily.

"Yeah. Yeah, I do. But I'm not driving it at the moment. It's too risky. Somebody might recognize me. What made you ask about my car?"

"Well, I've always been curious about where you got the money to buy it?"

"That's a long story and I don't have time to tell you right now."

A faint chill ran up her spine. She noticed something evasive in Mike's reply. He was hiding a great deal from her. And the anger was still there. Could Mike have something to do with Daina's disappearance? He had met her a few times and had remarked on how pretty she was.

"And what now?" Anda wanted to end the conversation.

"I've read in the papers that this child porn thing is being investigated. In a little while, it'll be safe to get back to my normal life. But in the meantime, I need a place to hide. Anda…"

"No, Mike. No. I have Vilnis now. Things have changed. My sister is dead. Daina is missing. I can't help you."

Mike's body slumped. He looked pathetic but Anda could still sense the anger. She was not going to give in. She stared into her glass for a few moments, then looked up at Mike.

"Surely you must have friends. Umm…have you tried Ivan? You and my father seem to get along so well."

"Yeah, but you and me…"

"No. I can't Mike. I have to look after myself. And Vilnis."

Anda put her glass down. She watched as Mike poured himself another. Luckily for her, he was out of cigarettes. He downed the drink in one gulp. Got up unsteadily.

"So what did you do with the photos?"

"I did what you set out to do. I gave them to Arnie Dambergs. He even paid me."

"Arnie Dambergs? How did you contact him? How much did he pay you?"

"Well, I knew who Arnie Dambergs was from his *WOW!* magazine. And you had mentioned his name a couple of times. I figured that he might be able to help me find Daina."

Mike repeated, "How much did he pay you? I could really use some of that money right now."

"Look, it wasn't a lot and I've already spent it on Vilnis and his day-care."

"Can't I just crash here with you for one night? Come on!"

"No, you can't," Anda said firmly but then realized she would have to mollify him a bit. "You know, you're sort of a hero. Without those photos nothing would have happened. At least now there's an investigation. I don't know where it will lead but it's a beginning."

"Anda," Mike said softly leaning towards her, expecting a kiss. Anda turned away. Resolve turned her eyes to flint. She spoke calmly but there was no mistaking the seriousness of her tone.

"I know you can take care of yourself," she said as she walked to the door and opened it.

Chapter Forty

It was Monday morning and Don Fischer had decided to take the day off. Time to work off some of his aggression. Luckily for him, the tennis courts on Kronvalda Boulevard had just opened for the season. It was a tradition with embassy people, foreign executives, expats and a select local Latvian elite to gather on the first day and hit some balls. Nothing serious. It wouldn't be till August and club championships that egos would be honed to the max and bodies ready to pound each other into the ground.

Don had hit some balls against the wall while he waited for one of his tennis buddies to show up. After ten minutes, he had had enough and went into the clubhouse for a beer. He recognized a handful of people out of the ten or twelve members, mostly businessmen. He picked up a copy of a local paper to read and, holding his beer in his other hand, found an empty table to sit at. Scanning the headlines made Don almost spit out his drink.

"Bullshit! Listen to all this crap attacking my wife and the beauty pageant!"

A few of the guys were sitting at the next table. Gordie Darlington, who worked at the World Bank, looked over and asked,

"So what do you think, Don? Is your wife going to win the Young Miss Latvia contest?"

The room exploded in laughter. Don felt the vein on his forehead puff up and throb. He threw his head back and laughed loudest of the group. Grabbing the conversational ball before anyone else could make another wisecrack, he asked,

"Anyone know what the pro is charging for private lessons this year?"

Don thought he heard Gordie muffle a snicker and say something like, "That old pro of his could give my wife lessons any day."

Ignoring him, Don continued,

"Who is the pro this year? Did they manage to get Bjorn Borg back for a second time? You know who I mean, Pauls whats-his-name."

One of the members told Don to look at the notice board for the pro's rates and that he was new, Russian, Boris Something. Something unpronounceable.

Don got up out of his chair.

"Looks like it could rain pretty soon. How about a game?"

There were no takers. And no wonder. Word had got around that Don was into some weird shit that nobody wanted to talk about, least of all Don.

The minute he turned his back, it started.

"Fischer trips on all that diplomat shit," Gordie said to Ken Thompson who was wearing extra-short tennis shorts. "Makes him feel powerful. His tennis game sucks so he has to compensate."

"All the same, I wouldn't mind all those trips to London. Do you realize there isn't any place in this city where you can buy a button-down blue Oxford cloth shirt. You see these tennis shorts I'm wearing? I had to order them from Lands End and they took a month to get here."

Gordie rolled his eyes. He could say, see this T shirt? I picked it up at the market for a pack of smokes but he didn't bother. Ken went on.

"You know what they say about Don's old lady? She's got cement for brains."

"Yeah, well, but what a body! I wouldn't push *her* out of bed."

Gordie didn't like men who said mean things about women. He looked at Ken, at Ken's tennis outfit and wondered, *is he?*

A brisk wind had sprung up out of nowhere. Not good for tennis. Don had a shower, changed out of his whites and decided to drive over to the newly opened Radisson Hotel in Pardaugava. He'd have lunch there. Perhaps run into one of his acquaintances from the political world. The bunch at the club were yahoos. The club itself was just a breeding ground for gossip and scandal. There were no real athletes there.

And no point getting paranoid even though there were people he now wanted to avoid. He knew better than to be seen at the Bistro. It looked as if Uldis Baltins was about to take the fall for the Young Miss Latvia scandal. Don worried. Uldis was unpredictable, scared as a rabbit. At any time, he could flip and start telling stories on his buddies. Don was the strong one, or so he thought. Well, at least he had a passport and enough cash to get the hell out if things really heated up. Whereas Uldis... Don didn't like to think, nor did he want to know, how a local without money would get out of a mess.

Before setting out for the hotel, there was something else that had to be done. He had been forced by that bitch to make one more payment on the damn office on Gertrudes Street. But that was it. She wasn't going to get another penny. He was going to make damn sure of that.

Don stopped his car at the nearest pay phone. When he finished his call he had made all the arrangements for a meeting later that same night. He planned carefully. Mace might not be enough protection. He decided that he'd better take his Saturday-night special which he'd tuck carefully into the right hand pocket of his dark Gortex windbreaker. And of course, the cash. A roll of American greenbacks. Russians were crazy for the crisp new hundred-dollar bills. Don laughed thinking of some of the old fools who had panicked believing that the old US bills they had been hoarding for ten years were now worthless.

The presence of his gun reassured him. He wouldn't take any chances with the type of guy he would be dealing with. This was about as low as life could get in Riga. Don knew he was riding a savage beast and, if he ever fell off, the beast would turn on him and devour him.

His room at the Radisson was empty. Don barely registered the fact that the boy had gone. He couldn't even remember his name now. Was it Oleg something? No, that was last week. He poured about two ounces of scotch into a glass and drank it down. Before setting out, he pulled a cap down over his eyes and raised the collar of his jacket up around his face. He had to make sure he couldn't be recognized. He even hunched down low as he walked to his car trying to make himself look shorter and older. Little did he realize that it made him a more likely target for a mugger. Don felt his gun snug beneath his left arm. He knew he could draw it at a moment's notice.

The wind flailed through the bare branches of the trees and shrubs. Rain had started to fall. There was no one about, no one to notice as two cars pulled up on an unlit street in Pardaugava far from the Hotel Radisson. In a secluded corner of a parking lot, a deal was made.

Chapter Forty-One

Maija was sure Don was keeping a woman at the Radisson. A woman? Well, at least she hoped it was a woman. She had never been able to bring herself to contemplate any other alternative. She knew that Don probably wouldn't call her to say that he wouldn't be back for dinner. Right now, his absence suited her just fine. She needed time to herself. Time to think.

She had awakened that morning feeling she was somewhere in the middle of the ocean tossed around on a tiny raft. She sat up in bed as nausea washed over her. She made it to the bathroom just in time to throw up into the toilet. A Russian baby for chrissake, she muttered as she splashed cold water on her face. Well, it could be worse. It could have been Don's. After the initial shock, she felt a surge of excitement. She adored children. Had never been pregnant, not once despite her many relationships. She had assumed that she couldn't have a child, but now, just after the big 40, she was sure she was pregnant.

Her excitement made her want to blurt out the news to everyone. She knew she'd have to be careful, make plans, get some money and get away from Don. With a shock, she realized that her desire for Sasha had vanished. Only the baby mattered. Now she had someone to really love, a new life to look forward to, a child to protect.

Her entire life had been about not feeling. With the help of alcohol and sex she had learned not to feel. She had learned to keep the pain away. Now, the suppressed longings and emotions swept through her in such a rush that it took her breath away.

Her narcissism was what had made her unaware of anything improper going on at the beauty contest. She had been too self-preoccupied to take in much that didn't concern her directly. Now she kept wishing she could tell someone about the baby and realized, with dismay, that she had no real friends here in Latvia. But then who could she get to teach her to knit? Before she could solve that riddle, the phone interrupted.

"Hello. Fischer residence."

Whoever it was hung up. Maija shrugged. It was annoying. Fortunately, they didn't get many wrong numbers. She sat down in the breakfast nook with her second cup of tea and planned her day. She should go to the office and get her messages. Should she buy a home pregnancy test or make an appointment with a doctor? The only clinic she trusted was the ARS Medical Company on Skolas Street where most expats went. She decided to do both but she'd have to hurry. She had a hair appointment and had scheduled a massage and a pedicure for later in the day. She hadn't slept well and felt the need to fit in a nap.

Her nerves had started to hum even before she opened her eyes. Something had awakened her. She stared blindly into the dark.

The phone? The phone was ringing. Maija worked her way up against pillows, fumbled around on her bedside table and picked up the receiver. There was only the dial tone. She was alert now. Could she have dreamed that the phone had been ringing? There was now some other kind of sound. It was faint but it was there.

She didn't have to look over to the other side of the king-size bed that Don had ordered from the States to know that it was empty. Maija stared at the luminous numbers in the dark: 3:35AM. She had been asleep since eight pm and now felt wide-awake.

She lay back against the pillows again, taking a few long deep breaths to still her pulse. She felt a sense of unease. Something tickling the nerves at the back of her neck. Perhaps it wasn't the phone that had awakened her. What could it have been?

Maija continued to lie there motionless, attempting to identify the sound that could signal an intruder. The heavy curtains in the bedroom muffled street sounds and kept out the faint glimmer of light from outside. The room seemed small and airless. She felt claustrophobic, as if she was sealed off from everything. Should she get up?

Suddenly, her body went rigid. As if picking up the current from an electric field, she sensed danger. She could feel a presence, almost hear someone breathing. Straining to listen, she became aware of the almost imperceptible sound of someone's footsteps coming down the hallway towards the bedroom. For an instant, she wasn't breathing. Her heart seemed to stop. Some instinct told her she was not safe in bed. Danger was palpable in the air, wafting in from the hallway, creeping in under the door. She smelled it, the sour sickening stench of vomit, the smell of garbage, the stench of evil.

In that instant of dark silence, she knew for sure there was someone inside her apartment. She knew it wasn't Don. A silent scream swelled in her chest. She could hear the slight pressure of footsteps coming down the bare parquet floor of the hall. The floor always creaked in front of the bedroom. She waited for it. Listened intently. Don! Maija wanted to call out. But she didn't.

Her heart tripping over fear and horror, without losing a second, she slid out of bed. Grabbing the phone, she raced to the bathroom just as the bedroom door opened. Soundlessly, she turned the lock. At that very moment, she heard the *whomp* of a heavy object hitting down on bedclothes. It was followed by angry muttering, a man's voice, incomprehensible, enraged. Then footsteps.

Maija huddled on the floor. Her mouth was dry, her heart seemed to beat out of rhythm. Who could she call? What number could she call for help? She didn't dare move or make a sound. The man in her bedroom would hear her voice, would kick in the door. Clutching the phone, she curled up on the floor and hugged herself. *Don't try the bathroom door. Don't. Don't. Don't*, she prayed, silently pleading with the intruder. Her brain had locked. The same words kept repeating themselves over and over. *Don't. Don't. Don't.*

Her heart jerked crazily. God! He had heard her. He was moving in on her. Panic swept through her. After a long agonizing moment—which seemed like eternity—he seemed to be moving away. Very slowly the wave of panic began to subside. Or was he moving away? A part of her continued, the rhythm of the words caught in her mind like an ancient gramophone record, the needle stuck in a groove. Was she breathing? She must be breathing. She wasn't dead. Reason took hold. Yes, now she was sure. He was moving away. He was leaving.

Minutes went by. She couldn't tell how many. Finally, she heard the front door of the apartment shut with a soft thud. She stretched out on the cold bathroom floor, her body cramping from the immobility. She exhaled in one long sobbing sound. Relief, terror, an uncanny mix of emotions made her stay down on the floor. She fought for control. Inhale, exhale. Deep deep breathing. *It's over, it's over*, her brain bombarded her with good news. A car door banged shut. It could be any car, Maija thought, not just *his* car. But he was gone. It was over.

At least ten minutes went by before Maija pulled herself up off the bathroom floor. She flipped on the light in the bathroom. Opened the door to the bedroom. The smell from the intruder's hideous body odour made her gasp. Fear, dirt, alcohol—it all combined to create a stench that permeated her bedclothes, her drapes, her rugs.

Not touching anything, she left the room in darkness. In bare feet, she went out into the hall. It was cold on the uncarpeted floor. She turned on all the lights and examined the lock on the front door. To her amazement, she realized that the chain had been tampered with. It hung loose by a screw. But the lock on the door had not been broken. Nothing had been disturbed. Maija felt dizzy. Cold sweat trickled down her side. She realized that the intruder had a key to her home.

Maija's pulse was still running hard. She shivered. To warm herself, she put on a jacket from the hall closet and hugged it tightly around her. She couldn't go back to what she thought of as the crime scene. In her mind, she saw a yellow police tape stretched across her bed. Her lifeless body lay there, her head bashed in, her brains and blood spilling out. No one would find her killer. Probably no one would even look. They'd bury her somewhere out in the country. A home invasion or a robbery gone wrong, they would conclude.

Then anger rolled in, dispelling her fear like sun burning off mist. Who had wanted to kill her? Well, this lady knew *exactly* who it was. It was Don's hired hit-man. She didn't think he'd try it again after Chicago. But she had been wrong. She had seen right away that someone had removed the screw from the security chain and of course it had been Don.

In the States, she would have immediately called the police. What would be the point in this country? She paced for a few minutes up and down the hallway. This steadied her. She got out the toolkit and made sure that the chain was firmly in place. Then, with determined steps, she walked into the kitchen to make herself a cup of tea.

As she sipped from her mug, Maija's eyes wandered around the kitchen. Don had an obsessive need to control his environment. It was neat and functional, just as he liked it. It had been recently renovated and equipped with all the latest appliances but there was nothing of her in this place. No knick-knacks, no personal touches. In the past, her kitchens had always been a cozy mess of cookbooks and herbs growing on windowsills and loads of fridge art. In this sterile new kitchen that she shared with Don, the linoleum floor and the arborite countertops looked industrial. She wouldn't miss a thing.

Her marriage to Don had been useful, had been tolerable for a while, but now it was over. Don had always been a control freak. This time he had really overstepped. So this was how he was going to handle a little blackmail. She got the message. And putting down her teacup, she went to pack.

As Maija looked around the apartment for the very last time, night was dissolving into the ghostly light of early morning. Out in the street, a car horn sounded, a bus lumbered by. A gentle rain was falling through the fog, leaving the streets slick and soggy. Water dripped from the ancient trees. Slowly the city was waking up.

Chapter Forty-Two

Arnie sat at the kitchen table. He had finished reading all the papers Peteris had just brought him. There had been major fallout over his articles. A cabinet minister had resigned and speculation was that other heads would soon be rolling. Parliamentary investigators had gone so far as to link the Prime Minister to the scandal. Vociferous denials were issued as well as accusations that opposition parties were trying to destabilize the government. Insiders were blamed and outsiders were blamed as businessmen and foreign investors were being fingered as influential pedophiles involved in the child sex cartel. Arnie couldn't help but think that corrupt government officials were to blame. Corruption at such high levels seemed to have turned Riga into a pedophile's paradise.

Even Arnie had been surprised to learn that the trail had led as far away as Chicago where a night-club owner had just been arrested for keeping two Latvian woman as sex slaves. Don Fischer had been implicated in an article in *The Baltic Observer,* 'Prominent Chicago businessman, in Riga as Commercial Attaché at the American Embassy, linked to Young Miss Latvia contest, now under investigation.'

Arnie shook his head. Teflon no more. Just plain ordinary Don. Don Fischer and his friend, restauranteur Uldis Baltins, were found to be in the planning stage for a Young Mr Latvia contest and right from the start, the rotting smell coming from this unholy alliance had attracted a media feeding frenzy.

Vizma had told him about the rumour started by one of the secretaries in the Embassy visa office. She had insinuated that Don Fischer's marriage was a cover for his pedophile activities. And then, there was the maid at the Radisson who had information she was ready to sell to the press. So far, nobody had come up with the outrageous ante.

From what he knew of local politics, Arnie could expect that a Latvian scapegoat would have to be found to silence the public outcry and he instinctively knew that Uldis Baltins would be fingered for the fall.

Of course, ordinary Latvians were incredulous. In the proletariat paradise of the Soviet era, it was public policy to maintain that pedophilia didn't exist and was exclusively a vice of the West. This was all new, horrible, outrageous and the fact that their elected officials might be involved was incomprehensible. Slowly, the realization sunk in that freedom had a price. The naked truth was ugly and brought with it a nation-wide loss of innocence.

In one ear and out the other, Arnie thought to himself. He knew that the scandal would probably last just a few days before it was replaced by something else that would fill the TV channels and front pages of the dailies. Public hunger for novelty would continue to be fed. And Arnie was just one among the many suppliers.

The blame game would go nowhere. Perhaps the government would ban under age beauty contests for a year or so, at most. Everyone would go back to his own reality, the struggle for political power, money, or just plain survival. Investigators would get temporary blindness and be rewarded with a bribe for their co-operation. Political deals would be brokered. New scandals would float across the nation's collective consciousness in tickertape format, lasting no longer than the time it took for six words to cross everyone's TV screen, only to disappear into the black hole of old news. And many in the new Latvia would be conned into believing that this was real progress toward the Valhalla of western democracy. It made Arnie wonder at his own success.

"So, you're not dead after all," Peteris said as he plopped a new batch of papers in front of Arnie.

"Let me have a look. Amazing! Who could have leaked that?"

"You should know. Don't you?"

Arnie shrugged. Well, there were his two ladies and, this time, he voted for Anda. Any Latvian journalist could have pried that out of her. As a professional, he also knew that some journalist would gamble on a rumour to get a headline. Well, this Rihards Plavins had hit the jackpot and it had probably been good for a raise.

"That blew your cover, didn't it?"

"Listen, I just have to make one phone call and I'll be dead again before you know it."

"So I can count on you for more farm work next week?"

"No, Peteris. I'll have to go. There are things I have to do in Riga."

Arnie went to the phone and telephoned *Diena*. He spoke to Plavins. Both journalists knew how to manipulate the public and how to help each other.

The planted story worked. The next day's headline read

ARNIE DAMBERGS DEPARTS FOR CANADA

There was even a picture of Arnie at Riga International Airport. Peteris had taken the whole day off to drive Arnie to the airport for the photo shoot and then to the post office to send Vizma another Happy Birthday telegram.

After his busy day in the city, Arnie was sitting on the stoop of the farmhouse enjoying the early evening. Marta had handed him a stein of their home-made beer and Arnie sipped on it, savouring every delicious drop. He felt a twinge of regret knowing that this was his last night in Marupe with Marta and Peteris. A veil of smoke drifted out of the chimney and weaved its way through the streaky white clouds. In a few weeks, the sky would stay milky all night long and he couldn't wait to come back to enjoy the magical twilight of the northern summer.

Arnie lit a cigarette. He had almost quit smoking, allowing himself only five cigarettes a day. He had made friends with Peteris and Marta and felt that, finally, he was experiencing the real Latvia, not just the hothouse world of the expat community. He wanted to meet their two sons, get to know the whole family. But it was a fantasy. Peteris and Marta were sheltering him, doing him a favour. He didn't have the right to expect more than temporary hospitality.

Arnie sketched out his future. Life would change, at least in the short term. The pedophile scandal had put him in the spotlight. How long would his fifteen minutes of fame last? He grinned. No matter how long, he would revel in it! Perhaps it wasn't as good as a Pulitzer but it certainly would open doors. His magazine had not been published in April and now he was hard at work planning the May edition. He had decided to take a more serious tone, cut some of the gossip and focus on investigative journalism. He liked being thought of as a watchdog, clearly a step up. Still not Gore Vidal or Truman Capote but at least a notch removed from Mad Magazine.

Arnie wondered sometimes if he could ever go back to Ottawa. Across the forefront of his brain slipped grainy images of dusty streets, video rentals, Shawarma shops, strip malls and the treeless grubby stretches of Bank Street—and the endless political squabbles, the endless strings of hockey games, the endless royal visits. Arnie gave himself a mental slap on the forehead. God, how could he ever think that he could go back. He'd die of boredom!

As he got his backpack ready for the morning, he caught sight of himself in a mirror. No one would recognize him now. He looked more and more like a country bumpkin. He had lost even more weight and now could fit easily into Peteris' work clothes. Marta had given him a home-style haircut, a tiny bit of bleach to help his disguise and he looked like a typical working class guy. Arnie was all set, ready to re-enter the fray.

Chapter Forty-Three

66 This is a fucking nightmare!" Don Fischer swore and pounded his fist down on the coffee table. News travelled at the speed of light in Riga. He kept up the obscenities as he crumpled the pages of *The Baltic Observer*. He'd sue the bastards. What were they thinking by linking him to some sex slave thing in Chicago? Peonage, the cops called it. Don barely knew what the word meant. The article went on about some top-ranking foreigner picking up two young women at Riga's Central Train station and offering them a great job in America. The journalist didn't use Don's name but any fool could connect the dots.

The phone rang. He picked up, clenched his jaw muscles. Rage flooded his face. It would take six Valiums just to be able to lie horizontal. God, what he wouldn't give for some weed!

"I'll meet you in the lobby!" His voice was breaking, exploding with rage. Don banged down the phone. It was eight o'clock in the morning but the room was dark. The heavy curtains kept out the foggy morning light. Last night he had taken a room at the Radisson. He looked toward the bed. Misha was still sleeping, his face lost in the pillow. As if feeling Don's gaze, the boy opened his eyes.

"Okay, okay," Don gestured a soothing signal with his hand. In seconds, the boy was fast asleep again. Don walked out of the room, careful that the door had locked behind him. How could the guy fuck up! Maija hadn't been in her bed. The plan had failed. Don wanted to throttle the guy. Hit-man, he called himself. What a laugh! These guys in Riga acted tough, talked tough, but when it came to delivering on a job, they fucked up. They fucked up with Arnie Dambergs and his girlfriend, they fucked up with his wife.

Minutes took hours as the elevator stalled at every floor on its way down to the lobby. He found an empty oversized chair beside a potted palm and sank down as far as he could. He waited.

The guy was always late. Sometimes didn't show but would later call. Don waited. And waited. His mind slid back to the boy in his room. He was no longer interested. He wanted to know nothing about him. He had become a nuisance that Don was eager to get rid of.

What was he going to do with him? He had picked up Misha, if that indeed was his real name, in the Central Train Station. He had approached the boy, asked him to have a drink in his halting Russian. Within an hour, they were at the Radisson. It had taken Don a while to devise a technique for getting friends into his room. Bribes to the hotel staff had always bought him silence. Recently, there had been hints that more money was required. Don would have to do something drastic. He hoped the kid had picked up the money and left the room by the time he got back.

Life in Riga had been good. He was a somebody. He had a flashy sexy wife, a prestigious job and a city where illicit sex was cheap and available. But trouble had been brewing in his paradise. Maija had proved to be hard to control, her infidelity threatening his sense of domination. Then came the blackmail. And now, it wasn't just Arnie Dambergs and his crappy magazine, it was all over the media, TV, papers and the radio.

Don knew that his big mistake had been to let Mike get away with the photos. He had been wrong to count on Anatol. He should have followed Mike himself. He should have taken care of him.

Don had taken steps to look after the problem before the situation got blown sky-high but all his efforts had failed. Mike had disappeared and Arnie Dambergs was still alive. He doubted that bit about Arnie going back to Canada. He was in Riga all right. Probably running scared.

A squeaky sound accompanied by the smell of freshly cured leather, vodka and garlic announced the approach of Don's hit-man. There he was at last, only twenty minutes late, motioning to Don to follow him out of the hotel. And Don did but not before he gripped the cold steel handle of his Saturday-night special.

Chapter Forty-Four

If she hurried, Maija would get to the bank just as it opened and, more importantly, just before Don got wind of her plans. A few minutes earlier, she had purchased airline tickets on her gold Visa card.

Rigas Komerc Banka in Old Riga was one of the few financial institutions to have escaped the recent banking collapse in which hundreds of depositors had lost their life savings. Maija had seen angry crowds of pensioners demonstrating outside the Parliament Building and had felt sorry for the poor people who had been lured in by promises of astronomical interest rates. Don had laughed. "Greedy buggers," he had said. "Who would fall for a hundred percent interest?" Western style banking was new in Latvia. People had a lot to learn.

Maija smiled a cold tight little smile. This morning she was close to the front of the line. And there was no Don in sight. She realized that lining up was in people's blood. It had been a fact of life for decades. She had been to this bank before and knew her way around the grand building. It was the largest bank in the Baltics, majestic and sound with an air of permanence and invincibility. Armed guards stood at the inner door, eyeballing each person as they entered. The interior was ornate, all marble and brass with dark panelling and high ceilings. Maija climbed the grand wooden staircase to the second floor and joined another line-up. Then one more official. It certainly took patience but Maija was prepared for this. She fingered her large leather carry-all bag with its sturdy zipper. It would do nicely. Don was not rich enough to warrant a suitcase.

"I'd like to close this account and take my money in American dollars, please," she said in her best Latvian. The startled clerk eyed her carefully, examined her passports. Maija had two. American and Latvian.

"One moment, madam."

Maija shrank inside with alarm. Could there be a hitch? Had Don beaten her to it?

The clerk was back and smiled at her.

"For such a sum, you will have to see our director, madam."

Maija nodded. Following instructions, she found her way back to the main floor. She knocked on the director's door. A tall blond man wearing a dark suit gave her a quick perfunctory bow and asked her to sit down. Maija felt paranoia surge through her. Are they calling the police? she wondered as she crossed her legs and forced a calm businesslike expression on her face. Or are they calling Don? Thank God he was still probably sleeping in at the Radisson.

"Just one moment, please," the man said formally. His face seemed to darken as he keyed in information on the computer.

Maija's paranoia heated up from a simmer to a boil. *No, I'm not a victim of extortion and my husband hasn't been kidnapped*, she wanted to shout but, instead, she simply looked down at her well-manicured nails and waited. At least three minutes passed before he looked up again. Had Don got there before her and cleared everything out? She knew that his position at the American Embassy gave him privileges that ordinary people didn't have. Maybe someone had notified him. *Maybe he was on his way over*. The thought made her hold her breath. She felt as if she were drowning, sinking to the bottom of a terrible cold dark sea.

"Thank you for your patience," the man said coolly.

"Yes?" The word came out as a gasp.

"Please take this form to the cashier on the second floor."

In a rush of relief, Maija's shoulders collapsed for a moment and she dropped her head. Then lifting it, her glance swept over the bank manager's hands. They were rough and muscular with ragged nails. The white cuffs peeking out of his jacket were frayed. She thought to herself, he probably goes home every night to chop wood while his wife washed clothes in the bathtub—on days when hot water is available, that is.

Back on the second floor, she joined the line to the cashier's cage. She kept her face expressionless. She wasn't out of the woods yet. There could be no humorous comments or sudden outbursts to draw attention to what she was doing. And she had never dressed this severely in her life. Still, the armed security guard looked her over. Inwardly smiling, she mimicked Mae West, 'It's better to be looked over than overlooked,' and wondered if the guard could tell she was wearing her set of lacy bra and panties from Victoria's Secret.

Not skipping a beat, she switched back into worry mode. If word had got out that she was withdrawing a fortune, would someone be waiting outside to grab her bag? Sweat rolled in cold trickles beneath her blouse. She was next in line for the cashier. Scowling inside the cage sat a plump elderly woman with a frizz of orange hair. Stony-faced, the woman counted out thirty-five thousand American dollars. Without saying a word, Maija arranged the stacks of bills carefully inside her bag. Hardly touching the ground, she sucked in air and speed-walked to the front door.

Sunlight filtered through broken clouds as she stepped into the narrow cobblestone street. No one accosted her. Maija breathed easier as she crossed it. Looked around. Nothing suspicious. Being vigilant had become second nature to her. It had taken her a while to become acclimatized to the dangers of Riga—the unlit streets at night, the pickpockets, the street urchins who stalked the unsuspecting. Today there was an added danger—her homicidal control-obsessed husband. She patted herself on the back. She had pulled it off, had got her drop-dead money. It was time to bail.

Maija gave a snort of laughter as she passed her favourite building, the whimsical ochre Cat Building on Meistaru Street. Poised on each of its pointed twin towers was a black cat looking down on the city. The cats had always meant trouble. At the turn of the century, the sculptor who had been installing them, had fallen to his death. But the cats had survived. Safe on their perches, they arched their backs disdainfully and continued to piss down on their adversaries.

Maija looked up and smiled at them. Everything was going according to plan. Like a cat, Maija was genetically coded to land on her feet.

Chapter Forty-Five

A mirage, Vizma thought. Surely it was a trick, an illusion. Something about the man standing at the bus stop had caught her eye. She was puzzled to see that he was waving at her, grinning and waving. He was a tall slender man with colour in his cheeks, a shock of blond hair escaping from a worn looking cap. Not like someone she'd know. But still, some instinct made her stop. He looked like a farm-worker coming to the big city, on his way to the market, perhaps.

Vizma was baffled. She didn't know any country people. She put up her hand to shade her eyes and squinted in the sunshine. It couldn't be, she thought to herself. Or could it? Could it really be Arnie? No, she decided. But it could be a younger cousin, from Jurmala maybe. A healthy, good-looking cousin. Then her eyes widened. God! It really *was* Arnie. She was amazed. Her face brightened as he came towards her, smiling, and said,

"Let's go have a beer."

Her heart leapt. This was Arnie's voice. He looked as if the sun had rubbed gold into his hair. He seemed to be glowing all over. Vizma moved towards him. As he began to talk, she realized that his Latvian had improved. It was more fluent, more colloquial. She wanted to hug him, to hang on to him before he could vanish again. Arnie extended his hand. Vizma took it and held on for a long moment.

"Arnie, you look great! Really great! Let's go," she said with a happy smile even though she had no interest in having yet another Latvian beer.

They crossed Marijas Street and headed for Staburags, melting in perfectly with the crowd. They were two ordinary people enjoying the spring day.

In the restaurant, Vizma noticed a few foreigners and felt nothing in common with them. There they were with their bright phoney smiles and their fanny packs. They were outsiders, whereas she belonged. She even looked like a local with her plain brown slacks and beige sweater. Her dark hair-colour had faded along with the Russian perm and strands of grey peppered the mousy blond that nature had given her. For weeks, she had worn no makeup. She liked the feeling of being plain and ordinary. She could pass for a local—until she opened her mouth. She knew her accent would always give her away.

The menu looked interesting—cabbage soup, *piragi*, sauerkraut and sausages, *karbonade*, potato salad and herring, *kotlettes*. With a 'maybe later' look, she waved the menu at Arnie as she said,

"Tell me everything."

"Just let me catch my breath," he replied.

Vizma smiled and leaned forward across the wooden table.

"What's been happening? I feel so left out."

Just then another couple joined them at the long table and Arnie lit up a cigarette.

"I'm down to five a day. Proud of me?"

She grinned. The open fire in the 'ye olde' Latvian beer hall gave off a cosy scent as the wood popped and hissed.

"Did you go see Anda for me?"

"I certainly did, Arnie. I took her out for coffee and we had a chat. Daina hasn't come back yet. But Anda told me that she'd seen Mike on the street somewhere. So the guy must be around. And I think Anda did a major blab. The papers reported that you're alive."

"I sure am, Vizma. I'll drink to that."

"Me too, the minute the waiter brings our beer," Vizma said looking around. "We didn't get run off the story, did we. And we're both still here." She glanced down the table to make sure the other couple wasn't paying any attention and was glad to see that they weren't.

"Here's lookin' at you, babe," Arnie growled in his Humphrey Bogart imitation, letting his cigarette dangle dangerously from his lower lip as he lifted the enormous beer stein that the waiter had just banged down in front of him. Lifting her stein, giggling, Vizma drawled,

"Just whistle if you need me, sugar."

They both sat back, savouring the moment. They had earned it. By now the long communal tables were filling up and, after a bit, they leaned closer together again.

"The media's going wild with the scandal. Everyone's in an uproar." Vizma gave a cynical laugh. "And wait, it gets better. One of the ministers has gone on a hunger strike until he's cleared. How absurd! What planet does he live on? Doesn't he know that more than half the people here are starving?"

"Yeah, but there are a hell of a lot of them that don't want to know. They're busy lining their own pockets."

Arnie's eyes narrowed. He took a big drag of his cigarette before he stubbed it out.

"These freshly elected politicos aren't quite ready for all this new-found freedom. Or maybe, they just aren't as experienced at doing the cover-up as the guys in Washington or Ottawa. Seems like some of them are newly minted but still from the old Soviet mold."

"Yeah," Vizma said, not being sure of the territory. Then she added, "It seems that your friend Teflon Don is the leading candidate in this sex sandal. Apparently, he and a few buddies were videotaping contestants in the dressing room. The police found some hidden cameras."

"God, that creeps me out!" Arnie's face twisted into a grimace.

"Me too. And I used to hear a low murmur at the expat ladies lunch about illicit sex at the Radisson. I think it came from one of the chambermaids whose sister cleans house for Anne what's-her-name. It's some scandal about our side and we're all worried about the damage it could cause for us North Americanos, if it proves to be true. And I think it will."

"Well, I don't know," Arnie said reflectively. "These maids are from the country. Would they be able to spot illicit sex if they tripped on it? Even if they're right, I'm sure it's all behind closed doors."

Vizma leaned closer to Arnie. She felt she was onto something.

"What if somebody's recording all this illicit sex with a peeper camera? I floated that balloon at the last lunch I went to and I wish you could have seen their faces. Some of them were ready to freak because they were worried their husbands may get a tape in the mail."

Arnie gave a sardonic chuckle. "Wouldn't that curl your toes!"

Vizma shook her head and pursed her lips. "You know, I could be right."

"Yeah, you sure could." Arnie broke into a wry half smile. "I bet Teflon Don has a load on his plate. People see him in and out of the Radisson all the time. I wonder who his chambermaid is?"

The heat from the fireplace and the beer had put Vizma in a mellow mood. Still, she shivered with distaste at the whole topic.

"What's happened to Mike's photos of the kids? Do you still have them?" she almost whispered even though the couple who had been sitting next to them had left.

Arnie nodded.

"They're evidence."

"Well, I hope they're useful," Vizma said.

"What do you mean?"

She hesitated. "I hope it's all been worth it. To be honest, I doubt that anyone will be arrested as a pedophile even after all your work. Sure there'll be a fall-guy. Someone dispensable but the big shots will get away with it."

According to what she had read in the papers, there was a huge undercover operation going on. Several people had been arrested but no names had been released. Deals were more likely being made, reputations protected, alibis invented, bribes changing hands.

Arnie looked thoughtful. "You know, what you say is true. They'll target someone, a nobody, to be more exact. They'll pin the whole thing on this one guy."

"Yeah. They'll pin it on a patsy. Like Oswald."

"That's right. It won't be anyone important. The rest of the pervs will just vanish back into the woodwork." Arnie frowned, took a deep drag on his cigarette and continued. "There's no justice for the poor and powerless. Unless someone makes a fuss, forces the issue. That's what I tried to do but I think, in the end, the really guilty ones will get away with it."

Vizma fell silent. They both agreed and were powerless to do anything about it. The whole thing was too depressing for words. She took a deep breath. She needed a change, something fresh and positive.

"I'd love to come back with you. Spend some time in the country."

Arnie's smile was sheepish. "I guess I haven't had time to tell you yet. I've come back to Riga and I'm staying in this flea-bag hotel not far from the Central Train Station. I'll be looking for a new apartment in a day or two."

Vizma's mouth flew open in surprise. "Oh well, that makes all the difference." She decided to make the best of it. "Still, I hope we can go back sometime soon. Definitely for *Jāņi*. I'd love to spend Midsummer at the farm with Peteris and Marta."

"We'll see," Arnie said.

"Sounds like a plan," Vizma replied with a smile and, while Arnie started to talk about his next issue, her mind shifted to thoughts of getting her own life back together again. It would be the same old thing. She'd go back to her apartment, to her job at the Academy. Still, lucky for her, Arnie hadn't asked about his cat. She knew he would, sooner or later.

Sensing her mood, Arnie looked over at her. A smile tugged at the corners of his mouth.

"I was thinking…"

"What?"

"I was thinking you need another beer."

Vizma shrugged.

"And I was thinking…how would you like a job as my co-editor? The pay isn't much but you can set your own hours. There's going to be a ton of work to do to get the next edition out."

A minute of silence went by.

"I'll think about it, Arnie," she said slowly as she picked up a menu and looked at it with renewed interest.

Chapter Forty-Six

The elevator door opened and Don stepped out into the lobby of the Hotel Radisson, unaware that two pairs of eyes were intently watching his every move. Passing one of the mirrored panels, he admired his reflection and decided that the money he had hesitated to spend on his new Burberry had been well worth every penny. He longed to have the Embassy send him to London again. He just loved every minute of his visits and had contacts at the Embassy who wined and dined him royally. The additions to his wardrobe purchased on Bond Street, not to mention the custom made suits from his usual tailor, had assured him of one of the top three places on the best-dressed list in Riga.

Casually glancing about the lobby, Don checked it out for familiar faces. Finding none, he make his way to the revolving door and, pushing it lazily ahead of him, exited into the street to find a perfect Daugava morning to start off his week.

There had been good news and there had been bad news. The bad news he'd deal with right away. He decided he didn't need a hit-man after all. He knew from experience how to take care of a wife who was becoming a nuisance. And then, there was the good news. It seemed that none of the Young Miss Latvia scandal had managed to stick to him. He was back on the Ambassador's guest list. And the weather was perfect for the first tennis round robin to be held later in the week at the club where he had noted, with some relief, that the undercurrent of the humour had moved on to other more topical issues.

Don stood at the entrance for several minutes, taking in the great view of the Daugava River and enjoyed the fresh cool air. He was trying to decide whether to take the free shuttle bus to the Liberty Monument downtown or whether he would be better off driving in his own car. He failed to notice that he had been joined at the entrance by two other men. Nor did he remark on their grim determined faces, tatty appearances, scuffed shoes and bulging pockets. He was completely focused on the homicidal plan in his head. The sooner that was over the better.

Don was about to get into his car when he turned abruptly at the sound of his name. Suddenly, he recognized one of the faces from the entrance. It was Mike, the photographer he had seen at the Young Miss Latvia office, the guy who had absconded with the photos. Don, still feeling confident and superior, spoke angrily.

"Should I know you?"

"Yeah, you should," Mike replied insolently.

"What do you want? I've seen you hanging around the Young Miss Latvia office, haven't I? Mike something or other. Are you ready to give me back the photos you stole?"

"I have something better, motherfucker."

Don's eyes widened as he saw Mike reach into his coat pocket. He was sure it was going to be a gun. Instead, Mike pulled out a videocassette. Don's puzzlement showed on his face.

"What have you got here?" He didn't put out a hand to take it.

"Have a look. You might recognize your boyfriend from last night. You were having a really good time, weren't you."

"What's this? A shake-down, you Russian bastard?" The vein on Don's forehead had become a pulsating blue rope. He looked around, desperately hoping to find a potential rescuer to come to his aid. But there was no one.

"Don't think of trying something dumb. My buddy here will shoot you dead."

Mike's companion had not said a word. To Don he looked like a Second World War Russian army deserter. Don took in the huge cabbage fists, the squat muscular body, still tough and strong. The hombre's gym bag looked heavy and Don thought to himself that it was big enough to hold a machine gun. As the old fellow came closer, Don could smell hundred-proof breath.

An evil smile crept over Mike's face.

"This time we'll let you off easy. Twenty large. That's the price to keep your secrets. For now. Get in the car. We're all going to visit your bank. And don't try anything."

Don was amazed at Mike's English. He must have memorized the blackmailer's manual from A to Z. He certainly talked the talk and walked the walk. These locals were full of surprises.

Cold sweat rimed Don's forehead and his hands were clammy as he started his car moving in the direction of Old Riga.

"I hear you're not a very good tipper," Mike said sarcastically.

"What do you mean?"

"Well, how do you think the chambermaids get by when the guests don't bother to leave them a tip? You never noticed the video camera, did you? You just got right to it, didn't you? You couldn't wait, could you? You sonofabitch!"

As fear warred with anger, Don fought for control. He felt his pulse pounding in his throat and at his temple. He had to concentrate hard to keep the car going in the right direction. Maybe he could crash it. Get away. No, that wouldn't work. How stupid had he been! He should have gone after this Mike himself. He should have offed the fucker when he had the chance. Stupid. Stupid. He had been dumb to rely on Anatol. Now it was too late.

Sweat rolling off him, Don kept driving. He had taken Akmens bridge across the Daugava River and, within a few minutes, had parked the Embassy's black Mercedes. Now he wondered if the car would still be there when they came back.

The three men got out and headed on foot through Old Riga to the Komerc Bank. They rounded the corner of Smilšu Street and did a straight line for the entrance.

There was nothing to tell them that, had they arrived just twenty minutes earlier, they might have bumped into Mrs Donald Fischer carrying a heavy flight bag across her shoulders as she exited the bank. Mike's sidekick, the WWII Russian vet, still with his gym bag, was left to wait outside. In due course, following in Maija's footsteps from one bank official to another, Don was directed to the manager's office. A few minutes later, he re-emerged, ashen and shaken.

"There's no money in my account. It's empty. Nothing left." Don's voice came out in a rasping whisper as he mopped with his trembling hand at the sweat streaming down his face. He could hardly breathe.

"You fuckin' with me?" Fury contorted Mike's face.

Don clenched his fists, wanted to scream at this Mike. Wanted to kill him. Instead, a pathetic "God, no," came from his mouth. Avoiding Mike's stare, he hunched over like a very old man and Mike had to hold him up as he was just about to topple over.

Slowly, the two men made for the doorway, a perfect picture of an ailing father and the solicitous son. The guards barely gave them a glance as they moved through the exit door.

Outside, Mike and Ivan vented their frustrations by starting a heated argument in Russian. For a split second, Don wondered if he would take a chance and make a run for it. His chest felt hot and painfully constricted. He thought he'd faint if he made a break for it.

"The ball's in your court, Mr Tennis Player," Mike said as he grabbed Don's arm and held on tight. Moving in unison, the trio made their way back to the car.

Maybe he could still make this work.

"I've got some money at the apartment. And my wife has jewellery. If you give me time, I'll raise the rest. I don't know what happened at the bank"

"You're crazy to trust any bank, Mr Big Shot." Don knew that the guy was right. How could the bank have let that fucking slut take off with his money? And where was she now? Don wondered if they'd whack Maija if he offered them an extra ten grand.

"Or do you have all your money in Switzerland?" Mike's mouth twisted in an ironic smile.

Don shook his head. "I'll get it but I may have to wire Chicago. It'll take time."

Don could tell that the war vet wasn't going to cut him any slack. The Russian bastard wanted his money now or never. A furious argument ensued. Don knew this was his only chance to save himself. They were going to kill him anyway so he might as well risk it.

He lowered his head and, in a half crouch, bolted from the car, hoping to take shelter in a nearby doorway. The men stopped shouting. The gym bag flew open. Ivan came to life. He was trained to kill.

Don fell a second before Ivan pulled the trigger. He had beaten the bullet. He lay on the pavement, black dots dancing across his field of vision, bells starting to clang. But only for a few seconds. He made one final violent gesture clutching at his heart. Then he was still.

The next morning, Mike and Ivan were to read in the paper that the Commercial Attaché at the US Embassy had been found dead of a heart attack in Old Riga.

Chapter Forty-Seven

The pretty young girl who had just arrived at Riga Central Station on a train from Moscow greeted Maija with a perky smile.

"You look great," Maija said in Latvian.

The girl swallowed a 'you too'. It seemed to her that Maija looked weird, all flushed and nervous. And fat. She continued to prattle on.

"But we must hurry. Something wonderful has come up. You've got an interview with Wilhelmina in New York. Wilhelmina is the number one model agency in the whole world. If they take you on, you will be one lucky lady. I have the plane tickets all ready. When we get there, until you get oriented, you can live with me and help me look after the baby."

The girl wrinkled her nose and pulled a this-is-crap look. "Eeew," she said. "I don't care about this Wilhelmina and I don't care about a baby." Her eyes darted around the train station. "I want a Coke."

"Yes, yes. Come along now." Maija couldn't stop talking. "I will have a baby, very soon. And you can have all the Coke you want. But not right now because we have to hurry. "

"I don't want to hurry. Where's the bathroom? I need to go. And then, I want a chocolate bar. Or maybe ice cream. Or both."

Maija wanted to throttle the girl. But somehow she managed to control herself. She spoke firmly.

"You cannot pee here. I've been told never to use the toilets here. They are the worst cesspools in the world and they still want you to pay. The smell is enough to kill you. You'll have to wait."

The girl frowned. "Where's Don?"

Maija shrugged a 'who cares'. She felt a sudden stab of hatred for the man who had tried to kill her. She had moved half way round the world but she couldn't always shake off her waitressing past in Milwaukee.

"You and me both are well rid of that dickless sack of shit," she hissed between clenched teeth.

She had said this in English and was surprised at Daina's snickers. Daina had understood every word.

"Have you been working on your English, young lady?"

The girl grinned.

"Never mind, Daina. I'll have to be more careful from now on."

"You're cool, Maija."

Maija was taken aback at the use of her first name and yet, she did nothing to show her displeasure. It could wait till New York. She would deal with it later. They had no time to lose. She had not got where she was in life by ignoring her instincts. She hurried the girl out into the square in front of the station and steered her towards the long line of taxis.

Maija knew all about the sharks lurking inside each cab and offered the first one in line a flat rate to the airport. Three lats, that's what it was worth to her. Four if he got her there in less than twenty minutes.

"Okey-dokey," came the reply. Maija looked like a good tipper.

They piled in, Daina still whining about the bathroom. Maija was relieved to finally sit down. She had packed carefully. Her essentials, which consisted of all the jewellery that Don had ever given her and her makeup plus a small collection of her pill bottles topped off by a stack of bribe envelopes filled with crisp new fifty dollar bills, were in a carry on bag that she had slipped across her ample bosom. Now, in the cab, she kept the bag close to her right hip.

Daina had noticed that Maija kept smoothing down her front and patting her extended stomach. She thought to herself, That's going to be some big baby!

Maija, on the other hand, was enjoying the proximity to the cash from the joint account that she had carefully organized in a plastic garbage bag which was now firmly duct-taped around her body.

Until Maija was safely in the air, she would still be doing her shoulder checks in case Don was catching up to her. By now he must know that she had escaped the hit-man. Had he checked the apartment? The bank account? Or was he sleeping it off after celebrating her death? The flight to New York was direct. They had a little over a half-hour to make it to the airport.

The sun was low over the pine trees that lined the narrow road as they sped along towards the terminal. From time to time, old buildings, rusting and paint-peeled came into view. Smoke drifted out of derelict chimneys and disappeared into the late afternoon sky. Here and there, new house being put up stuck out like hothouse orchids in a field of nettles.

Maija kept checking her watch and would interrupt the cab driver's chit-chat to tell him that he wasn't going fast enough to earn the bonus. He would speed up for a few minutes but the speedometer would fall back as he launched into another tirade about how the Russians were poisoning the entire country with toxic alcohol, how they were plotting to take over the country again, how their Mafia controlled everything.

"I know lots of young people who don't drink," Maija interjected. She looked over at Daina who had disappeared behind a curtain of sullen teenage silence. The driver spent the remaining minutes of the trip telling Maija how corrupt the government was, how the Jews controlled banking, how the gypsies were stealing everyone's children.

Finally, they were there. Even before the taxi had come to a full stop, Maija had the door open and had swung her legs toward the entrance. Unfortunately, she listed to one side like the Titanic and, nose down, had to double over before she could heave herself out onto the pavement.

Barrelling through the automatic door while demanding that Daina hurry up, she puffed, "Just in time," only to find that the Lufthansa flight was delayed indefinitely. Rather loudly, she spat out, "Bummer!" People turned to stare and Daina looked embarrassed.

Seething with frustration, Maija felt clammy, as much from anxiety as from the sweat accumulating under the garbage bag. She worried that Don would now have another window of opportunity to finish her off. A small smile escaped as she realized that a bullet would have a real challenge against the duct tape and the greenbacks. She looked around furtively for a hit-man. She didn't see anyone carrying a sign. So far so good.

Just then, Daina started to whine about calling her mother, forcing Maija to revert to her big sister mode.

"Just imagine how thrilled and surprised your family will be when you call them from New York City," she cajoled.

Daina didn't look so sure but her face brightened as she pointed to a Coke machine.

"Alright, Daina, here's some change. I'll have one too but I want a diet."

"Me too. That's cool."

Two minutes later Daina returned with the Cokes.

"No diet, Maija," she said already slurping on hers.

"Fine," Maija said then added, "I know you've never been on an airplane before. Are you scared?"

Daina shrugged.

"I have a tiny tablet people take when they're a bit scared," Maija said softly as she took a vial out of her purse.

"Eeew. No way." Daina did a nose wrinkle and stared off into space. She still felt she should call her mother to say goodbye.

"Once you're settled you can invite your mother and Vilnis to visit. Won't that be an incredible treat?"

Daina lifted her head, smiled broadly and asked,

"Is it okay if I have another Coke?"

"Tch," Maija uttered, getting really annoyed. But she caved. "Knock yourself out," she said in English but Daina was already half way to the machine.

And back in a flash.

"When can I call?"

Hang in there, Maija muttered under her breath. She wasn't about to lose it at this stage. She made an effort to speak calmly.

"As soon as we're in New York. That will be the surprise. And you know Sasha told your mother how well you were doing in Moscow. He brought them the ad taken at the trade show. The one with you leaning against the Mercedes. You're famous now."

The girl's face scrunched up. She muttered something that sounded a lot like 'gimme-a-break'.

The next forty minutes were agony for Maija. She had wondered if they should both hide out in the ladies room until their flight was announced but then thought better of it. Knowing Don as she did, he'd find her there anyway.

After a pastry and a cup of tea in the restaurant, she kept them moving. On the third floor of the airport, she stopped at the bar and bought each of them another Coke. Finally, the announcement came. They were ready to board.

Maija and Daina had reached the second floor and were making their way down to the boarding gate when out of nowhere a hand reached out and grabbed Maija by the right elbow. She let out a shriek, tried to pull away while clutching at her right breast where she felt the garbage bag had just shifted. Had the duct tape come loose? Was this a security guard? A hit-man? The police?

"For heavens sake, Mrs Fischer. I just wanted to say hello."

Maija's shoulders sagged with relief. She saw that it was just one of the clerks from the embassy. Someone she had sometimes flirted with. She realized that he had wanted to be friendly, give her a little surprise. But she started to frown as he continued,

"Are you on my flight to New York tonight? Maybe we could sit together?"

"Oh sorry, Craig. I didn't realize it was you. We're in a rush. My niece isn't feeling well and we're going to board right away so she can get settled. Have a good trip," Maija said firmly as she took Daina's arm and hustled her to the boarding gate. What a putz, she muttered under her breath wondering how she could ever have found him even vaguely attractive. Well, that's what Latvia did to you. It made you do strange things.

Nothing else was going to happen now. Maija decided that once settled, she'd take a Valium. Her nerves were screaming.

Smart girl, Maija said to herself when Daina again refused the blue tablet. She herself took two, settled back in her window seat and breathed a deep sigh of relief. Exhausted, Daina had fallen asleep as soon as the plane reached cruising altitude. Maija had tucked a blanket around her.

From now on, she'd have to maintain a low profile. Considering all she'd gone through, she needed a breather. Just thinking of her close call with the hit-man still made the hair on the back of her neck stand on end. How had it all started? She shivered at the thought of Don's wife number one. Everyone had theories even though no one had accused him to his face of being a wife murderer. Everyone but his sister-in-law, that is.

As the Valium worked its magic, combined with the first gin and tonic and the purr of the engine, Maija nestled her head into the little pillow propped against the seat. She felt comfortable and more than a little buzzed.

The whole sex scandal seemed ludicrous to her now and so did Don, Uldis Baltins and the rest of them. She had often wondered if Don played both sides of the net but never actually wanted to head into what she considered restricted airspace and find out for sure.

She looked over at Daina, thinking back to the first time she had met her. It was the day Daina had come for her interview for the Young Miss Latvia contest and Don had just happened to be there. Right from the start, Maija hadn't liked the calculating way he had stared at the pretty teenager. Maija hadn't let it matter to her what Don and his friends did or didn't do but this was one kid they weren't going to get their hands on. Maija had met Sasha Atnikoff a few weeks before. Their affair had been sporadic— hardly an affair by Maija's standards, as it was way too early to call it that. Still, it had turned out to be her Last Tango in Riga. And she didn't regret a moment of it.

Maija had been surprised to see Sasha with the pretty teenager. She remembered her eyes narrowing at the sight of them together as a shaft of jealousy had shot through her. She had been even more surprised to learn that Sasha was Daina's stepfather. By some bizarre co-incidence, that very same morning, a request had come in for a young model to work in one of Moscow's largest auto trade shows. Latvian girls were known for their beauty and freshness and Maija had taken steps to promote opportunities in the modelling industry.

And so, Daina had been whisked away to Moscow. She had been excited by the adventure and had been assured by Sasha that he would clear it with her mother. Daina knew how desperately her mother and younger brother needed money and she had been proud that she would be able to bring some home.

Weeks had gone by. Daina was a success and had never seen so much money, even though Sasha was doling it out to her, keeping most of it for himself. He even returned to Riga to settle a car sale but never mentioned that Daina was in Moscow. Nor did he bring Daina the news that her mother was dead. Then one night he got word from Maija that she wanted Daina back. Why was none of his business, Maija had told him. Sasha knew from Maija's voice that she was not to be disobeyed.

They were high over the Atlantic now. Maija had been dreaming. In a way it was like watching a movie. Images floated through her mind. Maija the Goddess of Undiscovered Talent, Maija the Survivor, and the best—Maija the mother-to-be, the middle-aged Goddess of Fertility.

Hah! she thought to herself, hearing one of her aunts saying, "Maija, you idiot! At your age! Pray to God that it's normal. Have amniocentesis to make sure. And who is the father? Let me guess. Russian? Jewish? Black, maybe? How could you, Maija, after all we've done for you!"

Chapter Forty-Eight

"What!"

Anda's voice cut through the stream of excited words.

"I'm in New York! Can you believe that? It's just amazing. I keep pinching myself to see if I'm awake. I'm so happy. There was no answer at home, so I'm..."

"Daina! My God, it's you! What are you doing in New York? Never mind all the happy talk. Where have you been? Why didn't you call earlier? We've been frantic and your poor mother..." Anda stopped herself. She was fighting for control of her emotions. How was she to tell Daina about her mother?

Anda's mind was reeling. The predawn silence of an overcast Friday morning had been broken by Daina's call. Anda had been speechless with shock. Now she had to make a decision. Should she let Sasha tell Daina about her mother's death? Or was this the moment?

"But, Sasha said…"

Not knowing whether to be angry or glad, Anda took a deep breath and let it all out.

"Never mind Sasha. I haven't heard from you or Sasha in weeks. And where does Sasha fit into all this?" She stopped long enough to draw a deep breath. Then she continued.

"I've been worried sick about you. You just disappeared without telling anyone where you were going. I'm so relieved that you're alright but what were you thinking of?"

There was silence at the other end. Anda couldn't bear to continue. To her surprise and annoyance she started to cry.

"Oh, Anda, don't cry. Don't cry. Sasha said he'd tell Mum that I was alright."

Anda let out a final sob, then started to laugh as tears continued to slide down her face. It *was* really Daina. Relief flooded her entire body. It made her almost weak.

"I'm just so glad, so glad you're alright."

"I have *so* much to tell you, Anda."

Anda looked down at her skirt speckled with tears. She shut her eyes, leaned back in her chair and listened. She heard Daina telling her a bizarre fairy tale. Anger rose up. She could kill Sasha and Maija and the rest of them. Silvia had died because of the grief they had caused. Before the conversation ended, Anda made sure she got Daina's telephone number in New York.

Putting down the phone, there was no way Anda could calm down with all the adrenaline pumping through her veins. Even before calling her mother, Anda thought of Arnie Dambergs. Thank God he was back. He would know what to do.

Anda punched in his number. She was lucky. On the third ring he picked up, listened to her story and was furious.

"That bitch Maija! Who does she think she is?" Arnie knew who she thought she was. A tough babe, a flimflam *artiste*, the one and only Maija from Milwaukee.

But Arnie was no slouch. He was tired of her bullshit. Emotionally, he had placed Anda and her family under his protection. It would be a pleasure to chew out that brain-dead bimbo for all the grief she'd caused. Within minutes, he had Maija on the phone. He was ready to nail her ass.

"Get yourself a lawyer, Maija."

"Who is this?"

"Arnie Dambergs, Maija. Arnie. I'm going to have you thrown in jail. You've really done it this time."

"What are you on about, Arnie? What have I done?"

Maija sounded scared and evasive. Gone was her confident husky voice.

Arnie shook his head. He couldn't believe that Maija would try the innocent-little-girl act on him.

"You know what I'm talking about. You know how much time you'll do for kidnapping? You and Sasha are going to do time in his and her cells."

"I'm pregnant, Arnie."

"Oh, for God's sake! Who cares, Maija! Get that girl back on the next flight or you'll be giving birth in the slammer. You'll look good in an orange jumpsuit."

"But Arnie, didn't Daina tell you about the appointment with the Wilhelmina Modeling Agency?"

"To hell with Wilhelmina."

"Don't say that, Arnie. Do you have any idea what an opportunity this is for the girl, not to mention her family? How much money it could mean for all of them? It could change her whole life. Open up the world. This is the Big Apple, Arnie. Do you know how hard it was to get the appointment? Do you know how few girls make it into their stable? It's a handful, Arnie. Even if Daina doesn't make it, she should have the chance to try.

Let her stay for the interview, Arnie. You can explain it to her family to make them understand. It isn't as if I'm trying to put her into the slave trade, you know."

There was silence. Arnie was thinking. He decided against telling Maija about Daina's mother. He was trying to weigh the pros and cons of what Maija was telling him. He hated to admit to himself that the Milwaukee beer-maid might be right. It was the way she'd gone about it that enraged him. All the same, Daina deserved her chance at the brass ring.

"Look. You have her back here safe and sound in one week. Call me tomorrow to confirm the flight number. If she's not, I personally will see to it that they lock you up and throw away the key. By the way, Maija, who's the father? "

Chapter Forty-Nine

This was a rare privileged morning for Anda. She had slept well, even though she had awakened earlier than usual. For a while, she sat before the dark window, not wanting to move around, afraid of waking Vilnis. She contemplated everything that had happened. The worst was over. Daina was safe. This was her first day off in two weeks and her heart did a little tap dance at the thought of all this time to herself.

When the first light crept above the rooftops, she quietly walked into the kitchen and made herself a good strong cup of coffee. Sipping the delicious brew, she mulled over the events of the past few days.

The world had opened up for Daina. Anda felt a twinge of jealousy. She would have to go work in the bookstore for the rest of her days, just to earn enough money for the rent. At least under the old regime, the low rents never increased. Lately, she had noticed that the young girls that they were hiring in shops and bookstores had glossy lips and nails and flowing long hair. Although Anda was only thirty, she could no longer trade on her youth and beauty. How would she get ahead? The pressure to compete, earn money, succeed or fail, was too much for many of her acquaintances.

Anda saw the opportunities offered to people as a frightening new freedom. Part of her longed for the safety net of the old regime. She often felt that she was too old and too tired and too poor to compete in this new world of free enterprise.

As often happened when she had a moment to herself, she thought of her sister Silvia, old and worn out before her time, dead before her time, leaving grieving parents and two motherless children. Sasha had killed her. He abused her, drove her into drinking and lied to her about her daughter's whereabouts. He lied by omission. His greed greater than Silvia's worry about her child.

Anda still felt Silvia's presence. Saw her every time she looked at Vilnis. If she were still alive, Silvia would be thrilled at Daina's opportunities. She would have been thrilled at a chance to go to New York. If only she had lived. If only Anda had been able to protect her. Guilt and grief swept over her. Shivering, she crawled back into bed. There were still a few minutes before she had to wake Vilnis. She could huddle in the warmth of the blankets and force her mind to see something positive.

A few minutes later, the sun lit the wall across from her bed. It was time to get Vilnis up and start the day. Getting the little boy to his day-care had been rushed because he refused to eat his rye bread and butter. He had broken it into tiny pieces and kept trying to feed it to the new kitten and half of it had ended up on the floor. Exasperated with his doddering, Anda had dragged him by the hand. Vilnis was freaked about not letting the kitten near the door. Ever since the old cat had been run over, Vilnis went into a tantrum, stamping his feet and waving his little arms up and down, shrieking at her, "No, no, no, no, no."

Anda had been enjoying her solitary and leisurely stroll in the beautiful spring air. Suddenly she was bumped back down to earth by the sight of Mike and Ivan scurrying into her apartment building. The hair on the back of her neck rose. She knew they meant trouble. Running into them would ruin her day. She turned on her heels and headed in the opposite direction. The next minute, she turned back again, deciding she had better check out what they were up to.

She met them on their way back out. Like stray dogs, they followed her back to the kitchen, even though she had not asked them in. For a long time now, Anda had stopped thinking of Ivan as her father.

Taking down three mugs, she mixed instant coffee into hot water while saying nothing. Ivan's rough instructions flowed out like sputtering lava between his broken teeth. Her father had always been an embarrassment with his orange stained fingers constantly clutching a stub of cigarette. She suspected that Mike provided the never-ending supply of black market American smokes. She opened a kitchen window.

Slowly, their scheme came into focus. They had parked a black Mercedes behind the building and Anda was now expected to keep an eye on it. When Mike told her he would be spending the night, Ivan issued a 'me too.' Anda had heard enough.

"It's absolutely out of the question," she said in a loud angry voice.

"But Anda…" Mike got up out of his chair and came toward her.

"Leave now or I will call the police!" Anda was ready to go nuclear. Still, she was surprised at how quickly the men got the message.

Later that afternoon, Anda could hear a disturbance somewhere outside. This was not uncommon in her neighbourhood and she paid little attention to it until there was a loud knock at her door. Ignoring it, she looked out her kitchen window and saw a knot of people standing around a black car. An even louder knock sounded from the hallway and this time, Anda was sure it would be the police. Damn Mike and Ivan for dragging her into this.

After the police officer had spent a few minutes asking her preliminary questions, Anda was truthfully able to tell him that she had never seen the car before, that she didn't know who it belonged to and didn't know when it had been left behind her apartment house.

That evening, her mother phoned to say that Ivan and Mike had been arrested for car theft. She hadn't sounded surprised.

The next day it hit the fan. Newsbreaks on radio and television outlined the results of the investigation in the child porn scandal. A Latvian man had been arrested. Scapegoat, Uldis Baltins, had been led out of his restaurant in handcuffs. He had been an easy mark, a flamboyant homosexual who had come up with the idea of the Young Miss Latvia Contest. It had been his word against several government officials. There had been no other direct evidence that the officials were involved. Rumour had it that Uldis had been offered a reduced sentence if he kept his mouth shut. The politicos had nothing to worry about.

The following day, Uldis Baltins was found hanging in his cell. There was some question as to whether it was really suicide. Some said one of the guards had helped him along because of orders from higher up. Others said Baltins had been unstable for months and all the profits from his restaurant had gone up his nose. His restaurant had been reported on the edge of bankruptcy anyway because most of the staff were taking food out the back door. But many others said Uldis Baltins was just another person trying to make a living and had been made to take the fall.

When Arnie heard the news, he was flabbergasted. All that hard work and risk had ended tragically in the death of one man who probably bore a minimal amount of guilt in the whole disgusting business. It left a bad taste in his mouth to think of how little he had really accomplished.

Chapter Fifty

Daina, together with Maija, celebrated her fifteenth birthday by going to see *Cats* on Broadway. She was ecstatic at the performance and loved every minute of the whole experience. As another birthday present, Maija bought her a copy of the sound track on their way out of the theatre. Daina had even been excited about being in her first traffic jam on the way to the performance. She had never seen so many cars in her short life and all the horns seemed to be blaring at once. For Maija, it was a homecoming of sorts as she realized she had missed the excitement of mega-city life.

Earlier that day, Maija had taken Daina to the Gap on a shopping expedition and Daina had a ball. Their hotel, just off 7th Avenue was, by New York standards, 'older' but to Daina it was like a trip to the moon. The lobby was dark and cosy with its coffered wood panelling, polished tables and heavy brocade furnishings. Faux Tiffany lamps and dark patterned rugs created small intimate pools of jewelled light. Here, taking time out to rest her feet, Maija wrote her postcards, sipped on cappuccino, smoked a menthol cigarette and surreptitiously eyed the flow of hotel guests as they came and went. One or two of the distinguished-looking men had even seemed to smile in her direction.

Out on the streets, the pace was hectic. Maija had to be on her toes making sure that Daina didn't get left behind looking at all the luxury items in store windows or get separated in the incredible flow of pedestrian traffic. In the evening, back at their hotel, Daina spent an hour parading around in all her new stuff. Maija stretched out on the comfortable twin bed, enjoyed Daina's excitement. She hoped her baby would be a girl.

The morning of the interview with the modelling agency, Maija spend over an hour doing her makeup and hair. Daina, on the other hand, had showered, towelled off her Titian mop, pulled on her new Gap jeans and tee and was ready to roll. Maija had to take a Valium, making sure it was only one because of the baby.

The taxi pulled up in front of 300 Park Avenue and Daina bounced out first, looking as if she belonged right there. Maija, moving awkwardly because of her high-heeled slides, almost lost it stepping onto the curb and was struggling to keep up with Daina who was already half way through the revolving door.

The big moment had arrived. Maija couldn't help thinking as she sat alone in the waiting room that Daina was much prettier than any of the other girls there that morning. She was a natural.

Later, Daina told Maija that there had been a picture session and an interview. She had been told that her English still wasn't good enough. But if she were to study very hard for the next year and not put on any weight and practice walking with a book on her head every day to improve her posture, she would be considered again next year. If she did all that, the Wilhelmina Agency would send her two plane tickets from Riga to New York. Daina decided then and there that she would bring Anda.

Chapter Fifty-One

Winter lay behind like a long laborious journey. Once again the laughter of children echoed through the parks and the scented breath of spring swept the city clean of its shameful scandal. Sunshine spilled over grey stone buildings and, under a cloudless blue sky, trees unfurled their fresh new greenery.

Streets were as brisk as a beehive. Everyone had somewhere to go, something to do, something to look forward to. It was time to shake off the darkness and the cold. It was time to forget. People were breathing easier now. They had survived. All but poor Uldis Baltins, that is, and almost everyone soon forgot about him.

The rain when it rained was warm. The wind was gentle, ruffling blouses, lifting skirts, sending hats spinning playfully along the busy sidewalks. It was only the beginning of May but politicians were already starting to gear up for their annual holiday recess, while, recently burned by the sex scandal, pedophiles all over Riga scrambled back into their dark dingy holes. A pall had been cast over their world. There was very little activity on the kiddie porn Internet. Entire chat rooms had closed down. And that was for starters.

The fallout from the under-age porno scandal had cut deep. All juvenile beauty pageants were now banned. Charm schools felt a drop in business, hairdressers suffered, teenage modelling careers were cut short. The beauty industry as a whole had taken a hit. And all of this thanks to Arnie Dambergs and *WOW!*. Still, time had not stopped. Life went on in the dark underbelly of society as fresh scandals were waiting in line for a chance to raise their ugly heads.

Elsewhere, the pulse of respectable Riga continued to beat at a steady predictable tempo. Clocks in living rooms tick-tocked as faithfully as they had for years, daily rituals were the same, the same comforting routine they had always been. Traffic rumbled by, streetcars and trolleybuses making the ground vibrate gently as they passed on their daily routes back and forth across town and garbage trucks arrived at five pm on the dot. People rushed to work, rushed home from work, shopped, ate, drank, then, exhausted, slumped in front of their television sets for their nightly fix.

The sun burnt deliciously through the dusty window, through her thick orange coat, right through to her naked skin. Gerda opened her eyes, looked up from her grooming and sensed that this day would offer something special. Till now, her routine had passed undisturbed. In the afternoons, she snoozed on her favourite sunny windowsill in the grand old apartment building on Valdemara Street. She had a new life now. Her activities were predictable and comforting: wake up, scoot out the back door, examine garbage, yowl for warm milk, fight off the strays, chase a few birds, back inside, nap all day.

Gerda was used to human voices and footsteps, and people were used to her. As time had gone by, she had even learned to tolerate a certain amount of cooing and stroking in exchange for treats. Her old life had floated away, disappeared, had been forgotten; though, from time to time, she still went to the sixth floor and pressed her nose against the crack under a particular doorway.

Then one day, a strange thing happened. As usual, Gerda was in possession of the fourth floor window ledge when she heard something. Her antennae perked up. Her eyes widened. For an instant, she was bewildered.

What's this? she asked herself. Then her tail began to twitch with excitement as she heard familiar footsteps climb the stairs. In a flash it all came back to her. Her old life with its pleasures and annoyances flooded through her. It felt like coming home. She heard a familiar voice. It was his voice!

Soft brown eyes locked onto hers.

"Gerda! My God, your fat!" The words came out in a rush as he reached for her.

Gerda was not amused.

"She's probably pregnant, Arnie."

Another voice. A female. Oh yes, Gerda knew who that was. That was someone she didn't like. That was the girlfriend. Gerda gave her a disdainful stare, then let out a giant yawn. But the way Arnie looked at her, she saw that nothing had changed. She was still his ticket to heaven. He needed her like other people need air. She waited philosophically, then smiled her enigmatic smile. With a sigh of happiness, he cradled her in his arms, held her tight. "Ouuu…" he cooed, making silly kissing sounds with his mouth.

Suddenly, a shriek broke through their blissful moment. It was the Cat Lady herself, rushing at them along the hallway. As usual, she was in good voice and had started to hurl a steady stream of abuse in Arnie's direction—telling him to put her cat down, to leave her cat alone, to move along, to get out of her building. Then, best of all, she called him a country bumpkin standing there with his farmer's wife and told him to go back to milking his cows instead of bothering honest people here in civilized Riga.

Arnie turned around to face her and in his now fluent Latvian, he started to thank her for looking after Gerda while he'd been away. Pulling out his wallet, he asked her how much money he owed her for cat food. The Cat Lady fell silent, her jaw flapping up and down. Vizma and Arnie smiled, then laughed, then giggled until they couldn't stop and were doubled over.

Praise for Riga Mortis

The Baltic Times

Ilze Berzins' fifth murder mystery, RIGA MORTIS, is the most recent English-language thriller to take place in Riga, and, along with William Safire's SLEEPER SPY, one of the only ones. But where Safire's book lacks an intimate understanding of the city, Canadian-Latvian Berzins raises Riga to the level of a character in-and-of-itself.

RIGA MORTIS is a unique novel about the realities of mid-90s Riga and the complex relationship between the many "Latvians" that make up modern Riga, in addition to simply being a first-rate murder mystery, Riga-style.

The Ottawa Citizen

Life in Riga is no bed of roses, as Berzins points out, painting a painstakingly clear portrait of a post-Soviet society torn by freedom. Two expats, Vizma Gross and Arnie Dambergs, become entangled in each other and in a scandal that Berzins artfully ratchets up to a grand conclusion.

At this point, Berzins probably has entered that category of writer known as "prolific." This is her fourth book in as many years, all of them mysteries. But she first became known to Latvian readers with Happy Girl, the 1997 autobiographical tale of her attempted "return" to her ancestral homeland. Berzins clearly draws on that experience for much of the rich detail in Riga Mortis.

In Riga Mortis, Berzins digs deeper not only in terms of plot, but also in developing her characters and getting into their minds. There are so many that we almost need a guidebook to keep them straight. But that does make Riga Mortis a fun book; although I hesitate to use "fun" to describe the story, given its dark undertones.

Berzins uses detail well to paint the Riga of the mid-1990s. The Riga she describes is the one many of us know well: the architectural beauty and nostalgic feel of the Old City contrasted with the grayness and squalor of living conditions for many in the outlying districts

Despite the unsavory nature of the story, Berzins continues practicing her wit, particularly when detailing how expats used to the comforts of North America encounter the nascent consumer culture of Latvia. "She was having another of her bad expat moments," Berzins writes of Vizma in an early chapter. "Her mascara stick would soon dry out and God knows where she'd be able to replace it."

Printed in the United States
98002LV00005B/63/A

9 781420 835441